you
broke me
first

ALSO BY LORRAINE BROWN

The Paris Connection

Sorry I Missed You

Five Days in Florence

Couples Retreat

you broke me first

Lorraine Brown

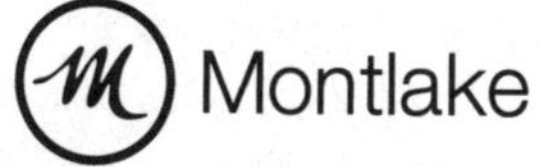

This is a work of fiction. Names, characters, organizations, places, events, and incidents are either products of the author's imagination or are used fictitiously. Any resemblance to actual persons, living or dead, or actual events is purely coincidental.

Published by Montlake, Seattle

www.apub.com

EU Product Safety Contact:
Amazon Media EU S.à r.l.
38, avenue John F. Kennedy, L-1855 Luxembourg
amazonpublishing-gpsr@amazon.com

ISBN-13: 9781662537639
eISBN: 9781662537646

Cover design by Emma Rogers
Cover images: © Lana Brow © alaver © Irina Strelnikova © Giuseppe Ramos © AlissaAlissa ©annaskurnia © Twenty-nine Feb / Shutterstock

Printed in the United States of America

you broke me first

Chapter One

I knew I shouldn't have come the second I pushed open the door of the theatre and was hit by a wall of pretentious conversation and the acrid smell of semi-expensive wine. Being around other people who appeared to be having the time of their lives was extremely unhelpful when your boyfriend, the love of your life, the man you'd assumed you were going to be with forever, had broken up with you and moved out overnight. And having thus far avoided telling a single person, I was finally going to have to say the words *Charlie and I have split up* out loud for the very first time and that terrified me almost as much as the thought of being without him did. Because it made it real, didn't it? And deep down I was still holding on to a miniscule amount of hope that he'd realise he'd made a terrible mistake and come crawling back. Not that I'd make him crawl. Pathetic as it was, at this point I reckoned I'd just throw myself into his arms with relief.

I spotted Mum and Cassie immediately, tucked away at a corner table and thankfully as far away from the throng of jolly theatregoers jostling for the bar as you could possibly get. No doubt they'd arrived about an hour early – my mum cared a lot about what other people thought of her and as a result had a pathological fear of being late in case she upset someone, even though I was pretty sure nobody noticed half the time. I fought my way through to them, swivelling my hips to pass a group of borderline-drunk posh people talking about themselves and their impressive, creative jobs. I wouldn't have been surprised if they'd started name-dropping which members of the cast they'd been to drama school with as I shuffled around their lithe, designer-label-clad bodies. Clearly I was making a *lot* of assumptions here, but it was that kind of a crowd, and I really wasn't in the mood. If it was in any way possible to say no to my mum and sister I would have been on my sofa watching early episodes of *Selling Sunset* right about now, which I intended to do the *second* this dismal-sounding low-budget play about addiction came to its unsatisfying end. My only hope was that it wasn't one of those extended extravaganzas that some self-indulgent director had been too caught up in himself (I just knew it was a man) to cut. I took a few slightly watery deep breaths, desperately trying to pull myself together – if my current disposition didn't swiftly improve, tonight was going to go *very* badly.

Mum looked up at me like a startled rabbit as I approached their table.

'Oh hello, Ava!' she said, as though we hadn't made plans to meet and that instead fate had brought about a chance meeting in Soho. This would have been extremely unlikely since the pair of them only ventured into London from Reading roughly once every two years.

'Hi guys,' I said, immediately clocking that Cassie looked very thin, although it could have been because she had on one of the chunky, oversized jumpers she insisted on wearing no matter the weather.

'Blimey, you're actually early to something,' teased Cassie.

'It has been known,' I said, ruffling the top of her hair and scooping her into a tight hug. Did she feel more fragile than she had when I'd seen her last? Not that she ever exactly looked robust.

Mum tried to stand up to give me a hug too, swiftly realising (after a bit of clunky to-ing and fro-ing) that she was wedged into her seat by the rather large man sitting on the table behind. I bent down to give her a peck on the cheek instead.

They'd saved me a stool, guarding it with their lives (and their coats). I scooped up their matching puffer jackets and sat down, having no choice but to place them back on my knee; neither Mum nor Cassie offered to take theirs, so I guessed I was stuck with them. It wasn't even cold out. And couldn't they have found a cloakroom? I was now smothered in a pile of polyester and was already burning up.

'I was just telling Cassie . . . the director is the brother-in-law of one of the doctors at work,' said Mum, clearly hoping to impress us with this very tenuous connection.

'Oh, interesting,' I said, fanning myself with my hand.

'He's been to see it and said it's fantastic.'

'Recommendation indeed,' I said, thinking he could hardly slag it off if a family member was in it, could he?

Mum worked as a receptionist in a GP surgery and talked about the doctors who worked there with a combination of overfamiliarity and barely contained awe. You'd have thought, then, that she might have been pleased when at one of my senior-school parents' evenings my chemistry teacher had suggested I had the potential to get into medical school if I got my maths grades up a bit. I remembered it like it was yesterday: despite Mum being offish with me all the way home, inside I'd been buzzing with a secret sense of achievement and the feeling that anything was possible, even if Mum quite liked me to think it wasn't.

'How's Charlie?' asked Mum. 'He is coming to Julie's wedding, isn't he? Because I've put him down as your plus one and they've made all the catering arrangements now, so he'd better be.'

Fuck. My cousin, Julie, was getting married in a posh hotel in Oxfordshire in a couple of months' time and now I was going to have to let Mum – and, even more humiliatingly, my entire extended family – know that Charlie would not be coming because he was, in fact, no longer my boyfriend.

'About that . . .' I said.

Cassie looked up with concern.

'Is he refusing to come? I know he's always banging on about hating weddings,' she said.

She was right, he did. He thought they were a waste of money and – other than for the bride and groom – a complete misuse of everyone's time. Saying that, there had been a few Whitfield family nuptials in the four years Charlie and I had been together, and after a bit of grumbling and moaning he'd always come with me in the end. Sometimes he'd even enjoyed himself, particularly if there was a free bar. Although I wondered now whether the invitation to Julie's wedding, which I'd surreptitiously left out on the kitchen counter for him to begin to get his head around, had been the thing to tip him over the edge.

I took a beat, attempting to exude calmness and acceptance, even if these were pretty much the opposite of the feelings that were *actually* swirling around inside me, which were more like anger, devastation and complete and utter hopelessness.

'Charlie and I have split up,' I said, swallowing the lump in my throat. Annoyingly, it was swiftly replaced by another.

'What?' said Mum, looking shocked. 'When?'

'Um, a few days ago?' I said, keeping it vague.

It had, in fact, been eight days, but if they knew that they'd only have had a go at me for not telling them sooner, and maybe it *would* have seemed like a bit of a red flag that I hadn't. If I was handling the break-up as well as I was trying to pretend I was, I wouldn't have had a problem announcing it, would I? And in keeping with me always having to be the capable, has-it-all-together sister, I felt compelled to give the impression that I was coping perfectly well with this life-changing turn of events. Broken up with my boyfriend of nearly half a decade, the man I'd lived with until about five minutes ago? No problem whatsoever. I could handle anything life threw at me, right? Except, suddenly, I couldn't. I was a mess inside, and part of me wished I could just admit it. Maybe Mum would be all caring and understanding like she was with Cassie, even if for as long as I could remember that had literally never been the case.

'Well, you're better off without him,' said Mum. 'Isn't she, Cassie?'

'Definitely,' agreed Cassie.

I bit my lip hard.

'It is a little bit sad, though,' I said, noticing my voice sounded all quivery. Shit. This wasn't how I'd wanted things to go, not at all.

I glanced at Cassie, who was worryingly quiet. Neither of them had particularly liked Charlie, and they both complained constantly that he never made an effort with them, but even so, Cassie hated change. Was she going to be okay with never seeing him again? Even as I had this thought I was somewhat aware that perhaps I didn't need to worry *quite* so much about her, or at least not all the time. But the thing was, it had been drummed into me that I should since the moment she was born (prematurely and very nearly not making it). She was twenty-six now and still I couldn't seem to stop.

'You seem to be handling it remarkably well,' said Cassie.

Really? I must be a better actress than I thought.

'Was it his decision or yours?' asked Mum.

Admitting I'd been rejected by the person I'd thought loved me most in the world was *not* what I wanted to be doing this evening. What I really wanted was to be lying on my sofa eating slabs of chocolate and drinking cheap wine like I had every other night since Charlie had left.

'Charlie was the one who ended it,' I said, digging my fingernails into my thigh because I suddenly felt a bit light-headed, which wasn't ideal with these two pumping me for information.

It was just that hearing the words *I don't want to be with you anymore* from the one person who'd always had my back, no matter what, was something I didn't think I'd ever be able to get over. Maybe if I'd had some warning – if we hadn't been getting on or something, but we had and it had felt totally out of the blue. He'd just come home from work the Wednesday before last and said he'd been dreading seeing me and thought that was probably a sign he didn't love me anymore and that he would be moving out with immediate effect. I'd been so shocked I'd had to grab hold of the kitchen worktop just so I could keep standing. Once I'd remembered how to speak again, I'd tried to reason with him – couldn't he stay until morning, at least? Surely we could *try* to work things out? Would it help if he told me what he thought the problem actually *was*? Mightn't there be a way we could salvage our relationship? How about couples counselling? Or a sexy city break? I'd nearly begged him to stay, if the truth be told, but luckily I'd stopped myself looking totally pitiful, even when he quite coldly said there was absolutely nothing to talk about and that he'd made up his mind and there was no changing it. I'd said okay and had helped him pack and then he was gone.

The flat had been quiet and empty without him or his clothes or the books he bought but never read. Only then had I let myself cry, but not for long, because I reminded myself that there were people far worse off than me, people with terrible, messed-up, traumatic lives, and I had a nice job as a freelance writer and a family who loved me even if they didn't understand me and a roof over my head (although how I was going to afford that now, I had no idea). I vowed I'd give myself one night and one night only to be upset – in private – and then I'd have to find the strength to accept that it was over and get on with my life. Except here I was, over a week later, still feeling like absolute crap.

'I'm surprised. I never thought *Charlie* would leave *you*,' said Cassie.

Was there a tiny flicker of triumph on her face, I wondered? No, surely not. She'd never want to see me hurt, definitely not, although I supposed I was pretending *not* to be that hurt, so perhaps I was giving her mixed messages?

'Remember how you thought he was going to propose to you last summer?' said Mum unhelpfully.

'Do we have to go there?' I mumbled.

In which universe would that be a good thing to say to somebody who'd just been dumped by their boyfriend? Sometimes my mum's complete lack of tact baffled me beyond belief.

'God, imagine if he had!' said Cassie, warming to the subject too. 'That would have made things really messy, wouldn't it? Is he moving out, then?'

'He already has,' I said, suddenly desperately in need of alcohol and wondering how long it would take me to get served at the bar. Hopefully long enough to miss the entire opening act so that I could meet my mother and sister later in the auditorium where it was dark and nobody could speak.

'Well, I'm glad he was the one to go,' said Mum. 'He's probably sleeping on someone's sofa, getting in *their* way and not making any effort to talk to *them*.'

Wow. Her feelings towards him were really coming out now, weren't they?

Anyway, he wasn't on someone's sofa, he was back in his childhood home where no doubt he was currently being fussed over by his lovely mum, who I already missed desperately. She'd be cooking nice things for him and doing his laundry and making his bed. I kept hoping she'd reach out to me with some words of wisdom – she was good at those – but she'd been tellingly quiet. Obviously, her loyalties lay with Charlie, but I'd thought she would have at least messaged to tell me how sorry she was about how things had turned out.

'You seem to be coping all right, though?' said Mum. A question that wasn't really a question. 'Less painful to do it now before getting married and starting a family and all of that.'

'Sure,' I said. 'That's what I thought.'

Never mind the fact that I'd wasted four fucking years of my life with a man who'd dropped me like I'd meant nothing to him without so much as a proper explanation. I was thirty now, and the pressure to be sorted financially, to have a life partner, to have babies before it was too late, suddenly crashed over me in a far more excruciatingly painful way than it had on my thirtieth last August, which was when I'd *thought* I'd start panicking about the dreaded ticking clock. Because I'd had Charlie then and he'd taken me on a trip to Rome where, yes, I'd thought he was going to propose, too, and had spent the entire time disappointed that he hadn't. It had been fine, though, I'd reassured myself, because we'd talked about getting married loads of times, and having kids – we both wanted two, and neither of us minded if they were boys or girls as long as they were healthy. He was going to propose to me at some point, wasn't he? It was what we'd always had planned.

Suddenly, I felt a burning sensation in the tips of my toes that rolled up my legs, over my hips, across my stomach, and finally lodged in my chest like a jagged shard of ice. It was unbearable and it was a feeling I'd never had before. Jesus, what was wrong with me?! I thought I might be about to either throw up or cry, neither of which I could do *here* in front of *them*.

I got up and flung the coats down on the stool, not caring that the sleeve of Mum's was now trailing on the floor in what looked like a puddle of beer.

'Need a drink,' I managed to splutter, although hearing my own voice right now was like having an out-of-body experience. 'And maybe the loo. Back in a sec.'

Feeling sort of robotic and as though my knees were about to give way, I followed the sign to the toilets and crashed inside one of the stalls, slamming the door shut behind me and leaning my back against it, my heart beating scarily fast and hard. As my face crumpled, I closed my eyes, bending at the waist in despair, succumbing to the tears that had been building up all evening. I willed myself to stop, tried not to think about Charlie and his safe and secure job as an assistant head at a secondary school and his lovely strawberry-blond hair and his terrible cooking and how it had felt when he pulled me close to him in bed. I missed him so much I didn't know how I was going to go on without him. And to make it worse, probably, I hadn't been able to say that to anybody, not even myself before now. I clamped my hand over my mouth, trying to quell the sobs; if I carried on like this, Mum and Cassie would know I'd been bawling my eyes out and Mum would tell me to pull myself together and Cassie wouldn't know what to say because I didn't think I'd ever cried about anything in front of her ever, although the hours I'd spent comforting her had known no bounds. I focused on my breathing, in and out, in and out, wondering if anyone could hear me and whether, even if they could, they'd care. And as my breath slowed, the pain of knowing I'd lost Charlie became slightly less acute. Good. I could do this. I could go back out there and I could watch the shitty play and then I could make the journey home to the flat I shared with absolutely nobody and spend yet another night alone. It was all right – this was my life now, and I was going to have to get used to it.

Chapter Two

It was half eleven on a Tuesday morning and I probably should have been doing something that at least resembled work, but instead I was lying flat out on the sofa watching daytime TV and wearing mushroom-print flannel pyjamas and, yes, they were as revolting as they sounded. Tellingly, it was the only item of 'clothing' I owned that wasn't currently crammed into my overflowing laundry basket, clearly an indication that I needed to do some household chores. But so what if I was a bit behind with it all? Except I couldn't let anyone else know that, could I, they'd know something was up. So when the doorbell rang, jolting me out of my stupor, I was forced to launch myself into the bedroom to rip off the pyjamas and pull on a pair of jeans and a jumper. Then I ran into the kitchen to shove the sinkful of washing-up into the nearest cupboard and swiftly removed empty crisp packets from the lounge coffee table. As a result, it took me so long to get out into the hallway that whoever was most inconveniently arriving unannounced in the middle of the day had rung the bell a second time – I really hoped it wasn't just a delivery driver after all this, although I knew I hadn't ordered anything because, well, what would be the point? I now lived in complete solitude and rarely went out, preferring to hibernate inside my flat with no desire to communicate with other humans. Using my fingers to comb my hair with limited, if any, effect, I power-walked towards the chink of daylight at the end of my hallway; actual sunshine was visible through the frosted glass, a gentle reminder that a world still existed out there.

I flung open the front door, clutching my chest in surprise.

'Why aren't you at work?' I exclaimed, standing back to let my friend Zoe in.

'Half day. I've got the dentist in a bit,' said Zoe, peering at me disconcertingly. 'You okay?'

'Yes,' I said, immediately on the defensive. 'Why do you ask?'

'Your jumper is on inside out.'

'Is it?' I said, craning my neck to look over my shoulder. Yep, there was the label, poking out, clear as day. I could hardly turn it round the right way now, could I, I had nothing on underneath.

'Is this because of Charlie?' asked Zoe, slamming the door behind her so hard the entire flat rattled.

'No,' I insisted. This was exactly why I'd put off telling people until I'd absolutely had to – the last thing I wanted was my friends watching me like a hawk in case I had a meltdown.

Zoe looked at me suspiciously. 'Really?'

I shrugged as she followed me into the lounge. It was easier if I didn't look at her, because we'd been friends for so long that sometimes it was like she knew how I was feeling before I did.

'I'm taking it one day at a time,' I lied.

It was the kind of thing people said in books and on TV, wasn't it, and I thought it sounded good and might get Zoe off my back.

I resumed my place on the sofa, albeit sitting upright this time. Earlier that morning, I'd been shocked to note that it had developed a sort of squidgy, lopsided sink hole on one side, possibly due to me lying on it for several hours a day of late. Once or twice I'd even spent the night out here, because it had felt all kinds of strange to sleep alone in the bed I'd once shared with Charlie. And night-times weren't generally the best – I tended to toss and turn, ruminating relentlessly about what I'd done to push him away, what I could do to get him back, whether I was destined to a lifetime of misery now and whether I would ever see him or his parents again. Thoughts that weren't exactly conducive to sleep, as you could imagine, and so I tended not to, and would spend the day napping out of sheer exhaustion instead and feeling permanently groggy as a result.

Zoe leapt on to the sofa next to me and I thought longingly back to a time when I would have had the energy to fling myself on to other people's furniture if I'd so desired.

'What are you watching?' asked Zoe, squinting at the TV screen. A celebrity chef was currently stirring a pot of a rather unpleasant-looking fish stew.

'*This Morning*,' I said, refusing to feel bad about it. What use was being freelance if you couldn't occasionally slack off and watch trash TV?

And yes, obviously I could have been doing something more productive, like writing, perhaps. But the thing was, I was finding watching semi-relatable presenters earnestly discussing unthreatening topics like red-carpet looks or somebody's new book exceptionally comforting. If I couldn't get myself together enough to enjoy my own life, I would live vicariously through others, and even better if they were rich, famous and on my TV screen.

My phone buzzed and I looked at it fake-nonchalantly, even though I knew, and Zoe knew, that if she wasn't sitting beside me I'd have launched myself on it in a matter of nanoseconds. It was never Charlie anyway, so I didn't know why I kept thinking it would be. Any hope I'd had that he was going to realise he'd made a huge mistake and come knocking at my/our door begging for forgiveness had waned somewhat in the last two weeks of radio silence; seemingly, he'd meant what he'd said. He'd sent me a couple of messages the day after he left – *I'm sorry* and then *I just couldn't do this anymore* – but that had been the extent of our communication, even though obviously I'd been tempted to call him about ten times a day just so I could hear his voice. But he didn't want to hear mine, did he, and that still felt unbelievable to me. How could he go from spooning me in bed one night to moving out the next? It continued to make absolutely zero sense.

'That had better not be him,' said Zoe, sporting the disgusted expression she'd started adopting whenever Charlie came up.

She was hating on him in a way that I wished I could. It seemed like it would be a healthy progression from the abject misery I was currently experiencing. Wasn't anger one of the stages of grief? I thought I was currently in the denial phase and was showing little sign of moving out of it.

I glanced at my screen, as casually as I could when my heart was hammering against my chest in an explosive manner. It *could* be him. Maybe a clean break had been what he'd needed and now he was ready to talk/declare undying love for me etc. etc. Of course I then had to hide my crashing disappointment when I realised it wasn't Charlie (stupid me), it was Cassie, with one of the excitable *Isn't it great that we can be single sisters together now!* type messages she'd taken to sending since I'd told her about the break-up. I supposed that if anything good had come out of this, it was that I'd made her feel better about her own disastrous love life, which mainly consisted of one-night stands that went nowhere and doomed 'situationships' with men who were clearly all wrong for her (and any other sane woman) from the start. I'd essentially normalised failing at relationships in our family, which was funny when you thought about it, because none of this felt normal to me in the slightest. Normal was me and Charlie sitting in front of the TV with a takeaway; me and Charlie curled up in bed together telling each other funny stories from our day – admittedly there wasn't loads of that, since he said he didn't want to think about school stuff once he was home and I mainly worked alone and therefore had no interesting interactions to share, but we tried. Me and Charlie doing couple-y things on a Sunday – coffee and a walk along Columbia Road, a matinée screening at our local cinema, buying up ingredients for a home-cooked roast. That was normal. Not this being on my own pretty much 24/7 and wondering if I'd ever truly feel happy again.

Zoe was looking at me expectantly.

'It's Cassie,' I said, putting her out of her misery.

My eyes were drawn back to the TV where they'd now moved on to a segment about the royals and had on one of those 'experts' who claimed to know everything about them. Despite sounding posh enough for this to be feasible, it was never quite clear how they'd gleaned this supposed 'inside info'.

'Ava?' said Zoe.

I dragged my eyes away from the screen to notice that Zoe had turned to face me with her mouth arranged in a sort of grim line, her glossy auburn blow-dried hair swinging perfectly into place. I felt a shot of humiliation at how much of a mess I must look in comparison. Perhaps sitting next to Zoe on my battered old sofa in a back-to-front sweater was precisely the wake-up call I needed.

'You look like you're about to tell me somebody's died,' I said. And then I panicked that somebody actually had and that's why she'd rocked up on my doorstep in the middle of the day. 'They haven't, have they?'

Zoe shook her head.

'Nobody's died. Not literally, anyway. But look, this *is* serious. I know you keep saying you're okay, but I'm really worried that you're actually not. For example, when was the last time you went out? And no, the theatre the other night doesn't count because Cassie asked you and for reasons I don't quite understand, you feel the need to pander to her every whim and demand. I just really want you to get out and about again. Remind yourself that you still have a brilliant life ahead of you, with or without Charlie. In fact, without him it might even be ten times better.'

Of course the theatre trip counted. Also, damn. How could she tell that things weren't quite as rosy as I was pretending they were? Nobody else had noticed.

'I've had a lot to sort out, that's all,' I protested. 'Rearranging all my stuff now I've got the flat to myself, that sort of thing.'

Zoe eyeballed me. Clearly, she was not to be fobbed off.

'You forget that I know your default is to shut yourself away when something bad happens. And that's fine, we're all different. But you *can* talk to me, you know. It's not like I've never broken up with someone; I know exactly how awful it feels. Maybe it would help to share stories of heartbreak. Chat it through. Slag Charlie off, whatever you need?'

Articulating actual feelings out loud was not what I did. Which made it quite extraordinary that my job as a journalist was to interview other people; to get under their skin, to pull stories – and yes, emotions – out of them and write them down in a way that made the people reading my articles feel something too. Funny that when it came to my own issues, I struggled to share them with anyone at all.

'I'm fine, Zo,' I reassured her. 'It was a bit of a shock at first, but I honestly think it was for the best.'

'Best how?' asked Zoe.

Shit. Good point. I must be able to come up with something.

'Because I wouldn't want to waste another four years with someone who was having doubts about our relationship, would I? At least I'm still young enough to find someone else.'

There, that had sounded convincing. And there was at least some truth to it – imagine if it had happened years down the line when we had two kids and a massive mortgage to consider, which was kind of what I'd always imagined for us if I were to have been pressed for a five-year plan.

'Break-ups are savage,' said Zoe gently. 'And you're bound to miss Charlie. It's okay if you're struggling, Ava.'

'Define "struggling"?'

I knew it wasn't exactly looking good, what with the whole not-working-and-not-getting-dressed thing – in fact, I was full-on wallowing when nobody could see me, but fundamentally I was totally surviving. I'd managed to send two work emails yesterday and had actually made myself something other than plain pasta with cheese for dinner the night before last.

'Okay. Well, for example, have you been turning down jobs?' asked Zoe.

'No! Of course not. I just haven't exactly been looking for any, either.'

I was usually extremely proactive – as a self-employed writer, you had to be if you wanted to eat – but I didn't have it in me to put myself out there at the moment and the idea of encountering yet more rejection was simply too much to bear. I had a few regular gigs and I was managing to get them done, even if it did feel like climbing Mount Everest every time I opened my laptop and attempted to string nice-sounding words together.

'How are you going to pay your rent?' asked Zoe.

This must be what they called 'an intervention'.

'I've got savings,' I assured her calmly, because I had. Savings for the flat in some nice, leafy part of London that Charlie and I were planning on buying once we'd cobbled together a big enough deposit. No point in keeping hold of that now, was there? I'd never be able to afford a property in London on my own.

'What are they, then?' asked Zoe, staring pointedly at the pile of brown envelopes on the coffee table. One of them rather unhelpfully had the words *Overdue Payment* plastered across the front of it in bright-red ink.

'Oh, those . . .' I said casually. For fuck's sake. Why hadn't I thrown them out with the crisp wrappers? 'I need to change them from Charlie's name into mine, that's all. The whole admin thing's a logistical nightmare.'

Taking his name off of every single household account *was* proving to be a mind-numbingly tedious task I could never be bothered to start, let alone finish. Because not only had Charlie moved out overnight, he'd left me to disentangle myself from him in every possible way without so much as an offer of help. The only nice thing he'd done was agree to pay half the rent until our contract was up in September, but I assumed he wasn't planning to contribute to other bills and I hadn't really had the headspace to consider whether any of this was sustainable. It was only a tiny, one-bedroomed place, so it wasn't even like I could sublet a room and get a flatmate, unless I did a Beth O'Leary's *The Flatshare*-type arrangement, although what's the betting my lodger would be *nothing* like Leon?

'Has Charlie given you any money towards all of this?' asked Zoe, waving her hand in the direction of the incriminating envelopes.

'Not exactly,' I admitted.

'Dickhead,' she said.

Fair enough. I'd called him worse myself in my head.

'Actually, I suppose your lack of financial security does bring me neatly on to the reason for my visit . . .' said Zoe, ominously.

'And there was me thinking you'd come to indulge my daytime TV addiction and assist me in polishing off a packet of Taste the Difference quadruple-chocolate cookies,' I said, swiftly realising I'd eaten the entire packet for breakfast a couple of days ago.

'You need more work now that your outgoings are bigger. Correct?' said Zoe, going for the jugular. 'And maybe writing your way through the pain will help. That's what they say, isn't it?'

'Who's "they"?' I asked, genuinely wanting to know.

Zoe's situation was far more stable than mine – she'd been freelance once, too, but six months ago she'd taken a permanent role on *Luxe*, a glossy monthly magazine that was one of the only print publications still selling shedloads and as a result attracted the crème de la crème of contributing editors, photographers, models and celebrity cover stars. And I supposed that if I was contracted to turn up somewhere to do my job, I would have had to by now and perhaps I'd feel better for it. I also wouldn't need to worry so much about money, because although I'd started to build a solid portfolio of work, I was still having to scramble around for jobs and persuade people I was good enough.

'I'm planning to get everything back on track,' I said, sounding far more convincing than I felt.

'When?' asked Zoe.

'Soon.'

'How about right now?' she asked.

I instinctively glanced at the TV. What, *right* now?

'Amanda's looking for someone to write a profile piece on that British tennis player, Marcus Taylor.'

'Marcus *who*?'

'Taylor,' said Zoe. 'You know the one? The press hates him. They've dubbed him "Racquet Man" because he's always smashing them up on the court.'

'Charming,' I said, a vague memory of last year's Wimbledon coverage filtering into my mind's eye. There had been some guy the media had gone to town on, calling him a brat and a bad loser and accusing him of bringing shame on British tennis. Presumably that was him. 'What's any of this got to do with me, though?'

'I persuaded Amanda that you'd be the perfect person for the job,' Zoe announced, looking at me triumphantly.

It took a second or two for me to compute what she was saying. Amanda Eddington was the infamous and utterly terrifying editor-in-chief of *Luxe*. She was constantly photographed at swanky industry parties, or on the front row of Fashion Weeks around the world. As if Zoe would even have mentioned me to her!

'You must have misunderstood her, Zo,' I declared.

Amanda could have her pick of writers, there was no way she'd trust an article of that calibre to a relatively unknown journalist like me.

'I haven't. She definitely wants to hire you and she's really excited about this one – apparently he won the Australian Open when he was twenty-three and played all this amazing tennis but since then he hasn't really lived up to his potential. She was having a nightmare finding the right person for the assignment and I immediately thought of you. I sent her that piece you wrote for *Refinery29* last year on why celebrities write memoirs, and she thought it was brilliant. Plus, she trusts my judgement. She knows I wouldn't recommend anyone other than an exceptional writer to her, best friend or no best friend.'

I swallowed hard, touched by Zoe going out on a limb for me and bigging me up. But in my experience, jobs this good did not get handed to you on a plate.

'What's the catch?' I asked her.

'No catch,' she insisted brightly.

'The interview's all agreed? Marcus Taylor and his people are all on board?'

'Something like that,' said Zoe breezily.

I narrowed my eyes at her. 'Tell me . . .'

Zoe sighed. 'Okay. Apparently, he's difficult. Which is obvious, isn't it, given how he behaves on the court?'

'Go on,' I said.

'And he may – *may* – have a rep for cancelling interviews at the last minute.'

'So basically it's a non-starter. He'll half-heartedly agree to do it but then he'll block the process at every turn so that it never happens. I've been on the receiving end of that before and it's a complete waste of time.'

'Amanda is hoping it'll be different this time. And I told her that if anyone could get Marcus on side, you could.'

I laughed hollowly. 'I appreciate you championing my journalistic capabilities, Zo, but I'm not a bloody miracle-worker. I bet Amanda's only said yes to me because nobody else wants the job.'

Zoe hesitated a moment too long. I *knew* it!

'It's not just that, Ava, you're a sensational writer. And so what if her usual slew of contributors have said no? This is a brilliant opportunity for you to put yourself well and truly on her radar. Imagine how fantastic a profile of a famously elusive celebrity will look in your portfolio? This could be your big break!'

Rationally, this was the point at which I should have said yes, and thank you, and I'd do it. I needed the work, and chances like this – to be hired by an industry powerhouse like Amanda Eddington – came about once in a blue moon. But nagging away at me was the thought that she was going to be expecting things from me that I wouldn't be able to deliver in my current state of mind. How was I, a jobbing journalist and occasional barmaid at the local gastropub, in any way deserving of an assignment as high-profile as this? I hadn't written a proper, full-length story in weeks – what if I couldn't, anymore?

'I'm going to put my foot down here, Ava,' said Zoe, trying to sound scary. 'I love you, you know that, but you *cannot* mope around in outfits like *that* watching *Loose Women*, or whatever this is, for one moment longer. I *insist* that you do this. Nobody has ever written an in-depth piece on Marcus Taylor before, and if you can pull it off, it would be a massive scoop for *Luxe*, a job Amanda wouldn't trust to just anyone. She believes in you. And so do I.'

Celebrity profiles were exactly the kind of thing I longed to be writing and if I did it right, this job could shape my entire future.

'But I hate sports!' I said.

'All sports?' said Zoe, looking confused.

'Yes! Have you ever known me to go for a run, or a swim, or a gym session? And as for team sports, even hearing the *word* football brings me out in a rash.'

'But tennis is different, right?' said Zoe hopefully.

'How? Because it's totally elitist, you mean?'

'Maybe, but what's not to like about Wimbledon? The outfits are cute and you like Pimm's and strawberries, don't you?' said Zoe.

Hmmm. I supposed the drinks and snacks side of things did sound a tiny bit appealing.

'Amanda needs a sports specialist,' I concluded. I'd always been *great* at talking myself out of things. 'I haven't got the right credentials.'

Swooping in to back up my argument, I could almost hear my mum's voice telling me not to get ahead of myself; that I – to use her favourite phrase – was getting ideas above my station.

'It might work to your advantage not to know much,' suggested Zoe. 'Our readers might well be in the same boat.'

'But how can I write about something I know absolutely nothing about?'

'Isn't that what research is for?' said Zoe. 'Pass me your remote.'

'Why?' I said, feeling strangely protective over it.

'Hand it over!' she instructed.

Tutting loudly, I reluctantly gave it to her; there was an interesting segment on spring knits coming up on *This Morning* that I'd been hoping to catch.

'Dare I ask what you're doing?' I asked.

After fumbling around in the Netflix search grid for a bit, Zoe pressed play.

'My mum recommended this documentary called *Deuce*,' said Zoe, turning the volume up so high I actually flinched. 'It follows tennis players as they travel around the world from tournament to tournament. Apparently, it's riveting.'

Highly unlikely, I thought. Playing sports was bad enough, let alone watching them on TV. I crossed my arms moodily when the opening credits of *Deuce* rolled over footage of something called the Rod Laver Arena in Melbourne where the Australian Open was about to kick off, whatever the hell that was. On the plus side, this did seem like one of those impeccably produced shows that attached the perfect piece of music to every emotion-infused encounter and made each location look achingly cinematic.

'Apparently, Marcus Taylor features a lot,' said Zoe, settling back in her seat.

I watched sullenly as two men in their early thirties began warming up on a cobalt-blue tennis court with stormy grey skies swirling over their heads. They were slamming the ball back and forth, back and forth, their muscular arms making light work of sending it spinning from one baseline to the other. I was already bored. Were they going to be doing this for long?

'That's him!' shrieked Zoe.

'Which one?' I asked, leaning forward, trying to make out their faces.

'The fit one with the dark hair.'

The camera went close in on the man who was supposedly Marcus Taylor. I couldn't help but notice that he had spectacularly sculpted calves, beautifully tanned skin (no doubt acquired from spending months training in the south of France or wherever the hell they all lived), and just the right amount of facial hair. He was quite handsome, I reluctantly acknowledged, but he had cold eyes and when he messed up a serve, he looked like he wanted to murder somebody, even though he was only warming up and hadn't even started the game yet, from what I could tell. Talk about a bad attitude.

Right on cue, the show cut to footage of Marcus competing in the quarter-finals of last year's US Open. I'd always thought that was a golfing tournament? Seemingly not, because a place called the Arthur Ashe stadium in Flushing Meadows, New York, was packed to the rafters with spectators, most of whom appeared to be chugging beer from paper cups and generally behaving as though they were at some rowdy frat boy party.

'Did he win this tournament as well as the Australian thingy, then?' I asked Zoe, as the camera zoomed in on the scoreboard. According to the voice-over, Marcus was leading by two sets to one and was ahead by three games to two in the fourth. I had no idea what any of that meant.

'Don't ask me,' said Zoe, who clearly wasn't a tennis aficionado either. I mean, who was?!

Michelle Obama, apparently, who was sitting in the front row wearing a denim dress that I made a mental note to google when I was back to wearing proper clothes again and actually leaving the house.

By this point, Marcus Taylor was looking all kinds of fucked off and had just produced three 'unforced errors' in a row. His opponent, Anton Bauer – a baby-faced Danish guy with a blond topknot – was crouched down, ready to receive his serve. For some bizarre reason, Marcus Taylor repeatedly bounced the ball on the ground, again and again. And again. Eventually (and after a ridiculous amount of time, in my opinion), his eyes narrowed as he tossed the ball into the air with his left hand, slid his right foot forward to meet his left and leapt fully off the ground in a powerful motion, like a tiger about to launch itself at some poor, unsuspecting prey.

Just as his racquet was about to make contact with the ball, someone shouted *Come on, Marcus!* at top volume, and instead of sailing over to the other side of the court like it was presumably supposed to, the ball slammed clean into the net. A hush descended over the stadium.

'Game Bauer,' announced the umpire.

The crowd roared.

Marcus Taylor's jaw tightened.

Given the Racquet Man moniker Zoe had described, I had a pretty good idea what was coming next.

True to form, Marcus marched over to the stands and *unleashed* on the visibly drunk guy who had put him off. The guy, to his credit, seemingly couldn't care less and was now jumping up and down with glee and pointing at himself on the jumbotron. I didn't see why it was his problem, either – if Marcus had messed up his serve, he only had himself to blame, didn't he? He couldn't expect total silence in a stadium that size. As Marcus continued his cringeworthy tirade of swear words and racquet throwing, I glanced across at Zoe, who was seemingly mesmerised.

'He's actually incredibly sexy to watch,' she said, sounding all breathy.

'Ugh. You have *terrible* taste in men.'

Mind you, I could hardly talk. Charlie was the polar opposite of Marcus Taylor and so conflict-averse that he'd clearly delayed ending our relationship until he couldn't stand it (me?) any longer and absolutely had to. According to the few words I'd managed to get out of him as he swept his toiletries off the bathroom shelf and into a shoe box, he'd been thinking about it for months, since before my thirtieth (so much for that proposal in Rome), but had kept hoping it was just a phase. Things between us hadn't been perfect, how could they have been, but I'd honestly been happy. He'd been the stability I needed and was relentlessly supportive through all the ups and downs with my work and my family and my friends and my finances. My parents and Cassie had never really liked him, but since I didn't value their opinion on most things, I'd always let their comments (about him being a little bit boring) wash right on over me. And I'd never really asked Zoe what she thought of him because they didn't hang out together anyway; my life had always been quite compartmentalised like that, and he'd made *me* happy and that had always been what mattered. I pushed out of my mind an image of Charlie's flushed, regretful face as he threw most of his belongings into bin bags and ordered himself an Uber, and focused instead on Marcus Taylor, who was really going for it now, smashing his racquet on the ground over and over again until the strings were torn to shreds; to add insult to injury, he then sent it flying into his chair at the side of the court. What a waste! It showed complete disregard for the fact that people were struggling to put a hot meal on the table while he trashed a perfectly good racquet that had probably cost hundreds of pounds.

'Actually, he is going a bit far . . .' said Zoe, hurriedly turning the volume down as Marcus started screaming insults at a terrified-looking ball boy.

'What is *wrong* with him?' I asked, genuinely perplexed.

'Who knows? Fascinating, though, isn't he?' said Zoe, winking at me.

'I can think of other words to describe him,' I said.

'I think this will be really good for you, Ava. It'll give you some purpose. Reignite that passion and ambition of yours.'

'It's not disappeared altogether, you know. It's just . . . resting.'

'You'll get to travel, apparently,' said Zoe. 'Amanda said something about covering a few of the tournaments happening over the next few months. Oooh, maybe there's another one in Australia!'

'I'm not going to Australia, Zo,' I said. God, I could barely make it to the corner shop.

'Shall I tell Amanda you'll do it?' asked Zoe, raising her eyebrows at me hopefully.

I closed my eyes for a second, struggling to make a decision. Could I really do this? Surely I hadn't lost the ability to write altogether, even if Marcus Taylor did seem like an absolute knob and I had no interest in tennis? And also, what better way to convince everyone I was completely fine about the break-up than to take on the biggest writing gig of my life? I'd hardly be able to do that if I was still cut up about Charlie, would I?

When I opened my eyes again, the first thing I saw was Marcus Taylor wiping his face aggressively with a fluffy white towel while storming off court with his racquet bag thrown over his shoulder.

'Fine. Tell Amanda I'll do it,' I told Zoe, needing to get the words out quickly before I could change my mind.

THE ROLEX MONTE-CARLO MASTERS

Chapter Three

After googling the weather in Monte Carlo (better than in London, unsurprisingly; sun likely, some light rain expected), I pulled clothes that might be in some way suitable out of my wardrobe and flung them into my suitcase. The only good thing about Charlie moving out was that I now had every single inch of the flat's limited storage space to myself. Also, if he *had* still been here, he would probably have put a dampener on my upcoming trip by ranting about how disgusting it was that millionaires chose to live in Monte Carlo to avoid paying taxes in their home country, the subject of which was guaranteed to make him turn beetroot with indignation (and, no doubt, envy).

My phone pinged and I paused the packing to read an email from Ruby, Amanda Eddington's very on-the-ball assistant over at *Luxe*. She'd done a great job of organising my travel at short notice after I'd had a Zoom call with Amanda and she'd hired me on the spot, chirpily informing me I'd need to leave for Monaco three days later. I was having to go from barely leaving the house to navigating travel to one of the most glamorous places in the world, not to mention somehow pulling off the biggest interview of my life. At least it had forced me to get dressed and make a serious dent in my laundry.

I skimmed through my itinerary for the next few days, which was an exhausting-sounding list of activities including drinks meetings with LA talent agents, observing practice sessions at the Monte-Carlo Country Club and watching Marcus play live at the Rolex Monte-Carlo Masters tournament. I sighed to myself, only about twenty per cent sure I was ready for any of this, but also aware that I essentially didn't have a choice since this career-changing opportunity to write for the UK's bestselling glossy magazine had presented itself to me out of nowhere. Sort of, anyway, because obviously it wouldn't have happened if I hadn't shared a flat with Zoe in university halls and she wasn't now my closest friend and biggest champion. I wasn't a fan of nepotism, but I was going to have to put my principles momentarily on hold because there was absolutely no way I could turn down the chance to see my byline on *Luxe*'s smooth, shiny pages. I could already see myself flicking through the magazine's November issue (Amanda wanted me to interview Marcus between April and July and follow him to four different tournaments) and landing on the piece I'd written – it was a dream come true. I'd already decided that I'd be arranging the magazine conspicuously on my coffee table, permanently opened at my article so that I could look at it every single day. It wasn't about other people seeing it, or needing to be congratulated for it or anything like that; it would just be for me. A reminder of how far I'd come. When I was growing up, being good at writing wasn't considered a skill to be celebrated (nor were most things that involved my achievements), but I'd learned over the years to find small ways to be proud of myself. And, as an added bonus, *Luxe* were paying well, and those gas and electricity bills were not going to pay themselves.

I did a quick sweep of my dressing table, zipped up my suitcase, checked all my electrics were switched off, watered my plants and gave myself a pep talk in the hallway mirror. *I can do this*, I told myself, like a boxer about to enter the ring. My confidence may have been knocked by the break-up, but somewhere deep inside me was a light burning bright with all the things I still wanted to achieve. *I am a great writer when I put my mind to it*, I told myself, and I could be great again. I stared my own reflection out: *Marcus Taylor is not going to know what's hit him!*

◆ ◆ ◆

A complete stranger (who'd better be *seconds* from missing his flight, because there could be no other acceptable explanation) rolled his size-of-a-house suitcase straight over my foot at speed, jolting me painfully out of the cocoon of isolation I'd been living in and leaving me fantasising about being back on my battered old sofa. After my self-imposed solitary confinement, it felt all kinds of wrong to suddenly be surrounded by about three thousand other people barging around me with giant backpacks and tired kids as they tried to work out which queue to join to check in for their flight. And the noise was deafening! I pushed my headphones into my ears as far as they would go and pressed play on my meditation app in an attempt to drown out the chaos. How did I interact with people, again? And why was everyone so loud and talky, I wondered? I sincerely hoped I wasn't going to be stuck next to somebody chatty on the plane, because if so, I was going to have to pretend to be asleep for the entirety of the flight.

When my turn came, I dragged my suitcase up to the desk, handing over my ticket.

'Good morning, madam,' said the chirpy British Airways staff member behind the counter of the bag drop.

He punched some numbers into his computer, glanced up at me, smiled smugly to himself and returned his attention to his screen. This was worrying – I hadn't checked my passport before I left. It wasn't out of date or something, was it? There was some new rule about having at least six months left on it, which I was sure I had.

'Everything okay?' I asked nervously.

'Oh, it's more than okay,' he said mysteriously, handing something to me. 'Your new ticket, madam. You'll be sitting in *business* class for your flight with us today.'

'Sorry?' I asked, not quite understanding.

The man lowered his voice and looked at me conspiratorially. 'We've upgraded you,' he said, looking exceptionally pleased with himself.

I instinctively glanced down at my outfit – perhaps it was the Sézane skinny jeans and black polo-neck combo that had done it. Clearly, this screamed 'money'. Either that or they were oversubscribed in economy, and I was the best of a bad bunch.

I motored through security, boycotting my planned trip to Boots and heading straight for the Galleries First Lounge because I doubted I'd be doing the whole business-class thing ever again and did not want to miss a *second* of the luxury I hoped was about to ensue. I paused and took a moment just inside the doorway; it was everything I'd imagined and more, from the delicious-looking food being whisked past on silver trays to the horseshoe-shaped bar that wouldn't look out of place in a five-star hotel. It was a *definite* step up from the plastic seating area by Starbucks I usually frequented at Heathrow Terminal 5. I casually checked to see if there were any celebrities around – discovering what famous people got up to when they were off-duty was my number one guilty pleasure, although the fact that they mostly managed to look stunning even when emerging from the gym with zero make-up on and sweat-soaked hair had been getting to me of late. It seemed to be mostly men in suits in here, anyway. The type of guys who made unnecessarily loud phone calls while pacing up and down the middle of the room to make sure that everyone knew exactly how important they were. I made a beeline for the bar. If the alcohol was free, I was going in, early hours of the morning or not. I needed *something* to calm my nerves, because this job felt huge and I had a sneaking suspicion that Marcus Taylor was going to make it very difficult for me. I ordered myself a glass of champagne and, as I watched it being poured, I considered whether karma might have been at play here; whether somebody somewhere had known I could do with a bit of a boost and had answered my prayers in the form of an upgrade, just when I needed it most.

I stayed seated on a stool at the bar because it gave me an excellent vantage point over the entire lounge and it was easy to order more drinks if I wanted them. The first person I wanted to tell about this stroke of luck was Charlie, a thought I'd had often since he'd left. When stuff happened – when I read something funny, or learned something interesting, or I had good news, or bad news, Charlie was the first person I wanted to call, even if towards the end even he had been a bit funny whenever I had something positive to report. I couldn't quite put my finger on why, except that I knew he was having a hard time at work – his school had had a bad Ofsted report and all the parents were up in arms. Maybe it was stress that had killed our relationship in the end, then, which felt easier to accept than it having anything to do with me as a person. Like, maybe I wasn't enough for him, or something. Or that in the end he'd got sick of my struggling writer routine and my volatile family dynamics. It was sad, really, that after so long together we hadn't even had a proper conversation about why things had ended.

I fired off a quick message to Mum – I supposed I ought to let her know I was going to be out of the country for a few days.

Instead of texting back, she rang me immediately. *Why, why, why?* If I'd wanted to talk to her, I would have called, wouldn't I?!

'What do you mean, you're going away with work. What work?' she said, sounding offish.

'A writing assignment, Mum,' I said. 'For *Luxe* magazine. You know, where Zoe works?'

She made a strange gurgling sound. 'Explain!'

I sighed. I purposely hadn't told her about the job in case something went wrong, like I found I couldn't write anymore and was unceremoniously fired by a vengeful Amanda Eddington.

'I'm writing a profile piece on a tennis player,' I reluctantly imparted. 'He's playing a tournament in Monte Carlo, so I'm going to shadow him for a few days, do an interview, meet his team, that sort of thing.'

She made the same gurgling sound again.

'Mum, are you all right?' I asked, suddenly concerned that there was actually something wrong with her and I was missing all the cues.

'Course I'm all right! I'm just a bit taken aback, that's all. I don't think I'll mention this to Cassie – she's a bit fragile at the moment, what with the girls in her office being all cliquey. She thinks they all hate her, and I don't think it would help to hear that you're full of the joys of spring and gallivanting around the south of France. Actually, where even is Monte Carlo?'

Gallivanting? There was no acknowledgement of the fact that a) I'd be working and b) I'd just broken up with my long-term boyfriend and therefore maybe some joy in my life would be a welcome addition. I bit my tongue – I didn't want to get into any sort of conflict when I was about to embark on what might just be the most luxurious few hours of my life.

'It's practically the south of France – between there and Italy. I'm flying to Nice,' I explained.

I didn't think I'd risk telling her I'd been upgraded to business.

'But what do *you* know about tennis?' asked Mum, clearly as perplexed as I was about this fortuitous turn of events.

I heard a scuffle in the background; the low rumble of Dad's voice. There was some sort of tussle on the other end of the line, involving Mum saying something like *No, Winston, she doesn't want to speak to you, she's working,* and Dad saying *Pass me the phone now, please, I want to speak to my daughter.*

'Anyway, lovely as this is, I've got a few things to do before my flight,' I said pointlessly, because they were both too busy bickering to hear me. 'Hello? Mum?'

There was a rustle on the end of the line.

'Ava? It's Dad.'

I signalled to the barman for another champagne. May as well.

'Hi, Dad.'

I could hear Mum grumbling in the background – clearly, Dad had had to force the handset out of her grasp.

'Mum said something about tennis. What's going on, then?' he asked.

'I'm flying to Monte Carlo for some tournament,' I said, checking the departures screen to see how long I'd have left in the lounge to enjoy myself once I'd got off the phone to these two. 'In one hour and twenty minutes.'

'You're going to the Rolex Monte-Carlo Masters?!' he said, sounding uncharacteristically impressed.

'Oh right, you've heard of it, have you? I'm interviewing a player called Marcus Taylor,' I said, perking up. This was the most interested my dad had been in my job ever.

'What, that Brit who's always breaking his racquets on people's heads?' he asked, seemingly incredulous.

'I don't think it's on people's heads, Dad,' I said. I was a stickler for getting my facts straight and my dad had clearly been sucked in by the sensationalised headlines.

'His game is excellent, but he hasn't lived up to his potential and he can't seem to keep his temper in check. He's a disgrace. A wasted talent. He should be ashamed of himself!' said Dad with passion.

'That's quite an extreme reaction . . .' I said, weirdly feeling as though I needed to defend Marcus Taylor, a man I'd never met.

Sure, I'd seen the *Deuce* footage and, okay, his behaviour wasn't great, but the show had probably been edited to make it look worse than it was. Anyway, I liked to keep an open mind going into an interview – after all, my job was to bring out the light and the shade; paint a three-dimensional picture of whomever I was profiling, not judge them before we'd even had a chance to speak.

'Look, Dad, I have to go.'

'Well, don't let me stop you,' he said, even though he and Mum *had* actually been stopping me for the last ten minutes.

I ended the call and opened up the articles about Marcus I'd saved on my phone, which were mostly newspaper reports with straplines like RACQUET MAN CRASHES OUT OF WIMBLEDON! and STROPPY MARCUS LOSES IT AGAIN! Blimey, the press hated him, didn't they? There were also a ton of stories about his love life, involving him partying in glamorous locations with a string of drop-dead-gorgeous models who all seemed to be clinging to him adoringly. What a player! I bet it killed him that instead of his phenomenal tennis, his biggest draws were his romantic pursuits and his propensity to kick off when a shot didn't go his way. One article gave a blow-by-blow account of a match at something called Indian Wells (I made a mental note to look up this mysterious-sounding thing/place), and I wondered why Marcus always seemed to be on the edge of something – teetering on the precipice of being either brilliant or mediocre, of winning or losing, of keeping it together or going completely off his head. Nobody had ever published a fully fledged profile on him before and it didn't entirely surprise me – he seemed like the kind of guy who assumed everyone was out to get him. Which they sort of were. But that didn't explain why he'd agreed to do *this* interview. Was he going to bail at the last minute again, like he had all those times before?

Business class on board wasn't quite as lovely as the lounge, but it did have roomy seats, pre-take-off champagne (yep, more of the stuff) and unusually attentive air stewards. I had the disturbing thought that now I'd had a taste of the high life, I was going to find it *very* difficult to go back to Economy, although clearly I was going to have to. And the best thing about Business, in my opinion, was that I would only have one person sitting next to me and was not destined to be sandwiched between a snoring stranger and a screaming baby. Or at least, I presumed I would have somebody sitting next to me – probably one of the corporate hounds I'd seen drinking espressos and scrolling manically through their phones in the lounge, although they were cutting it very fine to board.

I pulled down my table and set up my laptop, bringing up an interesting article about Grand Slam tournaments and why they were so important to players (big prize money, prestige and points – points for what, I wasn't yet sure). Last year, Marcus had reached the third round of Roland-Garros, also known as the French Open, but had he won the whole thing, he would have netted himself over two million dollars in prize money. I'd had no idea tennis was so lucrative, and never mind the sponsorships on top of that. You heard so much about footballers and their extortionate wages, and I got that tennis players weren't earning that amount every week, but I was shocked to learn that even those making it through to the second round of Wimbledon stood to earn around a hundred thousand dollars!

Just as the engines started up, somebody threw themself into the seat next to me, almost trampolining me out of mine. I wasn't sure why I'd thought people in Business would be any more civilised – money most definitely did not buy class. Out of the corner of my eye I could see that this person – a man, judging by his size – was wearing silky black tracksuit bottoms and some sort of expensive-looking cream-coloured chunky knit. I also couldn't help but notice his quite considerable thigh muscles, which were straining against the thin fabric of his trousers as though they were about to burst right through them. Not that I wanted to give him the satisfaction of looking up, but his face was bound to be a disappointment in comparison. You couldn't have it all, could you?

'Oh, great.'

The person next to me had spoken, but I wasn't sure whether it was to himself, to somebody on the other side of him, or to me. It couldn't be me he'd been addressing, because what would he be 'oh-greating' me about? I tried to focus on my article and not on his voice, which sounded vaguely familiar – deep, resonant, a very slight northern twang.

'Stalking me, or something, are you?'

This definitely sounded like it was aimed in my direction. I looked up, only to be met by the chiselled cheekbones and dead eyes of none other than Marcus Taylor.

Chapter Four

I'd been wrong in assuming his face couldn't possibly live up to his thighs, because Marcus was extraordinarily, dazzlingly handsome close up. I was suddenly finding it very hard to think straight with him glaring at me, his mouth mere inches away from mine, all pouty lips and thick, dark hair that you immediately wanted to run your hands through and a beard that made him look older than the thirty-one years I knew he was from my research. Shame he was such a massive arse.

'Stalking you?' I tried to joke.

'If you're not a crazed fan, why the hell have you got a picture of me on your laptop?' he demanded to know, using the same icy tone I'd heard him adopt when complaining to the umpire about the sun being in his eyes/noisy crowds/slippery surfaces/a shot he insisted had been incorrectly called.

Glancing quickly at my screen, I cringed when I realised I'd zoomed in on a photo of him mid-serve. It didn't look great that I was doing research so last minute, although, in my defence, Amanda had only hired me a few days before and since I knew absolutely nothing about tennis, I had my work cut out for me. I flipped my laptop closed.

'It's research,' I told him, stashing it under the seat in front for take-off.

'Research for . . . ?'

I met his eye, aiming to give off an air of self-assuredness and integrity. Who did this guy think he was? I'd never even heard of him before Zoe turned up on my doorstep dangling a best-job-ever-shaped carrot in front of my face, and now here he was talking down at me like he was Ryan bloody Gosling. Although I liked to imagine that Ryan would be ten times politer.

'I'm Ava Whitfield. The journalist writing the article on you for *Luxe* magazine.'

'What article?'

I swallowed. Fuck. This guy was a nightmare. My dreams of winning a Pulitzer Prize for this piece were fast fading in front of my eyes.

'*Luxe* magazine? The UK's biggest-selling women's glossy? You agreed to an exclusive feature on your life and career, and I'm the one doing it.'

Marcus scoffed. 'I agreed to no such thing. Because, as you'd know if you'd done your research sooner, I don't do press.'

I took a deep, steadying breath, wondering if it would help to have my meditation app playing in one ear.

'Which is why I'm delighted I'm going to be the exception to your rule,' I said, attempting – and failing – to deliver a coquettish smile.

'There are no exceptions. Ever.'

Aaaaaargh!

'I've literally been emailing your agent, Dean, back and forth!' I said, exasperation finally setting in. 'I'm meeting you both later. At your hotel in Monte Carlo!' I said, feeling ever so slightly desperate. This was the worst start to an interview I'd hands down *ever* had. Most people at least pretended to want to talk to me.

'Listen, Ada—'

'It's *Ava*.'

'Whatever. I don't care what Dean told you. I don't do interviews, so instead of flying all the way to Nice for something that I assure you is *never* going to happen, maybe you should get off the plane now, while there's still time,' he said, shuffling his body away from me and purposely facing the other way.

'Bit late for that,' I murmured, as the plane began taxiing along the runway.

Fucking hell. The British public had got him all kinds of right. Which didn't help with the impending feeling of doom that this massive opportunity was about to slip right through my fingers. I *had* to salvage the interview and persuade him to do it. As the plane took off and carved its way through the clouds, giving us jaw-dropping views of London in all its glory, I swivelled in my seat to face him, attempting to give off gentle, encouraging vibes.

'Marcus?'

'What?' he said, seemingly mesmerised by the back of the chair in front of him.

'Can I reassure you that it's going to be an in-depth piece covering all aspects of your life? Dean's arranged for me to come along to four major tournaments this spring and summer so that I – and *Luxe*'s hundreds of thousands of readers – can get to know who you really are and what makes you tick.'

He crossed his arms, sighing to himself.

'With a name like *Luxe*, I'm assuming it's going to be some sort of superficial nonsense about my abs, or my diet, or my workout routine, or what traits I look for in a woman?' he said, still stubbornly looking straight ahead.

He did appear to have great abs, but that was *not* what I was going to be leading with.

'Actually, *Luxe* specialises in thought-provoking articles on a diverse range of topics,' I insisted. 'Our readers don't want to know what you ate for breakfast. They want to know what goes through your mind when you walk out on to the court. How you feel when you win, or when you lose. How you keep your focus in a five-set match. What it would mean to you to win a Grand Slam.'

'I've already won a Grand Slam,' he said coldly.

'Another Grand Slam, then,' I said, kicking myself, because I knew about the Australian Open, I just hadn't realised that's what it actually was. 'They want to know where you came from. Where you want to go next.'

He finally looked at me. This was progress. If he'd liked something I'd said, I very quickly needed to work out what so that I could say more of it.

'I can't have somebody following me around 24/7, Ava, it would be far too distracting.'

He wasn't saying a flat-out no, was he? He'd listened to what I'd said and he'd thought about it, however briefly. *Keep calm*, I told myself. *You've almost got him.*

'I promise you I'll be extremely discreet,' I reassured him, mimicking the dulcet tones of my favourite meditation guide. 'You won't even notice I'm there.'

'Somehow I doubt that,' he said, his eyes boring into me for a second.

Irritatingly, my cheeks flushed involuntarily. I reminded myself that Marcus Taylor was not flirting with me, he was playing me. He probably thought that if he turned on the charm – or his misguided version of it, anyway – I'd be flustered enough to admit defeat and call the interview off. No chance – it would take more than good looks to dazzle me.

'A piece like this could completely change the public's opinion of you,' I said, wanting to seal the deal. 'Why not let them get to know the real Marcus Taylor? The likeable side we don't always get to see?'

He laughed, an annoyingly warm, rich sound that, by rights, somebody as insufferable as him shouldn't be capable of producing.

'Ava. Do you really think I care whether people like me or not?'

For some reason I liked it when he said my name, which was ridiculous. It was literally two syllables long – anyone could remember that.

'Doesn't everyone?' I countered.

'I really don't. Now, if you'll excuse me.'

He promptly produced a silk eye mask from his bag, slipped it on and placed massive black Beats headphones over his ears. I would not be deterred. The flight was two hours long, which meant that I still had a very small window of time to change his mind. Perhaps he'd be less defensive after a nap?

I tried to hold it in, but having downed three glasses of champagne over the last few hours, I was always going to need the loo mid-flight. Marcus hadn't moved for the last twenty-five minutes, so I'd sneakily carried on with my research, trying to find an angle, something I could use to convince him that appearing in *Luxe* would be as beneficial for him as it would be for me. I didn't have much to go on: he was born near Manchester, in a mid-sized town without so much as a municipal tennis court; he'd won a scholarship to some tennis academy in Spain and had travelled all over the world since turning pro at the age of eighteen. There were a couple of pics of him with his mum in the early days, an attractive, tired-looking woman with dyed blonde hair and pretty brown eyes like Marcus's, but she was strangely absent in the shots I could find from the last eight or nine years. He was currently ranked twelfth in the world, having reached the quarter-finals of both the US Open and Queen's last year, and was the British number one. As he'd been quick to pull me up on, he had indeed won a Grand Slam once – but that had been eight years ago. Apparently, he'd come out of nowhere to win it, got the British press and public all excited and then had failed to live up to the hype, getting knocked out of Wimbledon in the second round that same year. I wondered what had gone wrong – why another big win had eluded him, whether he wanted to be *world* number one, whether his Australian Open win was a fluke and whether deep down he knew it was. Other than the tournaments I'd heard of, there were lots of other less prestigious events all over the world that Marcus seemed to travel to, and I was struggling to get my head around what they all meant – if there was a way to write my profile on Marcus without totally immersing myself in the game of tennis itself, I was damn well going to find it.

Closing my laptop, I undid my seat belt and shuffled about in my seat a bit, hoping to alert Marcus to the fact I needed to get up. He didn't stir. Aaargh, how was I going to sneak past without waking him? Then I thought: *tough*. Everyone gets woken up on flights, you can't expect undisturbed sleep when you're sharing a metal cylinder with three hundred other people, can you?

'Excuse me,' I said, standing up, surprised to note that there was actually room to do that in Business.

Absolutely no movement.

I cleared my throat.

'Marcus, sorry, can I get past?' I said, upping the volume a bit.

He stirred, pushing his eye mask over his forehead. It took him a second or two to focus, his eyes eventually landing on mine.

'Really?' he said.

'Really, what?' I countered, purposely holding his gaze. I wasn't going to grovel. It was a perfectly reasonable request that he *move*.

He sulkily prised himself out of his seat, making a huge deal of unbuckling his seat belt and taking off his precious eye mask, huffing and puffing the entire time.

'Thanks,' I mumbled, careful not to touch him as I slid past.

◆ ◆ ◆

When I returned to my seat, Marcus's headphones were nowhere to be seen and he was scrolling absent-mindedly through his phone, stroppily standing up as I squeezed past. I reminded myself what was at stake here. Working for *Luxe* was my dream and this was probably my one and only chance to impress Amanda Eddington. Clearly, I was going to have to try even harder to get Marcus Taylor on side. Perhaps if he knew what I was trying to achieve . . .

'Would you like to read some of my work?' I suggested. 'I could show you a couple of my articles right now, if you like?'

'I don't think that will be necessary,' sneered Marcus.

Right, then. That hadn't worked. Maybe if I let him think he had a bit of editorial control?

'Why don't I tell you what I thought my angle could be for the story? How we could approach the article. Together. For example, we could talk about your pre-match preparation. How do you get yourself in the right mindset to play a tournament like the Rolex Monte-Carlo Masters and what does an ATP 500 event like this mean to you?'

Marcus turned in his seat to look at me.

'I think you'll find the Monte-Carlo Masters is an ATP 1000 tournament. Tut tut, *somebody* hasn't done their homework.'

Suddenly, a seat in economy had never looked so appealing.

'Slip of the tongue,' I said. Damn. I really thought I'd got a grasp of the ATP levels thing.

He raised one slightly unruly eyebrow at me, the only imperfect thing on his otherwise perfect face.

'Do you even know what the ATP is?'

'Yes,' I lied.

'Go on then.'

'Oh sorry, are we testing my tennis knowledge here or talking about the article I'm supposed to be writing about *you*?'

'As I've said at least twice now, I won't be participating in any articles, especially not written by so-called journalists who know absolutely nothing about tennis.'

'Well, that would be because my family couldn't have afforded to pay for tennis lessons, even if I'd wanted them. And in fact, I think you'll find that the entire stuffy tennis scene is set up so that privileged kids can thrive, much like most other things in life, and so no, Marcus, I don't know anything about it. I can think of far more exciting sports.'

'Like what?' he deadpanned.

At least he didn't seem too insulted by the fact I'd said tennis was boring and had practically called him a posh knob.

'Yoga,' I said.

'That is not a sport, Ava.'

'Who cares? I enjoy it. I have fun doing it. You should try it sometime.'

I grabbed my water bottle and glugged at it, hoping to reset so that I could act like a professional journalist trying to get somebody on side instead of this weird, outspoken version of myself. Perhaps I could explain that I'd just broken up with someone and wasn't feeling myself? I'd made an absolutely catastrophic start to the interview, whichever way you looked at it. And annoyingly, even though I hated him on sight, my journalistic curiosity had well and truly kicked in and I suddenly wanted this interview more than anything else; I *had* to persuade him to do it, even if he was – on first impressions – an awful person. There had to be more to him than back-to-back snidey put-downs, didn't there?

'Look, I think we might have got off on the wrong foot,' I said, which was obviously an understatement.

'You think?' he said sarcastically.

His voice was deep and resonant, but quiet and melodic, as though in another life he might have been loud and boisterous, but in this one he was forever holding something back. Except when he lost it out on court, of course, and then it was as though he released every single emotion he'd ever felt in one spectacularly visceral swoop.

'Why don't you tell me why you won't do interviews?' I asked, trying a different tactic. 'I might be able to alleviate some of your fears.'

'It's not about fear, it's about fact: the papers only skew stuff to make me look bad,' he said.

'Worse than you look already, you mean?'

Surely he had to take some accountability for his actions?

'Don't hold back,' he said.

Funnily enough, I *did* usually hold back, big time. If it wasn't because of Charlie, then it must be the champagne – quaffing three glasses of the stuff before 10 a.m. had clearly been a bad idea.

'Go on, then. Sell yourself to me. If you don't usually write about tennis, which clearly you know absolutely nothing about, what *do* you write about?' asked Marcus.

'Well,' I said, mentally scrolling through my CV, 'you might be interested to learn that despite being twenty-one and with marriage the furthest thing from my mind, I started out as an editorial assistant on *Your Wedding* magazine.'

Marcus snorted. 'I thought you were a serious journalist?'

'People are very serious about their weddings, I'll have you know. Anyway, it was the first paid writing gig I was offered out of uni, so I wasn't about to turn it down, was I? I had a little thing called rent to pay?'

'Not interested in marriage, you say?' said Marcus.

'That was then.'

'Changed your mind?' he asked, his tone teasing.

Charlie's face flashed into my mind's eye again, as it still did about fifty times on a good day. I was in dangerous territory here, but needs must.

'Currently undecided,' I said. 'You?'

'Is this part of your interview technique? Start talking about yourself and then slip in a question?'

'I didn't think you'd agreed to an interview?'

I had him, I had him, I had him! Surely. Didn't I?

'Carry on. What came after writing about other people's weddings?' he asked.

'Features assistant on one of the Sunday supplements,' I said, trying to gauge if he was still interested.

'I suppose that's marginally more impressive,' said Marcus.

'And now I'm a freelance journalist, so I can basically write about anything.'

'Except tennis.'

'Trust me, I can get up to speed in no time. I mean, it's a game, isn't it – how much can there be to learn?'

'I think you'll find it's more than just a game. And if you're serious about writing about my life, I suggest you start giving the sport the respect it deserves.'

My heart leapt. Even though he'd just essentially told me off, I was holding on to the fact he was talking about the interview as if it was actually happening. All I had to do now was not say anything else to mess this up.

I tucked my hair behind my ear, self-conscious for the first time since we'd met. 'I can assure you, I'm taking this very seriously. Dean would never have agreed to this if he didn't think it was important for your career. And for me, having an article of this calibre in a magazine like *Luxe* could be the big break I've been waiting for.'

'Are you using emotional blackmail on me, Ava?'

Dammit, he was more astute than I'd thought.

I was about to deny it when I was distracted by a flurry of movement out of the corner of my eye. It took me a minute to realise that a woman was heading purposefully in our direction with her phone held aloft, seemingly trying to take a photo of Marcus. By the way she was swaying up the aisle, I could only assume she'd had even more free champagne than I had.

'I thought it was you,' she purred in a thick French accent, shoving her phone in his face without asking.

Marcus put his hand over her lens, gently pushing her away. 'No photos, please.'

The woman clutched her chest in shock, as though it was her God-given right to stick her camera under the nose of a complete stranger. She might feel like she knew him, but he did not know her. I felt my very first pang of sympathy for Marcus Taylor.

'Just one tiny little picture. It is for my daughter. She is *big* fan,' insisted the woman, her words ever so slightly slurred.

'I'm sorry, but no,' said Marcus.

I cringed internally. I understood that it wasn't ideal, that he just wanted to sit quietly on a plane, but other passengers were looking over now. Couldn't he just say yes to the photo and get it over with? Between the two of them they were causing a huge scene, and for what? One measly little selfie? I was tempted to say something but bit my tongue; that was hardly going to help me get him on side.

After what felt like ages, during which all eyes in the business-class cabin were trained exclusively on Marcus, she finally gave up and backed off, waving him away in disgust, hissing what I guessed were expletives at him.

'Any idea what she's saying?' I asked, thinking it was probably better not to know.

'Nope, and I couldn't care less,' he said dismissively, pulling his eye mask aggressively out of his pocket and putting it on again.

Great. We were back to the silent treatment, and I still didn't have my interview.

◆ ◆ ◆

Marcus sprinted off the plane the second we landed, calling a derisive *It's been delightful talking to you, Ava* over his shoulder as he strutted down the aisle. It had taken all my mental strength to stop myself lunging after him in one last-ditch attempt to win him over. His agent had arranged for the three of us to meet at their hotel that evening and I had no idea whether Marcus was planning to show up. I was edging towards not, but a glimmer of hope was pulsating somewhere inside of me.

I didn't see him again until we'd retrieved our luggage from the carousel and I happened to fall into step beside him on the way out. He was sporting an iceberg-sized racquet bag slung over his shoulder and the requisite moody demeanour as we emerged into the bright lights of the arrivals hall. I felt tiny next to him, which was no mean feat since I was five foot eight and almost always felt too tall, especially if I was wearing heels. Marcus was six foot four, according to his official stats. I revelled in the need to strain my neck to look up at him.

'Still stalking me, then?' he said, glancing down at me with irritation.

'Your ego really does know no bounds,' I quipped.

'Marcus, over here!'

Suddenly, there was a flurry of camera flashes so bright that I physically had to hold my arm in front of my eyes. I'd never encountered actual paparazzi before, and it was shockingly intense. God, was this what it was like to be famous? All of the time?

Through the crook of my elbow, I noticed a young, denim-clad photographer snapping brazenly away in our direction, and he wasn't the only one: there was a guy wearing a cap, too, and another one kneeling on the ground, presumably wanting to get a shot of Marcus from a different angle. It seemed they'd had intel that some of the British players would be flying in for the tournament that day.

'What the hell are you doing?' yelled Marcus, striding over to the one in denim and pushing his camera quite violently so that the photographer almost dropped what was clearly a very expensive piece of equipment. The enormous lens alone must have cost a fortune. 'Get your camera out of my face. Now!'

I was rooted to the spot, somehow unable to look away even though every part of this spectacle made me recoil in horror. I'd only met Marcus a couple of hours ago and there'd already been a *lot* of drama, mostly involving the taking (or not) of photographs. Surely being papped came with the job? Now that I'd seen it first hand, I could vouch for the fact it wasn't a pleasant experience, but he must be used to it by now? If I got the chance, I vowed there and then to get to the bottom of his overreaction, because I refused to believe that anyone did this much shouting for the fun of it.

Eventually tearing myself away from the scene unfolding in front of my eyes – the photographer was now threatening to call the police, while Marcus stomped off in the direction of the taxi rank with a stressed-looking driver running after him – I searched for the car *Luxe* had booked for me, feeling somewhat unsettled. Marcus wasn't helping himself behaving like this – it couldn't be good for his blood pressure or his tennis career, not to mention the unfortunate people he unleashed his temper on. Surely there had to be another, calmer, *nicer* side to him somewhere, which I was determined to uncover. Now all I had to do was persuade Marcus to let me.

Chapter Five

At a quarter to seven I waited for my taxi in the unassuming lobby of my perfectly nice three-star hotel, hovering near the door but also careful not to block the entrance for any other guests who needed to come in or out of the hotel. There was a young-ish vibe about the place; studenty types wanting somewhere relatively low-budget to stay on their way through to the French Riviera, or to Italy if they were heading in the other direction. Anyone with money would surely be staying at one of the slew of ultra-luxurious hotels I'd enviously scrolled through on the Condé Nast Traveler website, Marcus's being one of them. Still, I definitely wasn't ungrateful – getting to travel at all with my expenses paid was a perk of the job I'd never, ever take for granted.

Marcus's manager, Dean, had emailed a couple of hours ago to confirm our meeting, which had been a relief given Marcus's antagonistic attitude on the plane. I'd been worried that he was going to call the whole thing off, so this had to be a good sign, didn't it? Maybe Marcus hadn't been in Dean's ear the second we landed, refusing to set eyes on me ever again. So after showering and changing into a black satin Zara minidress (hoping this was the kind of generically chic thing one might wear for casual drinks in a swanky Monégasque hotel), I'd touched up my make-up and slicked my dark hair back into a wavy ponytail, leaving a couple of tendrils falling loose at the front. This had been easier than washing it and straightening it from scratch, an arduous task I was unenthusiastic about at the best of times. I stifled a yawn, wondering when the double espresso I'd just downed was planning to kick in – today had been more eventful than the last fourteen put together, and the energy required was taking its toll.

I rested my head against the windowpane as the taxi glided along Avenue Princesse Grace, which, according to my research, had once been named the world's most expensive street. It curled around the bay, sending us sailing past the Japanese gardens, a Rolls-Royce showroom, and a run of Vegas-style hotels with glimpses of the sea shimmering away behind them. When I looked the other way, all I could see were stunning apartment blocks in whites, pale yellows and pastel pinks rising up in tiers as far as the eye could see, some with pretty, wrought-iron balconies, others sleek and modern, hanging over the cliff's edge like something out of a James Bond movie. I didn't dare to imagine how much any of them would cost and I thought it might make me feel physically sick to google the local real-estate prices; London was bad enough.

My taxi dropped me off on the sweeping driveway of Marcus's hotel. I took my time walking up the rather grand front steps, noticing the uniformed valets and the supercars parked out front, feeling like Cinderella arriving at the ball (minus the amazing dress). Once I was inside the spacious, marble-floored lobby, I had to force myself not to do an actual double-take at how beautiful it all was. It was the kind of place that probably had an achingly hip rooftop restaurant with a months-long waiting list and a plethora of intense-sounding gym classes that I likely wouldn't have signed up for even if I *had* been staying there.

Dean had requested that I meet him and Marcus in the hotel's poolside bar and as I followed a sign directing me out on to the terrace, I spotted them immediately, perched on stools at a high table with their backs to the sea, framed by the sunset and the pretty, private pebbled beach that I bet looked gorgeously enticing on a warm summer's day. Mentally preparing myself, I approached them, focusing my attention mainly on Dean and ignoring Marcus, just for a second, because his scowling would only put me off. Then again, maybe I should be grateful that he'd turned up at all.

'You must be Ava,' said Dean with a Hollywood smile, sliding off his stool to greet me as I approached.

'I am indeed,' I replied, attempting to exude professionalism and confidence with one rather clunky handshake.

Dean was senior vice-president at WCG, a behemoth of a talent agency based in Los Angeles, a city I had visited twice and loved, even though, to all intents and purposes, it should be the sort of place I hated. Clean-shaven, with golden-blond highlights, Dean had an expensive-looking set of veneers and was wearing a suit I reckoned was Armani or similar; clearly, I was in the wrong game. Not that I'd ever be cut out for a career in agenting, mind you, given that I avoided difficult conversations like the plague and hated chasing people for money. To be fair, I'd found Dean pretty amiable so far, which was not to be sniffed at given there were some seriously terrible management teams out there. One of my worst days ever at the Sunday supplement had involved being screamed at by the publicist of a C-list reality star because I'd offered her vegan client a Gail's sausage roll. The reality star herself hadn't seemed bothered at the time and had just declined it like a normal person would. Except that she must have complained to her publicist about me afterwards, so she'd instantly gone down in my estimation. Another one living up to the rep – Marcus Taylor was not alone.

I could sense Marcus watching me as I edged myself on to a stool – I'd have been much better off on one of the squidgy sofas. Perhaps, like cats, Marcus felt more powerful when he was sitting up high. He appeared to have changed out of his ludicrously overpriced sportswear and into an ensemble consisting of a grey

T-shirt, a black blazer and indigo jeans. Perhaps the working title for my article should be: *How Can A Man This Attractive Be So Utterly Unlikeable?*

'I've told Dean I won't be doing the interview he set up for me without my permission,' said an icy-toned Marcus, right on cue.

Great start. We were back to square one, then, by the sounds of it. Did Dean have the power to force him to do it?

Dean gave him a look. 'Marcus. We've talked about you being more of a "yes" man . . .'

'*You've* talked about it,' replied Marcus.

Dean didn't look remotely fazed. I thought I might like a 'Dean' fighting my corner – I didn't suppose he got messed around very often, and as a freelancer, getting money out of people was an unnecessarily stressful part of the job. Chasing unpaid invoices was my own private kind of hell.

'As you know, we've been thinking long and hard about how to propel you firmly into the hearts of the British public,' said Dean with enthusiasm. 'Hell, not just British fans, but fans all across the world. How do we reel them in and make them love you as much as we all do?'

If that was Dean's intention, boy did he have his work cut out for him.

'As you must be aware by now, the public's opinions are irrelevant to me,' said Marcus.

Before I could remind myself where I was, I snorted in disbelief, because I just didn't buy it. We all cared what people thought of us, as much as we tried to persuade ourselves we didn't. Surely? Or was Marcus Taylor really that sure of himself?

'Something wrong, Ava?' asked Marcus, narrowing his eyes at me.

'Sorry,' I said, coughing for effect. 'Had something in my throat.'

Marcus gave me a look that indicated he didn't believe a word of it before turning his gaze back to Dean, shutting me out completely. 'Dean. My goal is the same as it's always been – to play the best tennis I can. To win another Grand Slam. Whether or not people like me is neither a priority nor within my control.'

He sounded very convincing, if you could call a robot convincing, but he wasn't fooling me. It would break me to walk off court after playing my absolute heart out (this was taking a great deal of imagination) only to have at least half the stands booing, stamping their feet and hissing at me. I'd literally be a wreck. And Marcus might not be as sensitive as I was to the judgement of others – people rarely were, I'd found – but surely he felt *something?*

'But we care what the general public have to say about you. Don't we, Ava?' said Dean, nodding encouragingly at me.

'Um, yes?' I said, thinking only of the article; of the piece I'd already started to plan. I'd say whatever he needed me to say if it meant Marcus was going to agree to let me interview him.

And anyway, it was *kind* of true; I did care about Marcus's reputation, insofar as I wanted my readers to feel *something* for him by the time they'd read through to the end of my article. They didn't have to like him – I thought that might be a bridge too far, anyway – but I wanted them to at least begin to understand him. To empathise, perhaps. But in order for me to write something like that, Marcus was going to have to be honest with me, and I was beginning to think that this level of openness was something he might not be capable of.

Dean, however, was not to be deterred.

'Ava wants to write a beautiful piece about you, Marcus. Something that shows *Luxe* magazine readers who you really are. We know you're much more than the Racquet Man the press has dubbed you. You're not just a playboy throwing his toys out of the pram, you have layers. You have actual feelings, like all of us do. But I think that maybe you need to show us what's in your heart and prove to people that you can tap into your emotions as much as the next person. Do you hear what I'm saying?'

'Sounds like you're asking me to give up tennis and take up poetry,' said Marcus in the sardonic tone I was becoming all too familiar with.

'All I'm saying is, we need to show fans that there's a softer side to you,' insisted an impressive Dean. 'Yes, you're incredibly serious about your tennis and yes, it takes extreme dedication and commitment. But I want Ava to see the Marcus your team sees.'

'Which is . . . ?' he asked.

I was gagging to know, too, because so far he seemed exceptionally one-dimensional.

'I want you to show them *fun* Marcus,' said Dean, leaning forward to hammer home his point. 'Generous Marcus. Hard-working, kind, thoughtful, introspective Marcus.'

Was Dean talking about somebody else?

'And how is Ava going to achieve this, exactly?' asked Marcus, possibly thinking the exact same thing. Although this was good, he wanted details. Could I be back in?

'Well,' I said, clearing my throat. 'For a start, I'd like to shadow you for the next few months.'

Marcus rolled his eyes. '*Shadow* me? Planning to join me on court, are you?'

I smiled sweetly. 'Presumably you do occasionally do things *other* than play tennis?'

'Yes, Ava. What do you take me for?' he said.

'Go on, then, like what?' I asked. 'Have you got a secret hobby I should know about?'

'I don't see how any of this is relevant,' he said, waving me away with his hand.

'It's just that if everything in your life is all tied up with tennis, perhaps that's your problem?' I suggested boldly, meeting his eye.

He raised an eyebrow at me for the second time since I'd met him. 'And who says I have a problem?'

Dean leaned on the table, looking from one of us to the other and smiling to himself. 'You two are really hitting it off, huh?'

A waitress came over to take our order and Dean – rather prematurely, I thought – asked for a bottle of champagne and three glasses.

'You know I don't drink the night before a match,' grumbled Marcus.

'A sip won't hurt you,' said Dean. 'We need to celebrate.'

'Have I missed something?' I asked. 'Celebrate what?'

'Look, Marcus. I know talking about yourself is difficult,' said Dean, lowering his voice by an octave so that he sounded all sort of gravelly and persuasive.

I got where Marcus was coming from for one very brief moment. Talking about myself had always been discouraged and now I found it practically impossible, too. Interviewing people was one thing, but the idea of it being the other way around didn't even bear thinking about.

'Ava here comes highly recommended. *Luxe* magazine in the UK are offering you a four-page spread, including an exclusive photo shoot,' said Dean.

'You didn't say anything about photos,' said Marcus, his expression now so dark it was like an eclipse.

'We're open to you choosing your own photographer,' I added. 'If you have one in mind?'

'It'll be fun, no?' said Dean. 'You get to take control. To say who and where. We could shoot here in Monaco. Or in a studio in London, or Los Angeles? Whatever you want.'

Marcus put his head in his hands.

I dared to glance at Dean and he gave me a cursory nod, which I took to be a sign of encouragement.

'Let's go, Marcus. Let's shake this up, let's make a change. And having the lovely Ava following you around for the next twelve weeks won't be that much of a hardship for you, will it?'

I winced.

'Do I have to answer that?' said Marcus, slowly raising his head again as though in extreme emotional distress.

Thankfully, our champagne arrived and Dean poured us all a glass. If I got the chance at some point, I'd ask Marcus about his pre-match routine, even though he'd already warned me off mentioning his diet or his abs. For some reason I involuntarily glanced at his stomach, flat beneath the rippling fabric of his designer T-shirt.

'To our collaboration,' said Dean, raising his glass and holding it hopefully between us.

After a few moments of hesitation, I did the same. 'To our collaboration.'

Marcus wasn't moving. The air was thick with anticipation – was this it, the moment I'd been waiting for since eight o'clock this morning when I'd boarded my flight? Was Marcus going to agree to do this, or was this going to be another of the myriad times I'd heard him say 'no' already today? My foot fluttered lightly underneath the table as I watched his hand slowly reach for the stem of his glass. He picked it up and painstakingly slowly tapped first my glass and then Dean's.

'To our reluctant collaboration,' he said.

I smiled at him, I couldn't help myself. Obviously it wasn't reciprocated, but I didn't care. He'd said yes, that was all that mattered. Over his shoulder I saw two very dressed-up, giggly young women taking photos of us – I hastily looked away again, hoping Marcus hadn't noticed. The last thing we needed was another kick-off and I wasn't sure the girls were prepared for the full force of Marcus Taylor's disapproval. But he seemed to have a sixth sense for cameras and looked over his shoulder. The girls giggled harder and waved.

When he turned back, fuming, I decided to begin my get-Marcus-on-side campaign in earnest.

'It must feel quite intrusive sometimes,' I said. 'The last thing you want after a long day of training or whatever.'

Marcus took a sip of his champagne. 'It's only really the die-hard tennis fans who want pictures and autographs. And it's worse when I'm at a tournament, obviously.'

'But this isn't what you signed up for, is it?' I said.

He shrugged. 'Comes with the territory when you play sport at this level. And it's not like "signing up for it" was a conscious decision. I had the opportunity to change my life and my family's and I took it. I wouldn't have been able to choose to do something else, even if I'd wanted to.'

This was already getting interesting. Had he felt forced into playing professional tennis when deep down he'd had other ideas, other passions? And was it his parents who had stopped him from pursuing them, like mine had?

'When are you going to start following me around, then?' asked Marcus, clearly delighted at the prospect. I wondered if he could sense that I was in writer mode now and that anything he said was, in theory, out there for me to quote and send to print. Of course I didn't want to break his trust, but I also needed to keep it real – if Marcus continued to be an arse, I'd have no choice but to document it.

'As soon as possible?' I suggested.

So that I can file my piece and get this torturous experience over with? I almost added. I gave him a look, hoping I could convey this sentiment without actually having to say it.

'Ava, if it works for you, I suggest you observe Marcus's training session tomorrow morning at nine at the country club. Then you can meet his coach, Patrick Ferretti, and possibly his physio, Nick Breakspear.'

'Perfect, I said, hurriedly scribbling down the names of his team members. Interesting that he was surrounded entirely by men – I could only imagine the testosterone levels in the dressing room.

'Can't wait,' said Marcus, catching my eye with a look I could only interpret as *There's nothing I'd rather do less.*

Behind him, the girls surreptitiously took another photo and I pretended not to notice.

Chapter Six

The circular, dark-turquoise pool glittered tantalisingly in the periphery of my eyeline as I scanned the drinks menu, silently baulking at the idea of spending eight euros on a single cup of coffee. Perhaps it had been the wrong call to leave the normality of my own hotel and head over to Marcus's so early, but I'd needed to make some preparatory notes for the day before I saw him and thought I might as well do it here. We'd arranged to meet in the lobby at 8.45 a.m. because Dean had said it would be easier than trying to explain how to get to the country club and find the practice courts. Marcus had seemed less than enthusiastic about this idea, as you could imagine. In any case, I'd walked over in the morning, deciding I needed some exercise and wanting to see a bit more of Monte Carlo. I was glad I had, because I could now confirm that Monaco's most notable district was even more spectacular than I'd imagined from the pictures I'd seen in magazines or on film. For starters, the pavements, some of which seemed to be made out of actual marble, were the cleanest I'd walked on in my entire life, with zero signs of dirt, litter or any of the other unsavoury things I regularly had to avoid when walking on the streets of a somewhat less pristine London. A metallic purple Maserati had been parked up outside the entrance to a hotel and seconds later a red

Ferrari had roared past, the driver revving his impressive engine as though he was motoring around the Grand Prix track, which he might literally have been doing because the infamous hairpin bend was less than a mile away. Despite almost every square inch of land having been built on, this part of Monte Carlo felt airy and green thanks to the living walls dotted along the roadside and the flower beds lining the pathways, packed full of fragrant jasmine bushes and exotic birds-of-paradise with their dark-green, paddle-shaped leaves and bright orange flowers. The sun was already out and was gently warming the back of my neck as I walked, so much so that I'd pushed up the sleeves of my white cable-knit sweater (thought I'd give a nod to tenniscore, even if I didn't fully understand what it actually was). I'd even got my sunglasses out, which, given it was only early April, felt like the height of decadence.

I'd found a seat on one of the slouchy orange sofas in the grounds of the hotel, carefully avoiding the rock-hard stools Dean and Marcus had gravitated towards the night before. In the light of day, and with blue skies already soaring overhead, the beach looked even more enticing with its crystal-clear water and luxurious sunbeds laid out for anyone who wasn't going to the tennis to relax on. Carved into the cliffside were several wooden bungalow-style rooms with floor-to-ceiling windows, each with its own set of rickety steps down into the water – I wondered if Marcus was staying in one of those, or if his room was housed in the main building of the hotel. I made a mental note to ask whether tennis players always travelled in luxury. Did they pay for accommodation themselves or did the tournament put them up? And was the size of their room in direct proportion to their world ranking?

I ordered myself a cappuccino and began to formulate a list of the things I wanted to ask Marcus and the rest of his team.

I'd made a start on researching Patrick Ferretti (what a name!) and knew that he was Swiss, that he'd played tennis professionally until his retirement in 2001 and that he'd coached some of the all-time greats, including a ten-time Grand Slam-winning former world number one. Apparently, he had a rep for telling the players he coached exactly what he thought of them, and could often be seen screaming instructions from the sidelines – which, from what I could gather, he wasn't really supposed to do. He currently lived just down the coast in Cannes, where he owned his own tennis academy, and he trained Marcus exclusively, travelling with him around the world as he competed in various tournaments for around ten months of each year. He was divorced (hardly surprising if he was away all the time, was it?) and had two teenage children, both of whom were exceptionally good at tennis but who quite sensibly didn't want their father to train them. He'd been working with Marcus since just before Christmas and I was looking forward to meeting him, hoping he'd give me some valuable insight into the workings of Marcus's mind when he was out on court.

By the time I looked up from my note-making, the hotel was suddenly about three times busier than it had been half an hour before when I'd first arrived. There seemed to be lots of early-morning meetings going on, with laptops out, phone calls in progress, and very little of the relaxing holiday vibes I would have expected from a beachside hotel. I wondered if these people were all part of one of the tennis teams, meaning this was a working day for them, just like it was – in a way – for me. There wasn't even a single person in the pool. And I supposed the flurry of activity made sense because apparently the proper tournament started today, with the qualifying rounds (for some of the lower-ranked players who hadn't been given automatic entry) having started the day before yesterday. There was a buzz of excitement as everyone grabbed coffee and breakfast before heading to the venue, many of them, like me, going with a bit of a tennis theme – perhaps a sweater wrapped casually around their shoulders, or a white linen shift dress paired with a chic designer bag. Outfits that, with a bit of tweaking, could almost have been worn on court at one of the exclusive tennis clubs they were no doubt all members of. The temperature was hotting up and I was going to have to take my jumper off at this rate – hopefully, it would stay that way, as I was planning to watch Marcus's first match tomorrow and I didn't want it to be rained off because then everything would get pushed back. I was staying until the end of the week as things stood, hoping that Marcus would make it to the final, or at least the semis. But of course there were no guarantees, and if he was knocked out in round one, I supposed it wouldn't make sense for me to hang around.

When my phone rang with the trill of a video call, I was so into my prep that I assumed it was my mum gushing about the photo of the beach I'd sent her and answered it immediately, without thinking. It wasn't my mum, however: it was Charlie. My pulse hammered in what felt like every cell of my body.

'Hey,' said Charlie, chewing on his thumbnail. He did that when he was nervous. I'd always found it adorable.

For a few delightful seconds, I thought he was about to tell me how much he'd missed me. Was going to declare his undying love for me after all and admit that he'd gone mad for a minute there and that it was me he wanted, not his freedom, not anyone else, not to experiment, just me. If that was the case, I was going to have to pretend to make him work for it, obviously.

'Hello, Charlie,' I said. Even saying his name out loud felt strange now.

Other than my mum with her incessant *Heard from Charlie?* queries, everyone had stopped mentioning him, possibly hoping that by not talking about him, I'd somehow miraculously move on.

I hadn't, needless to say, and sometimes it felt as though the pain of the break-up was getting worse, not better.

'It's good to see you,' he said.

I drank in the sight of him, happy to see his face in real time rather than only in my imagination. He looked exactly the same – a little tired, maybe – and was wearing one of his extensive collection of fine-wool polo necks. If I was honest, this burgundy one clashed with his hair, but clearly he thought he could pull it off, so who was I to judge?

'How's everything?' I asked, secretly wanting to hear that his life was terrible now. Did that make me an awful person?

'Fine. Good. Mum sends her love. She said to tell you she's been thinking of you.'

Not enough to reach out to me, though, clearly.

He squinted at his screen. 'Where *are* you, by the way?'

I closed my notebook, keeping half an eye on the time. It was past eight-thirty – I couldn't get stuck on this call and be late for Marcus, he'd never let me forget it. Charlie always did have impeccable timing.

'Monte Carlo. I'm working, so I haven't got long.'

'Working?'

'Tennis. I'm writing a piece on a player.'

'That's great!' he said.

I bit my lip. He'd always been so invested in my career, so encouraging; my own personal cheerleader. Now I was going to have to do it all by myself again, like I had before I met him.

'Zoe blagged it for me. It's a four-page spread for *Luxe*.'

'Wow. Fantastic, Ava, really well done. Good that you're back out there, anyway, because I'd heard you weren't . . .'

He trailed off, his voice faltering to a halt.

I put my chin casually in the heel of my hand. 'Heard I wasn't what?'

'Doesn't matter.'

'Go on,' I insisted.

'Quite yourself . . . ?' he said, looking at me with sympathy.

'And who did you hear that from?' I asked, dearly wishing I could vehemently deny it and tell him he was deluded.

I was a bit miserable at times, but so what? Being broken up with out of the blue was hardly cause for celebration, was it? And if I was worried about anything it was likely to be money, thanks to him leaving me in the lurch with bills.

'It was nothing,' lied Charlie. 'I can't remember who mentioned it.'

'Sure.'

He cleared his throat. Good, I was making him squirm.

'Did you call for a reason?' I asked, determined to regain some small semblance of control over proceedings. I flickered my eyes to the time at the top of my phone: 8.34. I was cutting this very fine, and immediately hooked my foot into the straps of my bag and dragged it along the ground towards me. Then, without breaking eye contact with Charlie, I slid my notebook and pen into it.

'I wanted to know when I could pick up the rest of my stuff?' he asked, having the good grace to look sheepish.

After four years together, *this* was what had prompted him to contact me? There was no hope he was calling to ask me to get back with him, then.

'Well, as I said, I'm away,' I told him. 'So it'll have to wait.'

'When are you back?' he asked.

'Not sure,' I said, being deliberately vague. 'It depends when Marcus gets knocked out.'

'Who's Marcus?'

'The tennis player I'm profiling. Who I'm supposed to be meeting in about thirty seconds. Sorry, Charlie, I'm going to have to go.'

He'd managed to go this long without the one remaining bag he'd left at ours/mine, which, as far as I knew, consisted of winter jumpers and a pile of ancient DVDs. Surely another week wouldn't make any difference?

'It's just, I've got a trip coming up,' he said. 'So I could have done with some of my warmer stuff.'

'Sorry. Not much I can do,' I said, aware that I was now dangerously close to welling up.

Because he was clearly enjoying his freedom to the max and wasn't cut up about losing me at *all*. And who exactly was he going away *with*? Because if it was a friend or his dad or something, he would have just said, wouldn't he? My mind was working overtime now – was it possible he'd met somebody else already? Or even that this someone else was the reason he'd ended things with me in the first place?

'Fine. Let me know when you're back and I'll send an Uber to collect it,' he said.

Great. He couldn't even be bothered to come and get it himself. Was the prospect of seeing me really that unbearable for him?

'Take care, Ava,' he said, moving his face closer to the screen. 'And I really am sorry. I hope you'll find a way to be okay.'

'I'll be fine, Charlie. I'm not going to fall apart just because we're not together anymore.'

'Oh I know,' he said. 'I know. That came out wrong. I just meant—'

'I'll see you around.'

He waved at me sadly until I forced myself to end the call because otherwise I was probably going to cry. For some bizarre reason, I ran my fingertips across the now-empty screen. It had been better when I'd made myself forget he'd ever existed, because his call had totally made me relapse. Which I did not have time for because it was now EIGHT FORTY-FOUR! I launched my phone into my bag, scrambled up and power-walked around the pool, feeling nauseous and tearful and not at all in the mood for Marcus bloody Taylor.

◆ ◆ ◆

He was already in the lobby waiting, of course, standing next to a huge oval table housing the most gigantic vase of fresh flowers I'd seen in my entire life. He was wearing a pale-blue tracksuit with navy trim and a Lacoste logo on the chest. Perhaps he was sponsored by them, and I made a mental note to ask, and also to find out what they thought of his despicable on-court antics.

'Afternoon,' said Marcus sarcastically, picking up his racquet bag and hoisting it over his shoulder.

'Oh, I'm sorry, did we not say eight forty-five?' I snapped, plucking my phone out of my bag and waving it in his direction.

'I think you'll find you're late,' he said.

'What, by one minute?' This guy needed to lighten up. What difference was sixty seconds going to make. 'Shall we go, then?'

'Oh! *Now* you want to go?' said Marcus.

I tutted and stalked off but then I had to wait for him outside the main doors because I had no idea which direction we were going in.

'You do know I'm not staying here? That I had to walk across town to meet you?' I said, on a mission to justify not being on time by about a millisecond.

He turned right and headed uphill. I hurried to fall into step beside him, already feeling the pull of my breath as Marcus effortlessly powered along and I had to work ridiculously hard to match him step for step. For fuck's sake, couldn't he do *anything* at a normal pace?

'And yet you arrived at the hotel in plenty of time,' said Marcus.

'How do you know what time I—'

'I could see you from my balcony,' he said, cutting me off. 'So whatever it was that made you late, it certainly wasn't the walk over.'

Great – he was totally in one of those posh bungalows up on the cliffs, wasn't he? I felt uneasy at the thought of him watching me without me knowing. I could have been doing anything; something unprofessional (I wasn't sure what). Had he been watching while my cappuccino arrived, while I sipped it, while Charlie threw me off with his pointless call about clothes any normal person wouldn't wear until at least November?

'Any chance we could talk about something other than my timekeeping?' I asked, making the executive decision to change the subject. 'I'm here to interview *you*, remember?'

'Don't remind me,' he said.

'How are you feeling about your chances at this tournament? Do you have a game plan?' I asked him.

He squinted across at me. 'You're not seriously expecting me to tell you?'

'Why not?' I took my phone out of my bag. 'You don't mind if I record this, do you?'

'Yes, I do mind. Because my "game plan", Ava, is classified information and it remains firmly in my own head.'

This was frustrating, because if he didn't give me permission to record him, I was going to have to remember every single thing he said and furtively make notes once I got to the courts. I followed him as he marched across the road, up towards a huge turquoise marquee at the top of the hill, which I presumed was the famous Monte-Carlo Country Club, where apparently Grace Kelly used to play tennis for fun during her reign as Princess Consort.

'But Dean must know, right? And Patrick. And maybe even Nick?' I asked, momentarily so smug about having retained the names of the key members of his team that I almost forgot why I was having to mention them.

'Dean is my manager. He doesn't get involved in strategy,' said Marcus, unzipping his bag, pulling out a lanyard with an annoyingly perfect photo of his face on it and shoving it around his neck.

'You don't value his opinion?'

'I value it greatly when it comes to business. But not when it comes to my game,' he said.

'And Patrick?'

'Patrick works on my technique, my serve, my shots. He knows my weaknesses and my strengths. We talk objectives, goals. But we don't discuss my opponents, or how I'm going to use what I know about them to help me win the game.'

'Wouldn't his input be helpful?' I asked, as we bypassed a coach-load of fans pulling up by the kerbside, a bus dropping off a bunch of crammed-in locals, some of whom were wearing a uniform suggesting they were working at the tournament in some capacity, and a smattering of chic-looking people arriving on foot. Because it was so early, Marcus managed to go unnoticed for a second or two, until one person spotted him, setting off a run of *Good luck, Marcus!* and *Over here, Marcus!*, all of which he proceeded to ignore, keeping his head down while striding on by. I wondered why he couldn't find it in himself to give them so much as a cursory nod of thanks.

Marcus showed his pass to security and explained who I was, that I was a journalist and that I had a press pass waiting for me at the desk. They let us through, directing us to the official accreditation stand.

'To answer your question, when I walk out on that court, I'm all alone,' said Marcus. 'Patrick isn't allowed to coach me. Any decisions I make, I make by myself. And so the strategy has to be entirely mine, so that I can flip it whenever I need to. So that I'm not relying on anyone else to do it for me.'

I couldn't argue with that. I also hoped I could remember what he'd said word for word because despite his questionable personality, this man was a veritable hotbed of headline-ready quotes.

◆ ◆ ◆

Dean had put my name on the press desk and, having shown some ID, I was now kitted out with a lanyard declaring me fully accredited and Access All Areas.

'You can explain our tardiness to Patrick,' Marcus said huffily as he led me through the VIP village and out into a pretty square, which had marquees selling expensive sportswear and novelty tennis-themed gifts around its periphery and a pop-up café in the middle. I could have killed for another coffee, but I didn't dare ask to stop.

I made another mental note: *Marcus is obsessed with timekeeping!!*

I followed him down some steep steps, and then around for a bit and up on to another level with what looked like several courts at the top. The steps were flanked by tumbling beds of colourful flowers, neatly planted displays of daisies, marigolds, pansies and other plants I didn't have the knowledge to identify. A sign said we were on route to the practice courts and I could already hear the pop of balls being hit back and forth with considerable force. Stopping for a second to catch my breath, I looked behind me, thinking what a pretty venue it was. The sea was glittering in full view just beyond one of the main courts and, below me, the tournament was laid out on different levels, as though it had been carved into the side of a cliff like a village. The colour scheme appeared to be white and that lovely turquoise I'd seen from the bottom of the hill in the form of parasols and tents, with quaint white benches for people to sit on and bars and crêperies dotted around for when people wanted to spend the equivalent of their weekly salary on a glass of wine and a Nutella pancake.

After navigating yet more steps, we arrived at court number nine. Marcus ushered me through the gate and inside a sort of green mesh cage housing two of the bright orange clay courts I'd seen on that *Deuce* programme. A couple of players were already training or warming up and I didn't recognise either of them, which was probably a sign that I was going to have to force myself to learn more about tennis – not only the game itself, but the key players on tour. It didn't exactly fill me with joy and, if I had my way, I'd put it off until it was absolutely necessary.

Meanwhile, while rather distractingly peeling off both the top and bottom of his tracksuit ensemble, revealing white shorts and a T-shirt underneath, Marcus introduced me to Patrick, who was in his early fifties and was as suave and handsome as I'd imagined. He approached me with a sort of sexy intensity that only people with a French accent can pull off and said 'Welcome, Ava' loud enough to distract one of the players on the other court and make him abandon his serve in mid-air. Although Patrick and Marcus hadn't worked together for very long, they appeared to have a very similar disposition, and both looked as though they were about to go on trial for murder rather than hit a few balls back and forth across a net. I was being facetious, obviously, and clearly it was a serious business (as it should be, given the *947,000 euros* winner's prize!!) but this was just a training session. Would it have killed either of them to smile?

'Dean says you are hoping your article is going to make the British public fall in love with Marcus,' said Patrick, simultaneously unzipping his own racquet bag.

'That's the plan,' I said, laughing and then wishing I hadn't because nobody joined in.

'Don't get your hopes up,' said Marcus flippantly.

'Now, now, Marcus,' said Patrick before turning to me with the first glimmer of warmth I'd seen. 'Ignore him. He warms up eventually.'

I was far from convinced.

'Is it okay if I perch here to watch your session?' I asked Patrick, pointing to a bench handily placed at the side of the court. I'd have my back to the sea, which was a shame, but a perfect view of the court action.

'Go ahead,' said Patrick, already striding out on to the clay, ready to begin.

'How long will you be out here?' I asked him, thinking they'd probably be an hour or so max.

'Two hours,' said Patrick over his shoulder. 'At least.'

Marcus must have seen my face fall or something because he said snippily: 'If it's too much for you, Ava, feel free to leave at any time. Wouldn't want you to be bored, or anything.'

I sat down and defiantly got out my notepad. 'Oh, I intend to stay until the very end,' I said breezily, even though I'd formerly had no such intention.

I wasn't going to let Marcus Taylor dictate what I did or didn't do – he might have his team running around after him, but I was here to cast an unbiased eye on proceedings. Plus, I needed to understand the rules a bit more ahead of Marcus's first match the following afternoon and maybe this would help.

'Have a good session!' I called after him as he jogged with high knees over to the other side of the court and began squatting and lunging like there was no tomorrow. It wasn't *unpleasant* to watch.

Ninety minutes later, I was beginning to regret my rather premature declaration to Marcus, but of course pride prevented me from leaving now, because he'd only accuse me of not being able to cut it and would use it against me. So I ignored the fact that the slats of the wooden bench had officially turned the backs of my thighs numb, and that the sun had moved overhead and was now beating down on the top of my (hat-less) head, and I studiously took notes about Marcus's game. If nothing else, it was keeping my mind off of Charlie, which could only be a good thing. Marcus was right-handed – I'd made a note to ask Patrick/Marcus if this was an advantage or not – and he had a cool serve: he effortlessly tossed the ball into the air in the exact same position each time, casually stepped his feet together and then out of nowhere he sort of launched himself off the ground like a jet taking off. Was this a normal technique, or was there something different about the way Marcus served, I wondered? Something else I noticed was that Patrick kept telling Marcus to 'go into the net', which he seemed to have an aversion to. From what I could tell, he appeared to be happiest when he was slamming balls from one baseline to the other, his shoulder muscles rippling beneath his T-shirt, his biceps engaged as he brought his racquet through to make contact with the ball. His white shorts had already turned a subtle shade of orange, stained by the clouds of dust flying off the court every time the ball ricocheted off the clay.

While Marcus and Patrick took a break to talk and – in Marcus's case – glug about two litres of water, I began mapping out the introduction to my article. It always felt good to get words on a page, even if they weren't particularly good words. At this stage in the process I liked to write down anything that came into my head, with a view to finding the natural tone of the piece. Since nobody would ever read it and barely any of it would appear in the finished article, I felt free to note my honest impressions of Marcus and the elite tennis circles he moved in (spoiler alert: they weren't good).

> *Marcus Taylor: International Tennis Star. World Number Twelve. British Number One. Absolute Tool. These monikers have all been used to describe the man I've been assigned to shadow for three months between April and July – and on first glance, I don't disagree with a single one of them.*

Our initial meeting unexpectedly took place on a British Airways flight to Nice – unluckily for me, the one and only upgrade to Business I was likely to blag in my entire life was somewhat hijacked by the fact that Marcus Taylor had been seated next to me. What are the odds?! It quickly became clear that he's not a fan of journalism. He also appears to detest his fans, refusing to engage, sign autographs, take photos or show appreciation to people who have potentially travelled thousands of miles – and spent their hard-earned money – to see him play. Ignorant doesn't cover it. Arrogant is an understatement. And utterly obnoxious pretty much sums it up. And perhaps it's actually an industry-wide problem, because from my limited contact with male tennis players so far, I've never witnessed a group of men with such fragile egos in my entire life – one missed serve and their tightly coiled little world comes crashing down around them. In the case of Marcus Taylor, toddler tantrums are likely to ensue, involving racquet smashing, bag throwing, generalised stomping and red-faced tirades aimed at anyone from a teenage ball boy to a spectator whose only crime is to have quaffed a few too many glasses of Pimm's. The tennis scene is shockingly toxic and unsurprisingly privileged and my opinion of Marcus Taylor in particular can, quite frankly, only improve from here.

Pleased to have at least made a start, I put away my notebook and picked up my phone. I'd not looked at it once since we'd arrived on court because it would hardly look professional, and also I was finding the training session slightly more engaging than I thought I would. But as we neared the two-hour mark, I didn't think a subtle scroll would hurt, even if Marcus would no doubt take it personally if he caught me looking at anything other than him and his tennis prowess. I flicked through Gmail, Insta and TikTok, reassured that I wasn't missing out on anything whatsoever, finally scanning through WhatsApp where there was a message from Amanda's assistant, Ruby, presumably with some last-minute info about the tickets I needed to collect from the press office for tomorrow's match. I scanned through it, surprised to see she'd sent me a link to an article entitled: *Marcus Taylor's Secret New Girlfriend!* Ruby had added a few words underneath: *This just popped up on an obscure digital celeb gossip column I follow. Could be useful to know for your piece?*

This was surprising. As far as I'd worked out from my research so far, he'd never even been in a relationship lasting more than about five minutes. Glancing at Marcus, who was now practising volleys at the net, I sighed, clicking on the link – I supposed I was going to have his achingly beautiful girlfriend hanging around now when I was supposed to be spending time alone with Marcus and getting to know him intimately (in a professional capacity, of course) for my piece. Which was why it took me several beats to acknowledge the full horror of the blog-style column, culminating in my phone dropping out of my hand, landing face down on the clay and sending my own cloud of dust fluttering into the air.

With a few people – Marcus included – looking over, no doubt wondering why this strange woman had just launched her phone into mid-air, I bent down to sweep it up, cleaning the screen with my sleeve and immediately regretting it because now my white jumper was smeared with orange clay too. With a slightly shaking hand and a head that was literally spinning (this was *not* just a turn of phrase), I made myself look at the photos and headline again. *Concentrate, Ava*, I told myself. This could not be what I thought it was. Could it? Because from where I was sitting, the insinuation seemed to be that Marcus's secret new girlfriend was . . . well, me!! For reasons I didn't have time to unravel, I felt the tiniest sense of relief that at least this meant he didn't have an *actual* girlfriend to put a spanner in the works, an emotion that was swiftly followed by sheer, unadulterated panic. What if somebody I knew also subscribed to this column?! I immediately thought of Charlie, and while there was no way he'd be interested in celebrity gossip, any number of the other teachers at his school might be. And my parents and sister would think I'd lost the plot entirely – I'd only met Marcus five minutes ago and now I was supposed to be embroiled in some sort of passionate love affair with him? It made absolutely no sense! I swiped manically through the handful of pictures accompanying the story – the first was of me and Marcus sitting on the plane, which I presumed had been taken by that sly French woman. I bet she'd been snapping away before she'd even approached us! In the grainy shot, I was being all expressive with my hands and Marcus was looking at me with disdain (there had been a lot of those moments, it could have been any of them). The 'source' had quoted that we'd had a 'heated argument' but soon made up, 'cosying up over a glass of champagne'.

Cue a second picture of me holding a glass of bubbly. In this shot, we were looking at each other in a way that could easily have been mistaken for romantic longing, if you didn't also know what was going through my head at the time – i.e., wondering how I was going to get this egotistical man on side so that I could write the damn article I was being paid to write. In a split second, my entire obsession with celebrity gossip was shot to pieces – if they'd got this so wrong, was *any* of it true? And then I spotted the killer photo – the proof, if you like, that 'Racquet Man' and his 'exotic brunette lover', a description I'd never in a million years have come up with for myself, were in fact going public. Because there, in technicolour, my face as clear as day, were the paparazzi shots of Marcus and me entering the arrivals hall together. And the short exchange we'd had about whether or not I was stalking him had somehow given the impression we were engaged in an actual conversation, like any couple might be. A sort of: *let's go and find our taxi, darling!* Or: *shall we stop off at a romantic cliffside restaurant for lunch before we head to our delightfully luxurious hotel?* There was absolutely no indication that he'd accused me of following him on purpose, or that I was desperately trying to make him not hate me enough to agree to being interviewed for my story. The paparazzi – nay, the entire media industry – was an absolute joke! And why hadn't Ruby warned me, instead of casually sending me a link to photos of my just-off-a-flight face splashed across the web? It took me a few moments to remember that Ruby and I had never met – I'd never even been into the *Luxe* office, so in reality she had absolutely no idea what I looked like, and, of course, the writer of the column hadn't known my name. Ruby hadn't connected the dots at all and how could I blame her?

I slung my phone into my bag, my chest rising and falling with indignation as adrenaline rushed through every muscle of my body. Even the tips of my fingers were tingling as I tried to open my bottle of water. Was I going to faint, I wondered? I closed my eyes, tempted to put my head between my knees but realising that would attract the kind of attention I currently did not need. Marcus was going to go mad when he saw the pictures. He wasn't going to do the article now, was he, and my one chance to impress Amanda Eddington at *Luxe* had been ruined. My career-defining moment was about to be whipped out from under my nose because of a handful of stupid, misleading, incriminating photos, and right now it felt as though there was absolutely nothing I could do. Marcus would not, under any circumstances, want to be romantically linked to someone like me. And now I was going to have to face him. And if, by some miracle, Dean hadn't already seen the story, I'd have to break the bad news to him, too.

I looked back at Marcus charging around on court, an oblivious Marcus who wanted nothing more than to focus on the tournament and probably dearly wished that he'd never set eyes on me in the first place.

Chapter Seven

After another excruciating fifteen minutes of hitting, grunting and generally getting annoyed with himself, Marcus finally strutted off the court. He stopped right in front of me, a deliciously cool shadow falling across my face.

'What's wrong with you?' he said, training his piercing brown eyes on me. Sweat was pouring off him now, running down his temples in rivulets and dripping on to the white towel slung around his neck.

'Nothing,' I said, struggling to utter even the simplest of words.

Marcus crouched down in front of me and peered at me with a frightening intensity. 'You look all grey and sweaty, even though the only exercise you've done is to lift your pen. Have you got sunstroke, or something? You should have gone inside if you were too hot. Here,' he said, rummaging in his sports bag and pulling out an ice pack. 'Hold this against the back of your neck.'

He twisted the plastic pouch to pop it, shook it and handed it to me. Even though I probably didn't have sunstroke, I did as I was told. If nothing else, I was stalling for time. I'd emailed Dean the link and had asked for an emergency meeting – he'd requested that Marcus and I meet him in the restaurant in the VIP village as soon as they'd finished training. Hopefully, this meant that he was going to be the one to tell Marcus what was happening.

'What is wrong? Does she need a medic?' asked Patrick, now standing over me and peering at me too. He looked to Marcus for help. 'Is she diabetic, or something?'

'How the hell would I know?' snapped Marcus, standing up. 'Ava, do you feel unwell? Should we call for a doctor?'

'I'm honestly fine,' I said, keen not to appear completely pathetic. 'I'm not ill. I'm just a bit . . . thrown by something.'

'Thrown by what?' asked Marcus.

What had I gone and said that for? Now he'd know something was up and would try to force it out of me while I was feeling vulnerable and didn't have Dean to back me up. To distract him I got up, keeping the ice pack on my neck because, funnily enough, it *was* actually calming me down.

'Dean wants to meet us,' I announced. 'Urgently.'

'Where?' asked Marcus, still eyeing me suspiciously.

'Le Village. Shall we go?' I said, picking up my bag and trying to act vaguely normal, although it was difficult with an ice pack on the back of my head and Marcus and Patrick staring at me as though I was about to keel over. As I headed for the gate, trying to keep what little dignity I had left intact, I noticed another tennis player and his coach looking furtively in our direction. Had they seen the story?!

While I grappled with the lock on the gate – why wouldn't it open?! – Marcus grabbed his tracksuit and ran to catch me up.

'Ava, you're acting very strangely,' he said, sliding the lock effortlessly open for me.

'I know,' I said, choosing not to elaborate.

It was gone eleven o'clock now, meaning the main gates to the tournament had been opened. As a result, a group of fans had already gathered just outside the court, standing patiently behind a chrome handrail with their cameras held aloft.

'Morning, Marcus!' said one male fan chirpily as I followed Marcus down the steps, back towards the VIP village.

'Morning,' he grunted reluctantly.

A few people shoved notebooks and scrappy bits of paper in his direction, which he mostly ignored.

'Marcus! Sign this for me, will you? Please? Please, Marcus?'

I kept my head down, noticing that the only person Marcus stopped for was a little girl who wanted him to sign a giant green tennis ball.

◆ ◆ ◆

Dean was on the phone when we arrived at the restaurant, one of the plush places I'd spotted in the VIP village earlier. It had a marquee-style roof and proper linen tablecloths and food that looked as 'exotic' as I'd been described in the showbiz column I never wanted to set eyes on again. He waved us over as he ended the call.

'Thanks for joining me, guys. Ava, did you fill Marcus in?'

'Fill me in on what?' asked Marcus coldly.

I scraped back a chair and sat down, with Marcus moodily following suit.

'I thought it would be better coming from you,' I said to Dean.

Surely that was fair – this whole thing was humiliating enough without me attempting to put the unfortunate string of events into a coherent sentence. Plus, Dean knew Marcus best – he'd be well versed in how to manage things in a way that didn't cause Marcus to have one of his tantrums, although on this occasion I wouldn't blame him if he did. If I wasn't such a people-pleaser, I might have smashed a racquet up myself right about now.

'Can someone please tell me what's going on?' said Marcus, the dark look of yesterday reappearing. It was going to get even darker in a second, I was certain of it.

'You and Ava have been photographed by the paparazzi and it's splashed all over the press. They're saying she's your new girlfriend,' said Dean.

Blimey, he didn't mess around, did he? I cringed, probably visibly.

'Is this true?' asked a seemingly incredulous Marcus, turning to me.

'Yes,' I said. 'Somebody sent me a link.'

'Show me,' he said.

I opened up the column and handed it to him. You could have heard a pin drop at our table as he scanned the screen. The restaurant's other diners, mostly well-dressed tennis types who loved the sound of their own voices, were too caught up in themselves to notice that one of the best players in the world was metres away and currently a rather unhealthy shade of green.

'Fuck,' said Marcus, scrolling through the images with his thumb while shaking his head in disbelief. 'It was that stupid French woman, wasn't it?'

'Probably,' I agreed.

Here was a thought: maybe if Marcus hadn't been so rude to her, she wouldn't have done this in the first place! I decided against pointing this out, even though I was desperate to. The most important thing here was to keep Marcus calm. If he got too wound up, he might threaten to pull the interview altogether.

'What are we going to do about it?' said Marcus to Dean, still holding my phone in his hand.

'I was thinking nothing?' said Dean mysteriously.

Had I heard him right?

'Nothing?' I clarified.

'I like the idea of showing the public a different side to Marcus,' he said.

'Which side are we talking about, here?' Marcus quite sensibly asked.

Dean looked him in the eye, his confidence unwavering. 'A sweeter, softer side. The sort of side that might be more obvious to the general public if you were in a relationship with Ava, for example,' he said, sitting back in his chair and folding his arms as though he hadn't just dropped a massive bombshell slap, bang in the middle of our beautifully laid-out table.

'What are you *talking* about?' asked Marcus, using more or less the exact words that were on the tip of my tongue. Had Dean missed the point entirely? He was supposed to be ensuring the rumours went away, not making the situation ten times worse.

'Can I ask both of you to take a moment to think about this?' asked Dean, finally acknowledging the icy change of atmosphere.

Think about what, exactly? It was like he was talking in a foreign language all of a sudden, one that included utterly confusing vocabulary like *if you were in a relationship with Ava, for example.* At least Marcus appeared to be as blindsided as I was – this clearly wasn't a normal scenario for him, either, so it wasn't like it was an elite tennis world thing. I turned back to Dean.

'Just so we're clear, you're expecting me and Marcus to . . . do what exactly? Magically develop romantic feelings for each other, just because our picture was posted online?'

Dean laughed softly, which I took immediate offence to – how was any of this remotely funny? 'You misunderstand me, Ava. I don't expect you to have real feelings. I'm proposing that we simply let this play out for the cameras. Leave people to come to their own conclusions. And looking at those sizzling photos online, I have a sneaking suspicion that they're going to fall for those headlines hook, line and sinker.'

Sizzling photos? Was Dean looking at a different set of images? I took back everything I'd ever said about him, he was an utter *snake.*

'You're joking, right?' said Marcus, who now looked even angrier than he had the time somebody's phone had rung just as he was about to serve. Of course he found the idea of pretending to be in a relationship with me abhorrent, I was probably the furthest thing from his type.

'It's perfect,' continued a seemingly unfazed Dean. 'Ava has huge "girl next door" appeal, which the British public will likely relate to. The rumour mills are already out in force, anyway, and you'll have the tennis world speculating about whether you're an item or not in no time. The groundwork has already been laid. All we need to do is stay quiet and let people believe what they choose to believe.'

'Have you lost your mind?' asked Marcus, looking genuinely concerned. 'I can't stand the paparazzi, you know that. Do you honestly think I'm purposely going to *let* them take photos of me? In some sort of ridiculous fake-romance set-up?'

'I know it's a lot to take in,' said Dean, keeping his cool. 'And it's not a set-up: it's business.'

Putting Marcus's irrational dislike of photographers to one side, he did have some valid points, even if he could have put them across a little less aggressively.

'Is this something you do with all your clients? Because it sounds kind of unethical,' I said to Dean.

This was hands down the weirdest assignment I'd ever undertaken and I hadn't yet written a single word. Could I really endure another three months of this?

'It's not come up before now, actually, but that's not to say it won't. Anyway, half the relationships in Hollywood are fake, aren't they?' suggested Dean.

He had a point. But Hollywood was one thing – I'd had no idea the world of tennis could be equally cut-throat.

'You do realise I'm never going to agree to this,' said Marcus, which might just have been the most sensible thing he'd said since we met.

Let everyone think we were dating, indeed. As if! Although, I supposed pretending to be in a relationship with him might be *slightly* more tolerable than *actually* being in one (dating a man with an ego that big would be a full-time job in itself), but either way, it was not going to happen.

'I've got one word for you, Marcus: sponsorship deals,' said Dean.

'That's two words,' I pointed out.

'What about them?' said Marcus.

'You don't have any,' replied Dean.

'He doesn't?' I asked. 'What about Lacoste?'

'They cancelled their contract,' said Dean. 'They're seeing the clay season through, then they're out.'

'Does she really need to know all of this?' said Marcus, irritated.

'I think it's best,' said Dean.

'Do not put this in your article,' said Marcus, glaring at me.

Well, at least he was still planning to go ahead with it, I supposed.

'Fine, this is off the record. Go on, Dean, you were saying?' I prompted him.

'Marcus recently lost his two biggest sponsorship deals after having a rather . . . violent outburst at the Australian Open.'

'Oh! Was that when you threw your racquet so hard it nearly hit a ball boy in the face?' I asked him.

Marcus stared at me. 'It was an accident. And I bought him an Apple Watch to say sorry.'

No wonder Wilson or Head or whoever didn't want him representing their brand. Why would they, when he regularly smashed his racquets to pieces in front of an enraptured television audience's eyes? Hardly made you want to go out and buy one of their products, did it?

'So what we need from you, coming out of the shadows of this exceptionally bad press coverage, is a redemption tour. Starting right now, this season. Because if you want sponsors back in your corner, Marcus, something is going to need to change,' said Dean, bringing out the big guns.

I caught Marcus's eye – clearly, big-shot LA agents did not stop until they got what they wanted. Dean was bulldozing his way through this meeting and Marcus was about to admit defeat, I could see it.

'It wouldn't need to be forever,' said Dean. 'Let's say until just after Wimbledon. Enough time to shift public opinion, but not so long that it stops either of you from getting on with your actual lives.'

This was literally the worst idea I'd ever heard.

'Maybe I'm missing something here, but what's in it for me, exactly?' I asked.

I got that Marcus needed sponsors back on side, but if Dean thought the idea of five minutes of fame in *Heat* magazine was going to get me to agree to his ridiculous charade, he was seriously mistaken.

'Access all areas,' said Dean. 'A no-holds-barred, career-making interview.'

'You've offered me all of that already,' I countered.

'Dean, seriously. Be reasonable. There's no reason for Ava to get caught up in all of this,' said Marcus, clearly using me as additional leverage for his own gain. At least, presumably that was why he was protesting on my behalf. 'She might have a partner or something.'

I felt him looking at me. If only he knew how recently I could have vetoed Dean's suggestion because I *was* in an actual couple.

'Are you, Ava?' said Dean. 'With anyone?'

For four years, when anyone had asked me that question, I'd felt quite smug saying that yes I had a boyfriend and his name was Charlie and he worked in the senior leadership team at a secondary school in West London and that I thought he was probably 'the one'. Now I could barely bring myself to say his name.

'I've just broken up with someone, actually,' I said dismissively, hoping to convey that I didn't want to talk about it but also that it barely had an effect on me anyway.

Out of the corner of my eye, I was sure I could see Marcus react.

'Good,' said Dean.

'Good?'

Exactly how was me being dumped by the love of my life *good*?

Also, I might not be in a relationship anymore, but nobody was even *considering* the ramifications for my article. My career. Surely it would be wrong of me to write a profile piece on someone I had a personal relationship with, however fake we knew it was? If the *Luxe* team got wind of our 'situation', they'd probably pull the piece and I'd be back to using my savings to cover my rent.

Temporarily pulling me out of panic mode, my phone buzzed on the table and I snatched it up. Amanda Eddington was calling; for the love of God, it was like she had a sixth sense! I considered ignoring it, but also thought that if I had damage control to do, it would be best to face it now before any more incriminating photos surfaced online.

'Sorry, I should take this,' I said to Dean, getting up from the table.

I went out on to the balcony overlooking one of the courts to get some privacy, although there were still people milling about everywhere, players and their coaches and executives and big-shot managers. On the cobbled steps below, people were walking back and forth between courts, drinks in hand, shades on, enjoying the atmosphere. I wished life was that simple for me again, and that

I could be heading back to my hotel to type up my notes like I'd planned – suddenly, everything felt difficult in a way I hadn't anticipated. Had Ruby unknowingly shown Amanda the photos, not realising that Marcus's new love interest was none other than the Ava Whitfield she'd been emailing travel itineraries to?

'Amanda!' I said breezily, answering the call before I could talk myself out of it. 'Great to hear from you. How can I help?'

'I've seen the pictures of you and Marcus Taylor,' said Amanda, getting directly to the point.

Fuck. 'About those . . .'

'You're a dark horse, Ava,' she said, producing a deep, gravelly laugh.

'It's not what you think,' I said, desperately keen to convey that I hadn't lost my mind and copped off with an interviewee I'd known for all of twenty-four hours.

'It's brilliant news for us, of course,' said Amanda.

That was a weird thing to say.

'Is it?'

'Ava, everyone's going to want a piece of you and your burgeoning relationship, but it's *Luxe* who have got the exclusive. What could be more alluring than an intimate profile of British tennis's most enigmatic star written by none other than his utterly adorable new girlfriend, who also happens to be a brilliant journalist? It's genius! No wonder Zoe recommended you. She must have known about this, yes?'

'Ummmm . . . not exactly. Because there was – is – nothing for her to—'

'And because I just *know* what an amazing piece you're going to produce, I'm bringing your publication date forward and giving you the lead story for the September issue!'

I swallowed hard. This was big – the September issue was their bestselling edition by a mile, and the most prestigious offering in any glossy magazine's calendar.

'Are you sure?' I asked, my mind going fuzzy, because this was too much, it really was. I suddenly longed for the safety of my sofa and my pyjamas and Alison Hammond on *This Morning.*

'So sure that I'm giving you six pages instead of four and a cover line. I can't wait to see what you come up with, Ava!' trilled an over-excited Amanda.

I pinched the top of my nose. This was a dream come true. An offer I couldn't refuse. And yet it felt all kinds of wrong because even though I'd tried to tell Amanda that there was nothing going on with me and Marcus, it felt like she didn't want to hear it. Maybe the truth *didn't* matter as much as I thought it did in this scenario? As long as nobody was getting hurt, perhaps it was a case of neither confirming nor denying it? It might not sit well with me, but as long as I didn't have to out-and-out lie, it could be a win/win situation – Marcus could get back on side with his sponsors, and I'd get to have the career break I'd dreamed of.

'Now go get that story, Ava!' enthused Amanda.

Chapter Eight

On day two of the tournament, the players' lounge was a hive of mostly strenuous activity, and it seemed to be getting busier by the second. The Rolex Monte-Carlo Masters was a tournament for men only (no idea why – seemed odd) and Patrick had explained that because Marcus was currently seeded at number twelve, he'd be playing the first round, but that the top eight seeds got a "bye" straight into round two. I'd spent the morning in my hotel room watching YouTube videos about the rules of tennis – I thought I understood the basics now, at least, although I was still confused about the 'advantage so and so' bit. And don't even get me started on the tie break.

Feeling like an imposter, a familiar feeling if ever there was one, I busied myself with pretending to write notes and trying not to stare as players I recognised from *Deuce* warmed up with their trainers, some pounding away on the treadmills lined up against the far wall, others doing lunges and twists and intense-looking routines involving weights and medicine balls. Marcus was currently sweating away on a static bike, looking to all intents and purposes like he'd already done a full workout.

'Won't this tire him out before his match?' I asked Patrick, trying not to stare at Marcus's substantial thighs, which were shimmering with sweat as he pedalled away at a rate of knots, his head down, his breath coming in audible short bursts. Not that I'd ever even attempted this level of difficulty on a bike, static or otherwise, but if I had, there was no way I'd have been able to play a two-to-three-hour tennis match afterwards. Were these people even human?!

'Believe it or not, this is only a warm-up,' explained Patrick in his French lilt. 'The absolute last thing we want is an injury – that could mean Marcus having to take months off the circuit to recover. A good warm-up ensures that his muscles are nice and stretchy before he starts, giving him less chance of pulling something if he slips or falls. For Marcus, cardio work also helps him to feel switched on mentally. See how he is totally focused on the exercise?'

He had his headphones on again and I wondered what he was listening to – what his pre-game soundtrack was. And I tried to imagine what was on his mind as he frowned gently to himself, pushing through the last few minutes of his workout.

'Is he thinking tactics?' I asked.

Patrick nodded. 'He will most likely be running through the work we did in training yesterday. And the preparation he has done on his opponent himself. Marcus's game is very adaptable, in that he can shift and change it mid-match if he needs to.'

'And that's not something everyone can do?'

'Absolutely not. Some players, they plug away at what they're good at – it might be a strong forehand, or a powerful serve. If they're consistent enough, they hope that their opponent will make a mistake eventually, and that they will win the point by default.'

'But Marcus doesn't do that?'

'Not generally. If he feels like a match is not going well, you can see him making adjustments to his technique. His entire game plan can change in the blink of an eye.'

Marcus slowed down and stopped pedalling, the whir of the machine quietening as he came to a complete halt. He sat upright, pushing his headphones off his ears so that they hung around his neck. Grabbing the towel from the bike's handlebars, he rubbed at his face and neck, simultaneously sliding off the bike and launching into a set of deep hamstring stretches. He didn't look nervous, exactly, but I thought he seemed more closed-off than usual. Patrick had told me that the tournament was only one tier below the Grand Slams in terms of available 'points', which in turn affected world ranking. There was a lot at stake.

I watched him carefully as he approached us, approximately thirty minutes before he was going to have to walk out on to Court Rainier III in front of several thousand people, the majority of whom, according to Patrick, would be supporting his opponent, Dominic Griffiths, a very popular young Australian player. I unexpectedly felt a whole range of emotions for Marcus, the main one being worry that he wouldn't do well and I'd have to witness him kicking off in real time, which I wasn't sure I could stomach. Suddenly, I understood what he'd meant when he'd said it was just him by himself out on court – that no matter how well supported he felt by his team, during a match it was down to him and him alone to make every single decision.

'Getting what you need?' asked Marcus, approaching me and nodding at my notepad.

'Just getting started,' I said chirpily.

He nodded. 'I should go and get ready.'

He was standing very close to me all of a sudden, so close I could feel the heat rising off his body; could see a tiny drop of sweat hanging off the edge of his left eyebrow, which for some bizarre reason I wanted to catch between my fingertips.

'Good luck,' I said, and then instantly regretted it. Was it bad luck to say good luck, like it was to actors about to go on stage? Was there some other ritual for tennis players that I should have known about? Presumably it wasn't 'break a leg' – that wouldn't be the desirable outcome, and also it was entirely possible and far too close to the mark.

I waited for Marcus to snap at me.

'Thanks,' he said, flinging his towel around his neck and nodding at Patrick.

Okay, good, I hadn't said the wrong thing.

Patrick slapped him on the back. 'You've got this. If you play like you did yesterday, Marcus, it will be a breeze for you. Remember what we talked about – take risks, come into the net. Don't be afraid to push him to the baseline and really use the power of that forehand.'

Marcus nodded. 'Got it.'

He hesitated for a second.

'There'll be cameras out there. You might be photographed in my box. With my team,' he said to me.

While I was still undecided about whether or not I wanted to go along with Dean's fake romance plan, I *had* spent a bit longer than usual choosing my outfit that morning. Funny what the prospect of appearing in the gossip pages did for your inability to like a single item of clothing you'd packed. In the end I'd blatantly copied the women staying at Marcus's hotel, and had opted for black jeans, a white vest, a baby-blue cable knit tied nonchalantly around my shoulders and the loafers I was glad I'd decided to bring with me to Monaco, even if they had added a good few pounds to the weight of my luggage.

'Not a problem,' I said, surprised, in hindsight, that he'd managed to consider me at all when surely he should be focusing entirely on the game ahead. I'd read that tennis players were inherently selfish and Marcus had certainly seemed that way initially, but perhaps there was much more about him to learn.

He gave Patrick a high five and walked off in the direction of the changing rooms, dabbing the back of his hair with his towel as he went.

'Don't you go with him?' I said to Patrick as we stood, motionless, watching him disappear through the swing doors.

'*Non*,' said Patrick. 'Marcus does not like it. He likes to be alone before a match.'

From what I'd gathered so far, he liked to be alone, period.

◆ ◆ ◆

Patrick and I waited next to a deep-red velvet curtain with a sign bearing the words 'Players' Boxes' taped on to the wall next to it. After showing the steward our tickets and accreditation, we were directed to our seats pretty much courtside, which was a bit of a thrill, I had to say, because when I looked over my shoulder I saw there were at least fifty rows of spectators behind me. These little booths seemed to line the entire front section of the court on three sides, with the fourth end housing more fancy-looking seats leading up to what I presumed was the hospitality suite. Camera lenses poked out of the windows of the building – this, I assumed, was the press area, which I hadn't bothered to go to yet even though I had access to it. I preferred to hang with Marcus and his team when I could, as the whole point of coming here was to observe what went on behind the scenes, how Marcus prepared, how he treated his team. As I looked up there was a sea of photographers, no doubt capturing their own versions of the aerial shots I'd seen online – the orange clay courts surrounded by racing-green grandstand-style seating and, shimmering just behind the back row, the sea. Up high in the left-hand corner, a mini TV studio had been rigged up under a gazebo and I could see a blonde-haired woman in a beautiful pink jacket recording a piece to camera.

According to my ticket, we were in Loge J5. I made a mental note to look up the word *loges*. Did all tournaments have them? Were they reserved for press only? For friends and family? Or could anyone sit in them if they were prepared to pay the presumably top-tier fee? I noticed immediately that our loge was pretty empty, consisting of only Patrick and myself plus Nick, Marcus's physio, who was Australian like

Dominic Griffiths but presumably very much in Marcus's corner this afternoon. He had blond hair pushed up into a frizzy bun and a weathered complexion, and looked like he'd just breezed into Monaco on a surfboard. From the little I'd seen of him, his laid-back, smiley attitude was like the yang to Marcus's and Patrick's yin. I thought briefly about the absence of any of Marcus's friends (surely he must have some) and family, particularly his mum, and about why she never came to watch him anymore. This was definitely a question to ask Marcus once we were easier in each other's company, although part of me worried that he was so controlling over everything to do with his personal life, he'd never feel comfortable talking about it. What if he was too guarded to allow me to write the kind of in-depth, September-issue-worthy piece I was now under my own version of pressure to write?

The stands were filling up, with spectators filing back in having had a quick break between the last match and Marcus's. Patrick told me there was a fast turnaround in these early rounds – four matches a day on the two main courts, which were this one and the slightly smaller Court des Princes. There was a smattering of applause as the umpire was announced before emerging from one corner of the court and making his way to his stand, a high chair with a tiny green canopy over his head to protect him from the sun. Then out came the ball boys and ball girls, dressed in green, white and orange and clearly trying hard to contain their excitement.

I settled into my seat, already too warm but deciding I needed to keep the sweater around my shoulders for purely aesthetic purposes. I put on my sunglasses and pushed non-existent strands of hair behind my ears, acknowledging the strange feeling that I was being watched, that at any time an image of me doing something highly inappropriate could be hotwired to news agencies around the globe. I didn't think the Rolex Monte-Carlo Masters had huge international appeal, but then the fact that I hadn't heard of this tournament until I'd seen it on Ruby's schedule was hardly surprising given my lack of interest in sport in general. Turned out tennis was big news, even if I hadn't really noticed, and there were gossip and rivalry and upsets galore, all constantly being shared and updated in the press, on podcasts and on social media channels.

The time on the scoreboard read 12.59 and a huge cheer broke out as the screen flicked to live footage of the inside of the tunnel where Marcus was waiting, looking stern, composed and very tall compared to his opponent, twenty-three-year-old Griffiths, who was wearing a garish fluorescent orange headband over his floppy dark hair and was jogging on the spot like he had too much energy to harness. He wasn't even ranked in the top fifty, and yet he was acting as though the game was unequivocally his. Their approaches couldn't have been more different, and I wondered which was going to come out on top today.

'It's best of five sets, right?' I whispered to Nick.

He shook his head. 'Three. Five is only for the Grand Slams.'

I immediately jotted this down, annoyed with myself for not having known it before – it was just that with all the talk of female tennis players quite rightly demanding equal pay, I'd had the impression that women always played three sets and men five, which was the argument for men completely unfairly being more generously compensated. But if all the tournaments – and there were a LOT, I'd discovered – except the four big ones involved an equal number of sets, there was surely absolutely no argument to be made. I wrote *Check how much female players get paid for non-grand-slam tournaments* and put a star next to it.

Patrick and Nick had stopped talking and were focusing quietly on the empty court. Rap music blared out of a nearby speaker and the crowd erupted into an enthusiastic roar as Dominic Griffiths made his entrance, lapping up the attention and bounding over to his seat like a hyped-up Labrador. As Griffiths put down his bag and began preparing for the match, he waved enthusiastically at the crowd, stirring them into a frenzy before he'd hit a single shot. I wasn't sure whether I was supposed to be clapping for the opposition or not – did supporting Marcus mean that I actively didn't support Griffiths? I followed Patrick's lead and stayed still with my hands in my lap, feeling bad and a bit rude, and in the end I caved in and did a sort of half-hearted clap, not that Griffiths himself would notice – he had enough support on this court to last him a lifetime. Surely this was going to throw Marcus off? Unless I took him at his word when he said he didn't care what other people thought of him. The thing was, though, that felt to me more like bravado doing the talking and I was determined to get some real emotion out of him, not the robotic set of three or four 'feelings' (anger, disinterest, disappointment and disgust) I'd thus far seen him display on rotation.

The umpire made an announcement, first in French and then in English.

'And from the United Kingdom . . . Marcus Taylor!'

A graphic containing stats about Marcus – his age, height, weight, nationality and ranking – flashed up on the big screen as he appeared through the tunnel, freshly changed into a pristine white tracksuit top and mint-green shorts, his racquet bag on his shoulder as almost always. He kept his eyeline steady as he entered the court to a smattering of cheers from the small pockets of the crowd where maybe they supported the UK, if not Marcus himself, and a crescendo of boos from everyone else. Somebody half-heartedly waved a Union Jack in the air, but compared to Griffiths' reception it was positively underwhelming. My most recent deep dive into Marcus's professional history had revealed a tabloid headline from a few years ago dubbing him the GREAT BRITISH DISAPPOINTMENT because of his tendency to crash out in the first round, so maybe that explained it.

Patrick and Nick stood up and began to whoop as hard as they could.

'Come on, Marcus!' yelled Patrick. 'Let's go!'

I stood up because I thought I ought to do something, but I wasn't really the whooping type, so I clapped enthusiastically instead. A few cameras popped in my direction, and I felt a wave of anxiety as I wondered where my face was going to be plastered next. I immediately changed my facial expression to something I thought depicted warmth and encouragement, as it might if I was watching my actual boyfriend playing tennis at a tournament of this calibre. Was this what people in the public eye had to do? Were they constantly checking every look they threw at someone? I'd lived the majority of my life completely unseen, or at least it had felt that way. Part of what I liked about being a writer was that nobody really knew who you were, and that felt safe and familiar. Taking the limelight was something I'd never been allowed to do and even now the concept of it felt alien and uncomfortable. As I watched TV cameramen running backwards in front of Marcus with their long lenses in his face as he walked, I wondered how hard all of this was for someone like Marcus. For someone who, in Patrick's words, liked to be alone.

Marcus took a seat and unpacked his bag, pulling out several racquets and three water bottles, which he lined up by his feet. Thankfully, the boos died down as Marcus and Griffiths took to the court for a warm-up – hitting forehand to forehand, then backhand to backhand, then a flurry of lobs and smashes, finishing up with some practice serves. The air was thick with anticipation and the faint smell of crêpes wafting up from the food stands mixed with the expensive perfume that everyone seemed to wear in Monaco, the sort that might be overpowering if it wasn't so exquisite. As the umpire called Marcus and Dominic in for the coin toss, a hush fell over the stands, like in a theatre when the lights went down and you had a mini rush of adrenaline because you knew the play was about to start. Marcus lost the toss and Griffiths chose to serve first. As they took their places for the match to begin, my phone buzzed in my pocket. I ignored it – whoever it was would have to wait.

Griffiths tossed the ball into the air and served. Marcus hit it high, landing the ball just inside the baseline, on Griffiths' forehand. Griffiths returned it with Marcus immediately using a two-handed backhand to send it flying diagonally back across the court. Griffiths lunged hard for it, but it bounced just out of reach. *Love-Fifteen.* Patrick stood up again, yelling 'Yes, Marcus!' and I started clapping frantically, because it seemed like that was the etiquette. Surely I wouldn't need to do that every time Marcus won a point?

Griffiths served again, to the far side of the box this time. There was a longer rally, a run of slick, powerful forehands being hit from baseline to baseline, a position I already knew Marcus favoured. Eventually, Griffiths mishit a shot into the net. *Love-Thirty.*

The crowd slow-clapped Griffiths as he prepared for another serve; whether this put him off I didn't know, but he hit it too shallow and it slammed straight into the net. His second serve was more accurate, but looked easier for Marcus to return, and as predicted, he sent it careering down the sideline and Griffiths only just got it back. Marcus, meanwhile, had run into the net to intercept the ball and volleyed it on to the ground so hard that Griffiths didn't stand a chance. The umpire announced the scores in French first and then in English. *Love-Forty.* I knew we were at break point – and I could be wrong, but I suspected that a break of serve this early was a very good sign.

Griffiths, his bravado crumbling by the second, served twice into the net, one after the other. *Game Taylor.*

Marcus won the match easily in straight sets, 6-0, 6-2. The crowd were thankfully a tad more subdued as Griffiths made his way off court, leaving Marcus to face the television cameras.

'Marcus, congratulations. How do you feel that went for you?' asked a suited-up man I presumed was a commentator, perhaps for a local TV station.

Marcus cleared his throat. 'It went well, I think. I knew Dominic was going to be a tough opponent, and that he'd have the crowd behind him, and so I had to go hard right out of the gate.'

'Well, you certainly did that,' said the commentator.

I scribbled down what Marcus was saying word for word so that I could analyse it later, although the mass exodus from the stands was somewhat distracting and I wondered why these so-called tennis fans were more interested in taking selfies with the court as a backdrop than they were in listening to the winner's interview.

'Did Griffiths challenge you at all?' the commentator asked Marcus.

'Definitely more than is reflected in the final score. I had to push for every single point. And he had me running around more than I would have liked,' he said, attempting a wry smile.

To be fair, Marcus was much better at this than I thought he'd be – he was saying all the right things and was being nice about Griffiths, even though he'd thrashed him. I was marginally impressed and continued scribbling away until Marcus finished his interview and began walking off court, to much less applause than Griffiths had received. Was this what Dean had been talking about when he said he wanted the public to love Marcus? Were his meltdowns really so bad that he didn't deserve to be applauded when he'd won so impressively? With one defiant wave over his shoulder, Marcus made his way into the tunnel, stopping only to sign a couple more of those giant green balls, which people were dangling precariously over the side, presumably begging him for autographs. Would he have signed them if he'd lost, I wondered?

'What happens now?' I asked as we all gathered our things together and began heading for the nearest exit.

'Press conference,' said Nick. 'Oh, and don't make the same mistake I did when I first started working with Marcus . . .'

'What's that, then?' I asked, intrigued and thinking I'd probably already made it, whatever it was.

'Don't congratulate him,' warned Nick. 'Under any circumstances. He doesn't like people being positive about his game when he's just finished a match.'

I frowned. 'Don't say anything at all? Even though he crushed the guy?'

'Nope. Nothing. And always take the lead from him,' added Nick. 'That would be my advice.'

'Right,' I said.

Was Marcus really such a tyrant that he had his own team second-guessing what they were and weren't allowed to say when he'd gone and romped home with a match? Surely it was normal to say well done, what was so wrong with that? And surely Patrick, who was charm personified when he wanted to be but clearly had an 'edge', didn't tiptoe around Marcus too? I wondered what would happen if they didn't? What were they scared of? Losing their jobs? It wasn't clear what had happened with Marcus's last coach – the only write-ups I'd found on the subject said they'd 'parted ways' last November, which I took to mean either Marcus had fired him or he'd quit. Either way, nobody seemed to want to say, and yet it felt like the kind of thing *Luxe* readers would want to know.

'Will he head straight back to the hotel after the press stuff?' I asked, staying close to Nick and Patrick so that I didn't lose them in the crowd. Patrick, who it seemed was pretty recognisable on the circuit, pulled down the peak of his cap, presumably wanting to reach Marcus for a debrief without being accosted by camera-wielding fans.

'Marcus has an ice bath. And then we train,' said Patrick.

'More training?' I clarified. 'After all of that?'

'His serve was off,' said Patrick, ushering me up the steps towards the VIP village. 'He'll want to work on that and then maybe he'll have some free time if you need him for an interview. Then Dean is meeting us for a team dinner – you are welcome to join.'

Dean had other clients to look after, apparently, and was currently talking to potential sponsors with Mia Stephens, the women's number five.

'Sounds good,' I said, feeling my phone buzz in my bag.

I found a discreet spot in the back corner of the press area to wait for Marcus to make an appearance and took the opportunity to check my messages. Amanda might be trying to get hold of me and she seemed like the kind of woman who would wait for no one. I was semi-relieved to see it wasn't her checking up on my progress (minimal), it was Zoe. I read the message three or four times, thinking it would eventually make sense, or that there was a typo that had changed the entire context.

Do not, I repeat DO NOT, look at your Instagram.

This was very dramatic, even for her. What could possibly be so bad? Could it be that the photos of Marcus and I were no longer uploaded only to the obscure gossip website, but were also splashed across the sidebar of an infamous showbiz news column (which I knew she was addicted to)? I punched off a reply to Zoe.

My fingertip is literally hovering over the icon here – you're going to have to tell me why I shouldn't just click on it!

I half listened to a conversation between a couple of journalists sitting in front of me. One was slagging off Marcus, saying he'd been hoping he'd lose it on court so that he'd have something interesting to report on. I wondered whether Marcus knew he was unknowingly playing right into the hands of the media, who couldn't wait to tear him down.

Another message pinged through from Zoe.

Don't look!! Call me Immediately.

Oh God. It was the comments, wasn't it? Underneath the photo of me and Marcus. He, of course, would be looking glowing and gorgeous and in comparison I probably looked distinctly average at best. Everyone knew you should never read the comments under news stories (particularly not on Zoe's aforementioned website of choice, their readers were vicious). They'd be tearing me apart, I could imagine it now.

I sighed, immediately disobeying Zoe's weird instructions and opening my Instagram. I didn't need to be kept in the dark like a child; I would face whatever horrors were on my Instagram feed with dignity and resilience. Until I saw a series of photos of Charlie beaming back at me, that was. And not just Charlie, but Charlie and somebody else. He'd purposely kept her identity hidden, but it was definitely a woman, because he'd posted tantalising shots of her body parts – her lips; her pedicured feet; her hand HOLDING HIS!! The caption he'd so wittily come up with read: *Cosy spring vibes in the Cotswolds #datenight #newgirl #newromance #couplegoals* and was followed by three heart-shaped emojis. The Cotswolds? The same place he'd point-blank refused to entertain whenever I'd mentioned the words *Soho Farmhouse* and *romantic weekend away* in the same sentence? No wonder he'd wanted to collect his knitwear! I could only imagine the long rambling walks and cosy pub lunches he was currently indulging in with his NEW GIRLFRIEND!! God, had I meant that little to him? And who *was* she? I bet she was gorgeous, if her perfect feet were anything to go by.

Feeling sick and utterly bewildered, I looked up to see Marcus entering the room with Patrick by his side, his trademark grim expression taking hold as he took a seat at the conference table, adjusting the microphone, which was positioned far too low given his height. Cameras popped and the room, which was perhaps half full, became silent as the press director, a thin, impeccably dressed French woman in her late thirties, announced that Marcus would now be taking questions, and that anyone who had something to ask should raise their hand. A few shot up immediately. The first couple of questions were relatively easy for Marcus to answer. 'How much would a win at the Monte-Carlo Masters mean to you?' 'Did you have a game plan going out on court today?' 'What did you think of Dominic Griffiths' game?' Marcus said as few words as possible, answering each question with a sort of robotic efficiency. 'In the run-up to Roland Garros, this tournament is important in gauging how much work I still have to do.' 'My game plan is to win by any means possible.' 'Dominic is always a tough opponent and today was no exception.'

I tried to focus on Marcus, even though images of Charlie and his new love interest kept swimming in front of my eyes. It would probably help if I turned my phone off, but suddenly I didn't have the energy to do anything as complex as pressing a button.

A male journalist in his sixties, wearing a too-tight shirt with patches of sweat seeping through the back of it, shot his hand up. Marcus nodded in his direction.

'Yes?' said Marcus.

'How long do you think you've got left on the professional circuit?' asked the journalist.

I watched Marcus's expression darken.

'People are saying that you peaked at twenty-three. That you'll never get back to that form now. What do you have to say in response?'

I took an instant dislike to this guy, who was clearly trying to wind Marcus up. These journalists were smart, they knew what made a good story, and Racquet Man storming out of a post-match press conference would be one of them. They'd hit a nerve, I could see it clearly, and I felt for Marcus in that second, could see him trying to hold it together, the slight tightening of his jaw, the way his eyes had gone hard and cold.

'My tennis career is far from over,' said Marcus in a clipped, dismissive voice. 'And I am going to do everything in my power to prove my critics wrong.'

Chapter Nine

That afternoon, I perched on the end of a sun lounger on the private beach of Marcus's hotel, which I was ninety per cent sure was where we'd arranged to meet, but now I was wondering if I'd misheard because he was ten minutes late already and clearly timekeeping was of the essence for Marcus Taylor. Control freak, much? If I'd been in a different mood, I might have pulled him up on it, but the fact was, I didn't feel like doing anything at all now, except perhaps lying in a darkened room watching endless hours of *Friends*, my go-to TV choice when I was in emotional distress. Maybe after this I'd go back to my hotel and order myself a bottle of wine and finish it all in one sitting, along with not one but two desserts. Then again, I'd seen on the room service menu that they cost nearly thirty euros each, so perhaps I should refrain.

I checked my messages for about the thirty-fifth time that day, heartened to see another rousing vote of confidence from Zoe.

> *He's an idiot. You're well out of it – let this new girl deal with him!*

When I looked up, Marcus was jogging along the beach in my direction in a matching grey marl sweatpants and top combo, expensive-looking trainers and a cap that I suspected he'd been gifted by the tournament. I waved. He waved back and upped his pace.

'Apologies,' he mumbled, flinging himself on to the lounger next to me. He didn't seem out of breath, despite the run that would probably have had most mere mortals gasping for air. 'We trained longer than I'd thought we would. Had to keep bashing out serves until I got them back on track.'

'They looked fine to me,' I said.

'They weren't, I was way off. I wasn't hitting the spot I wanted. Too many missed first serves, and my second serve was passable at best.'

I'd hardly call his second serve 'passable'. And according to the stats I'd looked up after the match, Marcus had only given away two double faults as compared to Griffiths' seven.

'Go on then, pull me up on being late, I know you're dying to,' said Marcus.

'I'm not, actually,' I lied.

'Even though I called you out for it yesterday?'

'Some of us aren't bothered by trivial things such as somebody being a few minutes later than they said they'd be,' I said breezily.

A waiter delivered the drinks I'd ordered, a freshly squeezed orange juice for me and a coffee for Marcus. He looked at it, pulling the cup and saucer towards him.

'I grabbed you a cortado,' I said, having picked up on the fact he liked them.

'Clocking my hot beverage of choice. Nice touch,' he said.

'I'm nothing if not observant.'

'What was your take on the match, then?' he asked, putting me on the spot.

I wanted to get my notes out, to see what I'd jotted down during the one hour and thirteen minutes Marcus had been on court, but I also wanted to keep it casual and conversational. Marcus had a knack of making me feel like I was the one being interviewed – if I wasn't reeling off the details of my CV, I was warding off completely irrelevant questions about myself. Was this some kind of test? If I failed, or overstepped the mark, or said the wrong thing (whatever that was), would Marcus decide to share even less of his life with me?

'I thought you looked very focused,' I said carefully, keeping it vague. 'And I liked the way you dominated him from the off. It felt like he never really had a chance.'

'How do you imagine I dominated him?' asked Marcus, taking a sip of his coffee.

I looked at him quizzically. 'Are you testing my tennis knowledge again or something? Because I can tell you right now, it's utterly non-existent.'

'It's not a test, Ava. I'm interested to know what you thought,' he said, placing his cup back on its saucer and leaning back on the lounger.

I ran through the game in my head. What had stood out to me? What were my honest first impressions of his game, and could I say them? I pictured his stiff posture, his tight jaw, his grim expression throughout.

'I noticed that there was no real fun in your game,' I said.

I could bombard him with compliments, of course I could, he'd won easily, he'd been brilliant, there was no denying it. He'd been consistent, solid, not a trace of the temper I'd read about and had witnessed on TV. Every shot he'd played from the back of the court had looked to be going long, but when I'd watched it land, expecting it to be called out, it had pinged on to the clay just inside the baseline. But even though Marcus said this wasn't a test, it felt like it was, and my instinct told me that what he really wanted to hear was the stuff that hadn't been quite perfect. To see if I had the guts to stand up to him, I supposed, to tell him the things he didn't want to hear. Although why he thought that was my job, I had no clue. Wasn't that what Patrick was for?

'No fun?' he said, nodding to himself as he mulled it over, and then sitting forward in his seat. 'Expand.'

I looked out at the last vestiges of the day's sunlight glittering on the surface of the water, taking a moment to think about what I was going to say before turning back to him.

'It's just an opinion,' I said. 'But it didn't look as though you were enjoying it. You seemed tense. As though you had this huge pressure weighing on you. Like you might have had if this was the final and not round one, playing someone you must have known you could easily beat.'

'I see,' he said, reaching for his coffee again.

'Feel free to disagree,' I said. 'You could have been having a whale of a time, for all I know. Maybe this is actually your happy face,' I said, making a circular motion in the air with my finger.

Silence hung dangerously between us. There was a good chance I'd offended him, that I'd gone in too hard too soon. Mind you, he didn't have one of his *really* dark looks on, so it could have been worse.

'You're right, actually,' he said.

I swallowed the huge mouthful of orange juice I'd just sipped with a gulp so loud I was sure he must have heard me. Should I press him more?

'Why didn't you enjoy it?' I asked him.

He crinkled up his brow, as though he was trying to put his feelings into words, something I suspected he didn't do very often.

'I'm thirty-one,' he said. 'Which I presume you know from your research?'

'Of course.'

'Which means I'm nearing the end of my tennis career. Seems crazy, doesn't it, that everything you've worked for your entire life lasts the sum total of a little more than a decade. Just as mentally you feel like you've hit your peak, your body goes and gives up on you.'

'You've got a good few years, surely?' I said. 'Didn't Serena Williams play into her forties?'

'We're not all Serena. Realistically, I've got until I'm thirty-five, thirty-six at a push.'

'Okay. So let's say you've got five more years playing at this level. What's the pressure about? You're world number twelve. I'm presuming you want to go higher?'

'I want another Grand Slam win. And I think I can get it.'

This made sense. He'd been in finals and semi-finals of the big tournaments a few times since his Australian Open win eight years ago, but he'd never won another. I was going to have to do some research on why not – whether it was true what they were all saying, that it had been a fluke, that the British public couldn't rely on him to win anything.

'So that's your goal for this year?'

'Yes. Which is why I hired Patrick – if anyone can help me win a major tournament, it's him. He knows what it takes. He knows what I'm missing, what I need to do.'

I desperately wanted to write all of this down, but didn't want to ruin the moment. This was the most open he'd been with me, and it felt like he was beginning to trust me a little bit already. If I got my notebook out now, it would remind him that everything he said was liable to be printed in the press he hated, and that seemingly hated him.

'So he thinks you can do it?' I asked.

Marcus nodded enthusiastically. 'I'm injury-free, I'm fit, and I'm putting everything into this year that I can, because if I want that Slam title, it's going to have to be now.'

'Why's it so important to you? Isn't winning one Grand Slam in your lifetime enough?'

'That's a very complicated question, Ava.'

'Is it?'

He hesitated, as though he was unsure whether to say anything or not.

'It feels like I owe it to my mum. There, is that the kind of quote you're after?'

'Do you see me writing anything down?' I said quietly.

Marcus looked towards the shoreline, taking a deep breath. This felt important, like a bit of a breakthrough, and I wanted to keep him talking if I could.

'Was it your mum who got you into tennis?' I asked him, keeping my voice soft and gentle, so he didn't feel as though he was being interrogated.

He rubbed at his jaw.

'It was. She worked behind the bar at a tennis club near Manchester.'

I literally hadn't read this anywhere. 'Okay.'

'I hung out there while she did her shifts because she couldn't afford to pay for childcare. It was a way for her to keep an eye on me without having to fork out for after-school clubs or a childminder. Luckily, the owner of the club had a soft spot for her, because obviously employees weren't supposed to have their kids there.'

I rested my chin in my hand, watching him. He rubbed his mouth with his fingers, perhaps wondering if he'd said too much.

'Is this the kind of thing you want?' he asked. 'The sort of stuff you'll use?'

'Maybe,' I said. 'Try not to think of it like that.'

I wondered whether to push it further. I had so many questions about his past, about young Marcus and how he'd discovered he was a tennis prodigy. What he was like at school. What the other kids at the club thought of him – I could imagine, of course, that they were probably annoyingly entitled and then in breezed Marcus, the barmaid's son, blowing them all out of the water.

My phone buzzed again and Marcus looked at me expectantly. 'Need to get that?'

I shook my head. 'Sorry, I should have turned it off.'

'Any more photos shown up online?' he asked.

'Not that I know of.'

I'd barely thought about all of that since I'd seen the pictures of Charlie and the woman I was becoming increasingly convinced he'd left me for. I should probably ask him – it was a fair enough question when he'd posted it all over Instagram, wasn't it? – but part of me didn't really want to know the answer. When he'd called me yesterday morning, maybe he'd been planning to tell me he was already shagging somebody else but had bottled it at the last minute, banging on about knitwear instead.

'I've been thinking,' I said, gauging Marcus's reaction as I went.

'Don't wear yourself out,' he said.

'I'm up for it, if you are.'

There, I'd said it. I wasn't sure anyone was going to believe we were actually together, anyway – I mean look at us, we were like chalk and cheese in almost every way – but if it put the tiniest, most miniscule amount of doubt in Charlie's mind, if it made him realise that just because he didn't want me, it didn't mean nobody else would, I'd come to the conclusion that it would categorically be worth it.

'Up for . . . ?' he enquired.

Taking a deep breath, I said the words out loud – quickly, before I started to overthink it.

'I'll go along with the fake dating thing.'

Marcus cocked his head, looking utterly confused. 'Really?'

I cleared my throat. 'Really.' He still looked dubious, so I said it with more conviction. 'Definitely.'

If I said it enough times, maybe I'd even start to believe it.

'Why the sudden change of heart?' he asked, shifting in his seat and crossing his arms, as though he suddenly didn't trust that I was of sound mind.

'Some . . . new information has come to light,' I said, being deliberately vague and hoping he wouldn't be interested enough to push for more detail.

'Information about what?'

Damn.

'My relationship,' I replied.

'I didn't think you were seeing anyone?'

God, nothing got past him, did it?

'I'm not.'

He sighed, seemingly frustrated. 'Sorry, you've lost me, then.'

I closed my eyes for a couple of seconds so that I could think straight. I was going to have to come clean and tell him at least part of the truth.

'My ex-boyfriend has met someone else. And it's all happened very quickly. So quickly that maybe there was an overlap, if you know what I mean?'

'Right,' he said, as though he still didn't get it.

'And he's splashing photos of the two of them acting all loved-up across his Instagram feed.'

There, I'd said it, and it sounded even worse in the cold light of day. How could Charlie do this to me? What was it about this girl that made him want to shout about her from the rooftops? Already? And to not consider my feelings while he was doing it?

'Sounds like you're well shot of him,' said Marcus, his Manchester accent coming out thicker than I'd noticed before. I supposed with all the international travel it had been softened over the years and only came out in force when he felt . . . what, exactly? What was he thinking of me right now?

'Yeah. It's a bit crap, but I'll get over it,' I said, weirdly feeling tears well up in my eyes like a tsunami. God, please not now. Not in front of Marcus. The professional boundaries of our roles may already have been blurred by the whole fake dating set-up, but that didn't mean it was appropriate for me to start howling in front of an interviewee. I'd literally cried more in the last three weeks than I had in the rest of my life put together, and it did not sit comfortably with me. Bloody Charlie.

Marcus shifted on his seat. He was probably finding this exceptionally awkward since I was pretty sure he never cried about anything ever, mainly because every emotion he had seemed to manifest as anger. Maybe I could try that myself – it would be much less humiliating and having a good shout at Charlie might do me the world of good.

'You okay?' said Marcus half-heartedly.

'Yes,' I said, sniffing. 'Sorry.'

'There's no need to apologise, Ava.'

If he carried on being this nice to me, the tears were never going to stop.

'So yeah, there you have it. The exceptionally superficial reason behind why I'm happy to pretend to date you,' I said, trying to lighten the mood. Marcus was probably feeling like celebrating, not comforting a tearful woman he barely knew.

'Well, if it makes you feel any better, you can't get much more superficial than faking a romance to get your brand sponsors back on side, can you?' said Marcus.

This was a good point. He didn't *seem* money-obsessed, but that's all sponsorship deals were about, wasn't it? Or was there something more behind it? Some gentle digging might be required to get to the bottom of that one.

'On a different note, my boss at the magazine is loving the exposure,' I said, attempting to make myself look less like a jealous ex and more like an ambitious young woman who simply wants to open all the doors she can. 'She's bumped your profile up to the September issue, and is giving us six pages instead of four.'

Although, if we did go through with the pretending-to-be-into-each-other thing, I was going to have to find a way to reconcile the moral code of being a journalist writing an impartial piece on a celebrity with being photographed cosying up to him. Would people really take me seriously if they thought I was sleeping with him? I bit down hard on my lip, dragging the image of what that might look like from my mind. Not helpful. It was just, when you saw an elite athlete close up, it *was* kind of breathtakingly impressive. And yet, I reminded myself, he had a terrible attitude and the kind of aggressive, testosterone-fuelled manner I really couldn't stand. There, I could still be objective! Just because I was going to pretend to fancy him didn't mean I would go easy on him, not at all!

Marcus stretched out his arms, lacing his fingers behind his neck.

'I'm still not entirely sure we're doing the right thing,' he said.

'I feel the same way, obviously,' I said, secretly trying not to take what he'd said personally. He probably couldn't stand the idea of having to spend more time with me than was strictly necessary.

'I like to be straight up with people,' said Marcus. 'In case you hadn't noticed, it's a case of what you see is what you get with me.'

'That's definitely coming across,' I said.

'In which case . . . what are we going to say to people? People we know?' he asked.

'As little as possible? We let the pictures – if there are any – do the talking. We don't have to confirm or deny anything, we can just be sort of . . .'

'Enigmatic?' he suggested.

'Exactly. Leave them to fill in the blanks. That way we don't have to out-and-out lie. Which, for the record, I don't feel comfortable doing either.'

'Good that we're on the same page with this,' he said. 'We can get Dean to iron out the details later.'

'There's not going to be some weird Hollywood-style contract or anything, is there?' I asked, keen to avoid being sued if I slipped up, which knowing me wasn't beyond the realms.

'Don't worry, Ava, you won't be legally bound to pretend to like me.'

I pressed the palm of my hand into my chest, giving him a mock sigh of relief.

'Haha,' he said.

I smiled. Teasing him was actually quite fun.

'Are we done for today, then?' asked Marcus, no doubt desperate to get away.

'Sure. You probably need to prepare for tomorrow . . .'

He nodded, downing the dregs of his coffee.

'Round two,' he said. 'And it's not a great draw.'

'Sorry, I know you're probably sick of my questions, but who are you playing?' I asked.

This could be a useful conversation about his pre-match routine – perhaps I could gently ease the information out of him.

'Federico Rambetti. Italian, twenty-six years old. Difficult to beat on clay.'

'So the surface makes a difference?' I asked. 'Your game works better on one surface and not so well on others?'

'Exactly,' said Marcus, 'and clay is not my forte.'

'How come?' I asked. How much could what the court was made of change things – surely you could either play brilliantly or you couldn't?

'The ball bounces higher on clay,' he explained. 'So if my game is to hit fast strokes, preferably from the baseline, occasionally using the serve and volley, it means that my opponent is more likely to be able to return them. I'm naturally better on hard courts or grass.'

'So grass is Wimbledon?' I said, images of the enticing green courts popping into my mind, along with all the pomp and ceremony that came along with it every summer.

'Wimbledon, Queen's, Eastbourne, a couple of others.'

'And the hard courts?' I asked. This I had no idea about.

'Australian Open and US Open are the big ones,' he said. 'But also Miami and Indian Wells.'

'What *is* Indian Wells?'

He looked at me, amused. 'It's a place, Ava. In California.'

'Ah. Good to know. And where else has clay?'

'Roland-Garros – the French Open,' said Marcus. 'Obviously here, also Rome and Madrid.'

I nodded, thinking this was useful information to have. I was assuming most of my readers would know as much as I did about the game – some would be more clued up, but it would be good to put Marcus's game in context. From what I had deduced, he'd be hoping to reach the finals – and preferably win – at Wimbledon, and would give it a good go at a couple of the others, but probably wasn't going to triumph at the French Open. I presumed, however, that he never said never.

'How are you going to approach your match with this Rambetti guy, then?' I asked casually, hoping he would answer me before he realised what I was trying to do.

'Federico is a master of the unexpected,' said Marcus, leaning forward, warming to his subject. 'He does these stealth drop shots that are almost impossible to reach, although not so much on clay, and he has a great spin on his backhand.'

'Interesting,' I said. 'So you'll be doing what to try and beat him tomorrow?'

'You wouldn't be trying to coax my game plan out of me, would you?'

'Who, me?' I said, mock innocently.

'Nice try,' said Marcus, standing up. 'But you can see for yourself tomorrow, can't you?'

'It would be much more helpful to hear it directly from you,' I said, shielding my eyes from the sun as I looked up at him.

He laughed and went to walk away. 'See you at dinner?'

I nodded.

'By the way, is it true I shouldn't congratulate you on your win today?' I called after him.

I still couldn't believe it, and wanted to hear it directly from him.

'There's nothing to congratulate me for,' he said, slowing his pace and looking over his shoulder. 'I played terribly. I was sluggish, my backhand was all over the place, I didn't move him around the court as much as I should have.'

'But you won,' I said, incredulous.

'Luck,' he said, turning his back on me and walking away towards his bungalow.

Chapter Ten

A table had been booked for dinner that night at the glamorous-sounding Coco Bay, a trendy Thai restaurant near the casino. *Luxe* had agreed to cover a daily food allowance of twenty-five euros, which I assumed probably wouldn't even cover a starter, so I'd made a mental note not to get carried away with the food ordering, although things were likely to get awkward if everyone wanted to split the bill. I'd have to ask my accountant afterwards if I could write this off as a taxable expense if worst came to worst. It was part of my research, wasn't it, watching how Marcus interacted with his team while off-duty? And Dean's other client, Mia Stephens, was coming – I wanted to observe Marcus with another player. Would he feel instantly more connected to someone in the same industry? Were they close, given they had the same agent? Would anybody talk about anything other than tennis?

When I arrived at the hotel, Dean and Marcus were waiting on the soft chairs in the lobby. Dean looked pleased to see me, even if Marcus didn't.

'Ava! We were just talking about you!'

'Were you, now?' I said, taking a seat next to them.

'I was explaining to Marcus that I need you two to be more openly affectionate,' said Dean. 'The momentum from the first paparazzi shots is waning and we don't want people thinking your relationship is fizzling out before it's even begun.'

He had a point. So far, I didn't think we'd done a particularly good job of getting photographed together again – a family had snapped some photos of us as we'd talked on the beach earlier, but I hardly thought they had a hotline to *Hello!* magazine. Perhaps Dean had been a little optimistic in thinking that me being spotted with Marcus once on a plane was going to make people think he was suddenly relationship material.

'So what are you saying?' asked Marcus, looking pissed off.

'I've arranged for you to give Ava a tennis lesson tomorrow morning. It's the kind of cute thing couples do,' Dean declared.

'Are you sure about that?' I protested. 'Because believe it or not I've been in a couple before, and tennis has literally never crossed my mind.'

'First time for everything,' said Dean. 'And the photos will look great.'

I glanced at Marcus, who looked about as unhappy with the idea as I was.

'And I need you to touch each other. Stare into each other's eyes. Hold hands, for Christ's sake. I've also tipped off the paparazzi at Coco Bay,' said Dean, swiping up a glass of what looked like Scotch and taking a large mouthful.

I swallowed hard. Suddenly, things were happening really fast. Marcus and I could barely even look at each other, never mind hold hands – even if we did, it was going to look very obviously staged, surely?

'Oh, and I've told Mia you're an item. So for God's sake ham it up in front of her when she comes down to join us.'

Marcus looked appalled. 'Why on earth would you do that?' he asked.

'We'd already decided that we weren't going to lie to people,' I added, also getting slightly concerned. Marcus and I had had this discussion, and now Dean was going all rogue on us, putting us in positions neither of us felt comfortable in.

Dean shrugged. 'This entire exercise will have been for nothing if someone finds out it's not real. We need to stick to our story, and that means having to tell little white lies to friends, family, ex-lovers, whatever.'

I raised my eyebrows, suddenly on high alert. Had he said ex-lovers? Presumably he wasn't talking about me and Charlie, so he could only have meant there'd once been something between Marcus and Mia? I had a million questions in my mind, none of which a fed-up Marcus looked up for answering.

'Talk of the devil,' said Dean, standing up as Mia approached, gliding her way across the foyer like something out of a Victoria's Secret runway show.

She had a body to die for, of course, with long slim legs that were made even more impressive by the silver micro mini and heels she was rocking. I snuck a glance at Marcus to see if he looked in any way uncomfortable – talk about a baptism of fire. Not only was he going to have to pretend to be into me, he was going to have to do it in front of somebody he'd once had a fling with. How long ago had it ended, I wondered? Had it been a hookup, or something more?

'Mia, let me introduce you to Ava Whitfield,' crooned Dean.

I held out my hand to greet her warmly – there was no reason for me to assume she'd be anything other than lovely.

'Great to meet you, Mia.'

She gave me a stiff smile, swiftly extricating her hand from mine. If she could have got away with it, I reckoned she would have shaken me off in disgust.

'You too, Ava,' she said, for some reason elongating the first syllable of my name, putting an unusual emphasis on it, and I didn't think it was just because of her American accent.

Then she eyeballed Marcus.

'Evening,' he said with a nod.

'Well, Marcus, you certainly kept that one quiet,' said Mia. 'Dean tells me you and Ava are an item now.'

I really thought this was where Marcus would pull the plug. He'd said it himself, he was a straight-up kind of guy who said things as he saw them, but here we were, trying to fabricate a connection that simply wasn't there. I mentally prepared for him to come clean in front of Mia, upset Dean and then we'd have to deal with the fallout. But to my surprise, Marcus leaned forward in his seat, reached out and tucked my hair behind my right ear, letting his fingers linger on my neck for a few seconds, just behind the lowest point of my drop earring.

'Well,' he said, holding my gaze as I tried to remember to breathe. 'It kind of took me by surprise, to be honest.'

Even though my mind was reeling, I was aware of two things: the fact my skin was now burning where he'd briefly touched me, because it had been so unexpected, I supposed, and because Charlie hadn't touched me like that for months, fake or not. And the other thing was that Mia Stephens was currently giving me daggers, indicating that if something *had* happened between her and Marcus, it had been him who ended it.

◆ ◆ ◆

Dean had ordered us two cars to get to the restaurant, which was only fifteen minutes away by foot according to Google Maps, so I didn't see why we couldn't have walked. On the other hand, I was wearing heels, so I'd probably thank them later.

We all filed out to the front of the hotel and Dean ushered Mia into the first car with him, Patrick and Nick, conveniently leaving Marcus and I to share the second.

'That wasn't at all set up,' I grumbled under my breath as Marcus held open the taxi's door so that I could slide easily inside.

'Not exactly being subtle about it, is he?' said Marcus, shutting the door behind me as I strapped myself in and then striding around to get in on the other side.

We sat in silence to begin with. I was still in awe of Monaco, and this street we were driving down was like something out of a video game: smooth and straight, the strangely appealing central reservation filled with plants and palm trees. But then, after a while, it felt like somebody should acknowledge what had happened in the bar, how we'd upped our pretending-to-be-a-couple game. I wondered if it had been a moment of madness that he was now massively regretting.

'Hope that was all right?' he said eventually. 'That little display in there?'

I winced internally. How to even *begin* discussing that he'd just pretended to be so into me that he'd just *had* to reach out and touch me tenderly in front of a room full of people, one of whom, presumably, was his ex.

I cleared my throat. 'I suppose if we're going to do this, we may as well do it properly.'

'That's what I thought,' he said. 'Just wanted to make sure we were on the same page.'

I nodded, looking out of the window as our car snaked off the main road and up into a tangle of winding streets, away from the sea and into what I presumed was central Monte Carlo. The impeccable streets were lined with brightly lit designer shops – Dior, Louis Vuitton, Prada, Gucci, high-end household names that I could only ever imagine being able to afford. I'd found some random statistics for my article earlier, each one more surprising than the last: Monaco was smaller in size than New York's Central Park; over twelve thousand millionaires lived in less than one square mile, presumably due mainly to the country's zero income tax policy; there was supposedly a curse on the monarchy, otherwise known as the Grimaldi family, whose framed pictures I'd seen displayed proudly all over the city – photos of Prince Albert and his wife, Princess Charlene, were behind glass cabinets in hotel foyers, and beautiful black-and-white shots of his late mother, Princess Grace, took pride of place in every other shop window.

'Mia didn't seem happy,' I said, testing the waters. 'Did you two used to be an item?'

Marcus sighed. 'Is this off the record or on? Because I'm losing track here.'

'That's what happens when you mix business with pleasure,' I said with a shrug.

'And exactly which part of this arrangement are you finding pleasurable, Ava?' he asked, glancing sideways at me.

'Pleasure was the wrong choice of word.'

'Was it, now?' he said.

I could almost hear the smile playing on his lips, like he didn't believe me. Why would he, with an ego as big as his? He probably thought that I was finding every minute of being linked with him an absolute delight. And the truth was, part of me, the part of myself I was used to ignoring, *was* feeling more alive than I'd felt in months, but not for the reasons Marcus thought. It was more that I was fired up by the people I'd met, the way they didn't try to hide their ambition, that the players essentially put their souls on the line every time they stepped out on to that court. It was actually quite inspiring – shame they all had to be so arrogant about it.

'Mia and I spent one night together last season,' said Marcus, pinching the top of his nose as though telling me this was in some way difficult. 'I suspect she wanted more, but unfortunately that wasn't something I could give.'

Great. No wonder she was livid at the thought of him dating me.

As the taxi pulled up outside the restaurant, I felt like Julia Roberts in *Pretty Woman*, albeit with a slightly more salubrious job. The restaurant was housed in an ornate building that looked exactly like the photos I'd seen of the casino. It had been front-lit in a sultry red light and looked like something out of a movie, with its sweeping staircase and firepits blazing on either side of the entrance. Uniformed valets scurried about outside as a string of unbelievably expensive cars waited ahead of us to be parked – they were out in force tonight, the Ferraris, the Lamborghinis, their engines roaring, their reds and yellows and golds popping against the night sky.

'Wow,' I said.

'Flashy, isn't it?' said Marcus, as our car came to a stop.

'Are we really going to do this?' I blurted out as he reached for the door handle.

A cluster of paparazzi was already crouched at the bottom of the steps, ready to pounce, and I realised that if we were photographed together now there would be no going back. And I didn't want us to have a sort of will-we/won't-we moment in full view of everyone, I wanted to be clear – were we walking into the restaurant as ourselves, as Marcus Taylor, tennis star, and the anonymous woman who was interviewing him? Or were we pretending to be something more? Something more intimate? Something that would require me to revisit my somewhat rusty acting skills?

'We're doing it,' he said, catching my eye. 'Aren't we?'

I breathed in sharply, my heart suddenly racing, although I wasn't sure why. This could get back to my family now; to Charlie. And I was going to have to be prepared to lie – or at least avoid telling the truth – to the people closest to me. Could I really do that? It felt like maybe I could, but what kind of person did that make me?

'Let's go, then,' I said, bracing myself and swinging open my door.

Chapter Eleven

When Marcus came around to help me out of the car, I noticed he was wearing yet another beautifully tailored jacket, this time over a camel-coloured cashmere jumper with black jeans; the combination looked annoyingly slick. As he held his hand out for me to take, I swivelled in my seat, smoothing down the fabric of the white linen shift dress I was wearing – an H&M summer sale special – thinking about keeping my knees together, because wasn't that a classic, getting out of a car and being 'papped' with far too much on show? Not that I'd know; not that I'd ever *needed* to know. And then, as if in slow motion, because that was how it felt for some reason, I took his hand. It was big and warm and steady, and I held on to it for dear life as he half pulled me out of the car. He led me up on to the kerb and slammed the door shut behind me.

He bent to whisper in my ear. 'Ready?'

I squeezed his hand as a yes.

The entrance to Coco Bay was not doing things by halves, with a spotless bright-red carpet leading up to it that made it feel as though we were going to the Oscars and not to dinner. Blinded by camera flashes and rendered mute, I was aware of a few things as we made our way up the steps: my gold drop earrings swinging back and forth, knocking gently against my jawline; my heels sinking into the carpet; my hot palm pressed against Marcus's cool one. Everything else was a massive blur.

Marcus, who's that with you? Is this your new girlfriend? Did you meet on the circuit? Marcus, put your arm around your girlfriend, will you? Go on!

Marcus ignored them and kept walking, looking straight ahead. I tried to follow suit but had the distinct impression that I might have looked a little more rabbit in the headlights than cool and detached, a much-practised look that Marcus was pulling off with aplomb. After all, I'd never had people take photos of me arriving at an event before, why would they? Who had?!

The front door of the restaurant, which had seemed so far away when we'd got out of the car, was suddenly within touching distance. A doorman swung open the door to let us through and Marcus dropped my hand, placing it on the small of my back instead as he guided me inside. The door closed behind us and for a second it was just him and me in the relatively quiet space of the restaurant's foyer, the pop of the cameras out of sight although not entirely out of earshot.

'You okay?' he asked, looking down at me.

'Not sure yet,' I answered honestly.

And then the extremely beautiful twenty-something maître d' swanned up to us, exuding effortless French Riviera chic in a black trouser suit with nothing underneath. I felt a shot of envy for her confidence (and her flawless make-up) as she led us through the dimly lit, velvet-clad restaurant and showed us to our table, where Dean, Patrick, Nick and Mia were waiting. As we passed one table, Marcus waved to the people on it, one of whom was a player I recognised, although his name escaped me. I had a horrible feeling that I was going to have to up my research or risk making a humiliating faux pas.

Marcus didn't take my hand again, which was probably just as well, since Mia was already glaring at us as we arrived at the table. I didn't want to step on anyone's toes, or more importantly, hurt anyone's feelings. That wasn't what this was about – there should be no collateral damage, in fact the only people we could potentially be hurting were the two of us, and we knew what we'd metaphorically signed up for, so on our heads be it. Strange that he was the only other person who knew how all of this felt, and yet it wasn't exactly the same for him – whether he professed to hate it or not, he was used to being in the spotlight, but for me, it was the total opposite of my real life back in London, where I could walk down the street (when I wasn't in a self-imposed solitary confinement) and not one person would have a clue who I was. In actual, real life I was pretty much invisible, and I wasn't sure if that was how I liked it, or just how it had always been and I'd got used to it. I fleetingly thought back to my only experience of 'fame', not that you could have called it that at all. I'd been aged seventeen and in sixth form at Reading Comprehensive School and I'd somehow winged the lead in the end-of-year production of *Pygmalion*. I'd aced it, I knew I had, because everyone except my parents told me so. I'd toyed with the idea of acting as a career for ages after that; considered what it might be like to go to drama school instead of to university. There had been something addictive about all eyes being on me, of turning into somebody else for an hour and a half and having people watch me and enjoy my performance. But yeah, after weeks of my family banging on about what a terrible idea being an actress was, the sheen had come off and I'd given up on that little dream. Sometimes I felt annoyed with myself for being too cowardly to inform everyone in no uncertain terms that I wanted to be an actor and that I was going to go for it, no matter what they thought.

I was beginning to panic a bit as Marcus and his team ordered more and more food for the table and I started totting up the bill in my head – according to the self-important red leather menu, mains were around forty euros each and they'd ordered at least eight of them, plus several starters and two bottles of wine, which I could only hope were placed somewhere towards the top of the wine list and not at the eye-wateringly expensive bottom.

'Ava, tell us about yourself. Dean says you're a writer?' said Mia, eyeballing me accusingly, as though Dean had made that up and I was there purely to get my clutches into Marcus and his presumably quite hefty bank balance.

'That's right,' I said, only slightly distracted by the fact that Marcus's knee was currently resting rather satisfyingly against mine. Was this part of the show, or were his legs just so long that touching was inevitable when seated around a dinner table? 'I'm writing a profile on Marcus for *Luxe* magazine.'

'Get you, with all the publicity,' Mia said to Marcus. She turned to Dean. 'When are you going to get *me* an exclusive interview in a glossy magazine?'

'Working on it, Mia,' said Dean, in a soothing tone. 'I'm in talks with *Vanity Fair* as we speak.'

'Maybe I need to smash a few more racquets?' said Mia, smiling sweetly at Marcus. 'That's clearly what a woman needs to do to get noticed around here.'

'I wouldn't advise it,' said Dean. 'And Marcus is going to try controlling his temper on court from now on, aren't you, Marcus?'

'Try being the operative word,' he mumbled.

'We have been working on it in training,' said Patrick, looking up from perusing the menu. 'He is very hard on himself, Ava, did you notice?'

'I did,' I said.

Mia leaned forward on the table, looking from me to Marcus and back again.

'Are you two official?'

I took a mouthful of water so that I didn't have to speak, desperately hoping that somebody else would step in. I remembered what Marcus and I had said – no direct lying. Vagueness, mystery and ambiguity were the key words to remember here.

'It's early days,' said Marcus, thankfully taking the lead. 'We haven't known each other for very long.'

'Where did you meet?' asked Mia.

'On a flight,' I said, deciding a version of the truth was the best way to play it. Less margin for error. All I needed to do was ham up our initial exchange a little bit (okay, a lot), even if in my opinion it did seem completely unbelievable. Was anyone actually going to buy any of this?

'And what, it was love at first sight?' asked Mia.

'No need to put a label on it. We met, we hit it off, we're seeing how it goes. Now, I don't know about anyone else, but I'm starving and I'd like to enjoy my meal without being interrogated about my love life. Rice, anyone?' said Marcus, picking up an exquisite ceramic bowl and offering it around the table.

'Yes, please,' I said, grateful to him for shutting Mia down.

This was clearly a case of the less said, the better.

As the evening went on, we managed to ward off any more questions from Mia. Patrick and Dean were good company, and Nick made us laugh with his raucous Aussie sense of humour. I talked as little as possible while also wanting to appear interested and engaged, acutely aware of remembering anything that would be useful for my article. Part of me was glad when the dinner was over and I was in the car heading back to my hotel. As well as picking up the bill, Marcus had insisted on dropping me off, even though I'd told him I was perfectly capable of calling myself an Uber.

'Ubers aren't allowed in Monaco,' he'd informed me in no uncertain terms. 'I'll get my car to make a stop.'

Marcus rested his head on the back of his seat, letting out a huge sigh.

'How do you think that went?' he asked.

'Haven't got a clue,' I answered honestly. 'Although Mia was clearly a detective in another life.'

'If she spent less time worrying about what everyone else was doing and more time focusing on her game, she'd be moving up the ranks a lot faster than she is currently,' said Marcus.

'She's number five in the world, isn't she?'

'But she could be number one if she put the work in.'

'And what about you?' I asked, taking a risk. It had been a nice enough evening – did I really want to risk spoiling it by asking the wrong question? 'Is being world number one something you think you can achieve?'

There were a few beats of silence before Marcus spoke again.

'Of course. That's what I think every time I step out on court – that I can win, and then I can win again and again. Otherwise what would be the point?'

I got it. Sort of. It wasn't like you could go into a game with a defeatist attitude just because somebody was ranked higher than you. But I also wasn't a competitive person, and the thought of setting myself up for repeated disappointment, because being the absolute best in the world was the only thing that would make me happy, filled me with dread. What else made him tick, other than tennis? What else filled him with joy? Because I was yet to find a single thing.

'Are you going to put that in your piece?' he asked, turning to look at me in the dark.

'I don't know. Are you going to ask me that every time you say something profound?'

He smiled. I liked it when he did that, although it was only ever a half-smile, a sort of turning up of the corners of his mouth. Did he ever laugh uncontrollably about something, the sort of laugh that left you clutching your stomach with tears rolling down your cheeks? I doubted it. That would require a loss of control and that seemed like something Marcus was reluctant to do.

'You do know that you can pull out of our arrangement at any time, right?' said Marcus.

'Um, yes? That's what I assumed?'

What were they going to do if I changed my mind – *make* me pretend to fancy him?

'I hope you didn't feel under pressure to say yes to all of this – I know Dean can be extremely persuasive. And you've only just come out of a relationship. It could get messy when your ex finds out,' said Marcus.

His knee was dangerously close to mine again, but there was no point in us touching each other now, was there, with nobody here to see it?

'That's not something that concerns me,' I said, even though maybe I *did* want Charlie to find out. I wanted him to know what he was missing. That somebody else wanted me. And for him to know that he wasn't the only one who'd moved on.

My phone pinged. Marcus watched me with interest as I scrolled through a message from Zoe, wincing as I realised what she and other people I knew might have seen.

> *Um, Ava? Why are you splashed all over the OK! magazine website watching Marcus Taylor play with the caption: Racquet Man in Love??! Call me!*

Thankfully, the taxi chose that precise moment to stop outside the front entrance to my hotel. I needed to work out how the hell I was going to explain any of this to Zoe and I definitely couldn't do that with Marcus watching me out of the corner of his eye. She was going to think I'd gone mad – we told each other everything, so if I suddenly started being all cagey, she'd know something was up.

'Right. See you tomorrow afternoon at your match,' I said to Marcus, unclipping my seat belt and opening the door at record speed. I was sure I could see the driver checking us out in the rear-view mirror – surely he didn't read the UK gossip mags?

'I take it you've forgotten that Dean has arranged for me to give you a tennis lesson in the morning?' said Marcus.

'Oh yes,' I said. Shit – I *had* forgotten. 'Tennis really isn't my thing.'

'I bet you've never even played it properly. With someone who knows what they're doing?' said Marcus.

'No, but I've got the basics down – hit balls over the net, watch them repeatedly fly over the fence, spend half your time running after them. Rinse and repeat.'

Marcus tutted. 'Your respect for my sport is truly dazzling, Ava. Why did they pick you to write this profile again?'

'No idea,' I admitted.

My phone beeped again – Zoe wasn't the most patient person and she'd be dying to find out what was going on.

'Good to know,' said Marcus.

'Look, sorry, I'm just being grumpy because I know I'm going to make a total fool of myself and also I'm possibly the least fit person you'll ever meet.'

'It's fine, Ava, it's not like I'm dying to play with you either. I'll have Dean ping you the details.'

'Great. Can't wait.'

I flung myself out on to the pavement, slamming the door behind me. Marcus wound down his window.

'Me either,' he called after me.

Up in my room, I debated whether or not to call Zoe right away and get it over with, deciding there was no point in putting it off. She wasn't one to give up and her messages would only get more and more insistent if I didn't respond. I changed into my pyjamas (no, not the mushroom ones, not even I would pack those for a trip to Monaco), put my hair up, took off my make-up and basically made myself look and feel like a normal person again. The woman who had been photographed getting out of that car earlier this evening had not felt like a version of myself I recognised.

I lay on my bed, propped myself up with pillows and dialled Zoe's number. She snatched it up before it even rang my end.

'What is happening?' she shrieked. 'I've got everyone at work messaging me, although apparently Amanda knows about it already, and I've told them there's no way it could be true because you would have told me. Right?'

Of course I would have told her, if any of it was actually real.

'It just all happened so quickly . . .' I said enigmatically.

'What did?'

I held my clenched fist against my mouth – this was so hard! If I didn't want her picking up on what was really going on, I was going to have to go to town with the pretending.

'We've sort of . . . made a connection?' I said, knowing immediately that this was not the way I talked about men I liked, and certainly not to Zoe.

'What sort of connection? And Ava, why are you talking like a character from a Jane Austen novel?'

'Perhaps I'm tired?' I suggested, wondering why everything I said was coming out like a question. A question posed by Elizabeth Bennet.

I grabbed a glass of water from my bedside table and glugged at it, loosening my throat.

'What's all this about, then?' asked Zoe. 'Because last time I saw you, you had unwashed hair and were pining for Charlie and now you're saying you're falling for Marcus Taylor?'

'Something like that.'

'Is the feeling mutual?'

Ha, course it wasn't. Not that I had feelings for him either, but even if I had, I think I could safely say that they would not have been reciprocated.

'Ava?'

'Yes?'

'Have you had sex with Marcus Taylor?'

Nope. I couldn't do this. Zoe knew me too well and although we'd daydreamed about many a celebrity in our time – she'd never quite got over her Harry Styles crush and I was firmly in the Robert Pattinson camp – we'd always had the foresight to know that these were nothing more than fantasies. Hell, living with Charlie for years had soon made me realise the depth of what could actually be expected from a real-life romance. There would be no awards ceremonies or luxurious facials or personal trainers or exotic beach holidays for me and honestly, I was fine with that; what I'd had with Charlie had been more than enough. And yet, if I dug deep, being in Monte Carlo, spending time at the country club and at posh dinners – it *was* exciting.

'Ava, I'm getting really worried here. Are you drunk? You can't be jet-lagged, you're only just past France. What is *wrong*?'

Aaaaargh. Nope, sorry, I was going to have to come clean.

'Okay. But you're going to have to promise – no, *swear* – that you won't tell a single soul,' I said, my voice sounding grave.

'Tell them what?!'

'We're pretending to date. Okay? Marcus Taylor and I are faking a relationship so that he can show the press that he's not a total robot and I can make Charlie jealous. Oh, and Amanda likes the idea, so that's another reason for doing it.'

I fiddled with my fingernails, chipping away at the red polish I'd hastily applied the night before leaving London. Stupidly, I hadn't brought the bottle with me and couldn't do any touch-ups so I should probably stop picking at it. The type of woman who lived or stayed in Monaco did not have raggedy nails.

'You're joking?' said Zoe.

I adjusted myself, sitting more upright as I didn't think being slumped on a bed was the correct position for a conversation as important as this. And Zoe didn't sound happy. I was clearly going to have to fight my corner here. This was my decision, I reminded myself.

'I'm not, and I stand by it,' I said, holding my head up high even though Zoe couldn't actually see this attempt at bravado. Zoe could be tough, but I was fully prepared.

'Whose idea was all of this?' asked Zoe, clearly utterly perplexed.

I explained what had happened, from bumping into Marcus on the plane, to the pictures the French woman had clearly sold to the press, Marcus's temper and the repercussions for his sponsorship deals and Dean's initially unbelievable suggestion.

'And so in the end, we both decided that there were more pros than cons. We're both single, nobody's getting hurt here. So why not?'

'I can think of several reasons,' said Zoe, sounding massively disgruntled. 'You're extremely fragile at the moment, Ava. I'm not sure potentially being ripped to shreds by the British press is going to help you to repair your damaged self-esteem.'

'I hardly think a few pics of me watching Marcus play tennis will result in me being ripped to shreds.' At least, I very much hoped not. 'Also, I'm not fragile, I was just shocked and a bit blindsided when Charlie left. It's normal to grieve a relationship. Did you know there are several stages of—'

'Yes, you've already told me what you read in your self-help book about how to get over a break-up. I'm just not convinced you're thinking clearly,' she said.

'And so what if I'm not? What if pretending to date Marcus Taylor is, I don't know, fun?'

I frowned to myself. Did I mean that? Because how could it be? And yet, I had to admit that this was the most exhilarating thing that had happened to me in years, perhaps even a lifetime. It was the stuff of daydreams, wasn't it, a handsome sports star on your arm, being photographed while serenely watching Wimbledon (I could see it now, and had already been giving my outfit some thought). Part of me felt as though I deserved to do something just for the hell of it, because, up until now, almost every part of my life had been controlled by my parents, and then in a way by Charlie, not because he was controlling per se, but because I'd naturally put his needs ahead of mine in certain – most – scenarios. And sure, the fake dating thing might well go pear-shaped, but it couldn't feel any worse than Charlie moving out, and essentially Marcus had more to lose than I did. Amanda would be disappointed if she found out it was all a hoax, but I'd never exactly said the words 'I'm dating Marcus Taylor', I'd just let her believe what she wanted to believe. The worst thing she could do was pull the article, and honestly? Much as I wanted this *Luxe* piece to come off, more than any other job in my entire career, I'd lost out on stuff before, and I'd survived, and if it came to it, I supposed I would again.

'I think you should sleep on this,' said Zoe. 'Think about it carefully, Ava. Please don't rush into anything.'

'Good idea,' I said, thinking of the restaurant trip, of the photos of us that hadn't yet surfaced and were way more incriminating than anything that had seen the light of day so far.

I ended the call with Zoe, trying not to let her burst my bubble. And then I frantically texted her the most important thing I'd forgotten to say:

> *Promise you won't tell anyone about this, Zo, even if you don't agree with it. Marcus and I made a pact not to tell anyone. You're the only person who knows this isn't real!!!*

I watched as three little dots indicated that Zoe was typing. They kept disappearing and reappearing and in the end she just sent a thumbs-up emoji. Disappointing my best friend wasn't a great feeling, but also, she'd get over it. Turned out that upsetting people didn't feel as bad as I thought it would.

Chapter Twelve

Marcus had insisted on picking me up in his car at the godforsaken hour of 7.45 a.m.; I hadn't even had time to make full use of my hotel's above-average breakfast buffet.

'Couldn't we just have played at the country club?' I complained, thinking that surely that would have been a far better photo opportunity than this other tennis club, which appeared to be way out in the suburbs. The last thing I wanted was to have to struggle through a game of tennis without a camera in sight, making the entire thing a pointless exercise. I could have been writing by the pool with a caramel latte instead, it would have been much more pleasant.

'The courts will all be booked out. Sometimes even players involved in the tournament have to practise elsewhere,' he explained. 'Also, Dean reckoned it would look too obvious for us to be playing together there, too set up. He wants it – us – to look natural together, apparently.'

I sighed a little bit. 'Wonderful. Any advice on how to achieve that would be gratefully received.'

When we arrived at the club, the manager came bustling out to make a fuss of Marcus and then we were shown to the court we were using for our 'game'.

'If you need anything, anything at all, Monsieur Taylor, please do ask for me personally,' he gushed.

'Thanks,' said Marcus, turning his back on the poor guy and unzipping his bag, producing the kind of paraphernalia that might suggest he was going into a session with Patrick, not a knock-around with a complete novice.

'I don't own a racquet, by the way,' I said.

Marcus pointed to his bag. 'Take your pick.'

I bent down and looked inside, surprised to see at least ten of them placed neatly in there.

'Do you always carry this many around with you?' I asked.

'Yep,' he said. 'Sometimes if you're playing badly, it's good to switch things up. Or if the court is faster than you think, or if your serve isn't going well. Plus there's the problem of broken strings.'

'Throwing them about probably doesn't help?' I suggested.

Marcus gave me a look.

'What?' I said, all innocence. 'Just stating the obvious.'

'I'm well aware that you can't stand the way I let my anger get the better of me on court, Ava, but maybe you'll at least understand it a bit more by the end of our time together.'

'That is one hundred per cent my intention,' I said, glad he understood the point of the piece, even if he wasn't exactly at the opening-up stage. Then again, we hadn't actually spent much time alone together – maybe this would be a good opportunity to get him talking. Plus, the more I talked, the less I'd have to play, right?

I chose a racquet for no other reason than I liked the electric-blue trim and stood up, acclimatising to the weight of it in my hand; it was much heavier than I'd imagined. I wondered whether the fact he might have won a tournament with this very piece of equipment would bring me beginner's luck.

'Happy with your choice?' asked Marcus, making a show of stretching out his hamstrings. Should I be doing the same?

'You do know I haven't played tennis since I was forced to in a PE lesson circa 2011.'

'Well, that's what I'm here for. To show you where you've been going wrong all this time.'

'At pretty much every stage of the process, I'd say.'

He laughed. Like he had on the plane, but not really since. He was always so deadly serious when he was engaged in something tennis-related, and I guessed this didn't really count. Maybe a positive by-product of us doing fake couple-y things together would be that he'd feel relaxed enough to start talking.

'Let's just start hitting and see what we've got,' said Marcus, who of course was all kitted out in the kind of thing he'd just played the Rolex Monte-Carlo Masters in.

'Please don't work me too hard,' I said, looking around anxiously and noticing that almost everyone else playing at the club – most of whom were at least twenty years older than me and looked rich as hell – were really quite good.

'Wouldn't dream of it,' said Marcus, tossing a ball at me. Of course I fumbled it, didn't catch it and had to clumsily lunge around after it until it finally stopped bouncing out of reach. A fabulous start.

As I stood across the net from him and attempted to partake in a very basic rally, I was aware of how tight my shoulders were and how I kept sticking my tongue out every time my racquet made contact with the ball. Why was I doing that?! On the plus side, I *was* managing to hit the odd shot back and when I did occasionally make proper contact with the ball it made that satisfying thwack that I suspected could become addictive. Everyone had to start somewhere, didn't they?

'Not bad,' said Marcus generously.

After working on my forehand for what felt like an hour but was actually only about ten minutes, we moved on to backhand, which I found much trickier. There was so much to think about: getting into position, changing my grip, using my left hand more than my right, even though I was right-handed, following through after a shot and swinging the racquet over my right shoulder.

'Think of the racquet like a windscreen wiper,' Marcus said, executing a perfect backhand that looked nothing like the ones I was producing. 'Like this, see?'

I was already sweating and out of breath. How did Marcus play for four hours straight again? It was mortifying that I was so unfit and so I did my best to cover it up by commenting on the warm weather and taking fake water breaks, just so I had the chance to catch my breath.

'Right. Let's try a serve,' said Marcus.

'You're joking, aren't you?' I said, thinking of the complicated movement I'd seen him doing out on court, feet sliding here, arm swinging there.

'Not in the slightest,' he said, striding over to my side of the court. 'It's easy when you know how.'

He was suddenly perilously close. What was he doing?

'The paparazzi are here,' he whispered in my ear. 'Dean must have arranged it. Don't look.'

'You do know that when somebody says "don't look", it's really hard not to?' I said.

In order to avoid inadvertently making eye contact with one of the photographers, I was forced to keep my eyes on Marcus, which was a little disconcerting. I didn't think I'd been this close to him face on since we sat together on the plane, and even that had been from a weird angle, and also I'd had more pressing matters on my mind.

'Can they hear us as well as see us?' I asked, lowering my voice. Did they have listening devices as well as telescopic lenses, I wondered, their microphones primed and ready to capture some controversial snippet of conversation?

'I very much doubt it. So we can basically say anything to each other, as long as it looks like we're . . .'

I waited.

'We're . . . ?' I prompted.

'Into each other? I don't know.'

'Are you going to have to touch me again, then?' I asked, realising that had come out much flirtier than intended. On the other hand, if we were supposed to look as though we couldn't wait to rip each other's clothes off, I didn't think talking politely about the weather or the state of world politics was going to cut it.

'Would you like me to touch you again, Ava?' he asked.

For some reason, the thought of him getting *any* closer sent an intense fizzing sensation shooting down my spine. Annoyingly, the same thing had happened when he'd held my hand last night, and now here we were again – him with his golden tan and his perfectly trimmed beard and his pink lips that looked as though he might just have bitten down on them, sending blood pumping into that billowy raspberry-hued flesh. Damn. This whole thing would be much easier to manage if Marcus was, say, twenty-five per cent less attractive.

He took another step towards me, running his thumb along my cheek, cupping my jaw with his warm, soft palm, looking deep into my eyes.

'Is this authentic enough for you?' he asked.

I cleared my throat. 'You're actually quite good at this,' I said.

'And you're not, for the record. You're looking terrified, and as though I'm about to murder you, not kiss you.'

'Do not kiss me, Marcus Taylor.'

'Or what?'

I swallowed hard.

'Please tell me you're acting right now?' I said to him.

'Of course I'm acting,' he said, his voice gravelly and low. 'And it would be wonderful if you could at least *try* to do the same.'

My cheeks flushed. I'd show him.

I reached out, hesitantly at first, and hooked my finger into the belt loop of his shorts, pulling him closer to me.

'Still questioning my acting skills?' I asked, looking at him defiantly.

'This is definitely an improvement,' he said.

Then he very gently pushed me up against the green wire fence behind me. Other than his hands on my waist and mine on his quite considerable biceps, no part of us was touching, but it was oh so close, and probably looked much more intimate than it was from a different angle (i.e. from behind a bush on the other side of the court).

'People will see us,' I hissed.

'Isn't that the idea?' he asked coolly. Why was he so chill about this all of a sudden? 'Let me know if it gets too much for you, won't you?'

I wasn't sure what these feelings I was experiencing actually were, but I could *not* take much more of it.

'It's getting too much!' I shrieked.

He obediently removed his hands and took a step back.

'Since I am supposed to be teaching you how to play tennis, let's play a game. Best of three,' he called over his shoulder, walking back out on court.

I, on the other hand, was rooted to the spot. What had just happened? In less than twenty-four hours he'd gone from barely being able to look at me to pinning me up against fences – I guessed he really *did* want those sponsorship deals back.

Reluctantly, I took my place on the other side of the net, for the moment totally unable to look Marcus in the eye. Plus I absolutely did not want to play tennis anymore, especially now I knew that there were photographers lurking in the bushes just waiting to snap an unflattering shot of me missing a ball/falling over/repeatedly hitting serves into the net. It didn't help that my head was spinning from Marcus turning up the heat out of nowhere – by a *lot*. It had been years since anyone other than Charlie had put their hands on me and now, out of the blue, *this*! Talk about a baptism of fire.

'Ready when you are,' I whimpered.

Marcus, who seemed to have lost all sense of humour and had clearly switched into professional mode, showed zero mercy and absolutely thrashed me.

◆ ◆ ◆

Later that afternoon, I'd settled into my seat in Marcus's 'loge' and was watching him play his second-round match, even though I was still annoyed with him for his behaviour earlier. He hadn't even apologised for playing at what seemed like full capacity (though he insisted he was trying his best to match my standard of play) and not letting me win a single point! I knew he was competitive but that was just ridiculous. And it was mean of him, especially with the photographers there to capture every mortifying second. I'd decided I needed an Aperol Spritz after that and was now on my second, and I have to say my anger towards him had already dwindled.

Grey clouds covered the sky today and I felt much colder than I had at yesterday's match. Although I was somewhat regretting wearing a mini dress with bare legs, I was just going to have to suck it up. The press was out in force this afternoon and I'd had to make the difficult decision to choose style over substance. Was this the life of a tennis WAG? Wearing uncomfortable yet chic clothing while shivering courtside for hours at a time? I was sure there were lots of good things about dating a tennis player (Marcus's abs came to mind again) but I wondered how they were supposed to have careers of their own if they had to live out of hotel rooms for the entirety of the year?

Seizing the few seconds of time I had before play resumed, I quickly messaged the landlord of the local pub I sometimes worked at to ask if he had any shifts for the following week, i.e. as many as was humanly possible. I'd have about six weeks between returning from Monte Carlo and having to travel to Paris to watch Marcus play in his second Grand Slam of the year, Roland-Garros, and I was seriously going to need to make some money alongside pushing on with the article. I hurriedly put my phone away as music blasted out of the sound system and Marcus and Federico Rambetti prepared to play the next game after the changeover break. The score currently stood at one set all, with Rambetti leading by four games to three in the third and final set. Marcus not only had to hold his serve, but he had to break Rambetti's, too, or there was a chance it would go to a tie break. Patrick and Dean were talking quietly among themselves, clearly worried.

'He is losing his head. I can see it in his eyes,' said Patrick, making a disappointed whistling sound through his teeth.

'If he loses this game, it's a fucking disaster,' said a stressed-sounding Dean, rather unhelpfully, I thought.

Perhaps it was naive of me, and this was, of course, only the second full match I'd ever seen him play, but I fully believed Marcus was going to win. I reckoned he probably wanted this more than Rambetti did, for a start, and he had a much better serve. Unfortunately, however, the crowd was mostly Italian and therefore it felt as though Marcus had absolutely no support. Even his team seemed to have given up on him, and whether or not any of this was having an impact on him, I had no idea. I gripped the bottom of my seat, tempted to get up and shout some words of encouragement myself, but like what? And would Marcus appreciate it anyway? If I was really his girlfriend, what would I do? I tried to make eye contact with him, hoping to give him a subtle nod or something, anything to let him know I was watching and that I thought he could do this. As he chugged away on his water bottle, his face redder than I'd ever seen it, his usually voluminous hair plastered to his head with sweat, I felt certain he was looking directly at me. I self-consciously did the fist-pump motion I'd seen several of the other players do every time they won a point. It actually got a bit annoying after a while, and interestingly Marcus never did it, but perhaps it was universal tennis speak for *Yes! Come on!*

The umpire called time and both players took their places. Marcus slipped two balls into the pockets of his shorts, leaving one in his hand, which he bounced on the ground a few times. Then he looked at Rambetti, tossed it into the air and served. It was so fast, I didn't see where it landed, but Rambetti somehow managed to get it back. Marcus returned the shot to Rambetti's backhand and came into the net, at which point Rambetti lobbed it over his head, landing it just outside the baseline. *Fifteen-Love.*

Marcus had now started muttering under his breath to himself, which didn't seem like a particularly good sign. He took his position to serve, bouncing the ball for what felt like ages this time, finally lobbing it into the air. He hit the ball, but his angle must have been off, and it went way outside the tramlines. Marcus looked at it in disbelief, shaking his head.

'Let's go, Marcus!' shouted Patrick.

Marcus looked severely rattled as he set up his second serve, which I remembered he thought was sub-par. He managed to get it over the net but Rambetti returned it easily and the two of them proceeded to rally, playing shot after shot to the baseline, forehand to forehand. Then Marcus changed it up and sliced it across to Rambetti's backhand, then Rambetti hit a cunning drop shot. Marcus didn't make it to the net in time. The Italians went mad, stamping their feet, banging on metal from God knows where and breaking out into a deafening chant using words I couldn't understand, nor did I want to. *Fifteen-All.*

Marcus served again, his first going in this time, a shot so powerful that Rambetti didn't stand a chance of returning it. His fourth ace of the match. *Thirty-Fifteen. Come on, Marcus,* I whispered under my breath.

Rambetti won the next shot, producing a fluke of a return that Marcus thought was going out but wasn't. *Thirty-All.* The crowd were going nuts now, with the Italian flags out in force, a sea of red, green and white. I looked down at my hands, clasped in my lap;

this was properly tense. Marcus looked angry at himself, which I assumed might be a precursor to him losing it on court. Unless he could hold it together for long enough to win the point, and then the game, and then the match. If he just kept winning, he wouldn't need to shout at anyone, would he?

Marcus took his place behind the baseline, his body crouching and then unfurling as he served hard and fast. It went out, a couple of inches outside of the box.

'Second serve,' called the umpire.

Marcus served again. It went into the net, not even close. Marcus let out what I could only describe as a primal roar. I watched with increasing horror as he slammed his racquet on to the ground over and over again until it was bent in two and then launched it into his chair at the side of the court, leaving a trail of dust in its wake. The crowd began to boo. I resisted the urge to put my hands over my eyes.

'Warning – code violation, racquet abuse,' said the umpire, at which point the volume of the boos increased.

Marcus stormed off court, rummaged in his racquet bag and pulled out another, returning to court with a face like thunder. *Thirty-Forty.*

The final point of the game was over in seconds – a mediocre serve, a killer return. It was like the fight had gone out of him along with his broken racquet. *Game Rambetti.*

There was no break between games this time, and with the clock ticking, neither player had time to catch a breath before Rambetti prepared to serve for the match. Five games to three. If Marcus lost this, he was out of the tournament. They'd been playing for one hour and fifty-three minutes so far, during which time the sun had come out and it was considerably hotter than it had been at the beginning of the match. The crowd were sweating, the players were soaked through, their T-shirts clinging to their bodies, and all around us was a haze of flickering white as hand-held paper fans were fluttered in front of too-hot faces.

Rambetti hit an ace. *Fifteen-Love.*

Come on, Marcus, I silently tried to convey to him using the ancient art of telepathy. *Don't give up.*

The next point was better – a not great serve, an excellent return, a slice to Marcus's backhand, a winner down the line. Marcus's point. *Fifteen-All.*

After Rambetti won the next point, the crowd went wild. *Thirty-Fifteen.* Apparently Court Rainier III could seat ten thousand, and it felt as though at least nine thousand of those were on their feet, yelling for their countryman, willing him to win. Marcus sneered at them, putting his fingers together to make a 'blah-blah' gesture resulting in an even louder set of boos that went on and on.

'Code violation, unsportsmanlike conduct,' announced the umpire into his microphone. 'Point penalty, Forty-Fifteen.'

Marcus, who had been preparing to receive Rambetti's serve, stood up straight.

'What?!' he said to the umpire, approaching his chair. 'For what?'

I felt slightly sick. I really wasn't a fan of confrontation, and yet here was Marcus wading right in and asking for it, with an audience of braying Italians watching his every move. Aware that there might be a camera lurking somewhere, I tried to keep my face neutral, like I'd seen the real WAGS do.

'Because you told the crowd to be quiet and made a rude gesture,' said the umpire.

Marcus wasn't having any of it. 'How is what I did rude? If I'd sworn at them – which, honestly, they deserved – fine, I'd accept the violation, but this makes no sense!'

'Violation stands, Forty-Fifteen,' said the umpire, clearly unable to go back on his decision now, even if he'd wanted to.

'This is fucking ridiculous!' said Marcus, shaking his head and stomping back to his place.

'He will get another one if he does not stay quiet,' said Patrick.

'Marcus, come on, man!' shouted Dean.

To be honest, I felt like going down there myself and telling Marcus to stop. What was he doing? What was he hoping to achieve? He had one measly point left to turn this game around – did he really think he could play his absolute best tennis now?

Marcus took his place for Rambetti's serve, but you could tell his heart wasn't in it, and Rambetti outplayed him.

Game, Set and Match, Federico Rambetti.

I clapped half-heartedly as Marcus shook hands with Rambetti at the net. I felt bad for him but also thrown by witnessing his racquet smashing play out live and in real time. Perhaps the fear of losing helped some players to dig deep and pull something spectacular out of the bag, but for Marcus it seemed that thinking he'd blown it sent him spiralling off in a dark direction he was always going to struggle to come back from. At some point I would ask him what was going through his head at times like that, but I was definitely going to have to pick my moment with extreme caution.

A disappointed silence hung over our box as Marcus packed up his stuff and disappeared into the tunnel, and the cameras were set up for Rambetti's interview.

'Has he always lost his temper like that?' I asked Patrick.

Patrick shook his head. 'When he was younger, no. I'd say the last seven years. Since the year after he won the Australian Open – he went into the tournament a favourite and got knocked out in the first round by a guy ranked two hundred and fourth in the world. After that his mood and his confidence deteriorated more and more, although of course I was not coaching him then.'

'Why do you think he hasn't won a Grand Slam again?'

'It is a lot of things combined,' said Patrick, standing up wearily. 'And this attitude of his does nothing to help.'

As we left our seats to return to the players' area, Dean turned to me with a grim expression on his face.

'Ava, I'm gonna need you on board. We've got some fucking damage control to do.'

◆ ◆ ◆

The 'damage control' apparently consisted of me leaving the grounds with Marcus in the hope that media speculation about our relationship would supersede the negative press about his on-court meltdown. I agreed to do it because I couldn't think of a good enough reason not to, and also I thought it might be useful for the article to be alone in a car with him minutes after he'd crashed out of a tournament far earlier than expected. I knew clay wasn't his best surface, but it was clear he'd been hoping to get to the semis at the very least. I doubted he'd want to talk about it, but maybe I could pick something up that I could build on later.

I waited for him in the players' area while he had his ice bath and post-match talk with Patrick, who hadn't looked happy either. I wasn't sure if it was the tennis or the behaviour that hadn't pleased him, but I had the feeling he was going to tell Marcus exactly what he thought either way.

After a considerable amount of time, during which I took advantage of the free hot drinks in the players' lounge by ordering not one but two cappuccinos, Marcus finally appeared, his hair wet from the shower, his Lacoste tracksuit zipped up to the neck, his white Monte-Carlo Country Club cap pulled down so that it was hiding a large portion of his face, his expression darker than dark. The racquet bag, as ever, was on his shoulder and his water bottle was clutched in his hand, since presumably his body was in desperate need of rehydration. I'd read that apparently tennis was one of the most physical sports because you used almost every muscle in your body and also because the games could go on for so damn long. I was already dreading Roland-Garros, where I might have to watch a five-hour extravaganza. Just as well I was understanding the game a little more, and was just the tiniest bit more invested in Marcus winning. After all, he was far more likely to be an amenable interviewee if he was in a good mood, wasn't he?

'Hey,' I said to him, giving him a half-smile.

He nodded at me, barely making eye contact. 'Ready to go?'

He'd clearly already been briefed on what was going to need to happen – we'd be accompanied by two members of the tournament security team as we walked through the grounds to exit number 4 where a black Lexus with the registration number ending DHN would be waiting to whisk us the (no word of a lie) third of a mile back to Marcus's hotel. I got it – I didn't suppose you'd want to walk after that, what with the fans and the haters (more of those) swarming around, plus I had no idea if he'd be in any kind of physical pain after a match like that.

'Ready,' I said, more confidently than I felt.

We left the building together, with me scuttling along beside him. It might have been my own paranoia, but I sensed that all eyes were on us as I tested my own shockingly bad fitness to the absolute max by attempting to match him step for step as he motored through the grounds. He clearly had one goal: to get the hell out of here as quickly as possible.

'How are you doing?' I asked him, gasping for breath.

'How do you think?' he answered coldly.

Heads swivelled from all directions as we entered the main hub of the tournament and made our way down what felt like endless flights of steps, past pop-up shops selling tennis merchandise and some of the posher-looking bars linked to the hospitality suites.

'Dean said we had to—'

'I know,' said Marcus, taking my hand.

It was actually easier to keep my speed up now that he was half propelling me along. His hand was hotter than when I'd held it at the restaurant, and his grip was harder, as though he was scared he'd lose me in the crowd if he loosened it. I kept my head down because I couldn't bear watching everyone watching us, and also I was acutely aware that there were some steep slopes and I could very easy stack it, which although embarrassing for me might actually work very well for Marcus in terms of highly distracting media coverage. I wasn't aware of any paparazzi taking photos, although they were probably dotted about inconspicuously with their mega-long lenses, lurking behind bushes and up high hanging out of windows. When I saw our car, I squeezed Marcus's hand.

'That's us,' I said.

On the short journey back to the hotel, we barely spoke. I understood that he didn't want to and at least he managed a goodbye as he got out at the Monte-Carlo Bay, leaving me to travel on to my own hotel.

Since I had a few hours to myself, I set up a workspace on my desk in my hotel room and began trying to piece together a timeline of Marcus's game. He first appeared in the national newspapers in June 2012 when he was a finalist in the Boys' Junior Wimbledon competition. One of the papers had reported on it in their sports round-up: SO NEAR AND YET SO FAR – 17-YEAR-OLD BRIT BOY CLOSE TO SNAGGING JUNIOR WIMBLEDON TITLE. Wow, he was practically a child at the time and even then journalists were giving him a hard time – what was wrong with celebrating him having made the final instead of criticising him for not actually winning it? I peered at a photo of Marcus with the eventual winner, a Bulgarian player I didn't recognise – I wondered if he was still on the circuit? There was another photo of Marcus's mum, looking much younger than she had in the other photo I'd seen of her – she was beautiful, and she was clapping proudly with tears in her eyes. MARCUS MAKES MUM BLUB was the classy headline.

The next newspaper report I found was from 2017, which I thought was the year before he won the Australian Open. A specialist tennis magazine had run a profile on him in their Rising Talent section – Marcus was twenty-two at the time and there was a photo of him smiling to camera, then another one of him with his arm around his mum. Their eyes were exactly the same, brown and bright with long doe-like lashes. The article talked mostly about his game stats – apparently, he was known for his fast first serves, his impressive physicality and his ability to switch his game so that it was impossible for his opponents to predict what he might do next. I flicked back at my notes – that was what Patrick had said about him, so clearly this was one thing that hadn't changed over the years. I got as far as researching tournaments in 2018 before I had to start getting ready for dinner, and it had got off to a phenomenal start with Marcus winning the Australian Open in January of that year. G'DAY TO BRITAIN'S NEWEST TENNIS STAR! ran one headline. BRIT MARCUS TAYLOR PULLS IT OUT OF THE BAG IN OZ proclaimed another. I zoomed in on all the photos I could find. There were lots of Marcus smiling, of him running to the players' box to hug his then-coach, Marcus waving happily to his fans in a way he never did now. But there was not a single shot of his mum. Had something happened, then, between 2017 and 2018? Had they fallen out, and if so, had it got anything to do with his tennis? From what I could tell, she'd been cheering him on from the sidelines since he was a junior, so why on earth wouldn't she have been there in Australia to see him win his one and only major title? I made a note on my pad and circled it. FIND OUT WHY MARCUS AND HIS MUM FELL OUT.

Dean had insisted on taking Marcus and me out that evening as part of *Operation Distract the Press*, and as I busied myself choosing a cocktail from the extensive – and expensive – drinks menu, Dean appeared to have cheered up considerably. Our hand-holding exit from the tournament had seemingly had the desired effect; a few pictures of the two of us had popped up online already and had even made it to some of the American gossip sites. He showed me a couple of photos of the two of us walking through the grounds, and of course they'd caught the one time I'd looked up at Marcus so that my face was on full display. According to Zoe, I was still the talk of the *Luxe* office, but nobody else I knew seemed to be aware. Unless I'd jinxed it, because when my phone pinged with a message from my mum saying *Call me!!* I had an inkling that it was all about to come out. Dad was probably following the tournament results, and if he'd googled those, a story about Marcus having been knocked out might organically have led to these rather incriminating shots of Marcus and I clutching each other's hands as though our lives depended on it. I tapped back a message, delaying the inevitable: *At a work dinner. Call you tomorrow.* This wouldn't please her, but I hadn't had time to work out exactly how to play it with my family given their delicate dispositions, and I couldn't think about it now because I wanted to at least try to enjoy the stunning views over the famous marina, which I'd seen only on TV.

'The footage of you and Ava is great, but level with me, Marcus. What the fuck happened out there today? I thought we were on the same page here? I've already had Lacoste on the line,' said Dean.

Marcus didn't reply and when I dared to peep over my menu, I saw that he was sitting in a sort of deadly, simmering silence.

'I don't need to explain myself to Lacoste. If I had my way, I wouldn't be wearing them at all. They do not own me and unless they want to get out there and play at the level I do, they can keep their comments to themselves as far as I'm concerned.'

Dean tried a change of tack. 'We're just trying to help you out, here. Right, Ava?'

Huh? What was he dragging me into this for, I was just sitting there quietly choosing something to drink and had no intention of getting in the middle of whatever was going on there. Surely Dean had seen him behave like that myriad times before, so why was he getting so irate about it this time? Presumably, it was the losing of sponsorship deals that had done it, of which his agency WCG no doubt took a rather hefty percentage.

'What's Ava got to do with any of this?' asked Marcus.

'Yeah, I have to say, I don't think it's my place to—'

'This is precisely why you're here,' Dean said to me. 'To show your readers what goes on inside Marcus's head. And unfortunately, that doesn't include only the moments in which he's level-headed and winning, it means reporting on the more difficult times, too. Doesn't it?'

'Of course,' I said, getting fed up with Dean myself now. 'But if Marcus isn't ready to talk about it . . .'

I caught his eye. In my experience, you couldn't force things out of people. You had to gain their trust, let them know you were on their side (or at least let them think you were). Dean going in like a bulldozer wasn't helping anyone.

'You know what, guys? I think I'll leave you to it. Marcus, when you're ready to talk, you know where I am,' said Dean, throwing his napkin down.

'What an enticing prospect,' said Marcus.

'Oh, and next time I set up what is supposed to be a romantic tennis game for you, try not to totally thrash your date? Spoiler alert: you don't look like the good guy in this scenario,' said Dean, jabbing his finger on his phone.

Mine and Marcus's phones pinged simultaneously.

With a sigh, I opened the message Dean had sent, an article from an American gossip site with the unfortunate title: CRUEL TAYLOR FAILS TO LET GIRLFRIEND WIN A SINGLE POINT!

Aaargh. That wasn't good on any level, not least because I hardly looked my best with sweat sprouting out of every pore and a pissed-off expression on my face. On the other hand, the photos of us by the fence looked hot.

'Nice pics,' said Marcus, clearly on a mission to wind Dean up.

'Shame about the fucking strapline,' said Dean, pushing back his chair and stalking off.

We were currently seven floors up, sitting out on the terrace of one of the most beautiful rooftop restaurants I'd ever seen and I was craving my battered old sofa again, where thankfully the drama was usually confined to what I chose to watch on screen, and where I could change channels if it all got too much. Mind you, perhaps I should be careful what I wished for – since Marcus was out of the tournament and heading to Spain the following day to prepare for the Madrid Open, I'd asked Ruby to change my flights and I'd be back in London the following evening. I realised that living alone and barely seeing anyone from one day to the next was going to feel like quite the anticlimax.

Marcus cleared his throat. 'Sorry about that. It wasn't fair of us to have that discussion in front of you.'

He poured me a glass of water.

'Do you often clash like that?' I asked.

'Sometimes,' he said. 'He's hot-headed like me. I disappointed him, I get it. The problem is, it's impossible for people to understand where I'm coming from when I don't know how to explain it myself half the time.'

A waiter came to take our order – I went for a margarita and a Caesar salad in the end and Marcus asked for a burger, fries and a pint of beer.

'What happened to the clean eating?' I teased gently as the very polite French waiter scuttled off to the kitchen.

'I call it a commiseration dinner,' he said. 'It's a ritual of mine. If I lose a match, I eat and drink whatever I want for one night only, guilt free.'

'What happens if you win?'

'I rest and I drink water and I get an early night. It's nowhere near as much fun.'

I nodded. I supposed you couldn't properly celebrate unless you won the entire tournament, could you, and the chances of that were pretty low. I'd read somewhere that 128 male players were entered into the US Open, so essentially that meant one celebration and 127 commiseration dinners.

'Beautiful views,' I said, looking down at the marina below.

Yachts of all shapes and sizes were bobbing on the water, lit up against the dusky sky.

When our drinks arrived, Marcus was quick to take a mouthful of beer, seemingly savouring the taste.

'Sometimes it's worth losing just for this,' he said.

I ran my fingertip around the rim of my cocktail glass, enjoying the way it kept snagging on the salty crust around the edge.

'Do you want to talk about earlier? About the match?' I asked, fiddling with the stem of my glass now. Why did being alone with Marcus make me so nervous?

He chewed his lip; I could practically see his mind ticking over. *Should he? Would it help? Could he trust me?*

'I'm not really a talker,' he said.

'Neither am I, as it happens,' I ventured, gauging his reaction.

Often, celebrities didn't want to talk about anyone but themselves, and the private life of the person interviewing them was of absolutely no interest. I had an inkling, though, that Marcus might feel differently.

'That surprises me. Tell me more,' said Marcus, taking another mouthful of beer, this time leaving a line of white froth that I wanted to reach across and wipe off with my thumb. He licked his lips before I had the chance.

'I feel bad, sometimes, asking interviewees all these personal details about their lives. About their difficult childhoods, or their first heartbreak or their career failures, or whatever it is. Because I'm expecting them to open up to me in a way that I could never do myself,' I said, keeping my tone light, my voice barely audible.

Marcus looked confused. 'You had no problem telling me that your ex had left you.'

'Well, that was purely on a need-to-know basis. And I guess some level of . . . opening up has been forced on us with the situation we're in, hasn't it?'

I thought immediately of Mia Stephens and the fact he'd slept with her. I wondered how many of the other female players he'd hooked up with, because for every headline I found about his tennis, there would be two or three articles about his love life. One minute he was at an awards ceremony with a Czech model, the next he was at some rooftop party with a TV presenter. It seemed that Marcus Taylor was a player, and that because of his talent and the fact he looked like he did, beautiful women were up for playing. Whether or not he'd ever truly fallen for someone was yet to be discovered, but from the way he carried himself I'd say not. He had the air of someone who had never been heartbroken and although his career failures were plenty, he had probably never been rejected by somebody who was supposed to love him. I felt a shot of envy – life must be so much easier that way.

Marcus rested his arms on the table, leaning forward slightly. 'This pretending to date you thing is taking me way out of my comfort zone, if I'm honest. It probably won't surprise you to hear that public displays of affection are really not my thing.'

'It must be just *killing* you to have to hold my hand for the cameras.'

'Funnily enough, it's nowhere near as bad as I thought it would be,' he said.

He held my gaze but I absolutely could not hold his, and instead faked interest in the ebb and flow of my margarita as I stirred the liquid with my straw.

'What did you make of my little outburst today, then?' asked Marcus.

I looked up. 'I wondered what was going through your mind. Why you snapped like that.'

Marcus shrugged. 'If I could work that out, I could avoid doing it again, couldn't I, and my team would be a whole lot happier with me?'

'Think about it. It was that penultimate game. Something shifted at that end change. Maybe something came into your head, I could see your whole demeanour change. Patrick called it, too.'

Frowning, he took a few seconds to answer.

'Okay. I'm not sure if this is going to make any sense, but when I think I might be about to lose, I go one of two ways: either I change tactics or I start to believe I can't do it. That I'm not good enough, that I'll never amount to anything, that I'm about to let everyone down.'

'Where does that come from though, because it sounds as if it's entirely in your head. Did someone tell you that once? That you weren't good enough?' I asked.

'Everybody told me that,' he said, as our main courses were placed on the table in front of us. 'Now can we please talk about something less depressing?'

The conversation lightened up considerably after that – I hadn't wanted to get too heavy too quickly and thought a gentle approach to getting Marcus to talk was probably for the best. So instead we swapped stories about our favourite places in the world (mine had previously been Rome, but the Eternal City was now tarnished by the knowledge that Charlie had spent the entire trip trying to pluck up the courage to break up with me), the books we'd read, the music we listened to. Apparently, Marcus played Stormzy on his Beats headphones before a match; it helped him get hyped up. All of this was helping me build up a picture of who Marcus was outside of tennis, and the titbits of information I was gleaning would be extremely useful if I could remember any of them when I got back to my room. Because the thing was, I kept forgetting I was supposed to be working and found myself relaxing in his company and enjoying myself instead. I could have stayed out there chatting all night, and was now on my second cocktail, so had the sort of airy light-headedness that made me temporarily forget about my problems and enjoy the moment for what it was.

Marcus paid the bill again, although I tried to insist we went halves, and then we stood up and I ran my hand over the fabric of my Zara satin dress, the same one I'd worn on my first night in Monaco and had had to wear again because I was fast running out of evening wear. I'd worn my hair down this time to try to make it look subtly different, and had applied red lipstick instead of the neutral lip gloss I'd worn for our first proper meeting at Marcus's hotel.

As we walked through the restaurant, I noticed a few chic-looking people swivelling to look in our direction. Marcus was a handsome man, it could just have been that, but I also presumed that some of them would have been at the tournament today, perhaps in one of the hospitality suites, and so would have seen Marcus lose. I wondered if in some ways his temper made him more appealing – we always saw these polished versions of famous people, leading us to assume that their lives were near perfect all the time, but of course this was an illusion, Everybody struggled sometimes, and absolutely nobody got everything they wanted. At least with Marcus he was putting it all out there for everyone to see.

A group of nine or ten people were waiting for the lift down to street level and, as we joined them, a photographer seemed to come out of nowhere and started flashing away in Marcus's face, presumably capturing us both in the shot. I was torn – and possibly so was Marcus – and I could see that his instinct was to shout at them and push them away.

Instead he held his hand out in front of the lens.

'Come on, Marcus. Just one photo, what's the harm?'

The maître d' came rushing out, full of apologies.

'I am so very sorry, Mr Taylor, we are calling security right away,' he said, clearly flustered.

As the lift doors opened, I grabbed Marcus's hand, trying to indicate to him to stay calm, to not engage. It was just one photo, it didn't matter, and although it was a bit overwhelming to have a lens in our faces like this, it didn't really matter in the scheme of things, and maybe another shot of the two of us together would cheer Dean up.

The group in front of us probably weren't tennis fans, because they seemed utterly confused by the frenzy of camera flashes and the maître d' trying to jostle the photographer away from us, and Marcus mumbling under his breath about how this was invading people's privacy and shouldn't be allowed. There wasn't enough space for both of us to get in, really, but I couldn't stand much more of this, and so pulled Marcus into the lift with me, just as the doors were closing.

Silence.

The group started talking again. I was still holding Marcus's hand, but then his other one was somehow on my waist. We were pressed together so hard that my mouth was level with his clavicle and I could feel his warm breath on my hair. He bent his head a little to whisper in my ear, his free hand simultaneously moving from my waist on to the small of my back. It was like he was pulling me even closer to him so that there was no space between us at all.

'Sorry about that,' he whispered.

I looked up, because I suddenly wanted to see his face this close up. Even in the dim light I could make out the different colours in his beard – mostly dark brown, but also a smattering of red, and the tiniest flecks of grey.

'Not your fault,' I whispered back.

Our eyes were locked together as his hand moved slowly from my lower back to the middle of my shoulder blades, the heat from his palm burning into me, and for a second it was like we were alone in that lift, just him and me, suspended in motion, away from prying eyes and all the stresses of the day, his lips slightly parted and tantalisingly close.

And then the doors pinged open on our side, letting the bright lights of the lobby pour in. Even though I didn't really want to, I dropped his hand as we walked outside to the taxi rank.

ROLAND-GARROS

Chapter Thirteen

Visiting home – particularly if I had to stay overnight – almost always put me in a terrible mood afterwards. I'd never quite worked out why, but if I was going to dig deep on the subject, I'd say it had to do with being rocketed right back into being a teenager again and constantly having the feeling I was about to do something wrong. Dad had been a taxi driver then – or a 'chauffeur' as he used to prefer to call it, because he had an executive car and mostly did airport runs for businessmen who were prepared to pay a bit more (or their company was, more like) for a marginally more luxurious start to their journey. It had suited Dad – he loved cars, and although he wasn't particularly chatty at home, I reckoned he could be pretty jovial when he had a passenger in the back seat, plus he could choose his own hours. I assumed they needed the money because he seemed to be out driving almost all the time and often did night shifts at the weekends. As a result, it would mostly be me, Mum and Cassie at home, a dynamic I always felt distinctly on the outside of.

'The coals are hotting up,' said Mum, bustling inside to pick up the carefully laid-out barbecue utensils that appeared each year at the first hint of sunshine. It was now the end of May, just before Marcus's next tournament, and although the days were generally warm, it was typical that today wasn't. I shivered at the thought of sitting out in the garden for hours on end with goose-bumped skin and windswept hair while we pretended that we were all having a brilliant time.

'Lovely,' I said, looking up from prepping the salad.

We each had our jobs for Cassie's annual birthday barbecue and preparing the salad side dish had always been mine, along with doing absolutely all the clearing up, a task I'd long ago given up complaining about. I supposed Cassie couldn't be expected to do the dishes on her birthday, could she, but the thing was, she never did them on any other day either, even though she lived at home, and nobody ever appeared to challenge her about it.

Mum came up behind me. I could feel her peering over my shoulder, clutching her utensils like weapons.

'Don't cut the cucumber too thick, will you?'

'I'm not,' I protested. Did I really need direction on how to slice a cucumber?

I was aware that Mum was still hovering and thought this probably meant there was something she wanted to say. Might as well get it over with.

'You still seeing that tennis player, then?' she asked.

I stopped chopping, laying the knife flat on the board. Lately, I hadn't been able to focus properly when I thought too hard about Marcus, and I didn't think trying to talk about him and cut things at the same time was a good idea. It was fine if I was working on my article and thinking about him in a professional capacity, about his game, about the public perception of him. But if I thought back to him and me in that lift on the way down from the rooftop restaurant in Monte Carlo, I felt thrown for a few seconds, like I couldn't breathe. This was not good, even if it felt like it was, because I had to spend a lot more time with Marcus over the coming months and I absolutely could not start feeling things for him. Him of all people, who went through women like water and was clearly incapable of feeling anything for anyone other than himself. I was still badly missing Charlie and smarting from his rejection; the last thing I needed was to start lusting after a man who was never, ever going to like me back. He'd said it himself (or at least I thought he had): he was not prepared to allocate headspace to anything other than his career progression this year, and even if he had been, I didn't think I'd be anything close to his type. He liked Slavic blondes with athletic bodies and healthy bank balances – I had dark hair, was a solid size 12 and was almost permanently overdrawn. Therefore I could not – and would not let myself – imagine that there had been a spark that night. We'd been forced into close proximity out of circumstance, and it was only in my head – when I let it be – that there was anything more to it than that.

'He's away at the moment,' I said, doing what I always did when talking about Marcus to my friends and family – focusing on the half-truths. Avoiding answering direct questions about the nature of our relationship at all costs.

'At a tournament, or something?' asked Mum.

'Hmmm,' I said non-committally, reluctantly turning to face her. I really wished she'd put the utensils down, I was finding them quite intimidating. 'He's been in Rome for a bit and now he's in Paris preparing for Roland-Garros. Hadn't one of us better be in the garden? You're not supposed to leave a barbecue unattended. I'll go,' I said, attempting to walk away.

'Dad's out there,' said Mum sharply, touching my arm lightly with a black plastic spatula. 'Ava, have you got a second?'

What was this about? Mum wasn't one to have deep and meaningful conversations unless she was forced to, and I could really do without it myself.

'Sure,' I said, keeping it light. It couldn't be that bad, I told myself, ignoring the nagging memories of my adolescence when it felt like either Cassie, my mum or my dad were telling me off for something. Most of the time, I'd never quite understood what I'd done wrong.

'Is it serious, then? With this Marcus?' asked Mum.

Oh God, why was she still talking about him? She'd barely shown any interest in my relationship with Charlie, so why was she being so different this time?

'It's early days,' I replied vaguely.

'But you like him?'

I swallowed. 'Yes?'

She nodded. 'Thought so.'

'What makes you say that?' I asked, frowning.

As *if* Mum was tuned into the inner workings of my mind.

'It's the way your face goes all funny when you talk about him. And you've never been one to have your picture taken, but now you're splashed all over these celebrity magazines and you don't seem bothered. It's like he's changed you overnight.'

'Okay . . .' I said, unsure how to answer, when what I really wanted to say was my face looked 'all funny' because I was LYING to them all!

'What's your point?' I asked, knowing she wouldn't like me putting her on the spot because she'd never been very good at expressing what she was *actually* upset about.

'My point, Ava, is that your sister's been very quiet since all of this came out. She's been going for long walks on her own.'

'She's allowed to go for walks, Mum. What makes you think it's got anything to do with me?'

Mum sighed heavily. 'I think she's been struggling with all this . . . attention you've been getting. She was enjoying having you to herself when you split up with Charlie, but then about five minutes later you're off with the next one.'

I shouldn't really blame my mum, we were all guilty of it, trying to work out what Cassie was thinking or what she needed or what had upset her at any given moment. She never really told us but instead acted out in other ways. But she could totally be going for long walks because it was late spring and the weather was nicer, couldn't she?

'It's not just the walks, she goes straight to her room afterwards. And she's been late home from work some nights and won't tell me where she's been.'

'Mum, she's not a child. She shouldn't have to explain herself every time she's a couple of hours late home. Maybe she's finally getting on with the girls from work?'

Mum tutted. 'I doubt it, Ava. Do you think she's having one-night stands again?'

'I don't know, Mum. She's an adult, so yeah, probably.'

I didn't think all of us babying Cassie was the best thing, and my parents certainly didn't need to know the details of her sex life.

'All I'm saying is, please consider your sister in all of this,' said Mum. 'Because do you really think it's going to last with this bloke Marcus? He's a millionaire, from what Dad says.'

'His finances are none of my business,' I said.

'And he'll have his pick of women, won't he? Plus he always seems to be travelling, so where's the future in that?' said Mum, hammering home her point – i.e. that he wasn't going to stick around either, like Charlie hadn't. As if I didn't already know that.

I turned back to the salad, heaping it into a bowl, not caring how it looked, even though I knew there'd probably be some comment about shoddy presentation later.

'What are you trying to say exactly, Mum?' I said, irritated now. I couldn't bite my tongue any longer.

'That it's not all about you, Ava.'

I actually laughed, I couldn't help it. As if I'd ever thought it was. I picked up the bowl, needing to get away before I said something I would regret.

'Let's get out into the garden and try to enjoy the day, shall we?' I said, zipping past Mum before she could ask me any more questions or say anything else to annoy me. I didn't want to spiral into a bad mood.

I pushed through into the garden, the uninspiring square piece of grass surrounded by sparse little flower beds that Dad half-heartedly dug over once a year. Luckily, the roses must have been of a particularly hardy variety – they had to be to survive the onslaught of weeds that were visibly poking through the earth. And they had the audacity to comment on *my* presentation skills.

'Salad's up!' I trilled.

'Yum,' said Cassie, looking up from the book she was reading. She had her feet on one of the chairs and looked happy and relaxed in a way I didn't feel now, and probably wouldn't until I was back on my sofa in London.

Meanwhile, Dad was barely visible through the plumes of thick white smoke he was generating as he prodded heavy-handedly at the hot coals. A cloud of it was heading straight for next door's washing and it didn't appear to occur to Dad that maybe he should have suggested they take their washing in before he fired it up.

Surprisingly, the afternoon was a relative success. Cassie had picked at her food a bit, which usually had the effect of putting me off mine, but somehow I had the biggest appetite today and tucked into a burger, two sausages and a piece of chicken seasoned with jerk powder, Dad's summer speciality. Mum opened a bottle of prosecco and, after a glass and a half each, we actually had a bit of a laugh. Dad asked me a couple of questions about the tennis and seemed impressed with the knowledge I was gleaning, and he said how well Marcus had done in Rome – he'd reached the semi-finals, beaten by the world number four in three very close sets.

'Clay is his least favourite surface,' I said, pleased with myself for remembering.

'You can tell,' said Dad.

'Did he have any kick-offs in Rome? That's all I'm interested in, it's hilarious,' said Cassie flippantly, scrolling through her phone, which had been beeping constantly throughout the meal.

'Not that I know of,' I said, although I hadn't been following the footage avidly. It would have meant signing up to Sky Sports, which I wasn't prepared to do because it cost an absolute fortune. Also, I thought it might be a bit obsessive – as it was, he kept popping into my mind's eye at extremely unhelpful times. I didn't think watching him lunge around the court all sweaty and smeared with dusty red clay was in any way going to stop me noticing how gut-wrenchingly attractive he was.

I had a Eurostar to catch in the morning, which got me neatly out of having to stay the night in Reading. Cassie had disappeared up to her room pretty swiftly after lunch anyway, and by the time I'd cleared everything away while Mum and Dad watched *The Chase* it was gone four and time to head back. I was still umming and aahing about what to pack – was Paris more or less dressy than Monte Carlo? I wasn't staying as long this time, either, as Amanda Eddington quite rightly didn't think the budget could stretch to putting me up for two weeks in the hope that Marcus would make the final. I'd be there for his first-round match, and the second if he made it that far, which, judging by his performance in Rome and Madrid, he had a good chance of doing. According to Dean, it depended on who he got in the draw, which was being decided this afternoon, apparently, in a ceremony at L'Orangerie de Roland-Garros (no idea what that was, but it sounded perfectly lovely). I could have travelled a day earlier if I'd wanted, but I'd chosen not to because it was Cassie's birthday and I wanted to spend the day with her. Although since she'd spent most of it either staring at her phone screen or locked in her room, I felt slightly put out about that decision now, especially as Dean was pushing for Marcus and me to get ourselves photographed together at the earliest opportunity because according to him, things had gone a bit quiet on the 'romance' front. Marcus hadn't been in London at all since I'd seen him in Monaco, and apparently the press was likely to assume we were no longer together. Meanwhile, Charlie had continued to post photos of himself with his new girlfriend – whose identity was still a complete mystery – and I couldn't help being gutted that he was doing the same things with her on a Sunday that he used to do with me. Zoe had instructed me to mute his account immediately, and I kept saying I would, but I also had a masochistic need to know exactly what he was doing and with whom so that I could justifiably wallow in misery about it afterwards. Nobody I knew had heard from him, and we'd never really had mutual friends in the way that some couples did – they were firmly either in his camp or mine – so there was no information to be wheedled out of people that way.

I popped up to see Cassie before I left, already prepping myself to play down my upcoming trip. Paris in the spring sounded undeniably dreamy at face value, but it was also work, as I kept having to remind myself, particularly because sometimes it didn't feel like it.

I knocked on Cassie's door, my fingers already wrapped around the handle.

'Come in!' called Cassie.

She was sitting on her bed with her phone next to her. The TV wasn't on, so she must have been scrolling. I hoped she wasn't obsessing over influencers again.

'Just came to say bye. I'm heading off in a minute,' I said.

I sat on the edge of her bed, looking around the room. When we were younger, early-to-mid-teens, perhaps, I'd spent hours in here, slouched on a bean bag on the floor, doing my homework there, making the excuse that it helped to have background noise. Really, it was that she'd always be having a bad time at school and I hadn't wanted her to feel alone and thought it might help to have me there. The problem was, she had become kind of dependent on me and when I did actually have to concentrate – in the run-up to my GCSEs, for example – Cassie accused me of not caring about her anymore. She was only thirteen or so, I got it, and in the end I'd relented and had sacked off the library to resume my position on the bean bag, but I sometimes wondered why Mum hadn't offered to sit with Cassie instead, so that I could have done my revision elsewhere. It had crossed my mind once or twice that maybe – subconsciously, obviously, because she wasn't a malicious person – Mum didn't actually want me to do well in my exams. She'd made myriad comments about 'just passing' being enough, and not needing to get As, and I'd nodded along thinking: I *want* to do my best, though. I want to aim for As, because why wouldn't I?

'Looking forward to Paris?' asked Cassie.

I played it down, giving a little unenthusiastic sigh. 'I won't get much time to myself. And I'm not there for long, so I'll be writing or interviewing most of the time.'

'You can say, you know,' said Cassie, her expression softening.

'Say what?'

'That you're looking forward to seeing Marcus. That you like him. That you're excited about Paris. I won't fall apart if you do.'

I frowned. This was an extremely unusual reaction. Perhaps she was fishing so she could report back to Mum.

'I haven't seen him for a while, Cass. I don't even know if we'll—'

'Stop trying to hide things from me. I know you're into him, I can see it, and it's fine. Honestly. I'm a big girl. Sure, it would have been nice to be single at the same time for a bit. We didn't even get to have a girls' night out together before you jumped right back into a relationship again.'

'I wouldn't say it was a relationship,' I said.

'Whatever you want to call it. I'm happy for you.'

I didn't think she'd ever said the words *I'm happy for you* to me, not once, not ever.

'Are you feeling okay, Cass?' I asked.

She reached out and squeezed my hand.

'I'm fine. Now go and get ready for your trip. I appreciate you coming all the way out here for my birthday, but if I was going to Paris the next morning, I wouldn't have done that for you.'

Obviously, I thought.

I wondered briefly if these walks or whatever she was doing were helping. She definitely seemed more content in herself; she must be, to have said the things she just said. As I left the room, promising her a small gift from Paris, I felt lighter than I had since the day she was born. She was twenty-seven now and perhaps edging closer to thirty had given her the push she needed to finally start looking after herself. My phone pinged in my pocket as I put my shoes and coat on before poking my head around the lounge door to say goodbye to Mum and Dad. I checked my notifications, in case they'd cancelled my Eurostar or something. It wasn't about the train, though; it was a message from Marcus – I'd saved his number in my phone for official reasons, but until now we hadn't sent each other a single message, preferring – or at least having got into the habit of – communicating via Dean.

> *Ava, looking forward to seeing you tomorrow. Also, would you be free for a Parisian cooking class and wine-tasting the day after?!*

My heart did that thing where it felt like it skipped a beat and then produced an extra intense one to make up for it – it was the first time his name had popped up on my phone like that, that was all. I hadn't been expecting it. And a *cooking class?* Dean had obviously booked it for us, but I was surprised Marcus had agreed to it. I went back and forth over how to respond. What wasn't to like about a fun activity in Paris, and if we really were going to get the public on side with my 'girl-next-door' appeal, what could *look* sweeter and more romantic? I drafted a message and, after spending ages editing and re-editing it, I sent back what I hoped was an achingly cool response.

> *Nice idea. Let me check my work schedule and get back to you.*

Chapter Fourteen

Marcus's first-round match had been unexpectedly postponed due to a rain delay and instead of playing the previous night, he was now on first the following morning. It had meant that on arrival in Paris, I'd spent a delightful afternoon and evening at Résidence Juliette, a quaint, dimly lit boutique hotel in beautiful, buzzing Le Marais. The enormous bed had had the smoothest, whitest sheets I'd ever slept in, and even this morning they'd been practically *begging* me to lie back down on them. But Marcus was on at 10 a.m., so I was going to have to grab some breakfast and head straight over to Roland-Garros.

The receptionist ordered me a taxi and as soon as I got in the car I wound down the window, enjoying the early summer heat and the views of the Eiffel Tower over the other side of the river – it was much warmer here than it had been in London when I left and I put my sunglasses on, nonchalantly letting my cardigan slip off one shoulder, hoping I was suitably dressed for my first ever Grand Slam. I thought I was getting a little better at looking the part – today I had on a navy-and-white floral mini dress, black patent ballet flats and a fake Chanel handbag, which I'd slung across my body, plus a white cardigan in case the weather turned. I'd attempted to put my hair up into one of those French-style messy buns with bits hanging loose, and it had taken me ages to do and in fact I'd successfully managed it only when I'd given up, shoving my hair on top of my head in frustration without even looking in the mirror.

The taxi wasn't able to get close to the stadium because of the crowds. Who knew this many people liked tennis? Swathes of fans were heading up to the grounds, tickets clasped in their hands, the women mostly dressed a little bit like me (this was good). The level of security had been upped several notches from Monte-Carlo, including the presence of police officers with guns poised and seemingly ready to use them. I got out my phone, checking Dean's instructions: I was to follow signs for press accreditation, pick up my credentials and meet the team in the players' lounge.

The Stade Roland-Garros was around ten times bigger than the Monte-Carlo site and was a modern, purpose-built stadium named after a French aviator who had died aged twenty-nine after his plane was shot down in the First World War. The complex consisted of twenty courts, the biggest of which was Philippe-Chatrier – I wasn't sure who *he* was and made a mental note to check, because if Marcus got through to the second round, he'd be playing on it, apparently. Today he was on one of the smaller outside courts, which was another reason to be happy about the sun and the wispy white clouds skimming across blue sky. The grounds smelled like geraniums and Sauvignon blanc and I didn't immediately hear a single British voice, although I was sure there must be some. I'd read the French were particularly passionate about their tennis, often booing players from other countries before they'd even begun. This, I was sure, would not please Marcus.

Once I'd passed through all the necessary security checks, attempting to use my exceptionally bad French and in the end reverting to English about ninety per cent of the time, I found my way to the lounge via a long white corridor. On the walls was an impressive display of photos of past French Open winners that you would definitely have felt inspired by if you were in any way athletically inclined. I admired their winning spirit, even if I'd never been competitive about anything in my life. I would have taken a video for my dad if I didn't think that getting caught recording footage might get me thrown off the premises. I had to actively remember to breathe when I walked into the lounge and saw some of the faces I'd just seen displayed in the corridor. My eyes darted back and forth, looking for Marcus or a member of his team, desperately seeking a face I recognised. It took me ages to get my bearings and just as I thought I was going to have to turn back around and leave, I heard somebody call my name.

'Ava! We are over here!'

Patrick had spotted me. Relieved, I scraped together the last vestiges of my confidence and scuttled over to join him. He nodded a greeting as I approached, then Dean stood up to give me an LA-style air kiss.

'Marcus and Nick are finishing their warm-up in the gym,' said Dean. 'They should be out shortly. I know Marcus wanted to say hi.'

Patrick looked surprised – he wasn't in on our fake-romance "arrangement", presumably, and probably wondered why Marcus would care if I was here or not. I had mixed feelings about starting all of this up again, anyway, especially as for a second I'd actually thought Dean had meant it when he said that Marcus wanted to see me. It had given me a little burst of happiness I hadn't been expecting and I'd swiftly had to bring myself crashing back down to earth with a harsh reminder that this was all for show, even if our (fake) moments of intimacy had begun to flow more freely in Monte Carlo. Holding Marcus's hand when there were paparazzi around had become second nature, but it had been weeks without any contact now and obviously if we had been dating for real, there would have been phone calls and FaceTimes and morning texts, and messages before we went to bed, or was that just me? I was now going to have to fake a connection from the beginning again and we couldn't afford to ease into it. Amanda Eddington had been checking in regularly and I'd been forced to give the same vague answers to her as I had to everyone else: *Marcus is away at the moment in Europe. We're taking it easy, but things are going really well, yes.* Zoe was literally the only person I could be completely honest with. Although, saying that, I hadn't mentioned the super-hot pressed-together-in-a-lift situation to her – if I let on that I'd felt attracted to Marcus, even for what had amounted to less than ten seconds, she was going to have an *I told you it was a bad idea* field day.

I grabbed myself a pleasingly frothy cappuccino and listened to Dean and Patrick chatting away – unsurprisingly – about tennis, chipping in when I could, relaying how much UK press coverage there'd been around the Madrid Open and the Italian Open in Rome and the kinds of stories I'd seen printed about Marcus. They tended to be around the theme of shock – shock that Marcus had made it that far in a clay tournament, and shock that he'd lost a match without at some point smashing a racquet. Dean seemed pleased with this intel.

'We want the press focusing on his achievements, not on how many times he said *fuck* out on court,' said Dean.

Well, quite.

Of course, Marcus chose that precise moment to appear next to us, looking devastatingly handsome – having only seen him in grainy photos in newspapers for the last few weeks, I'd forgotten how impressive his physique was close up. This would be all athletes, I reminded myself. It was because I'd never really been around them before. Anyone would feel the same, wouldn't they?

'Talking about me again, are you, Dean?' said Marcus, briefly catching my eye.

'Always, Marcus, always,' replied Dean, not caring that he'd been caught. He appeared to have the thickest skin of anyone I'd ever met and I supposed he needed it in his line of work. In fact, I doubted that Marcus was anywhere near his most demanding client – Mia Stephens had seemed pretty highly strung in my opinion, and I knew that there'd be even bigger egos at play within his clientele.

I stood up to greet Marcus, trying not to overthink what I was about to do – I wanted to let Dean know that I hadn't forgotten I had an agreement to uphold and that I was all in and taking it seriously. And it had to seem authentic – if Marcus was my boyfriend and I hadn't seen him for a while, I'd want to kiss him. Wouldn't I?

'Hello stranger,' I said to Marcus, running my arm around his waist and pulling him into me.

To be fair to him, he hesitated only for a second before catching on and putting his hand on the small of my back, pulling me closer so he could brush his lips across mine. My stomach flipped and I nearly gasped out loud, right there in the middle of the lounge. His lips had just felt so . . . good! When he pulled back, we caught each other's eyes and smiled, each of us breaking into a soft laugh that from my perspective was a combination of mortification and my head spinning, because I still had my hand on his waist, and my thumb was dangerously close to the six-pack I kept finding myself daydreaming about at inopportune moments. Maybe I just needed to touch them once and get it out of my system.

'Wow. It is the lovebirds show,' said Patrick, seemingly unimpressed.

He was probably a) very confused and b) worried that this supposed love affair of ours was going to be distracting for Marcus, which I supposed it might have been if it was real. Then again, I couldn't imagine Marcus letting anything throw him off course, not this year, not when the possibility of a Grand Slam win felt so tantalisingly close.

I reclaimed my hand, which had somehow moved from Marcus's waist to the spot right between his shoulder blades, where I could feel his lungs expanding every time he took a breath. I let my arm hang by my side, trying not to look awkward, eventually hooking my fingers over the back of a chair for support and for something to bloody well do.

'What time are you due out on court?' I asked Marcus, hoping conversation would deflect his attention away from my flushed cheeks. If in doubt, revert to tennis, I was beginning to learn.

He glanced over at the TV screens lined up along one wall, each showing live footage of an empty court.

'I'm on court Simonne-Mathieu . . . they're planning to start on time, so I'll need to be ready for ten,' said Marcus.

'Who are you playing?' I asked.

'Anton Bauer,' said Marcus.

'The Danish guy with the topknot?' I asked.

'A topknot and a killer backhand,' said Patrick.

I thought back to *Deuce*, to sitting on my sofa with Zoe all those weeks ago – did Marcus beat Bauer, I couldn't quite remember? Given that the match had culminated in a racquet-smashing extravaganza of epic proportions, I was assuming not.

'I should go,' said Marcus, giving his obligatory high fives to Patrick and Nick and Dean.

Lowering his voice, Patrick gave him a few last-minute pointers.

'Remember how we have been working on sending your forehand straight down the line. If you serve wide, he will be expecting you to hit his return cross court, so give him a surprise, *non*?'

Marcus nodded. 'Got it.'

He looked at me, hesitated and then brushed his lips over mine again, just for a second this time, but long enough for my breath to quicken. I wasn't going to overanalyse it – it was simply an involuntary human reaction to having somebody's plump, pillow-soft lips placed on top of yours.

'Good luck,' I whispered.

He half smiled. 'See you after.'

I watched him go, noticing that he was taller than almost everyone he passed on the way to the dressing rooms. When I sat down again, Dean gave me a small nod of approval, which I was pleased about, because there was no point putting on what was essentially a performance if nobody noticed how brilliantly I was actually performing.

◆ ◆ ◆

That night, I waited in my hotel room for a call from Reception. Marcus had said he'd be there to pick me up for the cooking class at around seven, but that if he got caught up at the stadium doing press after his win, it might be a little later. I must have looked at myself in the mirror about ten times in the last twenty minutes, doubting the simple black trousers and white vest combo I was wearing (was I going to get flour all down my trousers? Probably), wondering if heels would look too much; if flats wouldn't say 'evening in Paris' because, even though we were making French bread, it sounded like the world's bougiest class, complete with cheese and wine at the end as we sampled our baked goods. And would it still be warm out? I slipped on a slouchy grey blazer and then immediately took it off again; I'd hold it over my arm, so that I had the option.

The phone next to my bed rang and I raced to pick it up, worried that I'd miss it and that Marcus would think I'd forgotten about our arrangement and had made other plans for the evening. Which was irrational, really, since Marcus didn't strike me as the kind of person to automatically assume he'd been stood up. Quite the opposite, I imagined – he was used to women flocking to him, judging by the photos I'd seen of stunning models sitting on his lap, hanging off his every word. It was strange, actually, because the Marcus I was getting to know didn't seem like the Lothario I'd assumed from the press – he seemed quiet and thoughtful and ambitious. Someone who actually cared about other people. So the fact he kept women at arm's length, moving on from one to another to another, didn't really make sense, even though there was actual photographic evidence of the fact – although of course he was a man, so perhaps that was all I needed to know.

'Madame Whitfield? Monsieur Taylor is in the lobby for you.'

'I'll be down in a second.'

Right. Work mode. The only reason I was keen to see him tonight was so that we could move the interview process on – I was pleased with the opener I'd already written and the information I'd gathered in Monte Carlo, but we weren't even halfway through our journey together and there was so much more about him to discover. If he was prepared to let me in, that was. I was hoping that he'd be in a good mood this evening – he'd beaten Bauer in straight sets and hadn't lost the plot once.

Giving my room a once-over – instinctively, I supposed, as it wasn't as though anyone else was going to see it – I grabbed my bag and jacket and left the room. My heart was beating a little faster than usual, and I had the sort of buzz of anticipation I hadn't felt for months, since way before Charlie had left. I was a little nervous and unsure of myself and even though I'd tried to bury it somewhere deep in my brain, I kept remembering kissing Marcus – or him kissing me – twice this morning. It wasn't exactly normal to get off with one's interviewees, was it? It was hardly surprising I felt on edge.

He was waiting for me in the lobby, sitting on the jewel-coloured sofas, all long limbs and a vaguely amused expression, wearing black jeans and a checked shirt with the sleeves rolled up and his bronzed, just-the-right-side-of-sinewy arms on display, his wrists a shade paler than the backs of his hands. The receptionist, clearly not a tennis fan, was tapping away on his keyboard, looking up only to greet me.

'*Bonsoir*, madame.'

'*Bonsoir*.'

I stopped, smiling at Marcus. He looked relaxed in a way I didn't feel, with one arm draped along the back of the sofa, his knees softly falling apart.

'Don't get too comfortable,' I said.

'Do I have to move?' he asked, his eyes glinting at me in the subdued light of the lobby, which had a sensual French boudoir feel about it thanks to the velvet drapes and the scented candles flickering away on each circular metal coffee table.

'Unless you want us to be at the mercy of Dean's wrath then yes, you do,' I teased.

Anyone would just want to slump on a sofa after playing nearly two hours of hardcore tennis that morning, wouldn't they? I was fully empathetic, but not empathetic enough that I didn't want him to come to the class with me. Maybe I'd be able to catch him off guard and get a gem of a quote out of him while he was kneading dough.

Gastronome was about a ten-minute walk from my hotel, housed beneath the arched arcades of Le Marais, and directly opposite Place des Vosges, which I thought might be my favourite square in Paris, although there were too many beautiful ones to choose from.

Marcus held the door to the cooking school open for me and I was immediately hit by warm air and delicious aromas as I stepped inside. Two long tables had been decorated with tiny little jugs full of bright-pink flowers – it reminded me of a French living room, complete with glass cabinets and piles of enticing recipe books.

'Here goes nothing,' said Marcus wryly.

'Are you a good cook?' I asked him, assuming not. I could be wrong, but where would he find the time?

'When I'm at home I have food prepared for me and delivered to my door. Does that tell you everything you need to know?'

I laughed.

'You?' he asked.

'Not great either. But I do love bread, so I'm totally in for tonight. Mainly the tasting afterwards.'

'Welcome!' said a lively French woman wearing a black tunic and trousers and a jaunty matching chef's hat. 'My name is Colette and I am one of the owners here at Gastronome. We are very happy to have you here with us! Please, come through to the kitchen and we will begin the class.'

We followed her to the back of the shop where six other people – mostly women – were already waiting behind a large stainless-steel table. Eight places had been laid, each with a chopping board and two ceramic mixing bowls. In the centre of the table was a shelf containing everything you might need to cook up a gastronomic delight – rolling pins, various utensils, baking trays, rolls of baking parchment. I was also pleased to see Colette was handing out glasses of wine and some of the other participants were already quaffing away. So far, so good; this was my kind of class.

During the requisite round table introductions it became clear that nobody here was a tennis fan, either, because although they all oohed and aahed when Marcus explained why we were in Paris, clearly nobody had heard of him. He had also casually referred to me as his girlfriend, which had thrown me for a second there. Although the whole point of this evening was to take as many photos as possible to send to Dean so that he could tout them to the press, it still blew my mind that Marcus seemed to lie so effortlessly. It should have turned me off, because maybe it meant he lied easily about other things, too, but I really didn't think that was the case. I thought he was just the kind of person to do everything well – he'd agreed to do this thing with us, and therefore he was going to give it his all, do it to the best of his ability. I might be doing the same thing if I wasn't also on guard – in my current fragile state, I was likely to misread signals and start imagining there was an actual spark between us rather than a connection orchestrated purely for the cameras. It would be nice to feel wanted by someone again, but I had to keep reminding myself that that person would never be someone like Marcus Taylor.

Once Colette had demonstrated how to make the dough for our baguettes and assisted us as we weighed out the correct quantities of flour and yeast, tipping them into our bowls, we slowly added in the water. The atmosphere was nice and relaxed, and I had to remember my goal – to write a profile piece on Marcus so good that Amanda Eddington would want to hire me again for another job. And for that to happen, I was going to have to start working out what made Marcus tick and piecing together the research I'd done.

I glanced across at him, smiling to myself as I watched him nervously adding water to the dough.

'My mum would have a fit if she could see me now. When I was a kid, she'd always try to get me to cook with her and I'd always point-blank refuse, preferring to run around outside or practise my tennis shots or whatever,' said Marcus.

'Was your dad around, too, when you were growing up?' I asked, thinking my question linked in nicely. He was the one who'd mentioned his family, it wasn't like I'd just plucked my question out of thin air.

'Not really,' said Marcus, focusing on his dough and surprisingly not looking as though he was about to shut me down. 'My parents split up when I was about two. He wasn't around much after that.'

Parents split up aged two. Didn't see much of Dad. This felt like an important piece of the puzzle. Did his dad have a temper, too, I wondered? Or was his dad the reason Marcus was so hard on himself – did he need to prove to his dad that he was doing just fine without him?

'What about now?' I asked. 'Are the two of you in contact? He must be really proud of what you've achieved?'

'He came to a match once, a few years back,' said Marcus. 'I was playing at Eastbourne. Apparently, he lives down that way now, Brighton or somewhere, and he just showed up, asked for me at the security desk. Told everyone he was my dad. They didn't let him in, obviously, but someone came to check, so I had to go out and see him so as not to cause a scene.'

'How long had it been since you'd spoken?'

'I tried to work it out at the time. He'd made a brief appearance at my tenth birthday, and then when I was fifteen he came to the tennis club where Mum worked and they had a row and the owner had to ask him to leave. That had been the last time I'd seen him before Eastbourne, so thirteen, fourteen years?'

'What did he say? What had made him just rock up there after all that time?'

Marcus shrugged. 'He started banging on about how much he missed me. How much he regretted disappearing on me. I told him I had a match to focus on, that it wasn't a good time, but as usual what I wanted didn't seem to count for a thing. In the end I had to threaten to call security if he didn't leave.'

'That must have been hard,' I said.

'It was. Is. Sometimes. It's worse that I don't really speak to my mum anymore. My dad I can live without, I've pretty much always had to anyway.'

Before I could ask him more, Colette brought the group together to watch her knead the dough in the bowl.

'Remember, keep checking the temperature of your dough. If it is too cold, we have a problem. If it is too hot, we have a problem. *Oui?* You understand?' she said.

We all nodded.

'And be aware of the texture of your baguette dough. When it is ready, it will feel smooth on the outside, but also soft, like a beach ball.'

'Why am I thinking this is the point at which this all goes badly wrong?' I said, grimacing in Marcus's direction.

'Ditto,' he said, prodding nervously at his dough.

'*Mesdames et messieurs*, please do not forget to flour your hands before you touch the dough!' instructed Colette.

'Well, you've ruined it now,' I said to Marcus.

He hurriedly dipped his hands in some flour and then returned to work his dough.

'We'll see about that. As you know, I never give up.'

We simultaneously kneaded in silence for a while, until my dough began to work itself together and I felt confident that it wasn't going to be a total disaster. Dare I go back to the conversation we'd been having before? I'd finally been getting somewhere with my questions about his parents, and I didn't think I should stop now – there might never be another opportunity this good. I'd keep it casual, off the cuff – he could tell me as much as he wanted to tell me.

'I was wondering why your mum never comes to watch you play anymore,' I said, keeping my voice light, as though it wasn't the one piece of Marcus's history I was just dying to know the truth about. 'Did you have a falling-out?'

Marcus paused, his hands hovering over his bowl. 'You want to talk about that now?'

'No time like the present,' I said. 'Also, it can be easier to talk about difficult stuff when you're focused on something else. It feels less intense or something.'

Not to blow my own trumpet, but that had actually sounded quite knowledgeable, particularly from someone who had a pathological hatred of talking about difficult things herself. If this worked on Marcus, perhaps I would try it on Cassie next time I was home. We could bake together, even if she would think that was an odd suggestion coming from me, and then I could slip in a question about her love life, or why she hadn't managed to make any friends, or whether she wanted to spend her entire life acting like a victim. That last one was a bit harsh, but I'd thought it, so it must – in my head at least – be true.

Marcus sighed. 'Fine. Sometimes I forget you're actually here to interview me.'

'Well, what else would I be here for?' I asked, raising my eyebrows at him.

'That is a very good point. So my mother . . .'

'Your mother . . .' I prompted.

'We were close when I was a kid. Because it was just her and me against the world, I suppose. We went everywhere together, partly because I had to because she couldn't afford childcare, but also because she liked having me around. If it wasn't for her, I'd never even have picked up a tennis racquet. I'd be hanging around the tennis club waiting for her to finish her shift and she'd persuade one of the coaches to give me a knock-around out on court. I don't think anyone had expected that I'd be good at it.'

'I bet all the rich kids at the club hated you.'

Marcus shrugged. 'I honestly couldn't have cared less what they thought. It made it easier for me to beat them out on court if I didn't like them.'

'Ah, so that's where you cultivated your *I don't give a damn what people think of me* attitude.'

'Oh, I had it way before that, Ava. I've always had it.'

I shook my head at him, baffled. 'How? Did you come out of the womb full of confidence and bravado, or was it something you learned?'

I ran my hands over my dough. Good, it was feeling smooth on the outside, just like Colette had said it should.

'No idea. You'd have to ask my mum, if she ever bothers to come and see me play again, that is.'

I chewed on my lip, wondering if that was enough for this evening, or if it was better to keep going while he was on a roll. Who knew if he'd ever open up this much again – perhaps there was something about the kneading of the dough . . .

'I've seen pictures,' I said, before I could change my mind. 'Of the two of you together in the early days of your career. Your mum looked so proud of you. What happened? Why doesn't she come and watch you anymore?'

Marcus wiped his brow with the sleeve of his shirt.

'Is it hot in here or is it me?' he said.

'Tell me,' I said quietly, not letting him deflect.

He winced, as though he was grappling with something. Was it possible that nobody had ever asked him this question directly? That he'd never had to put what had happened between them into words before?'

'She was part of my team, my mum. It was much smaller in those days, just my coach at the time, a guy called Mark, and my mum, who was basically my manager.'

'So she did what Dean does now?'

'A scaled-down version of that. I didn't have any sponsorship deals back then, but she arranged my travel for me, the odd interview on local radio, that kind of thing. But then the press started trying to dig up dirt on her, went out of their way to talk to people she'd worked with at the tennis club. Banged on and on about how we'd come from nothing, how she was a barmaid not a manager. If anything went wrong with my game, if I crashed out early in a tournament or whatever, they'd blame my mum. They'd say she had no clue what she was doing, that she didn't belong in the world of tennis and perhaps neither did I. One tabloid newspaper – it's closed down now, thank God – printed pictures of her drunk and then exposed her for being arrested for shoplifting when she was sixteen.'

'Wow,' I said. 'That must have been really tough for both of you.'

'I couldn't care less what they were saying about me, but it got to my mum. And at the same time, I'd started earning a bit of money, progressing in tournaments. It was the year before I won the Australian Open and I'd done well on the US swing.'

I looked at him, confused.

'The Miami Open, the US Open, Indian Wells,' Marcus explained.

'Ah, that mysterious-sounding place again,' I said.

'You'll have to come with me next time and then you'll know exactly what it is, won't you?'

Now it was my turn to freeze, with my fingers plunged right inside the dough.

'Did I just say that out loud?' said Marcus, tipping his head, making a joke of it. 'Never mind, as we were!'

Now wasn't the time to try to decipher what he'd meant by that comment, even if suddenly my entire body did feel warm and fuzzy and soft, like the beginnings of our baguettes. He'd have meant as friends, if anything. Maybe we would be, after all of this, although it was much more likely that once my article was submitted, I'd never see nor hear from Marcus again.

'So, yes. Your mum. You'd started to make money and . . . ?'

'And she started to spend it. Which was fine – that's why I gave it to her. I wanted her to be happy, to have access to the kind of life she'd never been able to have. But then she put an offer on an expensive house and asked me to cover the mortgage on it. She said it was for both of us, but if I'd wanted a house out in Richmond, or wherever, I'd have bought one myself, wouldn't I? Plus, I was travelling so much, owning a property was the last thing on my mind.'

'So you told her no?'

'Basically. She was trying to make me play in a tournament I didn't want to play and I put my foot down. I could tell I was getting burnt out and I wanted my body to be rested and ready for the Australian Open. The prize money for a win was particularly high, but I didn't want to do it.'

'And she wanted you to. So you could buy the house.'

He nodded. 'The funny thing was, though, we'd disagreed over stuff like that before and we'd always got over it. But when she had to pull out of the sale, I could tell I'd disappointed her. Every time

I called to try and patch things up, she'd pretend to be too busy to talk. She said she thought it was best if she resigned as my manager and I got a professional person on board, that she felt she was only holding me back.'

'Was she?'

He hesitated. 'Maybe. But I would have kept her on as my manager forever if I could. Without her, I wouldn't be here, would I? I felt like I owed everything to her. She used all of her earnings from the bar job to pay for my racquets, my lessons, the rent on our shitty little flat, food – she always made sure I ate well. I couldn't understand how things had got so bad between us that she was prepared to walk away.'

'When was the last time you saw her?'

'Last Christmas. She dropped a gift round for me. It's about the only time I see her these days, that and my birthday. We occasionally text, but it's just small talk. She doesn't want anything to do with my tennis anymore, she's made that very clear.'

I wondered, then, about his temper. Whether that had been the point at which it spiralled out of control when he was on court.

'How did it affect you, not having your mum come to matches?' I asked him.

'I was angry a lot of the time. In a way, I felt as though the game had ruined my relationship with her, and therefore if I played badly, or the match didn't go my way, I felt this uncontrollable resentment that I'd given everything up for tennis and I wasn't even winning at it. Plus, my mum had always been the person I'd talked to about my feelings – the only person. After she'd gone from my life, there was nobody. I was totally on my own, and when I was out on court, under all that pressure, it would sometimes just explode out of me because I didn't know what else to do with it.'

Without thinking, I reached out to touch his arm. 'That's really sad, I'm sorry, Marcus. You must wish things could go back to how they used to be.'

He looked at my hand on his arm and he just let it rest there for a few seconds before I realised my fingers were covered in dough, which was now smeared all over his (no doubt) very expensive shirt.

'Shit, sorry!' I said, whipping my fingers away, wiping them frantically on my apron.

'It's fine, Ava,' he said, his voice barely more than a whisper.

My breath caught in my throat. If either of us had thought to ask someone to take a photo, it would have made a brilliant shot – Marcus and I, covered in flour, staring at each other with thoughts running through my head that I really couldn't explain.

And then Collette bashed a wooden spoon against a stainless-steel bowl to get our attention and I swung my eyes away from him, although I could still feel the heat of his on me.

While we waited for our bread to cook, we all relocated to the tables at the front of the shop, where Colette topped up our wine and brought out plates of olives and cheese and butter for us to enjoy once our baguettes were ready to eat. Judging by the delicious smells emanating from the ovens, we'd all done a pretty good job, and Colette seemed pleased with our creations.

'So,' said Marcus, taking a large mouthful of his wine. 'Time to talk about you. That would be much more fun.'

'Fun for who?'

'Me, obviously. I've just told you all my family secrets and now it all feels a bit . . . unbalanced. Like you know loads about me but I know next to nothing about you.'

'Isn't that the whole point of *me* writing a profile on *you*?' I reasoned.

'Oh, I think we're a bit past that, don't you?' he said.

I swallowed hard, fiddling with my glass.

'Fine. What do you want to know?' I mumbled. 'By the way, how come you're drinking the night before a match?'

He shrugged. 'It's just one glass.'

'Am I a bad influence on you, Marcus?'

'No. Now, tell me about your ex,' he said.

'What about him?'

'Well . . . how long were you together? Was it serious?'

Charlie's face came into my mind's eye for the first time that day. I noted this was a definite improvement – it meant I could go hours without thinking about him, whereas at first I'd been lucky to go ten minutes. And I hadn't had time to miss him as much because I was either going off to meet Marcus or I was trying to write the best article of my life or I was thinking about Marcus or I was thinking about the article. I'd seen Zoe a few times and was back out there in the world like a normal, functioning human being, and even the housework was on track, although there wasn't the same need for me to keep the flat spotless so that Charlie didn't compare me unfavourably to his mother. I could never live up to his mum's high standards of cooking or cleaning, it seemed, and honestly, I had no aspirations to.

'We were together for four years. Lived together for two of those,' I said. 'And then one day he just came home from work and said he was leaving.'

'Why would he do that?' asked Marcus, seemingly almost as confused as I'd been at the time.

'Apparently, he'd been unhappy for months. It's difficult for me to explain because I honestly don't know what happened, but I'm starting to suspect that he left me for his new girlfriend.'

'Have you asked him?' said Marcus.

'There wasn't a chance to. He just packed up his stuff and left. I think I was a bit in shock, because I just let him.'

'Jesus,' said Marcus. 'What did you do then? Are you close with your parents? Who was the first person you called?'

This was going to sound strange, particularly when I'd been pushing him to open up, telling him that was the way to release some of the tension he felt on court, how talking was good.

'I didn't tell anyone. For ages, like a week.'

'What?'

'I know.'

'Why?' he asked, incredulous.

'Because when something goes wrong, I deal with it on my own.'

'Since when?'

'Since my sister was born. She was premature and nearly died. I was three at the time and was sent to live with my grandparents until she was home because my parents were too stressed out and worried to deal with me as well as Cassie. She's fine now. A bit fragile. She relies on my parents a lot, and as a result I have to be strong and capable so that they don't have to worry about me too.'

'So who does worry about you?' he asked.

For some reason, I felt a little bit choked up. See? It was much better when I buried all my feelings and forgot that any of this was happening.

'Charlie used to, but now that he's gone, it's really just my friend Zoe,' I said.

Slowly, I became aware of his perfectly muscular knee, right there next to mine, even though this table was pretty spacious and I was sure he could have avoided touching me if he'd wanted to. And even more alarmingly, I had no desire whatsoever to move.

'Perhaps we're more similar than we thought, Ava,' said Marcus.

'Why, do you feel lonely too?' I asked, realising I'd just revealed something else about myself that I hadn't meant to.

'All the time. In case you hadn't noticed, I'm not particularly popular on the circuit, probably because I don't actually *want* to make friends. For me, the only way I can win is to be ruthless out there on the court. If I start to care about the people I'm playing, I won't have the edge I need to beat them.'

'You're afraid you'll feel more emotional about your game?' I asked.

'Sort of. Although feeling anything at all isn't exactly my strong point,' he admitted.

He picked up his glass.

'Cheers,' he said.

I followed suit, tapping my glass against his, our knuckles knocking together. 'What are we celebrating?'

'I was going to say a fun evening, but I'm not sure that's quite the right word.'

'To a revealing evening,' I summarised, knocking my glass against his again.

'We should take a selfie,' said Marcus suddenly. 'Dean's going to kill us, we haven't taken a single photo.'

'Hmm, good point,' I said, ripping off my apron and touching my hair self-consciously.

'Plus the more photos there are of us out there, the more chance there is of your ex seeing them,' said Marcus, with a mischievous look in his eye.

I laughed. 'Are you serious?'

'Deadly. Put it all over your socials. Didn't he do that weeks ago with some new girl he was seeing? And if you think about it, maybe it's time we started doing this fake dating thing properly. Loved-up people put loved-up images of themselves on Instagram, or so I hear.'

'I guess you wouldn't know,' I said.

'That, Ava, is a conversation for another time. Right now, it's cosy photos time.'

I put my glass down, sitting back in my seat to observe him, amused. 'You're really getting into this, aren't you?'

'It *may* be more fun than I thought it would be,' said Marcus. 'And although I don't know the guy, I'd honestly take great pleasure in imagining your ex's face as he flicks through his feed and sees a photo of the two of us having the night of our lives in Paris.'

'The night of our lives, you say?' I said, my voice low and teasing.

'Well, it's not over yet,' he quipped, his voice equally soft.

I felt an intense fizzing sensation in places I definitely shouldn't have been having such a visceral reaction. Every part of me felt alive, engaged, turned on. Was he flirting with me? Or was it my imagination playing tricks on me because it no longer knew what was real and what wasn't?

I busied myself getting my phone out of my bag. 'Come on, then,' I said, shifting in my seat and manoeuvring the phone so that we were both in shot.

'Ready?' I said.

Marcus slid his arm around my shoulders. I felt myself go rigid under his touch and he must have felt it too, because I could sense him looking at me out of the corner of his eye.

'You do know we're going to have to make this look authentic?' he said.

'Obviously,' I said. 'I'm still fiddling with the shot,' I added as an excuse, flustered now.

The truth was that being this close to him was making me nervous. His thigh had literally slid up against mine, and his fingers, which were draped casually over my shoulder, were gently stroking the top of my bare arm. All of a sudden I was hyper aware of every single movement, the tiniest adjustment he made to his position. Needing to get this over with as quickly as possible, I dipped my head, pretending to nestle into him, noticing how broad his chest was, how he smelled so good, like the expensive perfume I'd caught on the wind in Monaco, something woody and exotic and out-and-out sexy. I breathed it in, feeling his chest rise and fall beneath my cheek. The feel of his cashmere jumper on my skin was so soft and comforting that part of me wanted to say to hell with the photo and just curl into him and stay there, and to be fair he didn't seem to be in a particular hurry to move either, and was still stroking me, his fingers applying more pressure than they had before.

'Ready?' I said, my voice light and breathy.

'Mmm,' he said, looking at the camera and smiling in the almost-not-smiling way I'd seen him do for publicity shots.

I snapped away, three, four, five photos.

'I think I've got it,' I said, not moving.

'Good,' he said, not moving either.

I put my phone in my lap, and sat up straight, still not wanting to move. I did a quick sweep of my fellow bakers, but seeing as they all thought we were a couple anyway, they weren't giving our selfie-taking a second glance. I noticed that we didn't look at each other for quite some time after that, pretending instead to be riveted by the conversation about croissant recipes and best patisseries in Paris and where to buy macarons to take home. We chatted easily about tennis – a subject I found myself genuinely wanting to know more about. Marcus felt under pressure to win the following day. He said that clay might not be his best surface, but if he wanted his opponents to see him as any kind of threat going into grass season, he had to do well at Roland-Garros, and that meant quarters at the very least.

And then a buzzer sounded and Colette announced that we must all return to our ovens to reveal our finished baguettes.

◆ ◆ ◆

When we left the shop, Marcus suggested a walk around Place des Vosges and I jumped at the chance.

'That would be a hard yes, because honestly? I've never eaten that much bread in one sitting in my entire life,' I groaned.

'Same,' said Marcus. 'And I'm begging you, don't breathe a word of this to Patrick. He likes me to eat lean protein the night before a match. Do you reckon baguette and butter counts?'

'Course it does,' I said, feeling satiated and relaxed after one of the nicest evenings I'd had for a long time. The company had been spectacular – Colette, my fellow bakers and, of course Marcus, who had opened up to me in ways I'd never expected, at least not yet. And I'd learned something practical – I fully intended to cook more baguettes the second I got home and thought I could quite happily live on homemade bread and butter for dinner until further notice.

A low moon hung just above the steep slate roofs of the gorgeous peach stone, seventeenth-century townhouses lining the square. Marcus made me stop to post the photo of the two of us in the restaurant on Instagram because he thought I might talk myself out of doing it.

'Also, it's called Insta-gram for a reason – you're supposed to post as things happen, not hours later,' said Marcus.

'Nobody does that anymore,' I complained.

'Well, I want *you* to,' he said, looking pointedly at my phone.

He was asking me to splash our selfie all over my social media feed when it wasn't my thing at all to gush about how wonderful my life was when that was only ever half the story, and these photos made it look as though my world was one big Parisian love fest. In order to keep it real, I should really be showing all the bad stuff, too, like . . . my mind had gone blank . . . obviously not everything had been perfect since I'd arrived in Paris. And yet, I couldn't think of a single thing I hadn't enjoyed. The hotel was adorable, the service impeccable, Marcus's team were far less intimidating now I was getting to know them better, the tennis was unexpectedly fun to watch, especially from plush front-row seats where I felt as though I was living every point vicariously through the players. And Marcus. Marcus was . . . more charming than the British press would have us believe, and I fully intended to redress the balance, but all in good time.

'Fine, I'll post it now,' I said, a thought popping into my head. 'But only if you do, too.'

Marcus laughed off my suggestion. 'I'm barely on Instagram.'

'You have one hundred and sixty-six thousand followers,' I said. 'I checked. And no, I'm not stalking you. That's one hundred and sixty thousand more than I've got. So if I'm going to announce our relationship to my friends, family and followers, then so are you,' I insisted, daring him to disagree.

He tutted, pulling his phone out of his pocket. 'You strike a hard bargain, Ava Whitfield.'

I pinged him across what I thought was the most flattering shot. Of me, that was – he of course looked stunning in all five of them.

I watched him frowning with concentration as we simultaneously uploaded the photo. I put a soft warm filter on mine, hamming up the dreamy Parisian light, and then I tried desperately to think of a caption that would hit the sweet spot between funny and romantic. I finally landed on: *Pre-match baking in Le Marais* with a hearts-in-your-eyes emoji. I absolutely was not going to add any schmaltzy hashtags à la Charlie, as that would simply cheapen the whole thing, in my opinion. And then I posted it before I could change my mind.

After circling Place des Vosges twice, we headed back to my hotel. Worryingly, I felt as though I could have walked around Paris with Marcus in the moonlight forever.

'How are you going to get back?' I asked him.

Marcus was staying near the stadium, in a room with nothing much about it other than excellent storage space and a spectacular view of the Eiffel Tower, he'd told me.

'I guess I'll jump in a taxi,' he said, making eye contact with me in a way that for a split second made me think that he was wishing he could stay over. No, he absolutely couldn't be. As well as the obvious reasons, he needed rest and sleep for his match, and to be near the ground the following morning for training. Why had my mind even gone there?

'See you tomorrow, then,' I said, fumbling around in my bag for my room key, more than anything so as to avoid looking at him. He was smiling down at me when I did look up, standing dangerously close.

'I was thinking . . . we should probably kiss or something. In case there are any photographers lurking around. It would look pretty weird if I just dropped you off without so much as a peck on the cheek, wouldn't it?' he said, tipping his head to one side while he waited for my answer.

'Um . . . really?' I said. 'You think they're out at this time?'

'They might be.'

My phone began to ping in my bag, which I could only assume was a reaction to the picture I'd just posted. I didn't want to look – there was the small matter of those horrible comments I dreaded – but I also knew that I wouldn't be able to *not* find out what people were saying in response. And as I was silently pondering that dilemma, Marcus took a step closer to me, sweeping his hand under my jawline, using the crook of his finger to lift my chin so that my eyes met his. That beard; that one messy eyebrow, that ridiculously shiny hair. Perhaps I should try to enjoy kissing him, whether it was for show or not. That's what single people did, wasn't it, kissed random people they only vaguely liked? I'd managed it before Charlie – surely I couldn't have forgotten how? I closed my eyes as his lips brushed across mine and then too quickly pulled away; I cupped his cheek and pulled him back towards me, kissing him this time, harder than I'd planned. I parted my lips slightly, which was a huge mistake, because somehow the tip of his tongue slid inside my mouth and it felt like my legs had disappeared out from under me and I was floating off into the warm Parisian air never to be seen again and never wanting to be. His hands were on my waist and moving slowly upwards. If I didn't do something now, we were going to go way too far. *Way* too far. It took every ounce of mental strength I had to push him lightly away.

'Sorry,' he said. 'That was a little—'

'It's fine,' I said, cutting him off, because it really was. It had been me as much as it had been him and so, if anything, I should also be apologising. 'I think we've convinced them, don't you?' I said, smiling weakly at him.

'I'd say so,' he muttered, seeming a little flustered too.

I made a move to leave, because somebody had to.

'Night, then,' I said.

'Night, Ava.'

I walked up to the entrance, feeling him watching me, pushing through the revolving door, entering the safety and absolute silence of the hotel's lobby, berating myself for coming on too strong, and for enjoying it more than I should have. Marcus could still pull the interview at any point and this – kissing him like *this* – wasn't how I was going to keep him on side. I was halfway through my interview, I couldn't afford to mess things up now. It was going to be good, really good. I had faith in my ability to write it, and in Marcus's ability to show me who he was in a way I'd doubted at first. As I took the stairs up to my room, I imagined him hailing a taxi out on the street, and decided that he probably wasn't even giving our kiss a second thought.

Chapter Fifteen

When Zoe rang the following morning, I was sitting outside a café feeling extremely Parisian on my red-and-white-striped woven chair, facing out on to the street so that I could people-watch to my heart's content. On the plate in front of me was a warm baguette, which I had to say was not a patch on the delights Marcus and I had made the night before, and a delicate cheese omelette. I was drinking orange juice *and* coffee, because I hadn't been able to decide which I'd wanted more, and so: when in Paris.

I put Zoe on speaker because I needed to use my hands to spread copious amounts of salty butter on to my bread.

'Hey,' I said.

A car honked its horn; a trio of tiny, yappy dogs trotted past.

'Where are you?' she asked accusingly.

'Paris.'

'I know, but where, exactly?'

'In a café?' I said, wondering why the sudden fascination with my location.

'Are you, you know . . . alone?' she asked.

'Um . . .' I said, glancing at the couple to my right and a businessman on his own to my left. 'Pretty much. Why?'

'I thought Marcus might be with you,' said Zoe.

'Marcus is not with me. In fact, he'll probably be pummelling away on a treadmill as we speak,' I said.

'You didn't spend the night together, then?'

The female half of the couple glanced in my direction and I hurriedly picked up my phone, taking Zoe off speakerphone *tout de suite.*

'You've seen the selfie, haven't you?' I said.

'Oh, we *all* have,' said Zoe knowingly.

'It was Marcus's idea,' I said, deciding that throwing him under the bus was the best way to get Zoe off my back.

I sat back in my seat, my mouth watering as a plate of delicious-smelling, warm, buttery croissants was served to the man seated next to me. Would it be too much to order one of those after I'd finished this? If you couldn't have double carbs for breakfast in Paris, when could you? It wasn't like *I* was playing tennis.

'The point is, I thought you were pretending and then I see this shot of the two of you looking really into each other. And you've got that smug, smitten look you used to get when you first got together with Charlie. And Marcus is smiling. You told me he never smiles. What had you said to him that was so funny?'

She was putting me off my breakfast here. There would have been little point in posting on social media and *not* looking loved-up. I suppose what worried me was that I didn't remember having to fake it. I remembered his thigh sliding into place next to mine, the way my head had felt on his shoulder. The way his beard had tickled the top of my head. Why hadn't it felt more difficult? I was supposed to be impartial, or at the very least feel nothing more than mild journalistic interest. Was it possible that I'd been having such a good time, I hadn't actually needed to remember to act like I was?

'We decided to up our game,' I said. 'And I know I've said this about a million times now, but you haven't said anything to anyone, have you? About it all being a set-up?'

'Ava, you can trust me, you know that. All I'm saying is, I see what I see. And he's smoking hot, so I wouldn't blame you if you did start falling for him.'

'I'm not falling for him.'

What a ridiculous suggestion.

'Is he a good kisser?' asked Zoe.

Yes, yes, yes.

'Can we change the subject?' I said, irritated now and wishing I'd never picked up her call. Way to ruin a perfectly good breakfast platter!

After managing to get rid of Zoe and rushing to finish my breakfast, which was slightly less appealing than it had been before she'd put stupid ideas in my head, I wandered down to the Metro and navigated my way out to Porte d'Auteuil, which was the nearest station to the stadium. It was packed. Everywhere! And after it took me about ten minutes to make it up the steps to street level, I realised I'd arrived at the exact same time as the approximately thirty thousand other people who were also going to watch tennis today, many of whom, I imagined, would be here to see Marcus take on Tomas Horvat on the iconic court Philippe-Chatrier. I spotted an entrance for press and decided that needs must – I got out my accreditation lanyard and swept past the queues, feeling mildly bad about it but also not wanting to miss anything that might be useful for my piece.

Our seats on Philippe-Chatrier were sensational – the court housed just over fifteen thousand people and the stands were filling up fast. We were in Marcus's players' box, two rows from the front, and slightly raised for a better view. Tubs of pretty cerise flowers divided the spectators from the court itself, which was that dusty red clay again. It had been raked until it was perfectly smooth, with no hint of the scuffing and sliding and (potentially) racquet smashing that was about to ensue on its hallowed surface. Behind me were rows of what I presumed were the VIP seats that rich tennis fans paid thousands of euros to acquire. Like at Monte-Carlo, they were housed in little booths that I'd learned were called *loges* but still didn't know why. As I settled into my seat next to Dean, my phone vibrated in my bag. I ignored it at first, focusing on taking in the atmosphere, the buzz of a match about to begin. But then it rang again. I opened my bag, fishing around for my phone. *Charlie Calling*. I frowned at my screen – this was everything I'd wanted, wasn't it? For him to have seen the photos and have had some sort of jealous reaction to them, prompting him to beg for forgiveness and ask to move back in? And yet now it was actually happening, the moment of triumph I'd imagined felt strangely underwhelming. I thought about Marcus preparing to walk out on to the court and rejected Charlie's call – I could hardly talk to him now anyway, could I, there were signs everywhere saying no mobile phones allowed.

'Here we go,' said Dean, as the umpire came out on court to a smattering of applause. Smartly dressed in a navy blazer and white polo shirt combo, he appeared to be enjoying the attention and gave the crowd a jaunty little wave. He didn't go up to his chair, choosing instead to chat to a couple of the ball boys and ball girls who had also made their way out to stand on the sidelines of the court. I wondered how excited they'd been about today, whether they were young tennis players themselves about to be inspired by seeing two of the world's best players battling it out right in front of them, while doing the complicated ball scooping and throwing routines they'd been taught. A row of TV cameras and photographers took up the front row of one full length of the court. I wondered if it was being broadcast in the UK and if my dad was watching.

On a big screen, footage of Marcus walking along a bright white corridor suddenly appeared. The crowd went wild, knowing we were about to begin. He had a white sports bag over each shoulder and was gently stretching his neck, first one way then the other. The camera stayed on him as he climbed a set of stairs, his trainers squeaking on the lino floor, and when he paused at the top, which was presumably just inside the tunnel, it zoomed in for an extreme close-up of his face. I looked up at the rows and rows of people and wondered how Marcus could do this – how he had the confidence to get out there in front of all these people. How could he keep his focus with so many eyes on him? I thought that for the first time I truly understood the pressure he was under – it wasn't about the money, or at least I didn't think it was just that. He was fighting for a place in history, the career milestone he craved, the second Grand Slam title that would prove to him and everyone else that his Australian Open win eight years ago had not been a fluke. I crossed my fingers in my lap, sending a wish out into the universe that he would win today, that he would triumph in front of all these people. Marcus, who perhaps was thinking something similar himself, was looking straight ahead, jogging lightly on the spot, kitted out in the mint-green shorts and white top with the Lacoste logo that looked so good on him but that he wouldn't be wearing next season once they'd snatched their sponsorship deal out from under him. Over the speaker system, an enthusiastic male voice spoke only in French. I didn't understand any of it except Marcus's name at the end and he began to walk, appearing at the corner of the court mere seconds later. Pumping dance music blared out as he waved at the crowd, only a smattering of whom were on their feet, although he seemed to be getting a slightly better reception than he had at Monte-Carlo. His name had been beamed on to the digital advertising boards around the perimeter of the court and was flashing in fluorescent pink font: *Marcus Taylor, Marcus Taylor, Marcus Taylor.* I clapped my heart out for him, as Dean and Patrick whooped next to me, and then I went for it and whooped too, immediately feeling self-conscious and reining myself in.

'Come on, Marcus!' yelled Dean.

His opponent had appeared on the screen and was now making the same journey Marcus had, along the corridor and up the steps.

Tomas Horvat was German, had cheekbones that could cut glass and looked so young that perhaps in another life he would have been lying on the sofa gaming while recovering from an all-nighter. The crowd roared as he entered the court; strange that he was getting a much bigger reception than Marcus. He was world number one, I supposed, a bigger name, so perhaps it made sense that hardcore tennis fans would be more excited to see him, but I still felt for Marcus. And then I reminded myself that he was able to block all of this noise out – that he became selfish, ruthless, intent only on winning the game. According to him, he couldn't care less whether people booed or cheered, he was there to do a job, and carrying that out to the best of his ability was the only thing that mattered.

Both men began unpacking their bags. Marcus walked over to what looked like a chest freezer (if chest freezers were sponsored by Perrier) at the side of the court and pulled out several white towels. There seemed to be constant movement in the crowds – latecomers arriving and struggling to locate their seats, others deciding that now was the perfect time to get up and use the bathroom. Wasn't all of this distracting for the players?

Once they'd warmed up, the umpire called them in for the toss. Marcus won and chose to serve.

'He is sending an early message to Horvat,' I heard Patrick say.

I presumed that the message was that he was not to be intimidated, but it was just a guess.

My phone buzzed again in my bag.

With two balls balanced on his racquet, Marcus took his place on the baseline, sliding one into his pocket and taking the other in his hand. Horvat prepared to receive – he was right-handed like Marcus, which was good, because I'd learned that playing a left-hander threw up a whole other set of challenges. There was a burst of slow clapping until the umpire asked everyone to be quiet and near silence fell over the stadium, although there was still a palpable, fizzing atmosphere in the air. A duo of ball girls took their crouched positions at either side of the net. Several rogue camera flashes popped and then all eyes were on Marcus as he bounced the ball (seven times, I counted) and tossed it into the air.

His first serve was deep and long, almost hitting the back line of the serving box. Horvat returned it easily, sending it cross court to Marcus's forehand. Marcus whipped it straight down the line on to Horvat's backhand – he, in turn, sent it sailing diagonally back over the net. Marcus repositioned himself so that he could use his backhand to hit deep. It must have been as powerful as it looked because Horvat sliced a clunky-looking shot into the net. *Fifteen-Love.*

Marcus served again – it went long. I knew he'd been working on his second serve with Patrick, so hopefully he was feeling better about it. He went again, only just getting it over the net, but it was in. Horvat returned long to the baseline. Marcus sent it across to Horvat's backhand – he seemed to be focusing on that side, was this Horvat's weakness? Was this part of Marcus's secret game plan? Horvat had manoeuvred himself around so that he was there waiting on the forehand and he sliced it straight down the middle of the court. Somehow Marcus must have anticipated where the ball would land because he was right there, using his forehand to send the ball into the now wide-open space in Horvat's right corner. Horvat charged across the court, hitting a diagonal shot to Marcus's own right corner, putting him off-balance and way outside of the tram lines as he lunged to reach it. He placed it in Horvat's mid-court. A more controlled Horvat hit a sneaky drop shot that had Marcus charging into the net, sliding across the clay to scoop it up before it bounced a second time. Horvat was waiting at the net to volley it straight back. It looked like it was going to sail right over Marcus's head, but at the last second Marcus spun around, reached for the ball and did a sort of backhand flick over his right shoulder at such a steep angle that Horvat had no chance of returning it. The crowd roared. *Thirty-Love.* I whooped again, I couldn't help myself. And then I released the breath I'd been holding for the entire point. Marcus was playing well, really well. If he carried on like this, he was in with a chance. And I knew that he would be thinking the same thing and that this would give him the boost he needed to push on.

Marcus took the first set 6-4. Tomas beat him in the second, 7-5.

Sweat began to prickle at the nape of my neck as the players took a changeover break and we waited for the third set to begin. Marcus was sitting with his back to us, glugging at water – he was already on to his third bottle – and then rubbing his face with a towel. In a split second he had peeled off his top – several female members of the crowd wolf-whistled in admiration, but it was over in seconds when he grabbed another from his bag and pulled it on in one swift movement. Then he threw the towel on the floor, did some hamstring stretches and ran back out on to the court, ready to begin.

Marcus took his position, taking a few beats to settle himself before executing what looked to me like a perfect serve. It was an ace, right off the bat. Dean pumped his fist next to me.

'Yes, Marcus! Let's go!' he yelled.

Marcus held his serve in the first game.

As the set went on, neither lost their serve, with each man matching the other's increasingly powerful shots stroke for stroke. It was the best I'd seen Marcus play. Neither of them double-faulted and the aces came thick and fast. There was a different feel to this set – not so much slogging it out on the baseline and more coming into the net. I wondered if this was due to fatigue, or whether one of them had purposefully changed tactics. Less of the running back and forth and more well-thought-out shots that caught the other off guard, forcing them to make a mistake. It was four games all, then five.

Marcus prepared to serve. His first went in the net, his second went long. *Love-Fifteen.* He shook his head, mumbling something to himself under his breath. Keep calm, I willed him. Don't lose your head, stay focused. He served again, but it was slower than usual and Horvat took full advantage of that, slamming it straight to Marcus's backhand so fast, it sailed right past him before he could even move. *Love-Thirty.* Marcus slammed his racquet on the ground twice, his face twisted in frustration. Fuck. This wasn't good. I glanced across at Patrick, who was calm and stoic, no doubt trying to show Marcus that he wasn't worried, that he had this, that it was just one point, two points. Although points that, because he'd lost them, could cost him the game and then the set.

The crowd, who I felt had been starting to get behind Marcus, were looking distinctly unimpressed as he served again. He seemed to have suddenly lost focus completely because the ball went into the net and he had to use his weaker second serve again, which Horvat took control of immediately with a sharp return to Marcus's far right-hand side. He lunged to return it, flicking it back across the net, but Horvat was there waiting for it and put it down the line. It looked out from here, and Marcus clearly thought the same as he gestured to indicate that it was wide.

Suddenly, the umpire was out of his seat, jogging over to the line, crouching down to inspect the clay. He called it in. Marcus went storming over to see for himself, pointing to something on the clay. I couldn't hear what he was saying, but his body language was clear – he was about to lose control and I didn't think I could bear it after all the progress he'd made. I got that he couldn't be expected to change entirely overnight, that this was Roland-Garros, that winning this match was a big deal and he had enough skill, he was almost there, matching world number one Horvat shot for shot. Maybe every point did count, but from what I'd seen, the umpires never, ever changed their minds after making a call, so what was the point in going on about it?

Marcus was still arguing, pointing at the clay, holding his head with disbelief and frustration, gesturing towards Horvat. It didn't look good. And as the umpire, clearly deciding he couldn't continue bickering about the call indefinitely, returned to his seat, Marcus threw his racquet across the court, sending it skidding across the clay. The crowd hissed and whistled. I bit my lip, finding it very hard to watch, perhaps even more so than the first time because I knew him now and I knew this wasn't an accurate depiction of who he was as a person. He looked like a bad loser, like a petulant child not getting his own way, and this wasn't what he was like, not at all. It was the pressure of the event, the disappointment with himself, this braying French crowd sneering at him from the stands. I got it. And maybe I'd been expecting too much – perhaps this would be an interesting angle for my story, anyway. A sort of one step forward, two steps back, as happened to us all. Maybe my angle was that he was human and made mistakes like we all did. It was just that, in his case, there were fifteen thousand people watching.

Somehow, against the odds – because when I'd seen him lose it before, his play seemed to disintegrate steeply from there – he held his game. At six games all, they went to a tie break.

'How does this work?' I whispered to Dean.

'They alternate serves, two each. The first to seven with two clear points wins the set,' explained Dean.

I nodded. As this was a Grand Slam, the match was best of five, so if Marcus lost this tie break he would be down two sets to one. There would still be a chance, but was it possible? Against the world number one, in this heat? Would Marcus's experience count for something, perhaps? He'd played Roland-Garros ten times at least, whereas this was only Tomas's third. But then Tomas was on a roll – he'd taken the US Open title last year, Wimbledon the year before. He knew what it took to win a tournament of this calibre. And he didn't look as tired as Marcus, which I supposed you wouldn't when you were twenty-one and at the absolute peak of your fitness.

Tomas won the tie break and, eventually, the match.

Chapter Sixteen

I waited in the grounds for Marcus to finish his press conference, deciding I needed some fresh air and a cold beverage more than I needed to watch him talk live about the match I'd just seen – I'd hear about it if anything interesting happened. Distracted by the lure of a glass of cold white wine, I hit one of the many bar areas and found a single chair and a shady spot for one, despite the crowds. The drama of the match had stayed with me; I thought it might have been the tensest I'd felt in my entire life, or at least for that length of time – nearly four hours! How Marcus had played at that level for that long, I had no idea. I had a new admiration for him, despite the fact he very nearly lost it at the umpire, because I'd witnessed what he was capable of when he played at his absolute best, even if he couldn't quite carry it through to the end. He might have slipped back into his Racquet Man persona for a minute there, but other than that he'd been brilliant – the match could have gone either way, particularly on a different surface. I wasn't sure if Marcus felt it, but from where I was standing, his hard work – and employing Patrick as his coach – was beginning to pay off.

When I checked my phone, I saw that I had several missed calls from Charlie and a text saying *Ring me, please.* My stomach fluttered involuntarily. Had those photos upset him rather than made him want me again? I didn't like disappointing anyone, obviously, but especially not Charlie. Even now, after everything he'd done, I felt the need to behave impeccably, to take the moral high ground even if he had taken the low one. I wasn't sure posting photos of me and Marcus together had been the best idea, in hindsight – I second-guessed everything I put on social media at the best of times. What if Charlie thought I was an awful person now? And – more annoyingly – why did I still care?

I returned the call, thinking about Marcus out there on the court – if he had the courage to do that, I could totally do this.

Charlie answered on the first ring, as though he'd been staring at his phone waiting for my call.

'At last,' he said huffily.

'Hi,' I said, as a gust of deliciously cool wind licked my face.

'So I saw your photos,' he said.

'Which photos?' I asked, as if I didn't know.

'You and that dick Marcus Taylor. Seriously, Ava? The guy's an animal!'

Now, after the way Marcus had just played, after I'd seen him leave his soul out there on that court, essentially, it took all my strength not to tell Charlie to fuck right off and end the call immediately. On the other hand, this was what I'd wanted, wasn't it? He was clearly rattled, otherwise why would he give a toss who I was dating?

'Know him personally, do you?' I asked, a little facetiously, I knew, but come *on*.

'We've all seen the footage of him, Ava. I'm surprised he hasn't seriously injured someone the way he throws racquets around. Why would you want to date someone like that?'

'Well, at least I've waited a respectable amount of time before jumping into something else. Could you have been any more insensitive, Charlie? Posting cutesy photos of you and your mysterious new girlfriend not long after you moved out. Who is she, anyway?'

I seemed to have rendered him mute, and I could almost feel him fumbling around for an answer.

'Why does that matter?' asked Charlie.

'Because if you're going to weigh in on who I'm seeing, it's only fair I get to do the same,' I said. He couldn't argue with that, could he?

'But the thing is, Ava, I didn't call to talk about me. We were talking about you and that . . . Neanderthal,' said Charlie, the king of deflecting questions he didn't want to answer.

I pinched the top of my nose, trying to keep calm. I didn't think screaming down the phone would be appropriate in the champagne bar at the French Open.

'You know what, Charlie? I think I'm going to go. Because I literally don't care about your opinion of Marcus – you're not dating him, are you, *I* am. And for your information, he is far more than just a man who gets angry on court. He's an elite athlete, more dedicated and hard-working than a single other person I've ever met. And he's actually very kind, and charming, and he listens – really listens – when you talk. And he's interested in me, which I have to say you stopped being towards the end of our relationship. So I'm actually very happy. Goodbye, Charlie.'

I went to hang up, feeling powerful and in control and also slightly reeling from the fact that I'd managed to name several things I liked about Marcus without even having to think about it.

'Ava, please. I'm sorry,' said Charlie, changing his tone, the aggression of a few moments ago gone. Now he just sounded desperate. What was *wrong* with him? Why did he care so much? Surely he should be putting all his energy into his new 'relationship' – because I was presuming it was official, and that it wasn't just a string of sexy nights away in boutique hotels.

'I think there's little point in prolonging this conversation,' I said, keen to get off the phone. Marcus might be ready to leave in a minute, and Dean wanted us to head back to the car together because this was a super-high-profile event and there were press here from all over the world, although I was pretty sure Marcus wouldn't be in the mood for photos. He probably just wanted to be alone.

'I miss you,' said Charlie. 'There. I've said it.'

I put my hand across my mouth, not quite believing what I was hearing. These were the words I'd imagined him saying over and over in the dark days after he first left; the reassurance from him I'd needed in the two weeks after he'd moved out, when he refused to answer my texts at all. *Now* he missed me. And I missed him too, but surely that was inevitable after spending four years with someone. Did it mean more than that, for either of us?

'It's probably a bit late for all that,' I said, wondering if I meant it or if I just didn't want to let him off the hook that easily. I didn't know, I couldn't think straight.

'Don't you still think about me? About us?' he asked, sounding a little bit tearful.

'Sometimes,' I replied, although it was less and less as time went on.

'Too busy thinking about Marcus Taylor?' he mumbled.

'Something like that. On which note, he's just finished a match and we'll be heading back to his hotel in a minute.'

'I saw he lost,' said Charlie spitefully.

Why was he looking up tennis results? He was a football man through and through and I'd never once seen him show interest in racquet sports of any kind.

'It was a very close match,' I said. 'He played brilliantly,' I felt the need to add.

'So what now?' asked Charlie. 'Can we meet up when you're back? Go for a drink or something? I really need to talk to you.'

I had a flashback to the night he announced he didn't want to be with me anymore. How I'd begged him – *begged* him – to sleep on it, to take the time to help me understand exactly what had gone wrong.

'You had your chance to talk and you point-blank refused,' I said, tears springing up at the memory.

'I'm sorry, Ava. I handled it really badly, I can see that now,' he said.

'You couldn't wait to leave!' I said, wiping a rogue tear away with the sleeve of my cardigan. It still stung that he'd left with so little regard for my feelings, after the years – *good* years – we'd spent together. 'You couldn't even give me until morning. You made me feel as though I was nothing to you.'

'No, Ava. That wasn't it, I just—'

'So no, Charlie. I don't want to meet up with you. And I'd prefer it if you didn't call me again.'

I ended the call, resisting the urge to sob because . . . photos. Marcus. I pulled myself together and went to find him.

It took a while for my heartbeat to return to normal as I sat quietly with the team in the players' lounge. Dean was up and down taking calls from LA, and Nick was with Marcus. Patrick had told me Marcus had had a wrist injury four years ago that flared up occasionally, which was why Nick travelled with him everywhere. At great expense, I imagined. Apparently, the press conference had gone well – Marcus had admitted feeling regret over the way he'd acted over the line call, which I thought was something different from him. When I'd seen recordings of post-match interviews before, he'd appeared to show little remorse, banging on about pressure and blaming the umpire/spectators/the weather and anyone else but himself. Perhaps, despite the setback, he was making progress after all.

When Marcus appeared, I knew immediately that he was beating himself up about losing. There was something different about the way he walked, about the dead look behind his eyes. Of course, it could just be exhaustion – I hoped it was – but I suspected there was something more. The second Grand Slam of the year and he'd been knocked out in round two, and perhaps in his mind it made little difference by whom, or how hard he'd fought for it. It meant he potentially only had two more chances to fulfil his dream of winning another Grand Slam this year – Wimbledon and the US Open – and what if he couldn't? What then? Would he try again the following season? Or would he be able to accept that everything else he'd achieved already was enough?

Marcus nodded at me and then turned to Dean.

'Is my car ready?'

'It is,' said Dean, giving him a sympathetic smile.

Despite what I'd initially believed, I didn't think Marcus's team were walking on eggshells around him. I'd felt a bit like I was at first, but I was nowhere near as worried about upsetting him or saying the wrong thing now as I had been at the beginning. I hadn't once seen him be unpleasant to any member of his team and, to my knowledge, his anger was always internalised. Or taken out on a racquet, obviously, but never a fellow human. Actually, that wasn't strictly true. There had been linesmen, umpires, ball boys and noisy spectators who had all felt the wrath of Marcus Taylor. So why did I feel so confident that he wasn't going to take it out on me?

He picked up his racquet bag and started walking towards the exit. As he passed Anton Bauer, who was sitting at a table with his team, Anton stood up and shook Marcus's hand.

'Commiserations, man. Close call.'

Marcus put his hand over Anton's. 'Thanks, man.'

As he walked on, I glanced at Dean. Was I supposed to be going after him? Because it really didn't seem like he wanted me to and I—

'Are you coming, Ava?'

Marcus was waiting for me by the door. A little self-conscious, suddenly, I hurried across the room to join him.

We held hands automatically as we stepped out of the stadium and headed for the pick-up area where a line of flashy black Mercedes minivans was waiting, presumably to whisk players back to their hotels whenever they desired. Behind a rope stood around twenty photographers, who immediately started flashing away and calling Marcus's name. I thought I felt him squeeze my hand as we ignored them and got into our van. The driver slid the door shut behind us, enveloping us in a dark, quiet cocoon that smelled of leather with a hint of pine. Marcus threw himself back in his seat, looking up at the ceiling.

'Well, that was a fucking train wreck,' he said.

I thought about how best to answer. And then I thought I'd just say how I felt and to hell with the consequences.

'You played really well,' I said, turning to him as we began to drive slowly out of the stadium. Fans were staring at us through the glass, not able to tell who was inside because of the blacked-out windows, although one of them took a photo anyway.

'I did not, Ava. And the most frustrating thing is, I had it all up here,' he said, jabbing his finger on his temple. 'I knew what I needed to do to beat him, I understood the shots I needed to make, but when it came down to it, I failed dismally to execute them.'

'Okay, but that's always going to happen, right? There's going to be things you do well, that you're proud of, that surprise you about yourself. And then at the same time you're going to make mistakes. Some shots are not going to work out the way you would have liked them to.'

'I want to play the perfect game, that's what I strive for, what I've always aimed for.'

'I know,' I said, wanting to show him that I understood. I knew nothing about elite-level sports, of course I didn't, but in my own way I was striving to be perfect too – with my sister, in my own career. I'd gone back and read articles I'd written and thought they were awful. But it never felt as bad as I could see this felt for Marcus.

'You get used to losing,' said Marcus. 'But some losses hurt more than others, and this is one of them.'

I nodded. 'You'll be okay,' I said.

I patted his knee lightly and although I was planning to remove it again, I felt the need to leave it there. We sat in silence for a minute or two, both of us looking out of our own windows as we drove along the streets of Paris. And then suddenly I felt him put his hand on top of mine. Curl his fingers in between my fingers. I squeezed hard, still looking out of the window, not able to take in the view now because all I could think about were the very pleasant sensations shooting up my arm and into my body, my mouth, my head. His hand was warm and strong. I could hear him breathing, quickly, gently, but I thought I might be holding my breath. I had the sense that he needed me to keep squeezing him and I wanted to do that for him, wanted to do anything to make him feel even the tiniest bit better about losing today.

'I like having you around,' he said after a while, his eyes not moving from the window.

I turned to look at him, even if he couldn't meet my eye, nodding gently. 'I'm not going anywhere.'

THE QUEEN'S CLUB CHAMPIONSHIPS

Chapter Seventeen

It took me a while to settle into the normality of being back in London. Marcus had been in the south of France with Patrick, preparing for the grass court season, so we hadn't seen each other for nearly two weeks, although there'd been the odd text back and forth. Dean had flown back to LA but had sent a message to say that our plan was working – there had been some good press coverage around Roland-Garros, not only of Marcus and I together, but of Marcus's performance against Tomas Horvat. I'd acclimatised to seeing photos of myself sitting on the sidelines of the court. The press had taken a shot of me cheering Marcus on in Paris and I'd realised that my emotions in those moments had become completely authentic. I wanted to support him; I wanted him to do well.

Zoe had sent me a set of photos of us walking in the Place des Vosges after the cooking class, pictures I hadn't even known existed. It still surprised me that images could be so misleading – it was dark, so they were pretty grainy, and I had the impression they'd been taken by a member of the public rather than by a professional paparazzo. Even so, we looked as though we were staring love-struck into each other's eyes for the entirety of the evening, mesmerised by the sheer sight of each other, his arm around my shoulders, mine slung around his waist. I hadn't even remembered walking like that, it had felt so natural and easy, and, okay, we'd had a glass of wine or two, but since when had we acted like a proper couple when we weren't even sure anyone was watching? No shots had surfaced of us kissing outside the entrance to my hotel, however, meaning that little set-up had all been for nothing. Not that kissing him had exactly been a hardship. And it *had* reminded me that kissing someone you didn't know that well could actually be quite nice, and that I could kiss random people now, if I wanted. Except that there was our agreement – I had a strong sense of not wanting to undermine everything Marcus and I had been trying to achieve. Our mission had had the desired effect for me – I'd succeeded in making Charlie jealous, and it had been much less satisfying than I'd thought it would be. I'd realised I couldn't forgive Charlie for the way in which he'd left me and also that there had been cracks in our relationship that I'd never even noticed because it had been enough for me that he was a nice guy with a nice family. But we weren't quite there with Marcus and his sponsorship deals. Dean said a few brands had been in touch to indicate that Marcus was back on their radar, but nothing was definite, and so for now our arrangement would remain.

I caught up with Marcus for the first time out on one of the practice courts, the day before his first match at Queen's. The club was in West Kensington, slap-bang in the middle of a residential area made up of beautiful four-storey townhouses that probably cost about eight million pounds each. The site was tiny compared to Roland-Garros and had the sort of neighbourhood tennis club vibe of the Monte-Carlo tournament, except with a stuffy, high-end London feel and crappier weather. I'd never seen Marcus play on grass before – he said his game was better on this surface than it was on clay, but when I took a seat on a bench to watch him hitting with Patrick, it looked exactly the same to me. Had he said the ball bounced faster or slower on grass? I honestly couldn't tell.

When he saw me, he said something to Patrick about taking a quick break and ran over, perching on the bench next to me. He stuck his long, bronzed legs, contrasted perfectly by his pristine white socks and white trainers, out in front of him. He was sporting almost indecently short shorts in the same silky material as the tracksuit bottoms he'd worn the very first time I met him on the plane, and a white T-shirt topped with the white Monte-Carlo Country Club cap I'd seen him in once before. It was a simple yet phenomenally effective combination. I knew Marcus had been training hard over the last couple of weeks and I could see that it had paid off – the shoulder muscles just visible beneath his T-shirt looked a little more defined and I was almost certain that his arms, still tanned from months of travelling in our winter, were a little bigger on the bicep.

'It's lovely here,' I said, looking around. 'I'm actually quite looking forward to the tournament.'

He frowned at me, his eyes in teasing mode. 'Ava, are you getting into tennis?'

'Now, that would be telling.'

'How have you been?' he asked, looking sideways at me.

I still found it quite difficult to look him directly in the eye when we were up close. I actively untensed my shoulders and forced myself to.

'Good. Busy writing up the article. I work in a pub sometimes and did a couple of shifts there.'

The bar manager had seen photos of me and Marcus in the papers and had been teasing me mercilessly about it ever since. My rule about not outright lying was getting harder and harder to stick to as time went on.

Marcus looked surprised. 'I had no idea you had another job.'

I shrugged. 'I'm not quite at the point of my career when I can survive on writing gigs alone. It's so up and down – one month I'll have a couple of commissions and the next I'll be lucky to pick up anything at all. And then there's the age-old problem of companies being slow to pay and having to chase them up the whole time. We don't all have a "Dean" to do that kind of thing for us.'

'Oh, believe me, I know how lucky I am,' said Marcus. 'If it was down to me I'd do everything for free. Even the whole sponsorship deals thing really doesn't sit well with me – if I didn't have to do it, I wouldn't.'

'How come you're doing all of this, then?' I said, indicating him and me. 'Because I thought the whole thing was about the sponsorship. The money. Getting it all back.'

He sighed. 'Yeah. It is, but not for the reasons you probably think.'

'Which would be what?' I asked.

'You probably assumed I was thinking about myself and my own bank balance. And sure, I'm not completely selfless, and a tennis career is short – I want to be able to support myself until I find something else to do afterwards. But really, it's for my team. They rely on me for their income, especially Patrick and Nick, but Dean too, in a smaller way, and my nutritionist and my psychologist.'

'You have a psychologist?' I asked, amazed.

'I do.'

'What do you talk about with your psychologist?'

'Almost exclusively tennis,' said Marcus.

I rolled my eyes, teasing him.

'And my temper,' he admitted.

'And your racquet smashing?' I asked.

'Sometimes,' he said.

'And your parents?'

He shuddered. 'Not yet.'

'So you have a whole team of people helping your body and your mind,' I said.

'I do. And I'd feel bad if I had to start letting people go. Or cancelling sessions or whatever. I feel I have a responsibility to them to change, to do well, to start bringing in sponsorship money again so that they can carry on doing what they love, too.'

'Can I quote you on that?' I said.

I made it sound like a cheeky request, but I actually meant it. This was exactly the kind of thing that would endear him to people – that readers would never have guessed about ruthless, ambitious Marcus Taylor.

'Sometimes I forget that you're actually a journalist being paid to follow me around. That anything I say to you may or may not be splashed over the pages of the UK's biggest-selling glossy magazine, as somebody once billed it to me,' said Marcus.

'Ah, well, that is my special power. Lull my interviewees into a false sense of security,' I said, smiling at him.

'Are all our conversations just about that?' asked Marcus.

'Course not,' I said, meaning it.

Our phones pinged simultaneously.

'What's the betting that's Dean checking up on us?' said Marcus, looking at his watch. 'It's like three a.m. in LA – does that guy *ever* sleep?'

'You look,' I said. 'Tell me what he says.'

Marcus scanned the message and did a sort of angry half-laugh.

'Well, that's not happening,' he said.

'What isn't?'

'He wants us to go to a gala dinner together – one of the tournament sponsors is holding an event at Claridge's tomorrow night. He's booked us a room.'

'*One* room?' I asked, aghast.

'Yep,' he said, putting his phone away. 'We can tell him no, obviously.'

Our phones pinged again. I looked at mine this time, reading out Dean's message.

'He says: Guys, I know you're about to say no way, but bear this in mind – Lacoste are close to being back in. But they like Marcus in a couple. Think it will appeal to their slightly older clientele, guys in their thirties and forties who aren't hanging out in bars picking up girls, they're at home with their wives and girlfriends and kids. Having the two of you photographed at an event like this could totally seal the deal.'

Great. *Really?*

'He's very persuasive, isn't he?' I said eventually.

'I think that's what you might call an understatement. Thoughts?' asked Marcus, staring out at the court, which I was glad of, because the thought of spending a night in a hotel room – at Claridge's – with him was making my cheeks burn. Scrap that, *everything* was burning!

'I'm thinking we should go. How bad could it be? And now you've explained to me why the sponsorship deals are so important to you, I really want to help you get them back.'

'But what's in it for you?'

'Don't worry, I'll think of something. It will probably involve a really intense question that you're going to feel obliged to answer because I've been so very accommodating with this whole thing.'

He laughed softly. 'After this, I deserve the most difficult set of questions you can possibly come up with.'

He stood up. Patrick was setting up cans at the back of the court that presumably Marcus was going to have to knock over.

'I guess I'll see you tomorrow night, then,' he said. 'Unless you were planning on hanging around until I'm done. We could grab dinner, if you want?'

Aaaargh. Dinner? Why did it suddenly feel as though there was nothing I'd rather do?! And no, I one hundred per cent wasn't ready to acknowledge that – for me, at least – my feelings for Marcus *might* have turned into something more. That slowly but surely I'd actually started to like him. To care about him a little bit, even. And of course he was beautiful to look at, but I'd always known that, even when I'd thought he was an arrogant arsehole, so that was nothing new. I didn't know what any of this meant, or what – if anything – I was supposed to do about it.

Feeling as though I needed to get away from his undeniably intense gaze, I began hurriedly packing up my stuff, grabbing my water bottle, my phone, my jumper.

'I think I'm just going to head home, actually. Want to make some good progress on the article today – Amanda's been on my case and I'm feeling the pressure.'

'No worries,' he said, smiling. 'Some other time, then.'

'Sure.'

No! Not some other time. In fact, never would be best.

'Marcus!' called Patrick, waving him over.

'Better get back to it,' he said, jogging off.

I sighed. He even looked beautiful from behind.

So much for pushing forward with the article. When I got home, managing to not put on the TV even though I desperately wanted to watch something light and easy and maybe even romantic (no, maybe not romantic) to distract me from thinking about the prospect of sharing a bed with Marcus, and started up my laptop, I realised I didn't have my notebook. After tipping out the entire contents of my bag – what *was* all that crap at the bottom of it? – I deduced I must have left it somewhere. Hopefully, it wasn't the Tube, because I'd never get it back then, would I?

I fired off a text to Marcus.

Did I leave my notebook on the side of the court?

He must have been on a break from training, because he began to reply almost immediately.

Yes. Want me to drop it somewhere?

It was kind of him to offer but I couldn't expect him to come all the way over here and, given my current frame of mind, I doubted my writing would be at its best today anyway. And a thumbnail for the new season of *Emily in Paris* had popped up on my home page last night and the idea of ploughing through the entire season in one sitting was proving impossible to resist.

I messaged Marcus back and told him I'd grab it from him the following day. When my phone pinged, I assumed it was him again, but it was actually my mum, asking how I was, saying they hadn't seen me for ages. It was true, I'd been avoiding them a little bit because I didn't want to have to lie to their faces about Marcus, so it had been easier to keep contact to a minimum for now. Then I'd tell them we'd broken up after Wimbledon and job done.

Haven't seen you for ages! Up to anything exciting this week?

It's Queen's so mostly tennis. Off to a gala dinner tomorrow night.

Sounds lovely. Somewhere nice?

Claridge's.

Very swanky. Beyoncé stays there when she's in London, apparently.

Ha, I'll keep an eye out for her. Will come up and see you all soon x

Chapter Eighteen

In the taxi on the way to Claridge's I purposely spent the journey re-reading articles on Marcus and the many women he'd dated. There was a tennis player he'd been photographed with several times last year, Zuzanna Kaczmerek. She was athletic-looking, tall, and world number ten – she was gorgeous, they were both passionate about tennis, so why hadn't it gone anywhere? A few weeks after the last photo I could find of them together, he was photographed on a yacht in Monte Carlo with some billionaire's daughter – she had dark hair, olive skin and was wearing a bikini that may as well not have been there. Yes, being confronted by evidence of his womanising ways was exactly what I needed ahead of having to share a room with Marcus that night – my only hope was that Dean had booked us a twin room. Surely he wasn't that cruel? Anyway, it should be fine now I'd reminded myself that stepping over the line with Marcus – or worse, developing any kind of feelings for him – was an exceptionally bad idea. Guys like him were obviously to be avoided. And if a very pleasant but relatively ordinary-looking secondary school teacher (i.e. Charlie) couldn't be trusted, what man could? No, as far as I was concerned, relationships were off-limits for the foreseeable. That wasn't to say I couldn't have some fun – it just could not, under any circumstances, be with Marcus Taylor.

◆ ◆ ◆

Marcus was already waiting for me in the lobby when I arrived at the hotel. I had to pause for a second when I saw him, and tell myself off – there was no need to feel intimidated just because I'd never seen him in a suit before and now here he was in a dark navy one with a burgundy tie, looking like James Dean in *Rebel Without a Cause*. It was just Marcus. It was just us, fake-dating away, just like we had been for the last nine weeks or so. Nothing had changed. Other than the odd kiss for the cameras, we'd always kept it very professional and we would continue to do so tonight, I would make sure of it. As a door-man lifted my small suitcase up the stairs, I felt a pang of something like guilt – since when did spending the night with an international tennis professional interviewee in a hotel in Mayfair become a thing? My life had always been small and quiet, the way I'd convinced myself I wanted it. As a kid, I'd never been able to stand out because most (all) of the attention had been on Cassie and I'd given up trying to make my parents notice me. I supposed some children would have gone the other way and become loud and boisterous and demanding, but I retreated into myself, losing myself in the world of books and school and the creative writing I'd loved. This – Claridge's, the epitome of London's five-star luxury hotel scene – felt like the kind of thing the other version of me would have done. I took a deep breath, taking in my surroundings. It was just as spectacular as I'd imagined, all thick cream carpets and uniformed staff and chandeliers, and the sort of subdued hubbub you got in places like this because everyone felt as though they had to talk in hushed tones.

Marcus was sitting in an armchair next to the restaurant, his Lacoste overnight bag by his feet, a disgruntled expression on his face as he flicked through his phone. My heart leapt a little bit, but I put it down to having to now face the inevitable – checking in to our room. 'Our' room. What a strange situation I'd found myself in.

'Hi,' I said, approaching him.

When he looked up at me, there was none of the usual smiling or teasing, it was like we'd reverted to the first time we met.

'Hello, Ava,' he said.

'Everything okay?' I asked, a bit needily.

'Why wouldn't it be?' he said, standing up and picking up his bag. 'Shall we check in?'

I followed him down an exquisite corridor with secret rooms housing goodness knows what leading off from both sides. If I had the opportunity, I wanted to take some time to wander around the hotel on my own, peeking into rooms that maybe I shouldn't be in, getting a sense of what really went on behind these walls.

Marcus took charge, checking us in, paying for the room (did I *really* hear the receptionist say it was costing £1,200 for *one* night?!), grabbing the key card. I was starting to feel slightly nauseous, not just because of Marcus's weird behaviour, but because this felt a little bit sordid, if I was honest. And I thought it might make me feel better to pay my way for the room.

'We're on the third floor,' said Marcus tersely, striding towards the lifts.

I fell into step beside him. 'I'd like to give you some money towards the room,' I told him. I would have offered half, but I did *not* have a spare £600 hanging around. 'So if you can ping me your bank details, that would be great.'

'There's no need, it's already covered,' he said.

'I know it's already covered because I saw you handing your card over, but it doesn't feel right. I'd like to pay my way.'

'Are you going to write it off as an expense or something?' asked Marcus. 'How would you explain a hotel room in Mayfair – research for your article?'

We stepped inside the lift, even though part of me wanted to turn around and march in the other direction, far away from him. So much for me daydreaming about romantic nights in hotels rooms on the way over here (yes, okay, I admit it, I'd allowed myself to fantasise about it just once before seeing sense and shutting the whole thing down) – he could hardly bear to look at me.

'If I've done something to upset you, I'd prefer it if you told me rather than doing this passive-aggressive silent treatment thing. Because I don't know about you but I'm not going to be able to fake *anything* tonight if we continue in this vein.'

As we stepped out of the lift on the third floor, Marcus turned to face me, his face devoid of any emotion, although perhaps I should have been thankful he wasn't angry, since that seemed to be his default in most situations.

'You're right. May as well get this over with. I read your notebook,' he said, crossing his arms defensively.

I frowned. Why was that such a bad thing? I mean, I was surprised he'd been able to decipher my handwriting at all.

'Right. And I'm guessing you read something you didn't like? Because it's just a rough draft at this stage, Marcus – if you don't like the direction I'm going in with the piece, then you can just say and we'll have a discussion about it.'

'Is that really what you think of me?' he asked, looking confused and, if I didn't know better, I'd say a little hurt.

'Um, yes? I don't understand what's so wrong? Is there a specific bit you don't like?'

'How about the entire opener?' he said, shaking his head in frustration. 'Ignorant? An absolute tool? *Toddler* tantrums?'

'Oh my God . . .' I said quietly, the words I'd written all those weeks ago coming flooding back to me in a horrifying wave. *Shit.* Why the hell had I left that stupid page in my book? And for him, of all people, to find?

'Why, Ava? I know we didn't get off to the best of starts, but I honestly thought you had a higher opinion of me than that. Perhaps you've been faking that, too?' he said.

'I haven't been faking anything except the thing that we both agreed to fake,' I insisted, mortified. I didn't blame him for being upset – what a horrible thing to read about yourself.

'I can't work out why you'd even agree to any of that when you clearly despise me,' he said.

'I don't, of course I don't. That was just me venting,' I said. 'That first day of training in Monte Carlo. You'd told me off for my timekeeping and other than our conversation on the plane, if you can call it that, I only had what I'd seen on TV to go by. Toddler tantrums probably was a bit harsh . . .'

'You think?' he said.

'I don't feel that way about you now, obviously. I get how hard it is for you out there. Most people would lose it in that situation. I *definitely* would.'

'I just . . . it was disappointing to read, that was all. I don't open up to just anyone like that, you know.'

'I know. And I'm sorry,' I said, lowering my voice, not allowing myself to dwell on why Marcus thinking I didn't like him was such a big deal and had affected him this much. 'I never meant for anyone to read it, I should really have ripped the page out and shredded it into a hundred pieces. Let me show you my actual opener. The one I wrote when I got back from Paris. It's very different.'

'Do I get to read the whole article, then? Before it goes to press?'

'If you want,' I said.

This wasn't usual practice, because if interviewees started wanting to take things out and put things in it could all become very difficult, and your entire piece could be skewed. But somehow I trusted him not to do that. And I hoped more than anything that he would love the finished piece, that he would feel seen and understood, and that I would be able to show *Luxe* magazine's readers the Marcus Taylor I had started to get to know, and not just the racquet-smashing side of him, which was just one tiny little bit of his personality. Everything else was surprisingly great. I winced. Damn. I wasn't supposed to be thinking good things about him tonight.

'Shall we go to our room, or just stand out here talking in the corridor all evening?' said Marcus.

'I'm totally fine out here, if you are,' I replied.

Ah, there it was. The smile was back.

'You look lovely, by the way,' he said, his eyes skimming my body.

I looked down at my dress self-consciously – it was nothing special, a cream satin midi dress with a side split and button detail from (you've guessed it) Zara.

'You too,' I said.

'Shall we?' he said, flicking his head in the direction of our room.

I nodded. We were here now, weren't we, with the room all paid up. It seemed a shame not to use it.

The room wasn't as big as I'd anticipated. It seemed £1,200 per night didn't get you much more space than a double room in a Travelodge, but it did get you a beautiful colour scheme, high thread-count sheets and a marble bathroom to die for.

'Hmmm,' I said, putting down my suitcase and looking around nervously.

It was all bed, bed, bed and not much else, which quite frankly was the very last thing I wanted to see right now with Marcus shimmering next to me in his suit.

'You seem worried,' said Marcus.

'Maybe there's a sofa hiding somewhere?' I mumbled.

'Don't think so,' said Marcus. 'I can sleep on the floor if you like?'

I hesitated. For some reason I didn't want that and I wasn't about to dig deep as to why.

'It's fine,' I said. 'I think the bed is probably big enough for both of us, don't you?'

'As long as you're sure,' he said, throwing his bag on to a chair.

Was he not at all concerned about this? Then again, I wasn't his type, was I, judging by the absolutely stunning women he'd been photographed with before. Sharing a bed with me probably wouldn't faze him in the slightest – he probably wouldn't be tempted to do anything at all except sleep.

'Maybe if I scoot right over to this side. And you kind of push over there,' I suggested.

'You don't want me actually falling *out* of the bed, I presume?' he said.

Not able to think of a suitable response, I wheeled my suitcase into the corner.

'Just nipping to the bathroom. And then shall we head down to the dinner?' I said, not trusting myself to stay in that room with him a moment longer than I had to.

'Let's do that,' he said, sitting on the bed and watching me with a grin.

I went into the bathroom and shut the door behind me, leaning my back against it and closing my eyes. It would be fine. *Fine.* I was sharing a room with one of the most attractive men I'd ever met who also just happened to be my pretend boyfriend and there was nothing strange about that, nothing at all. It wasn't like I was going to throw myself at him overnight, was it? Unless I drank too much free alcohol, which I immediately made a mental note not to do.

I touched up my make-up and tidied my hair, which I'd left flowing around my shoulders but had then decided to put up in a ponytail. I seemed to be perpetually flushed this afternoon and it was making my hair frizzy, particularly at the nape of my neck, where it had already turned into a tangled mess. I combed it out, clipping it up and out of the way, spraying about half a bottle of hairspray over the whole thing to smooth it out and then barely being able to breathe because of the lack of ventilation in the bathroom. I threw open the door, half falling out of it while gasping for air.

Marcus looked at me, bemused. 'Everything okay in there?'

'Hairspray,' I wheezed, taking a lungful of less toxic air.

And then we both laughed and it felt okay again. Sort of. If I didn't put too much emphasis on that extremely luxurious-looking bed that later that night we would have to share.

◆ ◆ ◆

The gala dinner at Claridge's was everything I'd imagined it to be – it was taking place in the hotel's stunning ballroom, which had a geometric black-and-white carpet, an art deco design throughout and beautiful chandeliers that made you so happy you wanted to swing from them. We'd only had starters so far, but I thought the smoked haddock soufflé they'd served us might have been the most delicious thing I'd ever tasted in my life.

Marcus and I were seated together, of course, and although he knew everyone at our table – a mixture of players, one tournament director, and a couple of commentators everyone except me seemed to recognise – the only person I knew was Patrick, on the other side of me. Everyone was lovely, but I was also quietly enjoying listening in on their conversations and joining in when I could without any real pressure to do anything; surprisingly, with Marcus by my side, I felt completely at ease.

'How's your article coming along, Ava?' asked Patrick.

'Good, actually,' I said, glancing at Marcus, somehow wanting his approval. 'I feel like I'm finally getting to know what makes him tick out on the court – now I just need to find a way to articulate everything I've learned about him to my readers.'

Marcus slid his arm casually along the back of my chair so that I was sort of nestled under it. It felt comforting and warm, like a place I might never want to leave, which was dangerous, because pretty soon he'd never be putting his arm around me again. I'd better start getting used to the idea.

'Are you excited for the grass court season, Marcus?' asked Patrick.

'I'm not sure I'd use the word "excited". "Pressured" feels like a better choice.'

'Marcus, this is not a now or never. One step at a time. You are thirty-one, not thirty-seven. There will be other chances,' said Patrick.

Marcus didn't look convinced.

'How are you feeling about round one?' I asked him. 'Who have you got?'

'Pedro García,' said Marcus.

I looked at him blankly. Although my tennis knowledge was much improved of late, Marcus regularly drew players I'd never even heard of, and Pedro was one of them.

'Spanish, twenty-nine, hit the top ten a couple of years ago but hovers around the low twenties now. But he does love grass. And he's been working hard on his fitness,' said Marcus.

'And so have you,' said Patrick. 'You did well in training today, Marcus. I have a very good feeling about this tournament.'

'Don't jinx it,' Marcus quipped.

'Marcus has always been driven,' said Patrick, 'but he has been working harder than ever before this season. We have got him changing a few things up, right, Marcus? Shots that weren't working before but that his old coach did not think it was necessary to adjust.'

'Is that why you split with him?' I asked Marcus. 'Did it feel like you weren't making the progress you needed to?'

He'd been working with an American guy before, who was now a co-coach for Mia Stephens.

'Partly,' said Marcus. 'Is this going in your article?'

'I think it's worth mentioning why you're working with Patrick and why now, at this point in your career?'

And then the waiter came to bring more wine, and I listened as Marcus and Patrick discussed rumours that were flying around involving somebody having an injury they hadn't fully recovered from and somebody else falling out with his coach.

It took me a second to work out what was going on when the waiter returned to our table and very casually let me know that there was someone in the hotel who wanted to see me.

'Me?' I said, thinking he must be mistaken.

'Got a secret admirer?' teased Marcus.

'They are seated at the bar, madam,' said the waiter. 'They asked me to let you know that it is your mother and your sister.'

My heart sank, or at least it certainly felt like it had. Surely they couldn't be here? They'd be at home in Reading. There must be some kind of mix-up.

'What, they're here, at the hotel?' said Marcus.

I cleared my throat, achingly embarrassed. What were they doing?? I should never have told them where I was going, but then I'd never expected them to do something like this, so why would I have kept it from them?

'Seems like it,' I said, cringing.

Patrick looked surprised. 'They are also here for the gala dinner?'

'No, they are *not*,' I said, snatching my napkin off my lap and throwing it on to the table.

Marcus stood up to let me out. He touched my arm lightly. 'Want me to come with you?'

I shook my head. That was the very last thing I wanted. 'Back in a sec,' I said.

Trying not to panic, I hotfooted it to the bar (a delight under normal circumstances, I was sure), where, to my horror – each sitting on a bar chair, dressed up to the nines – were Mum and Cassie. When they saw me standing there, probably with my mouth hanging open in disbelief, they smiled and waved, as though there was nothing at all strange about them rocking up at a restaurant in Mayfair – an area of London I was pretty sure neither of them had *ever* frequented – and to the very hotel I'd told Mum I was coming to!

Taking a calming breath, I tried to reduce my annoyance as I approached them, or at least internalise it – Cassie didn't deal well with thinking she'd upset people and took it very personally. But seriously, what were they *thinking*? They were clearly only here to nose at Marcus, and if I'd wanted them to meet him, I would have taken him to Reading, wouldn't I? Imagine if I'd done the same thing to Cassie.

When I reached them, Mum got in early with a ridiculous explanation.

'Now, don't be upset, Ava. We happened to be in the area and I looked up Claridge's and thought it would be nice to have one drink on the way back to the station so we could say hello.'

'Happened to be in the area? You live in Reading!' I hissed.

'Impromptu shopping trip,' said Cassie unconvincingly.

'If you were in London, why didn't you mention it before so that we could have met up?' I quite reasonably questioned. It made no sense whatsoever that they would come here for the day and not let me know.

'Last-minute decision,' said Mum. 'And I knew you were busy over at the tennis place.'

'I haven't even been to Queen's today, I've been working from home. You could have given me the option to come and see you, at least!'

'Oh yes, I suppose we could. Sorry,' she said, looking a little bit sheepish.

'Anyway, never mind logistics, where's Marcus Taylor?' said Cassie, looking over my shoulder.

'We're at a gala dinner,' I said. 'He can't just leave the table, and neither should I. His team are here and everything. I really don't think it's appropriate for you two—'

'If Marcus is so busy, why's he walking over here right now?' asked Cassie.

'What?' I said, turning around, just as Marcus slipped his hands around my waist, pulling me backwards into him. It did feel delicious. But also – in front of my mum? Brazen, or what? And it didn't go unnoticed, of course. I saw Mum and Cassie raise their eyebrows at each other as though they hadn't been expecting it – I wasn't sure which part of all of it was so shocking to them, but I could hazard a guess; I wouldn't have believed Marcus was that into me either.

'Aren't you going to introduce us, Ava?' said Marcus, his breath warm on my neck, the amusement in his voice noticeable only to me, I imagined. Was he actually *enjoying* this?

I gritted my teeth. I was partly enjoying Marcus's arms around me and partly wanting to kill him for bowling over here to interfere in the first place. As if I wanted him anywhere near the family drama that was bound to unfold, especially as Cassie was chugging wine – I hoped she'd checked the prices first. My plan had been to insist Mum and Cassie leave immediately, but I could hardly do that in front of him – as annoying as they were, I wouldn't want to embarrass them in front of anyone else, particularly Cassie, who took anything she deemed as rejection exceptionally hard.

'Mum, Cassie, this is Marcus,' I stuttered, incapable of saying anything more at this point.

'Call me Pauline,' said Mum, holding out her hand for Marcus to shake, which he did, of course, and then politely shook Cassie's too.

As he moved to stand next to me, I slipped my arm around his waist. For authenticity only, obviously. Okay, also maybe because feeling connected to him physically somehow gave me the boost of confidence I desperately needed right about now. Marcus could go out and play tennis in front of TV cameras and thousands of people – when you put it like that, I was pretty sure I could have a conversation with two family members in a bar.

'I'm so glad we bumped into you,' said Marcus, playing along with the idea that they'd just accidentally rocked up at the exact same place. 'Ava has told me so much about you all. And you've probably been curious about the man who's been dragging your daughter around Europe for the last few months.'

'Well, yes, we did wonder,' said Mum, who seemed to have turned into a simpering wreck on the spot.

'Can I get you both a drink?' asked Marcus.

'Um . . .' said Mum, looking startled, as though nobody had ever offered to buy her a drink before. Then again, my dad had never been one to put his hand in his pocket without careful consideration – he probably *hadn't* ever bought Mum an extortionately priced glass of wine at a swish Mayfair bar either, because there's absolutely no way he'd be in there in the first place.

Marcus, clearly realising that this was a decision too far – presumably it was Mum and Cassie staring mutely at the menu that gave it away – stepped in.

'How about a glass of champagne each?' he suggested.

'Only if you're sure . . .' said Mum.

'Of course,' said Marcus breezily. 'I'll get you one, too, shall I, Ava?'

'Yes please,' I said, trying my best to lighten up. Maybe this didn't have to be as bad as I'd imagined. And they'd have to head back to Paddington soon, wouldn't they? There were a couple of trains after midnight, but they wouldn't want to risk missing the last one.

Marcus squeezed my shoulder before taking his place at the bar. That helped. And at least champagne measures were quick to quaff.

Marcus was served immediately, meaning there was little time for me to glower at Mum and Cassie while they both gave me irritating fake-innocent looks, as if I was the one who was out of order here, which of course was usually how things felt for me in this family.

'Here we go,' said Marcus, handing a flute each to Mum and Cassie and then going back for ours.

'So, tell me about your shopping trip,' he said, looking at the bags strewn around their feet – Zara, H&M, Waterstones. Nothing special, but this definitely counted as a spree in my book.

Mum and Cassie proceeded to talk him through their purchases item by item, and while any other person might have found this as boring as hell, particularly a tennis star who probably only had his next match on his mind, Marcus looked focused and engaged, making positive-sounding noises in all the right places. I was having to work hard to match his energy so as not to seem like a sulky teenager in comparison, which unfortunately tended to be my default when I was around Mum and Cassie. I definitely didn't want Marcus to see this far less attractive side of my personality – not yet, anyway. And he was actually very good with them. It had taken Charlie years to win them around, especially Mum, but here they were fawning all over him in less than five minutes.

'We hadn't realised things were getting so serious with the two of you,' said Mum, somehow jumping from shopping to the one thing I really, *really* did not want to talk about. 'One minute there's a picture of you and Ava holding hands in some exotic place and next minute you're in London, looking *very* cosy together.'

That wasn't really a compliment, was it? It was a word you might use if you caught your boyfriend having a flirty conversation with a stranger at the bar, for example. A sort of *Well, well, well, you two look VERY cosy.*

'We're not making a big deal of it, Mum,' I said. 'Marcus is away a lot, so we haven't spent that much time together.'

When Marcus found my hand and held it tight, I wasn't sure which threw me most, the way having my palm pressed against his sent pleasure signals directly to my brain, or the look Cassie had given me when she saw him do it. I couldn't quite name it. And if I couldn't work out how she was feeling, how was I supposed to adjust my behaviour accordingly, because walking on eggshells around her and trying to please her had become an irritating habit. If I had to guess, she seemed kind of *pleased* about Marcus and I being together, but this in itself seemed odd. She wasn't usually happy when something went well for me.

'What have you been up to, Cass?' I asked gently. 'How's work?'

'Shit,' she replied with a shrug.

'Cassie . . .' said Mum ineffectually.

'Where do you work, Cassie?' asked Marcus.

I wished he hadn't, because Cassie's lack of career success was a constant source of disappointment for her, but I supposed he wasn't to know and if I'd realised they were about to gatecrash my evening, I'd have bloody well briefed him, wouldn't I?

'Ava hasn't told you what a loser I am in the job department, then?' said Cassie, trying to laugh it off.

'Absolutely not. Ava only has lovely things to say about you,' said Marcus, sounding kind and sincere.

I glanced at him out of the corner of my eye, silently thanking him.

'Cassie's actually met someone, too,' said Mum, immediately throwing her hand across her mouth as though she shouldn't have spoken those words out loud. 'Ooops, I don't think I was supposed to say.'

'You weren't,' said Cassie, tutting.

'Who's this then?' I asked, not getting too excited. It would probably be over within a fortnight anyway, because Cassie actively chose men who had red flags poking out of every single orifice. There'd been Richard, her married boss from work; Jake, who'd shagged around behind her back and then had a go at her for being upset about it; and Wes, a hoarder who lived with his parents and who, at thirty-three years of age, had never had a job and seemed to have little intention of getting one.

'No one,' said Cassie.

'Well, it must be someone,' I said, teasing her.

'I don't really want to talk about it,' said Cassie enigmatically.

'Okay,' I said, respecting her boundaries, even if she and Mum had totally failed to respect mine.

'Talking of romance – Marcus, would you be free to come to a wedding with Ava later this month?' said Mum out of nowhere.

'Mum!' I said. 'He won't be, he'll be at a tournament.'

'Which date in June?' asked Marcus, raising one eyebrow at me as though he was finding this highly amusing.

'The last Monday in the month, I think,' said Mum.

'Who gets married on a Monday?' I asked.

'Your cousin Julie, as you well know.'

'Actually,' said Marcus, taking out his phone and flicking through his calendar, 'I think I *can* make it. Queen's finishes on the Sunday, even if I do make it to the final.'

'I like your confidence, Marcus,' said Cassie.

'Thanks, Cassie,' he said. 'If you can't big yourself up, who's going to do it for you?'

Everyone laughed except me. I wasn't in a laughing mood now because I did not want to go to a wedding with Marcus. That would involve him meeting my entire extended family – Mum's half of it, anyway – and then what was I supposed to say when we 'broke up' weeks later? It would be utterly humiliating after the whole Charlie debacle. Plus, weddings were dangerous – everyone drank too much and did stupid things. I thought briefly back to our kiss in Paris – had that been a stupid thing? And to our luscious bed waiting upstairs – was there a chance we'd be doing stupid things in it? I shook the thought from my head. Of course there wasn't. Marcus might be all touchy-feely in public, but he was hardly going to ravish me behind closed doors, was he? There would be nothing for him to gain.

'What about Wimbledon?' I asked. 'You'll be prepping for that.'

'Doesn't start until the following Monday. I'll have to train in the mornings, though. Maybe I could come after that?'

'You don't have to come to *anything*,' I said decisively.

'He just said he'd like to,' said Mum, rolling her eyes at me and then looking at Marcus conspiratorially. 'Honestly, what's she like?'

Marcus laughed.

'Ava's ex-boyfriend, Charlie – she told you about Charlie, I take it – was supposed to be coming, but then they split up, and Julie had already given numbers to the caterer, so we've got a spare plus one,' said Mum.

'Way to make a guy feel wanted,' I said, glaring at her. Was she planning to stop talking at any point?

'Oh, I'm very used to being second best,' he said earnestly.

'Brilliant. It's all sorted, then,' said Mum.

I turned to Marcus and made one last-ditch attempt at putting an end to Mum's ridiculous suggestion. 'You know, the wedding is a way off. We might not even be . . .'

'Of course we will be,' he said, dropping my hand and draping his arm around my shoulders instead. He pulled me in for a tender kiss on the forehead, which I had to say made me feel better about it all, temporarily at least.

'Right, we'd better head off to get our train,' said Mum, shifting in her seat.

'Good idea,' I said.

◆ ◆ ◆

Once they'd gone, with promises of meeting up again soon (although not if I could help it), we were back at our table eating our semi-cold mains. Marcus had his arm around me, his fingertips making little circles on my bare shoulder.

'You do know that wasn't that bad,' he whispered in my ear.

'Maybe not for you,' I said, trying to stay calm when all I could focus on was the feel of him on my skin.

'They're nice,' he insisted.

'You charmed them, that's why,' I said.

'Am I charming you, Ava?' he said, his breath on my neck sending shivers along my spine.

And then, before I could answer (how would I have, anyway?), and as if he thought he'd said too much, he pulled his arm away again and asked Patrick a question about tennis and the moment was gone.

Chapter Nineteen

After dinner, a swathe of discreet staff pushed the tables to one side, creating a more informal space for guests to mingle and dance. The champagne was still flowing and a band had set up, with a woman of about my age belting out everyone's favourite hits from the last couple of decades in the most angelic voice. Everyone was dancing, even Marcus, even me – it wasn't something I'd ever done as a child because Cassie didn't like it and so none of us were allowed to get up on the dance floor at weddings and parties. Obviously, when I wasn't with my family I didn't hold back, but there was still something inside of me that couldn't fully let go the way some people did. The way Marcus danced surprised me – I would have imagined him to be like me, a little self-conscious, holding back, but he was really going for it, his body moving easily to the beat, his arms in the air. It was the most joyful I'd ever seen him and it was catching – even Patrick was swaying his hips to the music, a contrast to the controlled and emotionally reserved man I saw out on court.

When the tempo dropped and the band played the opening bars of Rihanna's 'Stay', I went to move to the side of the dance floor, but Marcus caught my arm.

'Shall we?' he asked, his gaze warm and relaxed.

'I don't know . . .' I said.

'Come on,' he said persuasively, holding out his hand. 'Indulge me. Tomorrow I'll be back to training and everything will be all serious again. Tonight I just want to have a good time.'

My eyes flitted around the room. Lots of people were dancing, it wouldn't mean anything.

'Dean would probably be upset with us if we didn't,' I said, letting him pull me with him into the centre of the wooden dance floor so that we were surrounded by lots of other couples, effectively making it feel as though we were cocooned and hidden from sight, even though there were cameras everywhere.

'I love this song,' said Marcus, twirling me around to face him and sliding his arms around my waist.

'Yeah?' I said, tentatively hooking my hands behind his neck, using the feel of him to give me stability.

We swayed in time to the music, our hips perfectly in sync. 'You're actually a really good dancer,' I said.

Marcus laughed. 'You seem surprised.'

'It's just that I've never slow-danced with somebody with actual rhythm before.'

'Oh, I've definitely got that,' he said, pulling me closer and swinging me around so that we were facing the opposite way.

Over his shoulder I could see what looked like a TV crew, their camera seemingly pointing right at us.

'What's going on?' Marcus whispered in my ear.

'Someone's videoing us . . .' I said, burying my head in his shoulder.

Marcus swung me back around the other way.

'There. Now you can't see them,' he said, as the music reached its rousing crescendo.

Instinctively, I wrapped my arms more tightly around him. It was risky – I could feel his body responding to my touch. In that moment, I didn't care about all the other girls he'd been photographed with, or whether he'd had this same connection with all of them. I deserved to have some fun, didn't I? I was dancing in the most exquisite room with a gorgeous man, and I was not going to ruin it by thinking about all the things that could go wrong. Nothing about it felt wrong, so maybe it wasn't? When he slid his hand up my back, I imagined how it would feel if my dress wasn't there, if he was touching my skin without anything in between. I shivered at the thought and acknowledged the truth to myself, there and then – I one hundred per cent did not have to fake liking him anymore.

'I should probably call it a night soon,' said Marcus. 'If that's okay with you?'

'Course,' I said, a whole host of emotions suddenly rushing through my head.

I couldn't be alone with him. I wanted to be alone with him. He liked me. He didn't. I liked him. I couldn't.

As the track ended, he took my hand and led me off the dance floor.

We'd said our goodbyes downstairs and had taken the stairs up to the room because the lifts were so busy – it seemed that quite a few of the gala guests had had the same idea and were staying here at the hotel. I'd just seen Anton Bauer and his girlfriend heading up to their room, and they'd waved at us as the lift doors closed on them.

We didn't speak much on the way up to our floor. I let myself into our room with Marcus close behind me. It was quiet inside after the music and laughter downstairs, and just the right side of cool. I slipped off my heels and looked at the bed.

'Well, that was fun,' said Marcus, coming to stand next to me.

I nodded. 'It was.'

'Shall I get ready for bed first, or did you want to?' he asked, pulling off his shoes, loosening his tie. He seemed calm. Easy. Everything I wasn't.

'You go for it,' I said, perching awkwardly on the end of the bed while he disappeared into the bathroom, closing the door behind him.

I used the time – all of about five minutes – to try to get my head together, failing dismally, of course. When he reappeared wearing joggers and a T-shirt, I almost lost my nerve completely and called myself an Uber. How could he look that hot in a simple loungewear ensemble?

'Your turn,' he said, smiling at me, still seemingly unbothered by how things were about to pan out.

'Cool,' I said, even though it was anything but.

I scurried into the bathroom with my wash bag, overthinking whether or not I should shower. Whether the cotton shorts and camisole combo I'd brought with me to wear overnight was too cutesy, or too see-through. Should I take my make-up off or leave it on? In the end, I just got changed, slicked back my hair, washed my face and used one of the lovely body lotions the hotel had laid out for us to sample. Then I cleaned my teeth and went back into the bedroom.

Marcus was already in bed. His top half was naked now and I could only hope that his bottom half was not, otherwise I was going to be in serious trouble here. The lighting was warm and cosy and I was sure the housekeepers had sprayed something in the room before we came up to bed because it smelled divine, like amber and oranges. The kind of sexy scent I loved.

'Coming in?' said Marcus, putting his phone down on the bedside table and watching me with an expression I couldn't quite place.

'I presume you have got *some* clothes on?' I said.

'Worried you won't be able to control yourself if I haven't?' he teased.

'Very funny,' I said, slipping into bed next to him.

Luckily, it was a super-king. I wouldn't need to touch him at all, if I just stayed right here, flat on my back, looking up at the ornate carvings on the ceiling.

'Alone at last,' he said.

'So many cameras tonight,' I said.

'Do we only kiss when they're around?' he asked.

Jesus.

'Well, what on earth would be the point otherwise?' I said.

'I can think of a point.'

I closed my eyes. If I couldn't see him, maybe it would all be okay. I'd just drift off to sleep, forgetting that delectable Marcus Taylor, tennis star, elite athlete, all-round hot guy, was lying half naked next to me.

'Ava?'

'Yes?'

'Do you think we should talk?'

'About what?' I asked, stalling for time.

'The fact that we're in bed together. That you're going to be sleeping right next to me for an entire night in *those* shorts . . .'

He liked my shorts.

I tentatively turned on my side. He was already on his, facing me, his mouth inches away. I could feel the heat of him under the covers.

'I really don't think this is a good idea,' I said, as he reached out and took my face between his hands, looking at me – really looking at me.

'You're right. It's a terrible idea,' he said, kissing me gently and then pulling back almost instantly.

'We should stop,' I said, groaning as his hand found its way underneath my camisole and he stroked my back so softly, so carefully that I almost caved in and pulled him on top of me.

'Remind me why?' he said, his breath warm on my mouth.

'It's already too complicated.'

'What's wrong with complicated?' he asked, his hand now skimming down the back of my thigh and sending waves of pleasure pulsating through my body.

'It's too soon. After Charlie,' I said, not quite meaning that, but not sure how to express exactly what I was feeling either. Which was that I didn't want to get hurt, not again, and that I was ninety-nine per cent certain that Marcus would end up hurting me.

'You're scared,' he whispered.

'I know,' I said.

'Me, too,' he lied.

Or at least I assumed he did. What would he have to be scared of?

'Let's just sleep,' I suggested.

He removed his hand from my leg and I ached for him to put it right back on again, but I had to stay strong.

'Ava, I have the feeling that this is going to be a very long night,' he said with a sigh.

And then we smiled at each other and I turned to face the bathroom and he turned out the lights and I heard his breath become slower and slower. Every time I swallowed I was sure he could hear it, and I wasn't tired in the slightest – how could I be, when my body was full of adrenaline? Because now, of course, I knew what it felt like when he *really* kissed me.

Chapter Twenty

Zoe and I took our seats in the front row of centre court for Marcus's first match at Queen's. Apparently, the space was usually just a patch of beautifully maintained grass at the front of the clubhouse, but once a year it became an arena seating nine thousand eager, mainly British tennis fans, keen to see their favourite players battle it out on home turf. According to my research, this tournament was an ATP 500, so not quite as prestigious as Miami, Monte Carlo, Madrid or Rome in terms of points. Perhaps because of its location, though, and because it served as a warm-up for Wimbledon (and often a good indicator of who was going to win), it attracted most of the big names.

'Oh my God, the atmosphere's so much better than it looks on TV!' enthused Zoe, chugging Pimm's and lemonade through a straw. 'It was so nice of Marcus to get me a ticket.'

A camera flashed in our direction.

'You might be in the papers tomorrow,' I warned her.

'Hope so,' she said. 'I didn't raid the fashion cupboard at work yesterday for nothing.'

There was never much time between getting to our seats and the match beginning. I quickly introduced Zoe to Patrick and Nick. Dean was in LA, although he'd be flying in for Wimbledon. I settled back in my seat, taking in the crowd and the way the beautifully smooth grass court popped against the red advertising boards lining all four sides. A well-spoken English woman came over the loudspeaker and announced first the Spanish player, Pedro García, and then Marcus, giving the crowd a few facts about each of them.

'*This is Marcus Taylor's thirteenth Queen's Championship. He reached the semi-finals in 2019, 2022 and 2023. Could this be the year he finally takes the trophy?*'

The English crowd were much quieter than the Europeans and very politely clapped and low-level cheered both players as they walked out on court, the requisite television cameras pointing in their faces, some sort of classical music blaring out, a stark contrast to the hip-hop in Monte Carlo and the rock tracks in Paris. Each tournament seemed to have its own vibe, and this was elegant and sedate. Everyone clapped and cheered, including Zoe, who was particularly loud. Marcus briefly caught my eye as he put his bag down and began unpacking it.

'Did he just look at you?' whispered Zoe, nudging me.

I shrugged non-committally. 'Not sure.'

I mean, he might not have done, but it felt like he had.

'What are they doing now?' asked Zoe as the two men took to the court.

'Warming up.'

'Ah,' said Zoe. 'How do they decide who goes at which end?'

'They'll toss a coin in a minute. Whoever wins gets to choose whether to serve first, the other gets to choose which end to start on.'

'And is it better to serve first or not?' asked Zoe, seemingly about as confused as I'd been only a couple of months ago.

I thought back to all the knowledge I'd gleaned from watching Marcus play, and my newfound tolerance, if not quite enthusiasm, for the game. 'I think it depends,' I said, keeping my voice low, so as not to draw too much attention to myself. Also, I didn't want to get something wrong and for Patrick to overhear. 'If you have a strong serve and you're confident about using it on this surface, it probably makes sense to go first, to try to get that first game done and dusted. If your opponent has a good serve on grass, it's probably best to go first, too, to stop them taking the lead early on.'

Zoe gave me a sideways glance.

'Is this the same woman who declared she knew nothing about tennis and couldn't possibly take the job?'

'Well, you pick things up, don't you?' I said.

Secretly, I was pleased with how I'd immersed myself in the tennis world. I thought this was shaping up to be some of the best work I'd ever done. Perhaps it was the decent amount of time I'd spent getting to know Marcus. I was trying not to give too much weight to the idea that I'd spent far too much time with him. Sometimes alone in hotel rooms. Once in bed with him, both of us half naked, longing for him to touch me but then inching closer to the edge of the bed so that neither of us would be tempted. I'd never have thought I was capable of pretending to date someone, of lying to my parents, of going out to dinner with my hot interviewees or of seeing photos of myself in the press and not minding. Like karma, this job – and Marcus – had come along at exactly the right time, pulling me out of the devastation of losing Charlie. I thought the way he put himself first, in a boundaried, ambitious way rather than a selfish one, might be beginning to rub off on me – I usually felt uneasy for days when I thought I'd upset Cassie, sometimes I even felt physically sick, experiencing symptoms that didn't go away until I'd seen her again and been reassured that she'd forgiven me. The fact that she'd turned up at Claridge's and I hadn't exactly been pleased to see them might usually have sent me into a tailspin afterwards. I'd have been going over and over things in my head, wondering if I'd been too harsh, if I'd made her feel unwanted, if I should have handled things differently. And of course some of those thoughts had crossed my mind, but I had also been able to talk myself down this time – Cassie hadn't *seemed* upset. She'd been a bit offish when I asked about the new guy she was seeing, but that was probably because she didn't want to say in front of Marcus. And also, I was allowed to have feelings too, to be annoyed when they did things I didn't like, like turning up unannounced and pretending they just 'happened to be passing'.

As Marcus and Pedro practised their lobs and smashes, I turned to Patrick.

'Do you think Marcus has a chance of winning here at Queen's?' I asked him, keeping my voice low.

Patrick nodded, not taking his eyes off Marcus, watching every move he made.

'Yes, but he must take his game to the next level. And not just his game, but the technique we have been working on, his attitude, his stamina. It must be perfectly aligned and if that happens today, like a beautiful synergy, he can do it.'

'He looks good out there,' I said, as he hit a brilliant serve.

Patrick turned to look at me.

'You know, he is much calmer these days,' he said. 'More able to contain his emotions out on court. And I think we might have you to thank for that, Ava.'

'Me?' I said, surprised.

Patrick shrugged. 'You are good for him. I was worried when I heard there was something romantic between the two of you, because he does not need distractions, of course. But in fact he seems much happier and more positive than he was before. There should be fun and joy in tennis, too, and finally he seems to be finding it. Whatever you are doing to him, do not stop now.'

I blushed at the thought of exactly what Patrick imagined I might be doing to him.

And I was confused, too, because how could anything I'd done have made a difference? The only thing I could think of was that I'd forced Marcus to talk about things he'd previously kept buried inside, and having them out there in the world – even just saying them to me – might have shifted something for him. But Patrick said he seemed happy. I didn't think being interviewed for a magazine would usually have that effect on someone. And I supposed, when I thought about it, I'd been feeling much better lately too. It was difficult to gauge, because I'd kind of been at rock bottom after Charlie left, so any state of mind was an improvement on that. But if I was really honest with myself, travelling to all these glamorous places and getting front-row seats at tennis tournaments and being taken out for nice dinners was only part of why the last couple of months had been so great. There was something about Marcus that made me feel seen in a way I'd never been before. I liked his quiet energy, his focus, the flashes of humour, the way he listened to me, really listened, and was interested. And even though I was going to try my absolute best not to, because it would end in tears, I knew it would, I had a sneaking suspicion that I was falling for Marcus and the more time I spent with him, the further I fell. We hadn't spoken much about us the morning after our stay at the hotel. We'd gone to breakfast together, he'd talked about the week he had planned, I'd filled him in on my suspicions about Mum and Cassie orchestrating a meeting with him, we talked a bit about tennis, and what the grass court season meant to him. And then we'd left the hotel and got 'papped' by photographers and so it felt that, all in all, the night had been a success. And yet there was now this lingering longing, this memory that came back to me again and again, of his hands on my body, of the two of us lying between those luxurious white sheets, and when I thought about it, it was like my skin was on fire.

The warm-up ended and Pedro García prepared to serve, having won the toss. He was tanned like Marcus, but was smaller and leaner with a pointier, clean-shaven face. Fierce concentration burned behind his eyes as he bounced the ball in front of him over and over again, waiting for the perfect moment to toss it into the air. Silence settled on the crowd, the only sound coming from a plane flying overhead, preparing to land at not-too-far-away Heathrow. Marcus was crouched outside the baseline, ready to receive, perhaps trying to anticipate where Pedro's serve might land. I still didn't know what his top-secret game plan involved, but I wouldn't put it past Marcus to have studied every single opponent he'd ever had to play, gathering information from footage of their games – were they left- or right-handed, which shot did they favour, where were their weak points?

García sliced the ball over the net. It bounced slightly lower than it did on clay, I could see that now, and Marcus returned it with an easy forehand. García lunged to reach it but the ball went into the net. *Love-Fifteen.* Zoe whooped loudly and I wasn't sure whether to tell her to be quiet or not, whether it might annoy Marcus.

'Um, he doesn't really like a lot of—'

'Whoo-hoooooo!' yelled Zoe.

She was still whooping one hour and nine minutes later when Marcus was at match point. He was up one set, and five games to two in the second. It was Marcus's serve.

He sent it fast and deep. García was clearly struggling, but he just managed to reach it. Meanwhile, Marcus raced into the net, using his backhand to send the ball sailing past García's right shoulder, landing it just inside the baseline, exactly where he'd been practising hitting the cans with Patrick. *Game, Set and Match Marcus Taylor.*

'Yes!' shouted Patrick, on his feet. 'Yes, Marcus!'

It had been a triumph and Marcus knew it. He'd dominated the match from beginning to end. He looked over at our box and when he saw us all on our feet – I had no memory of even standing up, but there I was, clapping and whooping – he ran over. First he high-fived Nick, then Patrick, who wasn't content with a high five and pulled him in for a hug.

'I am proud of you, Marcus,' I heard him say. 'This is an excellent start.'

Then Marcus saw me, sandwiched between Patrick and Zoe. He cupped my face in his hands and pulled me in for a kiss and I don't know why, but it didn't feel like it was for show, and either way I didn't care. I clasped his head between my hands, too, and kissed him back. When he pulled away I mouthed *well done* and he mouthed *thank you*. I was pretty sure Marcus didn't usually react this emotionally to a win, particularly not in such an early round – after all, he was seeded higher, he would surely have expected to come out on top. I thought the jubilation all round was to do with the quality of his shots, of his serve, the way he'd sprinted around the court, barely breaking a sweat. I supposed the length of the match had been nothing compared to the four-hour extravaganzas he'd had at Grand Slams in the past. And the crowd were whistling and clapping, too, in a way I hadn't seen them do before. Which I never understood, because racquet smasher or not, British players weren't exactly two a penny in the top twenty, so in my opinion they should be supporting the ones they did have. Marcus ran over to pack up his water bottles and his racquets, hauling the two bags I now knew he took out on court every time on to his shoulders, one on each, and waving at the crowds as he walked off the court. It felt like a moment. It felt like something had changed. And for some reason, I could feel Zoe's eyes burning into the side of my head.

'What?' I said.

'Nothing,' she said, but I knew she'd tell me over another Pimm's. Zoe wasn't one to keep her thoughts to herself.

◆ ◆ ◆

Zoe didn't have the right level of accreditation to get into the players' lounge, so we went to the marquee set up in the grounds and grabbed a drink there, although with the last match of the day having just finished, it was heaving. We couldn't get a seat, and so were propped up at a standing table. I wished I'd worn flats instead of heels, because not only were they pinching my toes, but the kitten heel had sunk into the grass without a trace.

'All I'm saying is, I know what I saw,' said Zoe. 'You're into him and don't bother denying it.'

I tried to laugh it off. 'It's not that, Zo. It's just that faking it is becoming easier as we go along. It *looks* more natural.'

At this rate I'd be convincing *myself* that that's all there was to it, even if I could still feel the pressure of Marcus's wet lips (I was hoping it was water rather than sweat – actually, scrap that, I didn't care either way) on mine.

'So nothing happened that night at Claridge's then?' she said accusingly.

Was I really going to lie to my best friend?

'Okay, we kissed. But that was it – it was nothing we hadn't already done.'

That wasn't strictly true. There were places he'd put his hands that night that he'd never put them before.

'Knew it. You're in denial,' declared Zoe.

'I'm not,' I insisted.

'I'm your best friend and I know when you like someone,' she said.

'I think I know what's on my own mind,' I said, irritated by the way she was making assumptions about my feelings, even if deep down I knew she was right.

It was true. I did like him. But then, who wouldn't? And sure, I'd got to know him now and he was more engaging than he'd seemed on first impressions, which only added to his appeal. And he was extremely manly, and nice to his team, and did very impressive things with a racquet and a ball. But there was plenty of stuff not to like, too. Even if, apart from the anger outbursts, I couldn't think of any right now.

◆ ◆ ◆

Zoe, weary from demolishing an entire jug of Pimm's by herself, headed home and I stayed in the marquee, doing some research on my phone in the twenty minutes or so I had until I'd arranged to meet Marcus in the players' lounge.

I'd got to the part of the article where I was talking about Marcus's childhood, his parents, particularly his mum, and I was still confused about why she'd been so present in his life and so supportive of his tennis and then nothing. It was like she'd disappeared from not only his team, but his life, and over what? A house she wanted to buy? A tournament he refused to play?

I began to search, cross-checking with photos and video footage of the matches Marcus had played nine years ago, the year before he won the Australian Open. The stories on Marcus's mum, who was called Denise (Taylor was her name; she and Marcus's father, Terry, had never been married), were ramping up at that time, particularly in the biggest-selling tabloid at the time. There were pictures of her staggering out of bars, having to be helped into taxis, wearing dark glasses at Marcus's matches, the insinuation being she was hiding something, like a hangover, presumably. This explained why Marcus hated the press so much – why wouldn't he, when they'd given his mum such a hard time? One of the nastiest headlines was MONEY MAD MUM, which was referring to a story about Denise being shown around a high-end property in Richmond, in which the journalist accused her of spending her son's money on big houses in one of London's wealthiest districts. I was about to click off the page when I noticed a hyperlink to a different article – it was in a small blue font and I could almost have missed it if it hadn't sparked a memory. Marcus had said something about his mum being popular with the owner of the tennis club she worked at. The title was TENNIS MUM SEDUCED CLUB BOSS TO GET SON FREE LESSONS. I hadn't seen anything like this before and clicked into it immediately, shocked to see a small article in the Sunday version of the tabloid that had been infamous for its sordid gossip around that time. It detailed how – allegedly – Marcus's mum had used her 'feminine wiles' to seduce the ageing owner of an exclusive tennis club in a posh part of Manchester to give Marcus free tennis lessons in exchange for sex. There were pictures accompanying the article, none of them flattering, showing Denise supposedly flirting with a much older guy, wearing 'revealing' clothing (a vest and shorts, basically) and drinking on the job. I cross-checked the date – it was the end of August, the year before Marcus won the Australian Open. Could this have had something to do with Marcus's mum dropping out of the team? Could it be that she knew the story was about to break and wanted to protect Marcus?

I googled tennis events from around that time and discovered that there had been a much talked-about tournament in Dubai – there were several stories in the press because it had a huge seven-figure prize attached, unusual at the time, it seemed. Most of the top players had taken part, but Marcus was notably absent. Had this been the tournament his mum had wanted him to play? Had their falling-out been triggered by her shame – that she had asked her son to buy them a house and tried to pressure him into playing a tournament to pay for it, coupled with the story she knew was about to come out about the tennis club owner? And if this was the case, did Marcus know about the allegation?

I was so caught up in my research that I then had to rush to meet Marcus, spotting him and the team immediately as I walked into the lounge. And I'd had no time to work out what – if anything – I was going to tell him.

'Hey,' he said.

'Well played,' I replied, kissing him lightly on the cheek in case anyone was watching.

He nodded. 'Shall we go?'

We snuck out of the back entrance of the complex, but even so, a group of die-hard fans and a slew of press were there waiting, cameras held aloft. For once, Marcus stopped to sign autographs and even agreed to have a selfie with one fan.

Once we were in the car, I turned to him.

'Did Dean put you up to that?' I asked. 'I thought stopping to talk to fans and taking photos wasn't your thing?'

'It wasn't. Isn't. I just felt like it today,' he said.

'Because you played well?'

'Partly,' he said.

'And the other part?'

'I don't know, Ava. I guess I just feel like being a bit nicer to people these days.'

'I like this version of you,' I said.

'The old version is still in there somewhere. It was still me. I'm still teetering on the edge of going back there. One bad loss and I could come crashing down again.'

'Then I should make the most of you being this amenable while I can,' I said.

He reached out, tucking a loose strand of hair behind my ear. The feel of his fingers was intoxicating, but we weren't doing this. We'd decided. And yet when he removed his hand, all I could think about was that I wanted him to put it right back on me.

'So I found something out today. Worked something out, maybe. And I'm not sure when would be a good time to tell you,' I said.

He raised his eyebrows. 'A good thing or a bad thing?'

'Bad, but with the potential for good,' I said. 'And I know you're in the middle of a tournament and that you need to focus and so I probably shouldn't have said anything. But on the other hand, I can't help thinking that it might, in a roundabout way, help you?'

He shifted in his seat to face me. 'Hit me.'

'What, now?'

'Why not? I'm a captive audience. And how bad can it be?'

'It's about your mum,' I said, wincing.

'Ah,' he said, looking uncomfortable. '*That* bad.'

I gave him time to stop me, to say he didn't want to think about that now, that having his mother on his mind might throw him off his game at a time when he needed to be at his absolute best.

'Tell me,' he said.

'Okay. Stop me if at any point it feels too much and you change your mind.'

'Noted,' he said.

Perhaps it would be easier to show him. I'd bookmarked the article on my phone and loaded it on to my screen.

'Now, before I show you this, I want to put it in context. Was the tournament your mum wanted you to play in Dubai? And was it so that you could use the prize money for a deposit on the house in Richmond?'

He looked confused. 'Yes, Ava, it was.'

'And was it just after you refused to play in that tournament that your mum distanced herself from you?'

'Correct,' he said, dubious, perhaps, about what relevance any of this had now.

'Okay, so hear me out,' I said. 'I found this article.'

Bracing myself – because I could be making a huge mistake here – I handed him my phone, watching his expression change as he read the horrible piece that had painted his mum in such a terrible light.

'And this was published when?' he said, his voice thin and strained.

'The same week the Dubai tournament went ahead without you,' I said.

He shook his head. 'I've never seen this. After Mum and I fell out, I stopped reading the papers, especially the tabloids. The last story about her I saw was the one of her being shown around that house. After that, I refused to look, and I told my team that I didn't want to be informed of any stories that showed up in trashy newspapers. Stories that weren't true, or had been exaggerated at the very least.'

'So this is the first time you've seen this?' I checked.

He nodded.

'What if your mum knew the story was about to break and didn't want you to see it? What if she felt she needed to distance herself from you because she thought that when it came out, it would reflect badly on you?'

Marcus rubbed his mouth. 'But why wouldn't she have said that? She could have talked to me about it. I would have told her I didn't care what the press had to say, that I knew the truth. Yes, she drank a bit much on occasion – she was a single mum, she worked hard, why shouldn't she have some fun? And it wasn't all the time, like the press made out.'

'Publications like this purposely sensationalise their stories without thinking about the consequences. They just don't care,' I said, feeling angry on Marcus's behalf.

'And it's not true what they said about the owner of the club. He saw potential in me and he was kind enough to help my mum out. He was married and twenty years her senior, for God's sake. He liked her, that was all, in a fatherly way. And maybe he felt a bit sorry for her, but not because he was sleeping with her,' he said, letting out an exasperated groan.

I stayed quiet, letting it all sink in for him. And I really hoped I hadn't gone too far. That I hadn't overstepped the mark and put his game in jeopardy. It would have felt wrong to know all of that and not let him know, but maybe it hadn't been my place to say. Or my problem to fix.

Chapter Twenty-One

I stared at my laptop, reading through the approximately twenty words I'd spent the last half an hour writing. I was working on my profile of Marcus, but felt stuck with it in a way that I hadn't before. The content I'd written since Queen's had begun wasn't flowing – it sounded too factual, too clunky, and I couldn't seem to inject the emotion into it that I knew I needed for my piece. That Marcus was playing better than ever didn't seem to be translating on to the page. I thought it might have something to do with the fact that suddenly I didn't know what was real and what wasn't. Was he who I *felt* he was when I was with him, or was he the guy who picked up girls on yachts in Monte Carlo?

I slammed my laptop shut. I'd wanted to get a couple of hours of work in before heading over to the club, but I knew from experience that there was no point trying to force it unless I had an imminent deadline, which I didn't. Instead, I ran myself a bath and ironed the dress I was wearing to that afternoon's match, a navy-and-white polka-dot number from my favourite French brand.

When I checked my phone before starting my make-up, I noticed that Marcus had sent me a text.

What time you arriving?

I replied with a smiley emoji. *Soon!*

After spectacularly winning three more matches – the round of 16, the quarter-finals and the semis – Marcus had made it to the final of Queen's. It was a huge deal – Dean was flying in especially, it was being televised live on the BBC and Marcus was receiving an unprecedented amount of coverage on TV and radio.

Come to training if you like?

I felt a pull to say yes, yes, yes and head over to the grounds immediately, but I reeled myself in. Keeping a professional distance was key here now, I thought, and the less time I spent in his company, the less all over the place I felt.

Not sure I can. I'll catch you in the players' lounge just beforehand.

See? I could still be cool and casual – from these texts, he'd never know that I'd been daydreaming about our night together in Claridge's on loop.

The players' lounge at Queen's was as plush as the pomp and ceremony surrounding the club would suggest. There were armchairs in muted pastel shades, TV screens showing the games on the main courts, food offerings, and faces I recognised. Dean called me over and I realised it was good to see him – having him around was a stark reminder of our fake-dating arrangement, which was exactly what I needed. There was nothing real about it, even if my body was telling me otherwise.

'Ava!' said Dean, standing up to hug me.

'Hi, everyone,' I said.

'You made it,' said Marcus, appearing from out of nowhere behind me and standing so close that I could feel his breath on the back of my neck. I wanted to melt backwards into him, to have his strong arms wrapped around me, to be pressed up against him again like we had been in that lift in Monaco.

'Can I talk to you for a second?' he asked.

'Sure. Here?' I said.

'Balcony?' he suggested, putting his palm on the small of my back and guiding me out there.

Part of the infamous clubhouse, it overlooked the prestigious centre court that Marcus would be playing on in around an hour's time. The crowds were just beginning to trickle in, dressed up for the occasion in frothy summer dresses and wide-brimmed hats, the men in linen blazers and boat shoes. Apparently, there was often a handful of celebrities present for the final, which under usual circumstances would have been something fun to gossip about later, but today all I cared about was Marcus. After the way he'd played this week, he deserved to win, but would he be able to hold his nerve?

'Feels like I haven't spoken to you properly in ages,' said Marcus.

'You've been busy,' I said.

He looked devastatingly handsome today, with a new, shorter haircut and the expensive-looking white hoodie that made his skin even more luminous than normal and his bright brown eyes pop. I wanted to clasp his face between my hands and tell him that everything would be all right, that he would be fine out there today, that I would support him no matter what, but I held back, like I had been ever since the night of the gala dinner.

'Well done for making it this far,' I said. 'Am I actually allowed to say congratulations now?'

'Not yet,' he said with a wry smile.

I nodded, accepting his rule for what it was. I understood it better now – if he celebrated too soon, it might have a knock-on effect on the drive he needed to win. He was going to have to play the absolute best tennis of his life today, and if he wanted the gentlemen's singles title, he was going to have to fight for it.

'I've missed seeing you, Ava,' he said.

'You've seen me. I've been at every match.'

'I know you have,' he said. 'But it feels like we haven't had a moment alone. Not since . . .'

I swallowed. He couldn't seem to say the words either. Not since the night we'd spent in bed together, when I hadn't been able to sleep, when it had taken every ounce of resolve not to wake him up and say *let's just do this. Let's just sleep together and see what happens.* He put one hand on my waist, tracing circles on my hip with his thumb.

'Tell me what you're thinking,' he said.

'You need to focus on your game,' I replied, glancing out at the stands filling up.

'You're right,' he said, looking over his shoulder. 'But being with you makes me feel calm. And the less tense I am, the better I'll play.'

'Does that mean you trust me enough to tell me your game plan?' I teased, trying my luck.

'Is this you with your journalist hat on?' he asked.

I shook my head, knowing without a doubt that this was not about my article. 'No.'

'You really want to know?'

'I really want to know.'

It probably wouldn't mean much to me anyway, but I wanted to push him, to see if he trusted me enough, and in turn, whether maybe I could learn to trust him. He was playing the world number three, a French guy called Alexandre Duardin, who had also done his fair share of racquet smashing in his time.

Marcus lowered his voice until it was barely a whisper. I had to move closer to hear him, so close that my body was touching his at several points: at our temples, our shoulders, our hips; my fingers had inadvertently laced through his. A tingling sensation ran down my spine, and I didn't think it was the anticipation of hearing what he planned to do out on court.

'Alex will serve big,' said Marcus. 'He rarely misses. And his reach is incredible – no matter where I put the ball, he's capable of getting there.'

'So how will you beat him?' I asked, keeping my own voice low.

'He never has a Plan B. So if for some reason his game isn't working, he can't change it up mid-match. So I have to make him feel like his game isn't working.'

'How?'

'I return his serves, no excuses. And if his focus drifts, even for a second, I take advantage. Get him running, keep him on the baseline, press him until he starts making mistakes.'

Extricating his fingers from mine, Marcus stood up straight, ruffling his hair, although there wasn't so much of it to ruffle anymore.

'I should probably go and get ready.'

'I believe in you,' I told him quietly. 'Go out there and win this.'

It seemed like the British public might finally be getting behind Marcus, too, as he made his entrance on court. Every single seat in the arena was filled and almost everyone stood as he emerged from the tunnel, looking very different from the man I'd seen enter the court for his first match in Monte Carlo. He'd lost the scowl and replaced it with quiet concentration – his face was softer as he waved at the stands, his lips widened out to form a half-smile, which I thought was the most he – anybody – could manage given the pressure of the enormous task ahead. My heart began hammering in my chest – I felt nervous for him. I knew how much a win would mean to him. Wimbledon, the world's most prestigious tournament, was just over a week away and triumphing today would take him one step closer to the ultimate prize. Had everything come together for him at exactly the right time?

Dean was seated next to me, with Patrick and Nick on the other side of him, and there was a tension in the box I hadn't felt before. As Marcus took his position to serve, I saw him adjust the grip on the handle of his racquet. He looked at Alexandre Duardin for a beat or two, then dipped his eyeline down to the grass, bouncing the ball five times. He'd told me it helped him find a rhythm for his serve, but it didn't always have to be five bounces, sometimes it was three, or four, or seven.

He delivered a strong serve to the corner of the box. Duardin flicked it back but only just and Marcus ended the point with a flat forehand that went spinning past Duardin, landing just in front of the baseline. *Fifteen-Love.* I realised I'd rarely seen Marcus hit a ball long – it must be one of the strengths his opponents took into account when they were creating game plans of their own.

He won the first game easily. Alexandre Duardin won the second – I could see what Marcus meant about his strong serve. Marcus had to work harder for the third game, but he won it on an advantage point. As the crowd roared, Marcus looked over at our box. It seemed to be Patrick he was searching for, but Dean was the first to his feet.

'Come on, Marcus! Let's go!'

I found myself pumping my fist without even realising it. *Come on*, I mumbled under my breath. I knew it was better to make an early break, particularly if his plan was for Duardin to lose focus and begin to doubt himself. Marcus had to try to break his serve, and the sooner the better.

The crowd were respectfully silent as Marcus took his position behind the baseline, crouching down, swinging his hips ever so slightly from side to side, gripping his racquet with both hands, entirely focused on what Duardin was about to do with that ball.

Duardin served straight at Marcus, almost hitting his feet. Marcus literally jumped out of the way and managed to hit the ball back over the net. There was a long rally this time, the first of the match, and I knew this was Marcus's sweet spot. Sure enough, after whacking the ball back and forth, back and forth, to the right, to the left, Duardin hit it into the net. *Love-Fifteen.* Our entire box roared, as did much of the crowd. He was winning them over, I could see it. If he could just keep his head. Keep playing well.

Duardin served again, missing his first. Marcus had told me this rarely happened. He was losing focus, just as Marcus wanted him to. He served again, Marcus hit it back cross court, Duardin lunged, making the return, but Marcus was already at the net, ready to volley it to the ground with an impossible-to-reach smash. *Love-Thirty.*

He was doing it. He could win this.

'Come on, Marcus!' I shouted, suddenly not paying attention to the part of me that worried about upsetting him. He said I calmed him down, so maybe hearing my voice might help in some small way. In any case, it had been completely involuntary and it was done now, and I wasn't the only one because Nick was yelling too. I felt part of the team, as invested in Marcus as they were, and I'd never wanted him to win so badly.

He won the game and the first set, 7-5. Everything was looking to be in Marcus's favour. Duardin had already smashed one racquet and had shouted at his team more than once. Marcus looked tired, but not exhausted – I knew he had it in him to push through, to take him in straight sets. But then, in the rest break, I noticed Marcus staring over his shoulder. It wasn't at us, at anyone in our box – he seemed to be fixated on somebody in the audience further down our row.

'What's going on?' I asked Dean.

Dean stood up, straining his neck to see. 'Oh fuck.' He turned to Patrick. 'His mother's here.'

His mother?

I leaned forward in my seat, trying to catch a glimpse of her myself. I spotted Denise immediately. Her hair was not as blonde as it had been in pictures I'd seen from a few years back, and was flecked with specks of grey. Her eyes were dark and intense, like Marcus's, and she was wearing a white blouse tucked into jeans. She was in her fifties, slim and angular.

I looked back at Marcus, who had his head in his hands, perhaps trying to block out the image of what – or who – he'd just seen. She hadn't been to one of his matches for years and it felt like too much of a coincidence that I'd shown Marcus that story and now she was here – had I inadvertently set something in motion that would damage Marcus's chances of winning?

'Time,' called the umpire.

Marcus got up and walked out on court. Everything about his demeanour was different; it was like the energy he'd had in the first set had been sucked out of him. He took his position to serve. The crowd hadn't noticed the change in him, of course, and were roaring away – it was only our box that was strangely quiet now, in anticipation of how all of this was going to affect him. Could he block his mother out? Could he imagine her not here, could he focus on what he needed to do and put his feelings for her to one side?

He double-faulted right off the bat, the first one I'd ever seen him do. *Love-Fifteen.*

His next serve went in, but Duardin hammered it back so hard that Marcus only just reached it in time, slamming it into the net. He let out a primal roar.

'Shit,' said Dean.

Shaking his head, Marcus served again. The first one was long, the second barely skimmed the net, but it was in. Duardin got it past him again. *Love-Forty.*

Come on, come on, come on, I begged silently. Don't let this throw you off.

He produced a decent serve, forcing Duardin slightly off balance. But when he tried for the shot he'd been practising, to the far-left corner where Patrick had relentlessly put his can, the ball landed just outside the baseline. Something else I'd never seen him do. *Game Duardin.*

The French members of the crowd went wild. And when Marcus flung his racquet into his chair, they went even wilder, booing, hissing and stamping their feet.

'Do you think he can come back from this?' I asked Dean, who looked as subdued as I felt.

He shrugged. 'I fucking hope so.'

After being annihilated in the second set (6-2 to Duardin), something seemed to change. Marcus had spent the changeover with a towel over his head. He did not turn around to look at his mum, and he didn't look over this way either. I wondered what was going through his mind, what he was saying to himself. I knew he would want to fight and that the match wasn't over yet – there was one more set and everything to play for.

From the moment he stepped back out on the court, he played like he had for the first forty minutes. Duardin's serve was solid, but as Marcus matched him game for game, you could see doubt beginning to creep in, which Marcus used to his advantage. He kept the ball long, the two of them slogging it out on the baseline, just how Marcus liked it, his phenomenal accuracy returning. Two out of three times, Marcus won the point because Duardin hit it long. Marcus didn't hit it long once.

At six games all, the match went to a tie break. I remembered Patrick saying that even the top players sometimes crumbled under the pressure of a tie break. I didn't think Marcus would crumble under usual circumstances, but today, with his mother watching, I wasn't sure.

Duardin served and won the point. *One-zero Duardin.* Marcus took the next two. *Two-one Taylor.*

The entire court was on tenterhooks. Dean was half sitting down, half on his feet, flying up and down as Marcus took three of the next four points.

Duardin served again, losing the point by fudging Marcus's return of serve. *Two-six Taylor.*

I was on my feet, we all were. Match point.

'Come on, Marcus!' I shouted, my voice drowned out by the thousands of other voices screaming the same thing.

'Quiet, please,' said the umpire.

Silence descended as Marcus took his place behind the baseline, crouching to receive.

The ball slammed over the net. Marcus returned it cross court. Duardin was there, whacking it down the tramline, forcing Marcus on to his backhand. But his backhand was his strength and he returned it easily, knocking it just inside the baseline. Duardin returned it and I assumed we were in for another long rally, the battle of the heavy hitters, until Marcus did something I'd never seen him do before. He sliced the ball, making it look like it was going to go long but morphing it into a perfectly executed drop shot that fell just over Duardin's side of the net. Duardin hesitated a split second too long before running in, using the full length of his body to reach for the shot. The ball bounced twice before he could get to it. Marcus had won not only the match, but the Queen's Club Championships. It seemed to take a moment for it to sink in before he put his head in his hands and bent double at the waist as the crowd went wild. I blinked back tears as I stood up and then I didn't bother to blink them back anymore, I just let them flow, yelling and whooping. Marcus stood up and glanced over at us, smiling like I'd never seen him smile. I raised my hands in the air, clapping above my head as Marcus looked directly at me. For a nanosecond, as we made eye contact, our faces beaming, the warmth we felt for each other shining through, I thought I might never have been as proud of anybody in my entire life.

◆ ◆ ◆

That night, Dean threw a party for Marcus at a rooftop restaurant in Kensington. He was so busy being congratulated by everyone that I didn't see him for much of the night and hung out with Dean and Nick instead, and occasionally Patrick when he wasn't schmoozing with the rest of the tennis crowd. It wasn't until gone eleven that I finally got to speak to Marcus alone.

'Want to get some fresh air?' he asked.

He had beads of sweat on his forehead and he was smiling, excited in a way I'd never seen him.

'Sure,' I said.

He took my hand and led me outside on to the terrace, a beautiful tree-lined space with views over rooftops and chimneys, the lit-up London Eye dominating the skyline. We leaned on the railings taking it all in, enjoying the cool breeze on our faces, the thumping music from inside the bar barely audible.

'How are you feeling?' I asked him.

He shook his head. 'I can't even put it into words. It's a strange mixture of not believing it's actually happened and knowing that it's exactly what was supposed to happen. Does that even make sense?'

'I think even if you feel like you deserve something, that it's meant to be, there's a nagging fear that it was a fluke, or a one-off, or that somebody's made a mistake and you haven't won this thing, or got this job, or whatever it is, after all.'

'Exactly,' he said, turning to face me. 'Exactly that.'

I bit my lip, not liking him so close to me and wanting him even closer all at the same time.

'Did you speak to your mum after the match?'

He nodded. 'Seeing her threw me off for a second there.'

'Did you know she was coming?' I asked, still feeling guilty for the part I must have somehow played in it.

'Not really. After you showed me that article you'd found, I called her to ask her if it was true. If she'd stopped coming to matches because she knew the story was about to break and didn't want to embarrass me.'

'And?'

'You were right,' he said softly. 'She wanted me to be able to focus on my career without worrying about which story about her was going to surface next. I told her I wouldn't have cared, that she was my mother and that I couldn't care less what people said about us. That she should have spoken to me about it instead of pretty much disappearing and making me feel like she'd . . .'

'Abandoned you?'

He shrugged.

I touched his arm. 'So she came to support you today.' I looked around. 'Is she here now?'

'I invited her, but she wanted to take it one step at a time. We've still got a lot more talking to do. But it's a start. And it's mainly thanks to you. I told her about you, and she said she'd seen pictures of us together and felt like she'd never seen me look so happy.'

I smiled.

'Ava, do you think we should talk? About what happened at Claridge's?'

'Nothing did happen.'

'But we both wanted it to. Didn't we?'

I didn't want to look directly at him, because when I did I couldn't be rational.

'It was best that it didn't.'

'Was it, though? Because I like you, Ava,' he said, taking my hands in his and pulling me off balance so that I had no choice but to fall into him.

It was like warm caramel was flooding through my body, sweet and comforting and delicious. I'd dreamed about him having feelings for me in the way I did for him and now here he was, actually telling me he had them.

'Get you, expressing an actual emotion about something other than tennis,' I said.

'Well, that would very much be down to you, Ava,' he said. 'You seem to have brought out a whole new side to me. And now it seems I can't stop thinking about you, which is strange because usually I'm very good at compartmentalising, and of course everything takes a back seat to the tennis. And yet, when it comes to you, I find myself giving you – us – an equal importance in my mind.'

Was I hearing this correctly? He'd been thinking about me? As much as he did about tennis? In pre-Wimbledon week?

'It's because we've spent so much time together,' I reasoned. 'It feels more intense than it might do otherwise. We've got carried away, that's all.'

The words felt empty as I said them, but I was no longer talking from my heart, I was trying to protect it. Maybe Mum had been right, because how could it ever work when he travelled so much and lived this glamorous lifestyle that was so different to mine? I'd be perennially anxious and full of self-doubt about whether or not I was enough for him and whether he'd still want me when he got back from whichever far-flung tournament he was competing in. And it wouldn't be fair of me to expect more from him than he could give, not with a career as pressured as his.

'I think we should see each other properly,' he said. 'After Wimbledon. Once our arrangement is done. Because whatever this is – and I really don't know, either, before you ask – it feels like something worth . . . exploring?'

My stomach flipped. If I said no, would I be missing out on something special because I was worried that one day it might go wrong? Wasn't that life for you, a sort of trial and error where some things worked out and others didn't, and this could be either one of those, so shouldn't I put myself out there and try?

'Do you think we should just be friends?' I suggested.

I'd have to stop feeling like I turned to hot liquid on the spot every time I set eyes on him, but it was better than nothing. At least I could still have him in my life in some capacity. It would be safer. Less margin for error. I could watch him play now and again. Perhaps the odd coffee if he was in London. I couldn't imagine going for dinner with him without doing the hot liquid thing, but perhaps it would be possible in time.

'The problem is, Ava, I don't want to be just friends with you,' he said, kissing me tentatively at first, as though he wanted to be one hundred per cent sure that this was what I wanted, and then more urgently, our hands tangled in each other's hair, my breath coming in short, ragged bursts of pleasure.

◆ ◆ ◆

It had taken minutes for Marcus to say a few goodbyes, particularly to his team who he hugged tightly, the genuine love between them all shining through. Then he ordered us a car on the way down in the lift and we waited outside in the dark. It was raining a little, and perhaps because of that Marcus pulled me to one side, pressing me up against a brick wall. I could feel its dampness seeping through my dress and I didn't care – all I cared about was being here with him, and the promise of what was to come once we were finally alone together again.

'It was very distracting having you in my players' box today,' he said, putting his mouth on mine before I could answer.

This time, there were no thoughts of cameras, or if I should or shouldn't. I just opened myself up to him, to the sensations coursing through my body, to his hot breath on my neck, the absolute deliciousness of sliding my hands under his shirt, gasping as I ran my hands over his taut body and the muscles I'd spent weeks pretending not to notice.

When the taxi dropped us off at mine, he closed the door of my flat behind him and before I could even slip off my shoes he was kissing me, his hands underneath the hem of my dress.

'We're finally doing this, then,' he said, his voice filling the narrow space.

My mind flashed back to a few months before, when I'd first heard him speak on TV. How had we gone from that to this?

I ran my hands through his hair because I'd always wanted to, and he seemed to like it because I felt him smile as he slipped his warm tongue inside my mouth. I tried to ignore the voice in my head, which had irritatingly appeared at the worst possible time. Would he find my naked body attractive? I wasn't like the women he usually dated, I wasn't taut and muscular, or skinny and flat-chested. Would he be disappointed?

'Do you have a bedroom?' he asked.

'I tend to prefer the sofa, but come,' I teased, taking his hand, leading him into the room with the bed I'd only ever slept on with Charlie.

I lay down, letting myself relax, watching as he slipped off his trousers.

'I really think you should take off that dress. You wouldn't want to get it creased,' he said.

I reached for the buttons that ran down the front of it – whenever I wore it, it crossed my mind that they might pop open at an inopportune moment, exposing me to everyone on the Tube, or whatever. Except that right at this second I *wanted* them to burst open. Every single one of them. I began fumbling with the buttons so that eventually Marcus had to help, impatiently popping them open from the bottom up. I slipped it off my shoulders. And then he crawled slowly on top of me, taking most of his body weight on his arms, his lips hovering tantalisingly over mine.

'I've wanted you since you sat next to me on the plane with that photo of me on your laptop screen,' he said, slowly unclipping my bra with one hand.

'And I've wanted you since I saw you smashing racquets on *Deuce*,' I replied.

'Have you, now?' he said, kissing my neck.

I half laughed, half gasped, letting the delicious sensations run over me as his tongue ran across my skin, feeling him dip lower and lower and . . . oh, God, lower.

Chapter Twenty-Two

The morning after had been as wonderful as the night before. Let's just say we *more* than made up for the missed opportunity at Claridge's and I desperately did not want him to leave my bed, even though Patrick was expecting him for training and I had Julie's wedding to get to.

'What's the plan for today, by the way?' he asked, flinging the sheets off him and heading for the shower. 'You need to give me the address for the reception.'

'You're not still planning to come to my cousin's wedding? Not now.'

'Not now what?' he asked, seemingly confused.

'You've just won Queen's,' I said, momentarily losing my train of thought at the sight of his muscular, naked body in my eyeline.

'I am aware of that, Ava, yes.'

'Haven't you got . . . stuff to do? A trophy to collect. Press to do, I don't know?'

He tilted his head, looking at me from an angle. 'Why are you trying to put me off coming with you to your family wedding? Are you embarrassed to be seen with me, or something?'

Obviously not. It was just . . . my mum, mainly. And Cassie. You never knew how they were going to react to anything and they could not be relied upon to behave like most other families would, especially – in Cassie's case – after a few drinks.

'Everyone will be asking us awkward questions,' I said, knowing as soon as the words left my mouth that it was a weak argument. He didn't care what people thought of him, but unfortunately the same could not be said for me.

'Could be fun, right?' he suggested.

'Been to any weddings lately?'

'Sadly not. I actually quite like them,' he said.

I laughed. 'You don't!'

'What's not to love? Good food, free drinks and a dance floor.'

I looked at him suspiciously. 'You must be the only man I know who doesn't do everything they can to get out of going to one. Are you actually saying you want to come? Won't you be tired from training?'

'My body needs to recover from yesterday, so Patrick will go easy on me, even if we do have Wimbledon prep at the forefront of our minds. I'll drive up as soon as I can get away.'

'Marcus, it's honestly fine if you can't make it. I won't mind at all.'

'It's just one evening, Ava.'

'Sure, but it's not like Oxford is convenient. You should be resting. Patrick and Dean will want to talk to you. If you get tied up and can't make it, I'll totally understand.'

'There is nothing I would rather do than come to a wedding with you today. Does that convince you?'

'I suppose so,' I said, pretending I hadn't minded either way, even though secretly I was over the moon that he was making the effort to come. Maybe sleeping with him hadn't been a mistake after all and I should have done it *much* sooner.

◆ ◆ ◆

Marcus left for training as soon as he'd showered, scattering me with kisses and promises to see me as soon as he could, and I set off for Oxford after breakfast. My train hit a section of engineering works and proceeded to crawl along the tracks at a snail's pace, although not even that could dampen my mood, even if it did mean I arrived late. I had to get dressed in the downstairs bathroom because I didn't have time to check into the hotel, and then leave my suitcase at reception before hotfooting it into the ceremony before the bride made her entrance. Mum gave me side-eye as I slipped on to the seat they'd saved for me next to Cassie.

'You nearly missed it,' she hissed.

'I'm here now, aren't I?' I said, as music began to play.

Julie glided ethereally into the room to Taylor Swift's 'Afterglow', and it made me very happy that she was marrying a man who didn't mind that she'd chosen a slightly naff pop song to walk up the aisle to. She looked beautiful on the arm of my Uncle Dennis, and what with the lyrics and Julie in tulle and the beautiful flowers wrapped around the pergola at the end of the aisle, I felt quite emotional. It was probably also partly to do with having spent the night with Marcus. Perhaps it was wedding fever, but I couldn't deny any longer that I was falling for him.

The wedding 'lunch' was served at four-thirty and I was seated on a table with eight other people I didn't know, which I was grateful for in many ways, not least because none of them would know I was supposed to have been coming with Charlie, although I did have to explain that my 'plus one' would be joining us later. I glanced over at a miserable-looking Cassie, who had been relegated to a table made up of mostly singles. She was already being chatted up by some drunk guy on her left and looked bored and pissed off, which was pretty much her default expression at any social event. I looked away again, dampening down the nagging feeling that I should do something. Anything. Rescue her, save her, make her happy.

'Is your boyfriend the famous one?' asked the woman sitting next to me, who was a friend of Julie's from work.

'I'm not sure about famous, but he's a professional tennis player,' I said, feeling a rush of pride, even if 'boyfriend' was pushing it.

She elbowed her partner, a cocky-looking City boy type, in the ribs. 'Told you! He's that guy who smashes his racquet around.'

'He won Queen's yesterday, actually,' I said, fed up with his racquet throwing being the first thing people mentioned about him. What about all the other amazing stuff? And what's the betting some of them would be smashing racquets in his position, too?

Irritated by her, I turned to the woman on the other side of me, who was also on her own and had apparently met Julie decades ago when they'd both been backpacking around Australia. As she told me how hilarious their trip had been and gave me all the intel on the questionable things my cousin had got up to aged nineteen, I surreptitiously checked my phone. Marcus had said he'd be here at about four, and it was already ten to five. I swallowed the rising panic that came out of nowhere – he said he'd come, so he'd come. He'd probably been held up. It might have been reassuring if he'd let me know, but perhaps he'd jumped in the car and hit the road, thinking it would be best to just get here.

◆ ◆ ◆

When Julie and her husband, Ben, took to the floor for their first dance just after 7 p.m., I watched from the sidelines with a lump in my throat – I didn't know why, but the first dance always got me more than anything else. It was the rousing love songs; the sight of two people being so wrapped up in each other that it was as if they were completely alone and not surrounded by two hundred moist-eyed guests aahing and awwwing at them. Added to that was the fact that Marcus still hadn't arrived, nor had he replied to the text I'd sent an hour ago. Unlike my mum and sister, I wasn't the type to catastrophise, but should I be? Was it possible he'd been involved in an accident or something? Because he'd been so insistent on coming when I'd basically given him an out, so why wouldn't he be here?

'Where's Marcus?' said Mum, bustling up to me with a look of disgruntlement on her face. 'I've told everyone he's coming, so he'd better show up. It'll be very embarrassing if he doesn't. Everyone's looking forward to meeting him. Ben's parents watched his match on television yesterday! They can't believe the two of you are actually dating.'

I imagined that would be the response from most people – what, *him*? And *her*?

'Did they?' I said, trying not to look worried. 'Well, I'm sure he'll be here soon. He's been held up, I expect. There's a lot to do after winning a tournament like that.'

'He has been in touch, though, I take it? He wouldn't – you know – just not come, would he?' said Mum, looking at me with raised eyebrows. 'Because he seemed very nice, but Ava, you don't always have the best taste in men.'

'Thanks, Mum, you say the nicest things.'

'I'm saying you could do better – that *is* nice.'

'Than Marcus?' I scoffed.

'No, not than Marcus. I'm talking about all the other ones.'

'You make it sound like there have been hundreds of them,' I said.

'I did try to warn you . . .' said Mum, crossing her arms.

'About which one, I'm confused?'

'Charlie. I said he was selfish. It took him months to ask me a single question about my job at the doctors' surgery, and he didn't give Cassie the time of day until very recently. You know how hurtful it is for her when people ignore her. I've never trusted him and I've been proven right, haven't I?'

'And your point is?' I asked, fast getting fed up with this conversation.

Mum sighed, as though I was the one being difficult. 'My point is, I hope your new boyfriend is nothing like your old one. Because if he lets us all down and doesn't show up this evening, it is going to be extremely humiliating for me.'

'For you?' I said, laughing. I couldn't help it. Of course she would be worried about herself first and foremost.

'You're being very spiky, Ava. I think I'll go and ask Dad to dance while you simmer down a bit.'

'You do that,' I said, as spikily as I could just to annoy her.

As she walked away, I was aware of two things: that I was acting like a fifteen-year-old again and had to stop doing that when Mum was annoying me, and secondly, that there was a very real chance that Marcus was not going to show.

A message from him finally came through just after nine. Mum had been glowering at me across the dance floor for at least half an hour and I – obviously – had not felt like dancing. What I really wanted to do was flee to my room and throw myself face down on the bed, but Mum and Dad would never forgive me if I made a scene. And as usual I felt compelled to brazen it out and pretend that it was completely fine that I'd been stood up AT A WEDDING and that it didn't matter a jot that my mum had been mouthing off to anyone who'd listen about my amazing new boyfriend who was so into me that he'd decided to let me down in front of half of my entire family – and the gossipy half, at that.

Ava, I'm so sorry, I'm not going to make it after all. It's been crazy here – I had to meet a couple of potential sponsors, do an interview with The Guardian and then Dean sprung a pre-Wimbledon promo on me. I haven't even had a second to call you! Are you okay? I hope this hasn't inconvenienced anyone. Wish the bride and groom well from me X

There was some serious burning going on behind my eyes and I felt as though I could just crumble to the ground right there, in front of everyone. Luckily, I made it to the nearest chair and slumped down on to it, re-reading the message, trying to work out the subtext. Because what was he really saying here? We'd literally just slept together – it hadn't even been twenty-four hours and already he was backing away, like I just knew he would. Why hadn't I listened to my instincts?? I'd known this was a bad idea from the start, but he'd lured me with his pretty face and his kindness (until now) and the words he'd used when he'd told me that life felt so much better when I was around. His life might be better with me in it, but mine was far, far worse now that I'd met him. All it had done was give me a glimpse of something really amazing and then whipped it right out from under me again. I was a very ordinary girl from Reading who should have known that fairy tales literally did not exist.

I put my phone away and annoyingly managed to catch Mum's eye a second later. She was shaking her head and tapping an imaginary watch. What she thought of all of this was the least of my worries. I got up and walked outside into the hotel garden, thinking some fresh air might help, and at least it felt as though I could breathe out here. There was only a smattering of people braving the cool air, the smokers mostly, and I perched on a bench and pulled my cardigan tightly around myself and acknowledged how awful I was feeling and that it was okay to feel like shit when somebody you'd just slept with and thought was lovely had treated you like you meant nothing to them. It was clear, now, that tennis was his one true love; it would always be that way and there was absolutely nothing I could do about it.

WIMBLEDON

Chapter Twenty-Three

It was the morning of Marcus's first-round match and instead of being excited to watch him play at the most famous tournament in the world, I was dreading seeing him. Not even my yoga class had helped, and I'd almost told him I wasn't coming to any of his games, but a deal was a deal and it was nearly over so the good girl in me wanted to see it through. Plus, of course, there was the article – I'd be submitting it in two weeks' time and I needed to be at Wimbledon to finish the story, because it would be the tournament *Luxe* readers would most want to hear about, even though Marcus Taylor was the last person on earth I wanted to see right now. He told me he'd had sponsorship meetings off the back of winning Queen's. That he'd been offered a lot of money to wear a particular set of clothes, to use this racquet, to wear this watch. It didn't matter whether it had been the positive coverage in the press about a newly romantic and calm Marcus Taylor or his phenomenal performance at Queen's that had done it – either way, we'd achieved what we'd set out to achieve when Dean first hatched his ridiculous plan. And Marcus was safe in the knowledge that his team would be well looked after financially by him for the following twelve months at least. Meanwhile, I continued to be angry at myself for letting myself fall for someone like him. I must have been deluded to think that he'd be interested in any more than one night with me – it was probably only because I'd represented a bit of a challenge for him that he'd bothered at all.

I came out of the Tube at Southfields, immediately knowing which way to walk because of the swathes of tennis lovers heading in the same direction, carrying straw hats and picnic baskets. Church Road ran from the Underground station to the All England Lawn Tennis Club, otherwise known as Wimbledon, in one straight line. Unless you'd been lucky in the ballot or had big money to shell out on hospitality seats, the only other way to get in was to queue, which people were doing in droves, or even better to camp out in Wimbledon Park, the expanse of green parkland that today was littered with multicoloured tents. According to my research, 1,500 tickets were given out daily to fans who were brave enough to rough it overnight in a field – 500 for Centre Court, 500 for No.1 Court and 500 for No.2 Court. If that wasn't dedication, I didn't know what was.

I went directly to the players' area on the first floor, which reminded me of the business-class lounge at Heathrow, which in turn reminded me of Marcus and the anticipation of meeting him I'd had at the time; the way I'd still been missing Charlie. That felt like a lifetime ago now. At that point, I'd had my journey with Marcus all to come, and now it was nearly over and I was trying desperately not to think about that today, to enjoy this time for what it was. I needed to focus on the article, to capture the atmosphere of Wimbledon, the details I could write about that would transport the readers there as they read my piece.

Straight away I spotted Dean on the phone and Patrick chatting to one of the other coaches, so I found a seat outside on the decking and got out my laptop, mainly to try to look as though I belonged among the throng of household names, top seeds, their trainers and their influencer girlfriends. Below us were panoramic views of the grounds and

Centre Court, which was covered in beautiful bright-green Boston ivy. Today, Marcus would be playing on No.3 Court.

When a shadow fell over my keyboard, I knew it was him immediately. I leaned back in my chair, shielding my eyes from the sun.

'Hello,' I said.

'Hey,' he said back.

He pulled up a chair and sat opposite me.

'You look very relaxed for someone about to go out on court at Wimbledon,' I said.

'Turns out I play better when I'm not all wound up and tense. Who knew?'

I tried to smile, I really did, but it struck me that this might be the last time I ever watched him play. If he lost today, that would be it – I'd file my piece and he'd do his photo shoot and the September issue of *Luxe* would come out and I would treasure it forever, but I would never see him again, not properly. Not like this.

Dean came over to join us, which was probably a good thing. Marcus needed to focus, and who better than his team to keep him on track? His nutritionist had apparently had him on a strict diet, Nick had him stretching every night and he was sharing a house in Wimbledon Village with a couple of the other players. He'd started texting me every day – a *How are you?* Or a *Where's my wedding debrief?* I hadn't told him that my mum and sister had been slagging him off ever since. Or how let down by him I felt. If I could do anything now, it would be to walk away from this with dignity and my head held high – we'd had one night together, and if I'd thought it would be anything more, that was on me.

I tapped away on my laptop as Dean and Patrick talked business with Marcus. I was listening with half an ear – yet more potential sponsors had come forward, impressed with Marcus's self-control on the court recently, and the new, much less volatile side to him, i.e. the fact he wasn't embroiled in screaming matches with the paparazzi every five minutes. He looked up and caught my eye when Dean told him this. I nodded and smiled. He thought he partly had me to thank for it, maybe – after all, would any other journalist have agreed to go along with the ridiculous fake-dating charade Dean had concocted? I doubted it. If it had been anybody else, they would have kept their professional boundary. Written a well-crafted piece. Done their best to understand Marcus on a deeper level with the time they were given. For me, I'd gone way beyond understanding him in the way I needed to as a writer – it felt like I'd shared things with him I hadn't with anyone else for a very long time, if ever. I'd spent a night (two nights . . .) with him that I thought about almost every minute of every day. He'd got under my skin when I was supposed to be getting under his, and if anything this was bad for my article because how objective could I be at this point? What did I leave out? How did I write about Marcus without it being obvious how hard I'd fallen for him?

'Ava?' said Marcus.

'Hmm?' I said, looking up, desperately wishing I could drag myself out of this melancholy.

'Wait for me after? I can drop you home?'

I could hardly upset him before his match.

'If you like,' I said.

And then everyone told him good luck and I stood up too, taking both of his hands in mine. 'You can do this,' I said.

He pressed his lips into my temple. 'I know I can.'

We took our seats on No.3 Court, which apparently housed two thousand, although it felt like much less. From our front-row position I could see the grass in all its glory, the perennial rye I'd read about that had to be 8 mm high, no more, no less. Apparently, it was the special soil underneath that gave the court its bounce, which explained why

I'd never been able to bounce tennis balls on our patchy garden lawn when Cassie and I had tried in those long school summer holidays. Because it was only day one of the tournament, the grass was vibrant and smooth, which I assumed it wouldn't be by the end of the two-week run. Today was tipped to be the hottest day of the year so far and I could already feel the sun beating down on the top of my head. I had an iced coffee in my hand, which I kept rubbing on my wrists to keep me cool. Wimbledon smelled like flowers and occasionally, when you passed a strawberries and cream stand, there would be the scent of plump red fruit. There was more noise than I imagined, too, the rumblings of voices and hissed whispers that only dropped in volume when the umpire appeared on court, signalling that the match was about to begin. I was fascinated by the ball boys and ball girls I'd read so much about – apparently, 250 of them were whittled down from 1,000 applicants aged fourteen to eighteen, who were all pupils at nearby (mainly state) schools. They'd spent months being put through their paces by a woman who trained them like it was a military operation, shattering kids' dreams of being let off school for two whole weeks by ruthlessly dropping them for a variety of semi-valid reasons, like being late, chewing gum on the job or not being able to stand still for ten minutes straight.

Marcus arrived on court first, to rousing applause. As he set out his water bottles and towels, he looked across at us and I tried to smile encouragingly, although I didn't think the warmth I was trying to project reached my eyes. I thought he looked a little less relaxed than he had upstairs, and I supposed this was the moment at which he had to begin his crusade to win another Grand Slam, and not just any Grand Slam but the one that meant the most to him.

Marcus's opponent, a young Norwegian player called Anders Nilsen, followed him out of the dressing rooms. He had slightly less support, if applause was anything to go by, but he seemed happy to be there anyway. He was only nineteen – it must have felt like quite the occasion.

'What's Nilsen like?' I whispered to Dean.

'It's his first year out of the junior circuit. He's good, but the pressure and inexperience might get to him. Marcus should be able to dominate if he plays like he has been over the past couple weeks.'

I nodded, reassured, watching as Marcus and Nilsen took to the court for their warm-up.

Despite Nilsen's youth and enthusiasm, Marcus won the match 6-2, 6-4, 6-0. He was off to a flying start.

A few heads turned as we left the lounge, and even though it probably wasn't me they were looking at, it was still a relief to slide into the cool leather seats of our executive car. We hadn't held hands as we'd left the building – I hadn't wanted to anyway, but I thought he might have at least tried so that I could have had the satisfaction of pulling away.

Marcus sighed as we slipped into the leafy back streets of Kensington.

'Is something wrong, Ava?' he asked.

I really should have thought about exactly what I wanted to say beforehand, but now I would just have to play it by ear.

'It's about the wedding,' I said, deciding I may as well be honest, even if he wasn't. 'I guess it didn't feel great that you didn't come.'

He turned to me, frowning. 'But you said you were fine for me not to. Didn't you?'

'Yeah, if you'd told me that from the beginning. But we were all expecting you and then . . . you just didn't show up.'

He ruffled the hair on the back of his head. Good, I was making him uncomfortable – that was nothing compared to the discomfort I'd felt that night.

'I'm really sorry. I honestly . . . I misunderstood. I thought you didn't particularly want me there anyway, and then I got caught up with stuff after Queen's. The day ran away with me. I assumed you wouldn't mind.'

'It's fine. You'd just won a tournament, of course that was your priority.'

'Also . . .' he said.

'Also what?'

He sighed. 'I guess my head was a bit all over the place after the other night. I kept remembering what you said about us being friends, after I'd pretty much just laid everything on the line. I thought maybe you weren't that into me.'

'Wasn't it obvious? Of course I'm into you, even if sometimes I wish I wasn't.'

'Why would you wish that?' he asked.

I swallowed. 'I don't know. Because I'm not your type?'

'You're totally my type.'

'Because tennis will always come first?'

'It won't, Ava. It doesn't.'

'You're just saying that.'

'What happened between us the other night – it meant something to me,' he said, reaching for my hand.

I shook him off. 'In that moment, sure. Just like the other nights you've spent with women that you never wanted to see again afterwards.'

'What women?' said Marcus.

'Do I really need to spell it out?' I said, getting frustrated now. 'You might not read your press, but everyone else does, and there are countless photos of you with models and actresses and Zuzanna Kaczmerek and rich girls in bikinis.'

'Because these are the people I meet, Ava. When you're in a scene like this, that just happens, and it's not something I crave or need. In fact, what I really crave is normality – I just want to be a normal person who happens to be quite good at playing tennis. To be doing normal things with normal people.'

I spotted a Tube station up ahead and leaned forward in my seat to speak to the driver.

'Could you drop me here, please?' I asked him.

He flicked on his indicator and began to pull over to the kerb.

I couldn't have this conversation in the back seat of a car when I felt all hemmed in and on the verge of being over-emotional. And despite everything, I didn't want to make Marcus feel bad, not when he was in the middle of playing the most important tournament of his life.

'Ava, please,' he said. 'It was easier to keep women at arm's length, and it was fun for a while, I'll admit it. But that was then. It's different with you. I find myself wanting to be with you all of the time. Running away from this hasn't even crossed my mind.'

I swallowed. I could feel my resolve going, and it couldn't – he was saying all the right things, but the evidence spoke for itself. He'd let me down at the wedding and he would let me down again and I COULD NOT DO THAT TO MYSELF.

'I'll leave you to focus on your game,' I said.

The car came to a stop and I unbuckled my seat belt and opened the door almost simultaneously, desperate to get out of there so that I could get my emotions under control again because suddenly I didn't trust myself to say or do the right thing. Marcus was stony-faced and looking straight ahead as I slammed the door behind me. I tried to put his grim expression out of my mind's eye as I crossed the road towards the entrance to the Tube station, blinking back hot, angry tears. The worst thing was, it felt like I didn't even know exactly what it was I was so angry about.

It was only then that I noticed Cassie. She was standing outside a pub in her work clothes, with her phone in her hand. What on earth was she doing in this part of town? I was just about to call her name when a man came up from behind her, spun her around and lifted her into the air. She laughed as he kissed her, eventually returning her to the ground, where they continued to beam at each other, talking softly, intimately. It took my mind a few beats to catch up with what my eyes were seeing, because something was very wrong. The guy she was kissing . . . it was unmistakably Charlie.

'Cass?' I said.

She casually glanced around at me, taking a few seconds to register who I was. Then a look of pure fear flooded her face.

'I thought you were at Wimbledon? Mum said.'

Which was when *he* looked at me, too, with a face like a lost puppy. Charlie. My Charlie. Kissing my sister.

'Does one of you want to tell me what's going on?' I asked, my voice sounding as though it was coming from somewhere outside of my body.

This couldn't be happening. I must have only *thought* I saw them kissing. She wouldn't do this to me, and neither would he. He didn't like Cassie. He said she was hard work and annoying and demanding. He said he liked me because I wasn't like her, I was strong and independent and I went after what I wanted.

'I can explain,' said Charlie, already sweating in one of his stupid polo-neck sweaters.

'Are you two . . . ?'

Charlie and Cassie looked at each other. Cassie started to cry.

'Will somebody tell me what the fuck is happening here? Cassie, is this the guy you've been hanging out with? Is *this* who you've been seeing?'

Her voice was painfully small. 'Yes.'

I wondered whether I was going to be sick, because I felt like I was. I felt like I'd been knocked sideways.

'How long has it been going on?' I gasped.

'Ava, it wasn't while we were together,' said Charlie, putting on the gaslighty tone he used sometimes when he wanted to convince me that something I was saying was madness.

'Is that why you ended things with me?' I asked him. 'To be with her?'

'No!' he said. 'It wasn't like that. Cassie reached out to check on me after the break-up and—'

'*You* contacted *him*?' I said, turning to Cassie, incredulous. '*You* instigated all of this?'

Cassie started crying harder. It was a tactic she used when she didn't want to answer people's questions anymore and I wasn't falling for it, not this time.

'You're both awful people,' I said, spitting out my words, although I would have chosen better ones if I'd been able to think straight. 'You're welcome to each other.'

I worried about Cassie almost all the time and wanted the best for her, even at the expense of my own happiness sometimes, and now it had been thrown right back in my face. There were so many things I didn't understand – had she always been into him? And had he always fancied her, because honestly, it hadn't seemed like it. Was it serious? And if so, had they ever planned to tell me?

I turned around, stumbling back in the direction of the Tube.

'I'm sorry!' screamed Cassie, running after me, making a scene and causing people to turn to see what the commotion was.

Fine, let Cassie explain herself in front of these strangers, because what could she possibly say to excuse what she had done? My chest was rising and falling as I tried to catch my breath, to think about what I could ask her before she had a chance to talk to Charlie and get their story straight.

'When did you start liking him?' was my first question.

'I don't know!' wailed Cassie, still crying. I wished she'd stop. She was trying to make me feel bad for her and there was a risk of it working, despite everything.

'Tell me exactly when,' I insisted.

She shook her head, exasperated. 'I couldn't put an exact date on it. A few months ago, maybe. After he broke up with you.'

Charlie ran up behind Cassie, seemingly unsure what to do for the best. This summed him up entirely – gutless. And he'd be hating this playing out in the street, making him look bad. Good!

'And what about you, Charlie? Because I'd never realised you'd been harbouring feelings for my sister. You'd certainly never given me that impression,' I said, spinning around to face him head on.

I wasn't going to hurt her by spelling out what he'd said, but he used to be out and out mean about her.

'I . . . look, it came as a shock to me, too, okay?'

'Were you ever planning to tell me?' I demanded to know, looking from one to the other.

'Yes!' said Cassie, slightly more enthusiastic at the prospect than Charlie looked. 'Of course. I wanted to see if it was going anywhere first, because I didn't want to upset you, obviously.'

'Obviously,' I said snippily. If that was her objective, she'd failed miserably, hadn't she?

'And it is going somewhere, Ava,' she said. 'I know it's not ideal, and I'm sorry, I really am. But me and Charlie have just clicked. And you've got Marcus now, so why does it matter?'

'Do I really need to explain?' I said, feeling like screaming myself. 'It's not that I want Charlie, far from it, you're welcome to him, Cass. What's hurt me more than you can ever know is that you would go behind my back and do this to me. You knew how upset I was about the break-up.'

'I didn't! You didn't seem like you were even that bothered, even Mum said so.'

'Because I didn't want you both to worry!' I shouted. 'Because I think about you in almost everything I do. Do you know, I even felt bad that I'd broken up with Charlie because I knew how much you'd enjoyed having him around recently, even if you hadn't really hit it off at the start, and I felt as though I'd taken that away from you. Little did I know that this was how it would turn out!'

For one brief moment, seeing Cassie's big, fearful eyes so full of tears and yes, at least some remorse, I almost backed down. My sisterly instincts hadn't gone completely – and I didn't trust Charlie to look after her.

'Please don't hate me,' she said in a tiny voice.

Hate. I remembered using that word in jest to describe what I had once thought about Marcus, but I didn't think I'd ever truly hated anyone for real, not even wild-eyed, pathetic Charlie. God, it had been Cassie in those photos on Instagram then, cavorting in the Cotswolds around the same time I flew to Monte Carlo, mere weeks after our break-up.

I turned and walked away, feeling a tug of guilt despite myself. When I glanced over my shoulder, Cassie was crying in Charlie's arms. Maybe it was time that I let other people look after her. It didn't always have to be me, and it wasn't always my job, especially not now.

'Ava!'

For some reason, Marcus was still here, standing by his car, looking concerned. He half ran towards me.

'What's happened?'

I kept talking to a minimum because I couldn't trust myself not to start sobbing, and I wasn't sure whether it would be about him or Cassie or Charlie or all of the above.

'Can you please drop me home?' I said simply.

Chapter Twenty-Four

It felt very much like *Groundhog Day* when the doorbell rang. I was experiencing a lot of the same sensations I'd felt when Charlie had left: grief, disbelief, anger, although the anger this time was even more potent than it had been then. Because people broke up all the time and it hurt and it felt unfair at first, but this – this was different. People didn't generally get it on with their sister's ex-boyfriend. People's ex-boyfriends didn't generally shag their ex's little sister mere weeks after they'd broken up. I still couldn't get my head around it all. If you'd asked me about their relationship when Charlie and I had been together, I'd have said it was a brotherly/sisterly one – he teased her, she looked up to him. I'd never seen one iota of sexual chemistry, but perhaps it had been simmering away the whole time, right under my nose.

In the hallway I could see Cassie's silhouette through the glass panel of the door, and I hesitated for a few beats before opening it. I was torn between not wanting to see her and wanting answers. Wanting the whole story, the whole sordid truth. I hadn't been able to talk to anybody about it, not even Zoe, not even Marcus, not really. He'd dropped me home, shocked when I'd told him briefly what had happened; he'd sent me messages to check on me and he'd asked me to come to his second-round match, which was this afternoon. I still wasn't sure whether to go, or how I felt about him after his apology. In the space of a couple of days, it felt as though every single person I thought I could rely on had let me down.

Cassie was standing there looking withdrawn and tearful like I'd seen her many times before, but never because of something she'd done to hurt me. I wondered how badly this had affected her – whether, if I was a kind person, I should forgive her on the spot, tell her it didn't matter, that I was glad she was happy, and that now I'd had time to think it through, I wasn't bothered about her being with Charlie. That she could have him and that I'd learn to be fine with it. I'd come to the conclusion that he'd probably chosen Cassie because she was clearly besotted by him and would do anything for him, just like his mother, which I had seemingly *not* done just by being me and having a modicum of career success that had sent him reeling into a spiral of self-doubt about his own life choices. Since Cassie had a job she hated, no social network and still lived with her parents, there was no need for him to feel inadequate next to her – he could be the powerful, successful one in their relationship, which I suspected was what he'd craved all along.

'Hi,' said Cassie weakly. 'Can I come in?'

I stood aside to let her through the door. Her arm brushed mine as she walked past, kicked off her shoes and went into my lounge. I was surprised she'd made the effort to come all this way – then again, she'd clearly been spending more time in London than I'd thought, since I doubted she and Charlie had been meeting up in Reading.

'Tea?' I said.

She shook her head. 'No thanks.'

I sighed, and sat on the armchair, putting as much distance between us as you could in one small, rather poky living room.

'I don't know where to start,' said Cassie.

I stayed silent. There was no way I was going to do the hard work for her by leading the conversation. She'd come to see me. She was here to explain it all to *me*.

'I'd always liked him,' said Cassie. 'I was always a bit jealous, if you must know. He was so in love with you. Nobody had ever looked at me the way I saw him looking at you.'

'Right,' I said, struggling to think back to those early days.

'When you broke up, it wasn't like I suddenly thought: *now's my chance.* I just couldn't bear the thought of not speaking to him ever again. You might have wanted him out of your life, but I didn't want him out of mine.'

'But I hadn't wanted him out of my life, Cassie,' I said. '*He* ended it with *me*, remember?'

'I know. I think I sort of glossed over that bit. And I decided it wouldn't hurt to have him as a friend, that either I wouldn't tell you, or you'd understand eventually,' said Cassie.

Of course that was what she'd decided – Cassie did what Cassie wanted. And until now, I did what Cassie wanted too.

'So what, you called him? Arranged to meet? When?'

'When you were in Monte Carlo.'

I frowned. 'But when I was there, I saw pictures of him in the Cotswolds with someone. I presume that was you?'

She floundered for a second. 'Okay. Just before you went to Monte Carlo.'

'How did this "friendship" you said you wanted turn into romantic weekends away so quickly, then?' I asked.

Cassie tucked her hair behind her ears. We both did that when we were nervous.

'Charlie was lonely. I was lonely.'

'I was lonely, too, Cass! Did you even talk about me at all?'

'Of course we talked about you! But you were fine, by then. Mum showed me pictures of you living it up in Monaco. You were already with Marcus and you looked really happy.'

I wanted to tell her that my relationship with Marcus had been nothing but fake at that point. But I couldn't go against our agreement – I'd already told Zoe, there was no way I wanted to admit how it had all started to anyone else, especially now our feelings had turned into something altogether different.

'Things aren't always what they seem, Cassie. You see what other people have got, make assumptions about how they're living their lives, but you have no idea what goes on behind closed doors. We'd never even had a conversation about Marcus. You shouldn't have assumed anything, or taken me being photographed with the guy once as carte blanche to basically seduce my ex.'

Cassie went to say something else but seemed to think better of it. What could she say? I knew her default would be to turn it around on me, to make me the bad person, which in her mind would excuse everything she'd done. But in this instance, there was nothing tangible for her to grasp hold of – it was probably killing her to realise she had absolutely no comeback.

'Did Mum know?' I asked her. 'About you and Charlie?'

Cassie shook her head. 'I told her last night.'

And? I wanted to say. And what was her response? Surely, *surely,* she couldn't think Cassie was blameless this time. I wanted to believe she was capable of sticking up for me, just this once.

'So where do we go from here?' I asked.

I wondered what I wanted her to say, what would make any of this better, but I didn't think there was anything because they'd done what they'd done and there was no going back. I had total closure with Charlie now, at least – he hadn't been the man I'd thought he was, and I should have known that when he walked out on me in such a callous way without helping me understand why. But it was different with Cassie – I still loved her, of course. But if Marcus had taught me anything, it was that it was okay to put yourself first sometimes. And look what had happened – I'd put Cassie first my entire life and this was how she'd repaid me.

'I want to carry on seeing him, Ava. Would that be okay?' she asked, looking young, still the vulnerable teenager I'd sat with in her room while I did my homework and tried to pretend that I was struggling at school as much as she was.

'Well, I'd be careful if I were you,' I told her, thinking of Charlie's tearful phone call when I was in Paris – he would have been with Cassie then, so what was he playing at?

'What's that supposed to mean?' asked Cassie.

'You'd better ask him.'

Cassie sighed. 'So you're not okay with it, then.'

'Not really, no. And if it's my blessing you want, I can't give it to you. That's not to say that I never will, but I can't give it now. And you're going to have to sit with that feeling, Cass. It's not something I can make better for you.'

'You hate me,' she said, a tear rolling down her cheek.

'I don't hate you.'

'I really am sorry,' she said.

I shrugged. 'I know.'

Cassie stood up.

'Maybe we can talk again sometime, if you're open to it,' she said. 'I just can't seem to find the words today.'

There was one thing I still wasn't clear on, something I wanted her to explain before she left.

'I still don't get why you decided to reach out to him, to go for it despite knowing how much it would hurt me, and please don't say you thought it wouldn't,' I said.

For a second, I thought she wasn't going to answer my question because she didn't *have* an answer. But then she turned back around and looked me right in the eye.

'Because your life is just so perfect, Ava. Everything comes so easily to you. You've got a thriving career, men falling in love with you left, right and centre, and you get to travel the world all expenses paid. You've always looked down on me and my sad, shitty life, and for once – just once – I didn't want to be the reject sister, the less successful one, the useless one.'

'I've never looked down on you, Cassie,' I said to her.

And it only seemed perfect because I never told her all the bad stuff. I realised then that by trying to protect her, by trying to be the good girl for Mum and Dad, I'd made Cassie think that my life was easy, smooth, a walk in the park. Perhaps it was better to be honest, then, to show people who you really were and how you really felt, instead of trying to pretend you were okay when you weren't.

◆ ◆ ◆

I decided to go to Marcus's game that afternoon, mainly because I needed to document his journey through Wimbledon for my article. He was playing on No.1 Court, which was just as well because it looked set to rain all day and it had a retractable roof, meaning play would be able to go ahead no matter what the weather. I sat in the players' box with Dean, Patrick and Nick, jotting down notes about the venue, the atmosphere, the fans, the snippets of conversation I heard from his team. At twenty-three minutes past three, Marcus entered the court, followed by his opponent, Dominic Griffiths, the Australian guy he'd played in Monte Carlo the very first time I'd ever seen him play in real life.

'We've had some good news,' said Dean, leaning in to talk to me. 'Marcus has secured several sponsorship deals for next season. Winning at Queen's, plus the campaign we designed for the two of you . . . well, it's worked.'

'That's great,' I said, squeezing his arm. I'd become quite fond of Dean and secretly wished he was my agent, too. I could only dream of the kind of kick-ass writing assignments he'd have no trouble securing for me. 'Good work.'

Dean turned to me again, dropping his voice to a whisper.

'Ava, I hope I'm not out of line saying this, but I think you and Marcus actually make a cool couple. Like, for real. I'd never have suggested any of this if I hadn't seen a spark between the two of you in the first place, you know that, don't you?'

I wasn't sure how much to say, but I trusted his judgement and his opinion was about as neutral as I could hope for, given he worked for Marcus.

'I think things have become more real for us over time,' I said. It was strange to say the words out loud. Not even Zoe knew the back and forth I'd been doing in my head: the longing, the recriminations, the embarrassment, the excitement – Marcus had got me feeling all kinds of things I'd never experienced before, at least not at the same time. 'With his career taking off, and me in London while he travels the world . . . I don't know. Maybe the timing's not right. Maybe it might not ever be.'

'You could make it work,' said Dean. 'He's really into you, I'm telling you. You've changed him and he's not an easy guy to be around sometimes, but when I see him with you, you make it *look* easy.'

'Has he said anything?'

Dean shook his head. 'He doesn't need to. The guy is easier to read than he thinks he is.'

I smiled to myself. Maybe he was. Honesty was his thing, he'd told me himself. So what if I should believe him when he said he liked me and had never felt like this about anyone before?

The match went smoothly, other than Marcus being about to serve for a game at one point and somebody deciding that was the perfect time to pop a champagne cork. Marcus had looked angrily over at them and the umpire had told everyone to please avoid opening champagne when a player was about to serve. At least Marcus didn't start shouting, and he went on to execute the best second serve I'd ever seen him do, so no harm done. He beat Dominic again, 6-4, 6-4, 6-2 and was into round three.

Chapter Twenty-Five

On the morning of the Wimbledon men's final, I was in my mushroom pyjamas on the sofa, watching the news. There was a lot of focus on the match – Marcus had made it, the first British player to reach the final in years, and the country was going wild. The BBC were interviewing the thousands of fans who had been queueing all night, hoping to get their hands on a much-coveted ticket, and there were beautiful aerial shots of Centre Court with bright-blue July skies framing the stadium – I couldn't believe that, later, Marcus would be walking out on to that grass and making his bid for the thing he wanted most in the world: another Grand Slam win, and more than that, to be a Wimbledon singles champion.

I was deciding what to have for breakfast when the doorbell rang. I sighed – who could be here at eight o'clock on a Sunday morning? I padded out to get the door, throwing it open, shocked to see Marcus standing there, all six foot four of him, dressed in a midnight-blue Lacoste tracksuit, his hands in his pockets, his cheeks a little flushed, his eyes shining. I braced myself against the door frame.

'Hi,' I said.

'Nice pyjamas,' he said, his eyes sweeping over me.

'I aim to please,' I said.

I should have felt self-conscious, but somehow I didn't. This was the raw, unfiltered version of me, and if he didn't like it – I mean, who would? – then so be it.

'Sorry to call so early. I've got warm-up at ten, so I'm on my way out to Wimbledon now.'

'Of course. How are you feeling about the match?' I asked.

'Optimistic,' he said. 'But I'm not here to talk about me.'

From behind his back he produced a large, pink, expensive-looking box and handed it to me.

'Don't get too excited,' he said as I took it from him.

'Is this a gift?' I said.

'Open it and you'll see,' he said, crossing his arms. Was he *nervous*?

I removed the lid from the box. Inside were two rolled-up yoga mats, one a beautiful pastel pink, one black with grey swirls.

Frowning, I looked up at him. 'What's this?'

'You said you love yoga.'

'That thing that isn't a sport? Yes, I do.'

'So I thought we could do it together,' he said, uncrossing his arms and running his hands through his hair instead.

'What?' I said, laughing lightly.

'I want us to do the things you like. Together. Because I'm aware that so far, the time we've spent together has been very focused on me, and on tennis – on what I like, and where I need to be. But I want to learn everything there is to know about you and why you enjoy the things you do, and I thought that maybe we could start with yoga. You can teach me,' he said, raising his eyebrows hopefully.

'Why are you doing this now?' I asked. 'On the day of the Wimbledon final?'

'I don't know. I just had to say it before I bottled it. Because I love being around you, Ava, and I don't want this – you and me – to end just because Dean says it can.'

I was holding my breath, I realised. If I could have done I would have sat down, right there on the doorstep.

'Come on tour with me,' he said, his voice low, quiet.

'How can I leave everything here?' I said, not understanding.

'Everything like . . . ?'

Good point.

'My home. This flat.'

'The flat you shared with Charlie? That you can't really afford, that reminds you of him?'

There were other things I couldn't leave. Weren't there?

'My parents,' I said, although that sounded feeble because how often did I see them, anyway?

Marcus gave me a look.

'Okay, what about my job?' I said.

'You can write from anywhere, can't you? And you can always fly back if you need to. And there's a little thing called virtual meetings.'

I let all of this sink in.

'Where would you be going next?' I asked, still very sure that I couldn't possibly go with him. He was getting carried away, he'd think differently if he won today, when he was back focusing on what was most important to him.

'I'll be heading to Washington after Wimbledon, then Toronto and Cincinnati. After that it's the US Open in New York. You wouldn't have to be at all of them if you didn't want to be. But you might want to be at some?' he said, wincing. 'I know it's a lot. And I wouldn't expect you to give up your entire life for me – I know you have your own career to focus on, and I'd want it to be an equal arrangement. I support you as much as you support me.'

'I don't know,' I said.

'It's a big decision, I get it. You have a life here. But it's not like you can never come back. And I'll probably be retiring in a few years' time, playing less at the very least. It won't be forever.'

Was he suggesting we had something that might outlive his tennis career? That there was a chance of *us* going on forever? This seemed unlikely. Could he really go from avoiding commitment at all costs and picking up different women on a weekly basis to imagining a future with me? Was it less me and more my calming presence that he wanted? Was I a good-luck charm that he didn't want to risk losing? Was I somehow unthreatening to him in a way that his exes weren't?

He reached out to tuck an unruly lock of hair behind my ear, looking deep into my eyes. 'I'm falling in love with you, Ava, just so you know.'

My eyes felt tight and bright. What if he was one of those guys who, once he knew he had you, lost interest instantly? He could have anyone he wanted. Why would he choose me? In the words of my mum when I was a child, what did I think was so special about me?

'I'll need to think about it,' I said, my throat tight with emotion.

'Of course,' he said. 'Take your time.'

'And you need to go and warm up,' I said.

The last thing I wanted was to throw him off before the biggest match of his life.

'See you on Centre Court,' he said.

I nodded. 'I'll be there. You've got this.'

I took my time deciding what to wear. It was already gone twelve and I needed to get going if I wanted to make it to the grounds in time for the match, because I could only assume the traffic would be horrendous on men's finals day. England was in the height of Wimbledon fever, even more so because Marcus was playing. The press had finally started to champion him. One newspaper had even printed a picture of him and me together with the headline HAS RACQUET MAN TURNED INTO ROMANTIC MAN? Dean's plan had worked like a dream. Marcus had offers of sponsorship, more than he could ever have imagined. But for all that Marcus had gained, something had been lost for me. My relationship with Cassie was going to take some time to recover, and I was going to need to process the fact that she and Charlie were together now, and that I felt differently about my sister as a result. Any happy memories of my relationship with Charlie had been trashed by recent events, which was probably a good thing. And my article was finished, I just needed to add in a line or two about Marcus's final match at Wimbledon. Amanda Eddington was impressed with what she'd seen so far – Zoe said she was raving about me in the team meeting, and that she wouldn't hesitate to hire me again – in fact, there was a profile of an A-list actor she was negotiating for and she'd already asked about my availability for August.

I laid my dress out on the bed. Zoe had persuaded me to buy it, and I swung between thinking it looked lovely and being convinced that I looked ridiculous in it. It was a showy dress. A cerise pink mini with puffed sleeves and a nipped-in waist. A look-at-me dress. If I wore it in the players' box, would everyone think I was pulling attention away from Marcus? And then I realised that it was my punishing voice doing the talking – my mum's voice, I supposed, that I'd somehow internalised and made my own. As if wearing a nice outfit would in any way take away from what Marcus had achieved and would go on to achieve today, whatever happened. I slipped it on. I was just about to leave when my phone rang. It was Mum. I checked the time – 12.20. She would have to be quick.

'I'm just off over to Wimbledon, so . . .'

'This won't take a minute, Ava,' she said.

I packed my bag while she was talking, hooking the phone between my shoulder and my ear. I'd need my tickets, my accreditation, tissues, money, credit cards, lipstick. Foundation and powder for touch-ups. Sunglasses. Sunscreen. What else?

'I know we haven't really spoken about Cassie and Charlie, but I wanted to have a proper think about what I wanted to say to you.'

Here we go, I thought. I'd somehow be to blame. Cassie would be a mess and it would be my fault.

'Mum, can we skip the recriminations? I really haven't got time for this today.'

A beat.

'That's not why I called, Ava.'

'Oh?'

'It might surprise you to hear that I'm actually quite disgusted by what Cassie has done. And I've told her as much.'

I raised my eyebrows. She was right, this was not what I'd been expecting, not at all.

'I'm not sure if I've told you about when Cassie was born,' continued Mum.

'You have,' I said. Several times, I nearly added.

I knew she'd arrived two months early, that she'd been in the neonatal unit, that she'd caught an infection and almost died. I knew that I didn't see my parents for almost two months because they were at the hospital and I had to go and stay with my nan and grandad in Slough.

'Well, I think it shaped everything from then on. Because we nearly lost her, and because you were so strong and healthy and capable, I think I felt I had to make it up to her. Had to make Cassie feel extra special, as special as you seemed naturally to be.'

'Mum . . .'

'Hear me out, Ava, I'll only be another minute. I want you to know that I'm aware I tried to dull your light. Me and Dad both did. We saw that you were destined to shine and we felt worried that Cassie would feel left behind. And . . . I'm sorry about that. It wasn't fair of us to do that to you.'

I swallowed hard. Mum had never said any of this to me before, I'd never had any idea this was how she felt.

'Sometimes I thought you actually disliked me,' I said.

'Never,' she said. 'And I understand now that I need to show you how much I care about *both* of you, not just Cassie.'

'Thanks, Mum,' I said, touched. I took a deep breath – it probably wasn't a good idea to get upset and ruin my make-up.

'And Ava?'

'Yes?'

'For what it's worth, I think Marcus Taylor makes you ten times happier than Charlie ever did.'

'Okay, you're embarrassing me now, Mum.'

She laughed and so did I.

'I'd better let you go,' she said.

'Yes please, unless you want me to blub all over my nice new dress.'

'Have fun, Ava. And tell Marcus good luck from us.'

In the taxi I messaged Zoe, thinking I should probably give her a heads up.

I think I'm in love with Marcus Taylor. Is that mad?!

It took too long for her reply to come through. Where was she? – it was a Sunday, so she wouldn't be at work. Why on earth wasn't she glued to her phone, waiting for a message from me she wasn't expecting?! What if it was a mistake to tell her while I was still a little bit on the fence – not about loving Marcus, because I finally trusted that he meant what he said, and honestly my feelings for him were too strong not to try, but about the travelling around with him bit. Was it crazy to give up everything I had here to follow him around the world? But whenever I tried to bring myself back down to earth, I had the sense that it was something I couldn't turn down – I'd loved spending time with him and the team over the last couple of months, why *wouldn't* I want more of it? And he was making an effort to meet me halfway – he did bring good things into my life. Without him, the situation with Cassie would have been so much worse, because learning from him, watching him, I'd finally learned that it's okay to go after what I want, even if it disappoints people along the way.

Zoe finally messaged back.

> *No, it's not mad, it's lovely. Go for it, tell him how you feel, and don't look back!*

I smiled to myself, watching south-west London life out of the window, wondering when I'd begun living the fairy tale I'd daydreamed about when I was young and would have done anything to escape the monotony of my day-to-day existence, the constant walking on egg-shells at home, the boredom of school. It was when I got upgraded to Business on the flight to Nice, I thought. That steward who upgraded me had changed my whole life and he'd never know it.

I didn't get into the grounds until gone two-thirty. The traffic had been at a standstill and in the end I'd got out of the cab and had had to walk miles in my heels, finally making it on to the site, running past the beautiful flower displays and the Pimm's stalls (I'd be having one of those later, for sure) and into the entrance to the players' box. There was a rope across the gate, meaning I'd had to wait until the players next changed ends. I could hear the ball slamming back and forth, back and forth. Marcus was playing Tomas Horvat again and Tomas grunted every time he hit the ball and so I knew which shots were Marcus's and I closed my eyes, willing him to do well, willing him to win. After every point, there was rapturous applause. They'd been playing for over half an hour now.

'What's the score?' I whispered to one of the officials on the gate, a man who looked to be in army uniform from *circa* 1924.

'Taylor is leading three games to two in the first set,' he said.

I nodded. It was close. Anyone's match.

Finally, the officer removed the rope and I filed in with a couple of others. Dean had left me a seat next to him in the box, but for a second I stood at the bottom of the stairs, wanting Marcus to see me, to know that I was there. As if he could sense me, when he stood up to run back out on court, he looked up. Perhaps the pink had caught his eye, perhaps that had been why I was supposed to wear it.

I smiled at him, nodding my head, hoping he'd understand what that meant. It meant a few different things, actually. It meant yes, I would take a chance on us. Yes, I'd come with him on tour. And yes, I knew he could do this.

He smiled and nodded back. He'd got it.

And then he turned and walked back out on court, the crowd fully behind him, cheering him on. And I took my seat to watch him win.

ABOUT THE AUTHOR

Photo © 2021 Maria V. Kaz

Lorraine is the author of five romantic comedy novels, with her debut *The Paris Connection* shortlisted for the RNA's Debut Romantic Novel Award. She writes screenplays alongside her novels and her romance movie *The Love Issue* is currently available to stream on Amazon Prime in the US. Lorraine previously trained as both an actress and a psychodynamic counsellor and currently works at a university, delivering counselling sessions to medical students. She lives in London with her partner and their son. Lorraine is on Instagram @lorrainebrownauthor.

Follow the Author on Amazon

If you enjoyed this book, follow Lorraine Brown on Amazon to be notified when the author releases a new book!
To do this, please follow these instructions:

Desktop:

1) Search for the author's name on Amazon or in the Amazon App.
2) Click on the author's name to arrive on their Amazon page.
3) Click the 'Follow' button.

Mobile and Tablet:

1) Search for the author's name on Amazon or in the Amazon App.
2) Click on one of the author's books.
3) Click on the author's name to arrive on their Amazon page.
4) Click the 'Follow' button.

Kindle eReader and Kindle App:

If you enjoyed this book on a Kindle eReader or in the Kindle App, you will find the author 'Follow' button after the last page.

PRAISE FOR LORRAINE BROWN

'Fresh, charming and wonderfully escapist'

—Beth O'Leary

'A wonderfully engaging tale of love and self-discovery'

—Mike Gayle

'Perfect poolside reading'

—Paige Toon

'A charming, romantic read'

—Sophie Cousens

'Utterly charming'

—Nina Pottell

'Fresh and romantic. This is feel-good fiction at its best'

—Nicola Gill

'The ultimate escapist romance'

—Sara Jafari

'A perfect-for-these-times novel about friendship, connections and finding love where you least expect it'

—Zoe Folbigg

'Plotted to perfection'

—Kirsty Capes